the EXRACTOR
Rise of Osiris

the EXRACTOR
Rise of Osiris

DEEK RHEW

Book One in the Osiris Series

Tenacious Books Publishing

Published by Tenacious Books Publishing

Copyright © 2020 Deek Rhew

All rights reserved under International and Pan-American Copyright Conventions. No part of this book may be reproduced in any form or by any electronic or mechanical means, including information storage and retrieval systems, without permission in writing from the publisher, except by a reviewer, who may quote brief passages in a review.

Published by Tenacious Books Publishing in 2020
Tenacious@TenaciousBooksPublishing.com

This book is a work of fiction. Names, characters, places, and incidents are either the product of the author's imagination or are used fictitiously.

Library of Congress Cataloging-in-Publication Data
Rhew, Deek. First edition.
The Extractor: Rise of Osiris / Deek Rhew
ISBN 978-1-7338974-3-3 (print)
ASIN B0868339PJ (e-book)

Cover Image: © ShutterStock
Cover Design: Anita B. Carroll www.race-point.com

Printed in the United States of America

www.TenaciousBooksPublishing.com

CHAPTER ONE

JEFF

My car sailed down the highway under a tearful Portland sky, the exact color of old bone. I let the auto's digital chauffeur drive so I could study the pamphlet in my lap.

Our lives are finite... Appeared at the top of the page, then the last part of the sentence materialized *...but our memories are infinite.* An image of a withered, wrinkled old man appeared then faded, replaced with a chubby baby in a diaper. A picture of a toddler overlaid the infant. The toddler faded to a gap-toothed boy. High school. Military. Marriage. Children. Grandchildren.

Step back in time with Dencephalon. History may forget, but you never will.

Still having no idea what Dencephalon did or why Calvin had insisted I come, I tossed the propaganda onto the passenger seat as the auto slid into one of the slanted parking spaces in front of an old warehouse.

I stared up at the huge, dilapidated building. "Lexi, are you *sure* this is the right place? It looks abandoned."

My digital assistant's face appeared on the dashboard monitor. "This is the address Calvin provided us, Jeff."

I looked up and down the drenched, desolate street, then returned my attention to the derelict warehouse. Nothing broke the monotony of concrete and stone, save a rusty roll up garage door large enough to fit a pair of semitrucks. A huge vampire skull had been digitally tagged across the wavy burnt orange metal. The live-paint graffiti's inferno-red eyes drifted as though in search of a new victim. As its gaze focused on my car, and more specifically onto me, it slowly grinned, revealing a mouthful of nail-sharp teeth. A glimmering, elongated ruby of blood rolled down one of its stalactite fangs and dropped from view.

I could practically hear the splat against the ground.

The relentless rain thrummed on the roof of the car while the undead and I stared at one another. My gut gurgled, and my skin broke out in gooseflesh.

I blinked. The vampire didn't.

Yep. That's my cue. Time to go.

Just as I opened my mouth to tell Lexi to take me back to the office, a side door swung open. Calvin, his hair sticking up in all directions like an electrocution victim, leaned out and motioned for me.

Staring at my friend, I contemplated the impact to our relationship if I left him standing there, waving at me like a lunatic, as I had Lexi drive me back to the office. Juvenile amusement lifted my spirit as I imaged his perplexed expression. Despite the unnerving circumstances, I almost laughed out loud.

But as I studied Calvin's Christmas morning smile and bright, excited eyes, the uneasy exasperation returned, melting my temporary joviality. As much as I wanted to at times, I could never do that to him. Though not by blood, we were each other's family, and family didn't do that… no matter how crazy he drove me.

Besides, when it came to technological advancements, and sometimes even acquisitions, I needed and trusted his instincts. Whether or not I liked it, he was the true brains of the operation. The patents listed me as the inventor of MindLink, but Calvin had been its creator. Without him, I'd probably still be puttering in my garage, trying to get the beta version working.

Not that I would ever admit that to his face. Not in a million years.

Glancing once more at the lurid graffiti, I cursed under my breath as I tried to pretend the vampire skull wasn't a gang's territorial mark, but simply an art-inspired vandal's way of expressing himself. I turned to my digital assistant. "Lexi, keep the engine running in case we have to leave in a hurry."

"Jeff?" she said. "This vehicle has no engine. It's an all-electric—"

Without waiting for her to finish, I flung open the door and stepped out into the pounding rain. Ignoring the vampire as it fluttered its black, forked tongue and leered at me, I strolled through the deluge to the side entrance.

Calvin shook his head. "You're such a Portlander."

Relieved to be out of the monster's gaze, I said, "Only out-of-towners run in our liquid sunshine."

He pointed at my DigiSleeve. "There's no need to run if you're smart enough to turn on your sonic umbrella."

Ignoring his comment, I hung my overcoat and hat on an old iron pipe jutting out of the grimy wall and glanced around the small atrium. Water stains, splotches of mold, and bubbling paint marred just about every surface of the room. Dirt, leaves, and dust bunnies littered the floor.

Boundaries. Gawd, I seriously needed to establish some. I sighed and wondered again why I hadn't just left the moment I'd seen the undead, nerd-devouring gang graffiti.

I considered getting out while I still could do so on my own two feet, except that I'd already wasted half my day and put myself in peril…again. Might as well see it through. "This is a great place, Cal. I heard that Condemned Interiors wants to feature it in their next show."

Calvin cocked his head. "This is just the entrance."

"Oh, so it gets better?" I snorted. "That hardly seems possible. Can't wait to show it off to our customers. What do you think they'll like more, the urban cannibals or the unique chance to catch dysentery?"

"Come on, it's not that skeevy," he said.

"You can't be serious, man," I said, folding my arms. "Even torpedo-armed police drones are afraid to come to this part of town." I took a deep breath. "Alright, I've risked my life for another one of your flights of fancy. What is this place?"

He smiled. "This is our future."

"Oh, obviously."

He turned and strolled down a shadowed hallway toward a door inset into the wall. "Don't judge a book.

Remember, we didn't always have a high-rise in downtown. When I started working for you, your first 'office' didn't look that much different than this."

Despite my irritation, I chuckled. Crammed full of computers, soldering irons, electrical parts, and empty pizza containers, that old space hadn't been much larger than a storage closet or much cleaner than this dump. "Touché. Okay, I'll try and withhold judgment then."

He typed a code into a small pad, pulled open the door, and ushered me inside. As I entered the room, frigid air froze my rain-soaked shirt collar and assaulted every inch of exposed skin. Calvin followed, closing the door behind him.

I started to ask him something, but when I looked up, the question died on my lips.

The darkness, deeper than a coal mine and blacker than a killer's soul, would have completely engulfed us had it not been for tens of thousands of twinkling stars. As if we'd stepped out onto the edge of space and freed from the laws of gravity, we seemed to be drifting in the furthest corner of the universe.

"Where are we?" I asked, marveling. "Did we cross over into another dimension?"

He laughed. "Funny, I thought the same thing the first time I saw *it*. Come on. I'll show you." He headed deeper into the mass of stars.

I hesitated. "It?"

Calvin didn't answer my question, so I started to follow him. Suddenly, he vanished as if he'd fallen into a wormhole.

Halting, I stared unbelievingly at the spot he'd been just an instant before. I looked in every direction, but without anything to fixate on, quickly became disoriented.

Damn, Calvin's abandoned me in the middle of the frigging galaxy to fend for myself. Typical.

"Come on, Jeff!" His voice floated from the distance.

Triangulating on where I thought I'd heard him, I hurried to catch up, while also watching out for space-time vortices and other phenomena I'd never dreamed I'd have to worry about.

In the distance, a haze of luminescent fog swirled out of the darkness. Still having no idea where Calvin had gone, I carefully made my way through the condensing mist toward a glowing, door-sized gap in the twinkling lights.

Reaching the void, I stumbled into Christmas in Vegas…only brighter.

In a room large enough to house the Great Sphinx of Giza, hundreds of pulsing neon ropes, starting from a single point in the ceiling, flowed overhead and down the walls. The luminous, throbbing veins all came together at the epicenter of the floor in a glowering purple swirl.

Calvin came up beside me, his gaze on the fury beneath our feet. "It's beautiful, isn't it?"

Stymied, it took me a minute to answer. "What is it?"

With his ghoulish grin, crazy hair, and wild eyes reflecting the angry, floor-bound storm, he looked as though he'd escaped a mental institution. "We're inside the only dark matter server in the world."

He did not just say that.

"No. No way. That can't be," I said. "The World Consortium of Scientists banned planet-side dark matter technology years ago."

He put a finger to his lips. "Sssshhhhh. I won't tell if you won't."

I scowled at him. "Did you really just shush my point about aiding and abetting international criminals?"

"*Technically*, there aren't any laws forbidding its use," he replied. "So *technically*, we can't be aiding and abetting anyone."

"There's no official law. That's your argument? At the very least, don't you think that building what is essentially a massive bomb within the city limits might break a town ordinance or two?"

He laughed. "Right? The mayor would have a conniption if she found out. Except that it's been stable and without incident for three years now."

I swallowed. "There've been 'incidents?'"

"I guess." He shrugged. "But not too many and none in three years."

This information did not help settle my apprehension. I studied the pulse of the arterial threads and the synchronized swirling vortex heartbeat under my feet. The system appeared sound. Maybe they really had figured out how to stabilize the technology in Earth's gravity, or maybe at any second, the core would collapse and vaporize half the town's population as the blast leveled the entire northwestern corner of Portland.

Calvin's purplish eyes remained riveted on the floor. "Will you look at this thing? It's gorgeous." He sounded like a cross between Dr. Evil and a first-time father holding his newborn baby.

"Dude, you're drooling," I remarked scornfully. I couldn't help but wonder if the designers of the Titanic had gazed upon their new creation with similar misty affection as it sailed out of Southampton.

Though I neither possessed the ability to see into the future nor the ability to converse with the manager of the universe, I nevertheless sensed an ominous presence lurking deep within the recesses of wire and silicon. As though this machine weren't a machine at all, but a maleficent entity come to life.

First the gang graffiti, then dysentery, and now the possibility of fiery molecular dissolution. Why the hell did Calvin think this was a good idea?

I'd been so preoccupied I hadn't noticed he no longer stood beside me. I glanced around to find him entering a side hallway. He paused and waved for me to follow. "Come on. You'll see why we need it."

We need it? I somehow doubted that.

As I hurried to catch up, I considered trying to convince him to leave. Abandon this insane notion before something awful happened. But the gleam in his eyes made me bite back my words. I could talk until we ran out of atmosphere, but I wouldn't be able to convince my friend of the potential dangers this machine posed.

Instead of a lecture, I turned to sarcasm. "Finally, I get to mark 'Spend the day in Wonderland' off my to-do list. Are we on our way to meet Alice?"

"Funny you should ask," he said, nonplussed. "I kind of think of him as a genius Mad Hatter."

The hallway emptied into a large open office. Rock and movie stars, both active and long dead, danced and gyrated across holographic posters stuck to the ancient brick walls. Elvis Presley, his lip curled in his trademark sneer and his hips pumping, seemed to be trying to "Jailhouse Rock" his way out of his rectangular prison.

As we passed the first in a series of large workstations, a man with vibrant green eyes and light-blue, plasticky hair that looked like a Picasso rendition of a tidal wave watched me. Perhaps he had heard me compare his company to a children's book because his hostile gaze remained riveted on me as he talked to a bald woman in a camouflage vest and a man sporting a plaid bow tie.

While the three seemed to be having an animated conversation, they were as silent as specters passing through our world on their way to another. A hazy wave domed their workstation like an igloo.

Ugh. Sound silos.

Since I wanted my teams to be able to talk to one another, I had strictly forbidden the use of isolation chambers such as these. Evidently, not everyone valued communication the way I did.

On the plus side, at least the guy with the plastic hair couldn't have heard me. So, he wasn't mad; he just had a severe resting bitch face.

A voice from behind me interrupted my thoughts. "You must be Mr. Braxton."

I stopped and turned around to find a man standing so close that I almost bumped him with my shoulder. Suppressing an urge to yell out in surprise, I took a step back from the interloper. "I am."

He bowed slightly at the waist. "I'm Rick Tieg. The owner and operator of Dencephalon. Welcome."

The man's foul breath hit me like a punch to the face. I casually retreated two more steps while trying to not look as though I wanted to gag. Grateful I didn't have to get close enough to shake his hand, I nodded. "Thank you."

I indicated the sea of people. "What is this?"

A mock smile twisted his chapped lips. "This is the most advanced development team in the world."

I almost laughed at his audacity but managed to rein in my surprise. He'd invited *me*—the creator of the most successful and progressive virtual reality gaming company on the planet—to visit, yet he had the gall to presume his obscure little startup was superior?

Puuh-lease.

I raised my eyebrows. "That's funny, I thought *I* had the most advanced development team in the world."

If my words offended or provoked him, he didn't show it. "I guess that remains to be seen."

"I suppose it does," I said, glancing once more at the sea of workstations.

My eyes locked with the man with the tidal-wave blue hair.

As he stared, he spun a glowing digital model of the human brain, tumbling it end-over-end like a basketball.

Something about him, besides his flaming green irises, gave me the heebie-jeebies. I held his gaze for a few heartbeats, then tore my eyes from his.

Suddenly, I'd had enough. Between crossing into gang territory, the potentially explosive and possibly illegal dark matter server, the creepy scientists, and now this fire-breathing imposter insinuating he'd intellectually trounced us, my patience had run out. I needed to either gain control of the situation or get back to the office because I'd had more than enough of these shenanigans.

Folding my arms, I leveled my gaze at Rick. "While the overclocked abacus in the other room and your team *look* impressive—and I'm trying really hard to be a good sport—I have to admit, fellas, I'm totally lost. I don't understand what any of this has to do with Virtual Adventures."

"I like a man that cuts to the chase," he said. "Come. It's easier just to show you." He stepped over to an empty workstation, pulled out a chair, and motioned for me to sit.

As I entered the noise-cancelling silo, my ears popped like a gong in my head. I yawned, trying to equalize the pressure that threatened to explode my skull like a poodle in a microwave. When I sat, the two men plopped into the seats in front of me.

Rick slid an arc lighter out of his pocket. He pulled the trigger and the tiny electric flame flared to life. As fluid as a magician, he absently began rolling it over and in between his knuckles. "Calvin has given me an overview of your inability to replicate tactile simulation in your virtual reality gaming system."

My inability?

He'd delivered the line as if mimicking the human nervous system should have been as trivial as high school algebra. This man either had zero interpersonal skills or had purposely decided to try and press every hot button on my emotional control panel.

I wanted to launch into a lecture on the complexities of neuroanatomy to digital conversion, but amusement danced in his eyes as if he could see my inner tirade. If I went on the defensive and began explaining what we'd tried—but failed—to do, I'd be giving him exactly what he wanted.

Choking down my arguments, I shoved my outrage aside and offered him my most placating smile. "It's not that *we* can't do it," I shrugged. "*No one* can. It's impossible. As you may or may not know, just replicating a simple temperature change is off the charts complex. The human body contains an infinite number of nerve endings, and for each one, there's an infinite number of sensations."

I paused before continuing, "I've published several articles on the subject if you want to learn more."

Calvin, who seemed oblivious to our less-than-friendly banter, smiled. "Rick and his team have found a way around the tactile limitation."

I barely refrained from reaching over and thumping his pointy little, electrified head.

Whose side are you on?

For reasons that eluded me, he seemed completely enamored with this skid mark. Once again, I reminded myself that Calvin had brought me for a reason. Maybe if we could get on with this dog and pony show, I could find out why. "Okay, you've got my attention."

Cal handed me a MindLink fob and a neckpad.

I took them and frowned as I studied the little piece of wizardry I'd used to revolutionize the world. Correction. The little piece of now-modified wizardry.

What the hell?

Though the fob still had the usual components that bridged the gap between the MindLink gaming system and the human brain, a thin circuit board had been sandwiched on top.

Internally, I seethed. First, I'd lost the controlling portion of my own company in a hostile takeover, and now this roadkill breath blowhard had monkeyed with *my* tech without the courtesy of letting me know ahead of time.

Though my pride raged, demanding I denounce this egomaniac's blasphemous modification to my baby, I held myself in check. As of late, things had been spiraling out of control, and before I jumped the gun, I needed to be smart and learn all I could. "This fob is almost twice the usual size."

Rick nodded. "Yes. The extra sensory simulation takes another layer of circuitry. We can talk about that if you enjoy what I'm going to show you."

When I hesitated, Calvin smiled encouragingly. "Don't worry, Jeff. It won't bite."

I glared at my "friend" and wondered what he'd gotten us into this time.

He grinned like he expected me to be impressed, or inspired, or excited, but he'd only pissed me off by allowing this poser to screw with our bread and butter. Calvin had better pray to the gods of geekdom that this tricked-out fob blew my socks off, or he'd get the royal smack down on his skinny little ass—hurt feelings or no hurt feelings—the second we got back to the office.

My gaze found his, and I tried to telepathically warn him of his impending doom. But, as usual, my message got bounced back to me as undeliverable. Instead of looking sheepish or worried, he appeared to be on the verge of having a nerdgasm.

I sighed, slipped the pad onto the back of my neck, and then, brushing my hair aside, touched the fob to my temple. It quietly snicked into place as the magnetic adapter latched on to the sensory tap embedded in my skin.

In spite of the circumstances, that tiny sound still gave me a few seconds of private joy. Every single time. Hearing it always took me back to the very first time I'd sat in our closet-sized office with the very first crude version of the fob.

Just as it had done all those years ago, in my peripheral vision, the little marvel's neon light started glowing like a green moon as it drew power from my body. My heart skipped a beat in anticipation, flooding my senses with a happy expectation.

Rick pulled out a mobile and typed something on the screen. The fob turned blue, then the world drained of color, everything in it dimming to monochrome, before fading to black.

MindLink had taken over.

CHAPTER TWO

JEFF

The smell of lilacs and hot electronics drifted on a cool breeze that ruffled my hair and tickled my skin. Muffled voices and snippets of conversation accompanied the whir of drones and the shuffling of feet.

A grayish crowd surrounded me as we waited for the traffic light to change on the corner of a busy intersection. The steel skeleton of what would become the city skywalk and blade bike track floated two stories above us. An automated garbage truck lumbered by, its throaty engine revving like a bass choir, while swarms of electric gray-colored cars buzzed past.

The signal changed, and I stepped into the street along with the throng of blurry-faced people.

I squeezed my fingers and realized that I held something in my hand. I glanced down. A briefcase. It perfectly matched my black suit pants. My shiny leather shoes, while light, squeezed my feet uncomfortably.

I hope these things break in soon. They're killing me.

As I stepped up onto the curb on the far side of the street, the screech of tires and the breaking of glass grabbed my attention, and I turned back. A muted yellow taxi had collided with another car in the intersection. Two men, one with a Brooklyn accent and the other with something more exotic, yelled and cursed at one another.

A man next to me stared at the wreckage. "Pretty soon the city's going to take away everyone's right to drive." He shook his head. "Maybe it's for the best."

I chuckled. "Maybe." I turned back around and immediately collided with a young woman.

My briefcase flew open. Papers caught in the brisk wind began to blow away.

"Oh, I'm terribly sorry," she said as she grabbed at the tumbling, scurrying documents.

I too reached for the papers, and together, we managed to gather the bulk of them. She stood and held out the crumpled mess. Her blue eyes sparkled in the bright March sunshine.

As I took the disaster that had been my annual sales report, my heart leapt with joy at the sight of her clear skin and girlish figure in the knee-length dress that exactly matched the blue of her eyes. "Janet?"

She scrunched up her nose and shaded her face from the sunshine. Her eyes flew open wide. "Rodger? Rodger Thornton? No! It can't be you!"

She dropped the brown paper bag she'd been carrying and flew into my arms. Her hip knocked the remains of my ruined report out of my grasp. The documents once again took flight in the city breeze, though neither of us paid them any attention.

My cheeks grew hot, and my heart hammered as she wrapped her arms around me and pressed her face to my chest. Her hair smelled of some kind of fruity shampoo—apple, or cherry, or something. I wrapped my fingers around her small, firm waist and pulled her close.

In a few years, that slim belly would bulge with our first child.

She looked up into my eyes and cupped my face in her long, slender—and ringless, I couldn't help but notice—fingers. Her cool palms cradled my flaming cheeks. "I can't believe it's really you. I thought you'd joined the military and went off to fight that awful war."

I nodded. "I did. But I got hurt and honorably discharged."

She looked me up and down. "Well, you look good to me."

I posed and brushed a fingertip down my leg. "You think I look good in this? Wait until the evening wear competition. I've got a ball gown that will knock your socks off."

Janet laughed.

Even after all these years, her voice sounded like a choir of angels. The war had called to me, as it had to so many of us after the brutal microbe attacks against our country. But now, nothing called to me like the beautiful light in my old girlfriend's eyes. The feel of her embrace. Her laughter. Her smile. I'd returned to the States nine months ago, but only now did I feel like I'd come home.

I tried to keep the grin on my face from being too cheesy, but evidently, I failed because she laughed again. "What are you doing in Portland?"

Trying to seem as suave as possible, I replied, "Looking for you."

"Really?" She cocked her head prettily.

"If I'd known you were here, then, yes, that's all I would have been doing," I said.

She held up her hands. "Well, if that was your goal, it seems you've succeeded. Now what?"

Reaching down, I picked up her bag and my briefcase. "Now, I take you to lunch."

I offered her my arm. She looped her hand through the crux of my elbow.

The scene around me faded, and my heart broke.

"No, no. Don't stop. I want to see what happens next." But despite my protests, I'd returned to the workstation and the two men staring at me.

Calvin grinned. "It's incredible, isn't it?"

With shaking fingers, I pulled the fob from my temple as my pits and back dripped with sweat. "Is there more?"

"Sorry." He shook his head. "That's all they could get."

Get? What is there to *get?* Simulations are not "gotten;" they are created. Then I realized they must have repurposed the word to refer to some element in their creation process. Companies did that all the time—changed the meaning of a term or a phrase and made it part of their vernacular. While internally it made sense, to an outsider, it usually sounded like Greek.

I let the odd word choice go and thought back to the simulation. Only, it had been more than a mere simulation. It had been a totally immersive experience. In an odd way, it had felt more real than real life, and I found myself longing to go back.

Despite my earlier convictions that Rick and his band of geeks were nothing more than a run-of-the-mill startup, I sickeningly realized that they, not us, truly led the virtual reality pack.

Dread settled deep in my stomach. The ominous beast I'd sensed earlier had not been the destruction of my city but the decimation of my industrial domination. My subconscious had been trying to warn me, but I hadn't understood the message.

I wanted to tell Rick that I hadn't been impressed—that his boasts of being the most advanced development team in the world had been outrageous and self-aggrandizing. But I'd be lying, and he'd see right through it.

I looked at his somber face. "This is…amazing."

"Yes, I know," he said.

I wiped my damp forehead as I waited for him to elaborate or brag or something. Only he didn't.

"Why are you showing it to me when you could be burying us with it?" I asked. "The marketing potentials are off the charts. We design state-of-the-art video games, but the worlds Virtual Adventures makes are like pencil sketches compared to this."

Rick shrugged. Though his face remained passive, his eyes gleamed with smug satisfaction. He still had the arc lighter out, slithering its electric flame between his fingers. "Yes, our software is decades more advanced than yours, and, yes, we've discussed entering the market on our own."

I'd asked, but I still cringed at his brusque bluntness.

Calvin smiled at my obvious distress. He'd insisted I come, yet while our company faced not only obsoletion and obliteration, he seemed neither concerned nor apprehensive about his upcoming future in the unemployment line.

Had Rick offered him a job? Perhaps he'd brought me here to gloat? It seemed unlikely, but at this point, I couldn't begin to fathom the purpose of this meeting.

My friend handed me a bottle of water. "While I think we can all agree that what they've done here is awesome, Rick feels that he and his team should stay focused on improving and perfecting this technology. They aren't an entertainment company; they're purely R and D and want to stay that way. If they try to branch out, if they broaden the scope of their purpose, they risk losing what makes them great."

Rick huffed as he leaned back in his chair.

I waited for him to contradict Calvin, but when he didn't, a tiny spark of hope flared to life in my soul. If they had no plans to enter our market, then that opened the door for a possible partnership…

I looked at Cal with a new appreciation. For the past few months, I'd been doing little besides whining and complaining about losing control of my company, and all the while, my friend had been trying to do something about it.

Dencephalon had somehow leapfrogged us, but instead of grousing and throwing in the towel, Cal the Visionary had finagled us into some sort of alignment with them.

I'd been giving him non-stop grief since I'd walked through the front door, and I'd even planned to dress him down when we got back to the office. *Gawd, I'm a schmuck.* He didn't deserve that. He and his phenomenal foresight deserved to have a bronze statue made in his likeness and displayed prominently in the center of our lobby.

While I couldn't apologize to Calvin right now, I could follow his lead and back him the way he'd backed me. I took a long drink off the bottle. The cool water quenched my parched throat. "How did you make such a realistic simulation? It was more than tactile. I felt…emotions. I had memories."

Rick sighed as if being forced to explain physics to a Neanderthal. "Unlike you, we didn't try and fake it. This isn't a simulation. It's a memory extraction."

I stared at him. "What does that even mean?"

After extinguishing the flame, he slipped the lighter into his pocket and folded his hands across his midsection. "I meant just what I said. Those are real memories."

"What?" I shook my head. More obtuse company vernacular?

Calvin gave me a big smile as he picked a tablet off the desk. "The gentleman's name was Rodger Thornton. The lady was Janet Morrow, who, as you probably guessed, eventually became Janet Thornton. According to his bio, they dated all through high school and into college. After the microbe attacks against Philadelphia, he joined the

Army and was shipped off overseas. She started seeing and got engaged to someone else, but she broke it off a couple of months after Rodger returned home."

Had they created a backstory to add yet more realism? None of these random pieces seemed to fit together.

Cal set the tablet down and leaned forward. "You know how we've always theorized that if we could send a signal to the occipital part of the brain, we should also be able to read one too?"

Is *that* what this is about? My flame of hope turned into a fire of outrage. They'd illegally enabled two-way communication on the fob and had been reading human thoughts right out of the brain. That explained what he'd meant by "real memories" and why their simulation had felt so authentic.

Shit. If they'd really broken this mother of all laws, I might have to turn Rick and his crew in after all. My company couldn't even peripherally be involved with them, or we'd be roasted over a hellfire and brimstone cauldron of liberal outrage and marched to the Gulags under the stank of a criminal scandal so thick it would make White-water look like a church picnic.

"Yes," I said, "but the Anti-Virtualists and the Civil Privacy Advocates went completely apeshit when the bill went to Congress to allow MindLink two-way communication. We can only send signals. It's illegal to read them. And, after the backlash we got, I would never dare propose such a thing again."

My cheeks burned as my blood boiled with indignation. I turned on Rick. "Is that what you did? You hacked our hardware and are breaking the law by downloading memories? If so, we could never be part of this operation. It would be political and financial suicide, not to mention it could land us all in Torpor Prison."

Rick sighed. "Calm down. Other than adding the sensory layer, I haven't touched your little darling. We understand the laws and would never dream of breaking them. But there is a loophole."

Startled, I stared at him. I'd read the regulations a million times and they seemed pretty ironclad to me. "What loophole?"

"Cadavers," he said as if the answer had been obvious. "The law doesn't apply to the dead."

CHAPTER THREE

SANDY

The dirty mesh bag covering my head smelled like rotting possum fur. Sun shining through the loose fabric blinded me and exacerbated the raging throb pounding through my skull.

I tried to pull my hands out from behind me, but my wrist bindings, evidently tethered to my ankles too, yanked my feet back. Searing bolts of pain raced through my shoulders and hips, and I took long deep breaths of the foul air, forcing myself to relax. As the tension within my muscles eased, so too did the strain on my aching joints and tortured ligaments.

"Sanford, *what* have you gotten yourself into this time?" my mother would have asked had she been here to witness my latest predicament. "All the neighbors have calm, polite sons. Why the Lord gave me such a rowdy hooligan, I'll never understand. Can't you stay out of trouble for a minute?"

Evidently not.

Lacking not only the maternal lecture but also any assistance its bearer might have provided, I began trying to liberate myself from this situation. Twisting my arms, I wrestled with the bindings but could gain no slack with which to free myself.

I ran my fingers over the rough rope. The knots felt complex and intricate. Perhaps whoever had tied them had been a seaman at one time? I pried at the knots, but they resisted my efforts and the hemp chafed my skin raw.

Sigh.

Who do I know that's ex-Navy with delusions of becoming a kidnapper?

I could only think of a couple of possibilities, but each seemed very unlikely. Could this even peripherally be related to my investigation, or had I just ticked off some bureaucrat who'd had the resources to put a hit on me? While the former seemed highly improbable, I *had* dealt with a lot of sketchy politicians who would like nothing better than to see me come to harm. Who had I pissed off enough to warrant getting stuffed into the trunk of a car?

Now that was a long list. Very long.

Regardless, I needed to get free. "Emergency protocol, charlie-tango-delta-six," I whispered.

I'd hoped for a ping of acknowledgment and my digital assistant's obedient reply. Nothing. I stretched my fingers up my forearm. As I'd suspected, my DigiSleeve had been removed. I twisted my hands around and yanked on the material of my shorts, pulling until I could grab the side pocket. No mobile either.

Though my legs had gone numb, I could still vaguely feel my feet. I curled my toes only to discover that my industrious little abductors had taken my shoes—and the tracking devices within them—as well. Damn. My sailor had the smarts and the foresight to remove all forms of communication before dragging me to his lair.

The brakes squeaked, and we came to a stop. Muffled voices wafted up from the passenger compartment, but I couldn't make out the muddy words. We started moving again and something underneath me clicked. Metal-on-metal. Maybe a tire iron or a jack.

Cars made in the last decade had rubberless treads and would have no need to carry such rudimentary tools. Those that had rolled off the showroom floor in the last fifteen years would have sound cancelation barriers, so I wouldn't be able to hear anyone within the auto itself. Not even peripherally.

I breathed deep through my nose. It could be that my little cell itself smelled bad, not the bag.

Given all that and the rotted-out trunk lid seal, my sailor must have picked this vehicle up from a third-hand dealer or a chop shop. Older cars lacked modern day tracking devices, making them invisible to the grid and, if discovered abandoned, would make them virtually untraceable.

Score one for Kidnapping School. Who says our education system has completely failed us?

I peered through the fabric, trying to decipher the images overhead as they blurred past. Unfortunately, the thin sliver of light seeping in around the trunk lid didn't provide enough context for me to make anything out.

Closing my eyes, I tried to piece together the series of events since I'd left my auto in the traffic jam. I'd talked to my wife, Harmony, promising to beat the car to the hotel. I'd changed into my gym clothes and then got out, leaving the auto to navigate the gridlock without me. As I ran through the park, I'd been assaulted by ghosts who weren't really ghosts at all, but men in liquid camo suits developed for special ops by Poltergeist Armor. After being knocked to the ground, I'd grabbed the throat of the man with giant bushy brows as he tried to hold me down. A bee sting to the neck and then nothing.

The suits had not only made my assailants invisible, but they would have masked their body heat as well, thus thwarting the hundreds of thousands of city scatter cameras and making my sailor—and his accomplices—undetectable. But you couldn't just waltz into an Army surplus supply store and pick up Poltergeist Armor. The military never let a single piece of it out of their control.

I opened my eyes and stared at the fuzzy images as they flew past the slit in the trunk.

My assailants had timed my capture so that the city gridlock kept the police and their drones preoccupied. But that seemed too convenient, their efforts too coordinated and well-timed. I frowned as I flipped the idea around and looked at it from another direction. When I'd been griping about the traffic, Harmony told me that at least six cities in the last two weeks had suffered similar navigation failures.

Could it be that my hosts hadn't been taking advantage of the gridlock but had somehow instigated it? Why do that? Why shut down an entire city?

The floor vibrated beneath my back as I mulled it over. Suddenly, realization dawned. They'd wanted the police, the patrol drones, and EMT services preoccupied so they could capture...me. I couldn't imagine what they wanted with me, but mobs of stranded, angry commuters roaming the streets would be the mother of all diversions.

I didn't know if I should feel flattered they'd gone to such great efforts to nab a piece of my ass, dismayed by the depths of their conniving, or impressed by their tenacious, brilliant underhandedness.

If my captors *had* managed to breach the city's central server with the intent of nabbing me, their ability to obtain Poltergeist Armor didn't seem as far-fetched.

Who had these kinds of resources and connections? Not the government—at least not the US government—because the car was too old. Protocol would have mandated something with the latest gadgets and gizmos.

Several reports had been circulating within the agency about a sharp rise in missing persons, particularly among government employees. What if these citywide shutdowns corresponded with other kidnappings? Could there be a correlation? I thought it over, examining the theory from all angles. But, if I'd pieced it together from a few secondhand reports and some simple reasoning, why hadn't anyone else?

I should have been given the assignment of finding those responsible instead of being tasked with reviewing the rubbish report shat out of the Secretary of Defense's bung hole.

Why had this not been made a top priority? Why hadn't a nation-wide manhunt been started? Even if the operation to find those responsible had been classified, I'd have heard about it. Someone somewhere would have leaked the intel.

I cursed as the pieces fell together. Six cities stalled. Military-grade camouflage. Organized coordination and kidnapping of a government defense contractor. It seemed improbable, impossible even, but being in this predicament *also* seemed improbable. If my suspicions proved true, I might be in a bit more trouble than a mere junkie trying to trade me for money.

The car slowed and turned. Gravel crunched as we shifted from pavement to unfinished roadway.

As we navigated terrain far rougher than city boulevards and highways, I got tossed around so violently that I rebounded several times off the lid of my steel cage. The car thudded through a pothole that must have rivaled the Grand Canyon, driving the air from my lungs. When it bounced again, my head ricocheted off the floor, and my world faded to black for the second time today.

∞ ∞ ∞ ∞

The next time I woke, the car droned smoothly, gently vibrating the floor.

Finally, some good news!

No more being knocked out on the rough gravel road. If I could stay conscious long enough, perhaps I could find a way out of this fix and be home by suppertime.

Unfortunately, some bad news accompanied the good. Based on the hum of the car's motors and tires, we had to be traveling at a high rate of speed, and due to my lapses in memory, I couldn't even begin to calculate how far we'd gone.

Trying to filter out the sounds of the car, I concentrated on ambient noises—a train, boat, or something else that could give me a clue as to where the hell we'd gone. But I couldn't hear anything over the whistling air pounding against the hull.

I looked around the trunk. Sunlight still peeked through the edges of the lid, but it had dimmed since the last time I'd looked. We must have gotten out of the city. Probably *way* out.

Just my luck.

I'd wanted to take a quick run and burn off some energy after a long day of meetings. But instead, I'd been roped like a prize cow and now headed for the slaughterhouse. Granted, being kidnapped and killed by these faceless assailants *was* better than reading the Secretary of Defense's report, though just marginally.

I needed to escape. Then I could improvise a way home and maybe even get back to that report.

What a great life.

The roof lay about three feet above my head, so the vehicle must be a sedan of some kind. Since the buzz of the electric motors came from beneath and to my right, and the buffeting wind to my left, I had to be in the front trunk. There should be an inside release. After I'd found and pulled it, the lid would fold back onto the windshield and all hell would break loose.

I just needed to get my hands free to fight off the terrorists holding me hostage—and pray they didn't have backup in a trail car—and hitch a ride home. Easy peasy. But first, I needed to get loose.

I twisted my wrists as far as the bindings would allow and started probing the floor. The rough carpet gave no purchase to pull against, but I found a small indentation beneath my hip.

Rolling onto my back, I used my body weight to push on the spot. When the carpet stretched, I doubled my efforts. My shoulders felt as if my arms would pop out of their sockets. But when the fabric began to tear, I ignored the pain and pressed even harder.

My fingers burst through the carpet, and I let out a pent-up lungful of air. I shoved my hand through the small opening. At first, I only found open air, but when I shifted my body and stretched my tendons, my fingertips grazed cold steel. The tire iron I'd heard earlier. Praising the god of old cars and cheap hoodlums, I wrapped my middle finger around the bar and pulled. At first, it resisted my efforts, but then it popped free.

Despite the ache in my screaming joints, I refused to let go and worked the tool until the sharp tip poked through the small gash in the floor. I yanked it out, dropped it, and lay on my side, panting.

I took a moment to catch my breath. The rotting possum air sludged in and out of my lungs, hardly a reward for a job well done.

Sighing, I rolled onto my back. Maneuvering the tire iron, I trapped the lug nut end beneath my hip and began to scrape the bindings against the sharp end of the tool.

While I ground away on the rope, the motors slowed. We turned, and, once again, the tires chewed gravel.

Discarding my original pulling-the-trunk-latch plan, I worked harder as I formulated a new one. Unfortunately, if I didn't get loose soon, I would need to come up with a Plan C in a hurry.

The car came to a stop, and I pulled against my bindings. The hemp held tight, but when I doubled my efforts, it snapped in two. I ripped the cloth sack from my head and loosened the knots binding my feet.

Doors slammed and heavy footsteps crunched toward my small metal prison.

I draped the rope over the top of my ankles, yanked the cloth sack back over my head, and twisted my aching body until it once again formed a convoluted pretzel.

I stared up into the light seeping in around the edge of the trunk. A shadow blocked out the sun, and, with a sharp click and the squeak of old hinges, the lid opened. Two men stood over me staring down as I pretended to be out cold, a task made infinitely easier by the hood.

Peering through a small hole in the bag, I thought I recognized Thug One's furry eyebrows. He reached for my legs while Thug Two reached for my arms.

As One grabbed my calves, I flipped the putrid sack off my head and yanked my legs out of his grasp. Arching my back, I thrust my feet into the air and grabbed the brute around the neck with my ankles.

Surprise had just begun to register in his expression when I slammed his face, along with his rodent-infused brows, into the lip of the trunk. His head ricocheted off the metal hull, and he flopped to the ground.

Thug Two's gaze lingered for a heartbeat on his fallen comrade before his misbelieving eyes found mine.

I shrugged and gave him a half-smile. *What can you do? The guy was obviously a putz, so I had to kill him.*

The thug's expression turned from confusion to outrage, and he leapt forward, swinging his fist.

I pulled the trunk lid down.

His hand and face collided with the metal, and he yelled some obscenity about my mother being a female dog.

Shoving the improvised shield back open, I brought the tire iron around in an arch, aiming for his head. For the briefest moment, I thought that I could end this before it had really gotten going—especially since he'd already resorted to insulting my mother—but at the last second, he lifted his arm to protect himself.

Instead of the steel rod crushing his temple, it clanged off his elbow. He screamed and reached for his injured limb, leaving his torso unprotected.

Amateur.

I flipped the iron around and shoved the pointed end into his hip. Using the makeshift leverage to haul myself out of the trunk, I drove the tip of the rod deep into his pelvis.

Thug Two screamed again and fell to his knees.

Once I landed on my feet, I grabbed his oily hair and smashed his head into the bumper of the car. He thudded into the dirt next to his partner.

"Don't ever say anything about my mom again," I told the brute.

Silence descended, and I wiped the man's nasty hair gel on my shorts as I looked around the deserted, overgrown parking lot. No trail car. No one coming out to help their fallen comrades. No one.

I knelt down to examine my former captors. Squat and muscular, Thug One looked to be about six inches shorter than me, but forty or so pounds heavier. He wouldn't do. Thug Two seemed approximately my size, so I removed his brightly colored sneakers.

Holding them up, I shook my head. "Really? Orange?" Muttering to myself about criminals having horrific taste in footwear, I slipped the shoes on. Even though I could now be seen from space, at least I could run if I had to.

I rummaged through the shoeless man's blood-soaked pockets, searching for the mobile tethered to the car. I had to be long gone before any of their—undoubtedly unpleasant—friends realized the brutes hadn't shown up for tea and biscotti and came sniffing around.

When I flipped him onto his back, he moaned and grabbed at the tire iron sticking out of his belly.

"Don't be such a pansy. It's barely a flesh wound." I swatted his hands away and continued my search but found nothing.

I turned to Thug One. Blood oozed from the deep gash across the bridge of his nose. If I'd been a betting man, I'd have placed a hefty wager that slivers of bone had been lodged into the front of his brain. I rooted through his clothing but couldn't find the mobile. It must still be in the car.

Thinking about the joyful expression of my Homeland Department buddies when I rolled in with a couple of dead bodies, I scooped up Thug One and dropped him into the trunk. Smiling at the satisfaction of making these brutes ride in the same place they'd held me captive, I turned to grab Thug Two, but froze mid-stoop.

A man—roughly the same size and build as a buffalo, only a lot uglier—leaned up against the side of the auto watching me.

I stared for a second at the long scar running along the base of his throat. *Could it be...?*

He held up a mobile in his beefy paw. "Is this what you were looking for?" His voice came out in a jagged rasp. He glanced at the man lying in the dirt. "You killed two of my men. I wish you hadn't done that. Good help and all."

I reached down and yanked the tire iron from Thug Two's belly, waving the bloody tip through the air. "Just toss the mobile onto the seat and walk away." I nodded toward the fallen brute. "You don't want to end up like your 'help.'"

He shook his huge head and let out a cancerous-sounding snort. "No, I don't think so. Tell you what, I'll make this easy on you. Put the toothpick down, and I won't hurt you...as much. If you give up, I might not break *all* of your bones."

"Come on," I said, smiling, "you can't be serious. They had me tied up and locked in a trunk, but now look at them. Just give me the mobile, and I'll be out of your hair."

He sighed and slipped the small device into his pocket. Pushing off the auto, he lumbered toward me.

I crouched low as he approached. He probably outweighed me by a hundred, hundred and twenty pounds, but I'd handled bigger. "You don't want to do this, my friend." My threat didn't even make him pause.

Some people needed to learn the hard way.

As he got within arm's reach, I sprang up, driving the sharp end of the tire iron into the flesh under his ribcage. Only, instead of the tool tearing into his abdomen, he grabbed it before it grazed his skin. We froze in a temporary stalemate.

For a second, our eyes locked, our noses almost touching, as we both pressed for the advantage. Tobacco littered his teeth. The acrid odor of it wafted on his breath. This man didn't mind the stink of his own sweat either.

He smirked, and the thick muscles of his hairy arms bulged as he twisted the iron.

I spun with the steel bar and fell to the ground.

Tossing the tool into the bushes, he loomed over me.

I rolled onto my backside and started sliding, trying to put some distance between myself and the hulking beast.

In a single giant step, he undid my pathetic attempt to get away from him. He brought his huge fist flying in from the side, and I barely got out of its way as it whizzed through the air half a centimeter from my nose.

Ducking down, I hooked my arms around his tree trunk thighs and pulled myself between his legs. I sprang to my feet and spun around, intending to leap onto his back. But as I finished my rotation, a cinderblock-sized fist connected with my face, and I landed ungracefully in a cloud of dust on my butt. Blinking hard, I tried to shake off the worst of the clang ringing through my skull.

He leered down at me. "Are you done?"

Despite the dizziness from having been coldcocked, I stumbled to my feet, though I remained hunched over at the waist. I paused, waiting for him to drop his guard so I could drop him.

The big man stepped forward. "I told you…"

I sprang up and swung with all my might. But connecting with the underside of his massive jaw was like punching a bridge pillar. Pain exploded through my knuckles, radiated up my arm, and reverberated through the muscles and tendons in my shoulder. The impact even rattled the fillings in my teeth and vibrated the marrow in my bones.

The big man shook his head and shoved me to the ground with the swipe of a giant paw. "If we're going to be working together, you're going to have to learn to behave yourself."

Back in the dirt yet again, I flexed my hand and rolled my wrist to see if I'd broken any bones. Things hadn't been going exactly the way I'd anticipated. I needed to change tactics or soon I'd be lying in the dirt alongside the Thug brothers. "There's nothing for us to do together. You're going to give me the mobile, and I'm going to go home. People know where I am and will be here shortly. I'm giving you the opportunity to save yourself."

Take charge. Tell him how things will go. Textbook tactics from *Brutes and the Men That Fight Them*.

He grabbed the front of my shirt and lifted me into the air, sticking his buffalo face into mine. "You're wrong. No one knows where you are, and no one is coming. Besides, you and I have a lot of work to do."

I stared into his bloodshot eyes, gagging at the gut-rot alcohol in his breath. "Look, Bub, I—"

He shook me so hard my teeth clacked together. "My name's Jesper."

My head pirouetted like a drunk ballerina. Stars whirled and spun in my vision, then began to fade as my sight slowly returned to normal. I held up my hands. "Okay, *Jesper*. First, you've made a mistake. I don't know who you think I am, but I'm nobody. I'm just a—"

He smacked me on the side of the head with a hand roughly as large and dense as a cast iron skillet. "I know who you are."

The clang, reverberating through my skull, blurred my world so much I had a second to hope that this whole scene would turn out to be nothing more than an elaborate nightmare. Perhaps in reality, a roving gang of ninjas had tried to mug me. Even now as my body ached and my face throbbed, maybe I lay in a hospital bed. Soon, I'd wake to find Harmony sitting at my side, beaming with relief and pride. The doctors, undoubtedly impressed by my heroics, would be reverently patching up my cuts and bruises while a team of morticians hauled off piles of mangled ninja bodies.

Unfortunately, as my vision cleared, the huge head of the king thug still loomed giant and vile in my face.

He sneered. "What's the second thing?"

Perplexed, I stared up at him. "Huh?"

"You said, 'first,' so I'm guessing there's a 'second' to go along with it."

I smiled. "Well, aren't you an observant one? You're right. And second..." I pulled back and then rocketed forward, my forehead connecting with the bridge of his nose. In all my years of training, I'd never done it better. Made a more solid impact. For half a second, I patted myself on the back for keeping my nerves cool and thinking straight, despite having been beaten and battered by three of the baddest in the business.

My trainers at the academy would have been proud... But only for half a second.

Jesper didn't flinch. He didn't, in fact, react at all.

When I tried again, he caught my face in his cast iron hand and shoved me back. This time when I fell to the dirt, my head thumped against the ground, and black encroached on my vision.

He stepped forward, staring down at me and shaking his head. "I warned you to play nice."

"Jesper, I—" But even as the words came tumbling from my mouth, he pulled back his fist.

Damn, it looks like I might not be going to DC tomorrow after all.

Then the huge brute put my lights out for the third time that day.

CHAPTER FOUR

JEFF

I blinked. "Pardon? Cadavers? As in dead people?"
Rick nodded. "Yes."
I squinted and shook my head.
Joking. These guys had to be pulling my leg.
"I'm trying to follow," I said, "but I don't have the slightest idea what you're talking about."
Rick pulled the arc lighter out again, lit it, and resumed rolling it around in his fingers. "Years ago, I was a med student who tinkered with electrical engineering on the side. One day I was doing an analysis of a woman who had died of complications from dementia. During one of my experiments, I noticed the vague outline of an image on the monitor. When I showed it to the instructor, he said it was the result of faulty equipment."
"But you didn't think so," I said.
Rick shook his head. "My instructor was an idiot. I knew I'd found something groundbreaking, so I ignored him and focused on reproducing the phenomenon. After

two days of probing, I did it again. This time the image was much clearer and undeniably *not* a malfunction."

He retrieved a mobile from his pocket. With his free hand he slid out the keyboard and started laboriously typing with his thumb. After a minute, a blurry image of a boy, maybe ten years old and holding a fishing pole on a pier, materialized a few inches above the device.

I frowned. "This is the picture that came up on the monitor?"

He nodded. "Though my instructor still blamed bad equipment, I tracked the woman's daughter down and showed her the picture. She said that it was her brother from when he was little. The woman with dementia didn't know her own name, yet I was able to retrieve a picture of her son from her long-term memories."

"But, since I couldn't get anyone to listen to me, I bought one of the supposedly faulty impedance imagers," Rick said, tossing the mobile onto the desk. "I tore it apart and figured out exactly how it 'malfunctioned.' Long story short, here we are two decades later. My old instructor retired without contributing a single thing to society. Not a thing. The company that made the equipment is long out of business, but we're still building on the breakthrough they had no idea they'd made."

Rick wanted us to believe that he'd not only figured out how to read thoughts from the human brain a good ten years before anyone else but he'd also done so by reenergizing, reanimating, and interpreting bioelectric synaptic signals from *dead* tissue.

Uh uh. No way.

His story blew way past science and technological breakthroughs and galloped right into fantasy land.

"No," I said. "I'm sorry, but that's completely preposterous. That's like downloading the contents of a mobile that's been first stripped of its casing, then beaten with a hammer, and then tossed into a lake."

"Your metaphor is totally inaccurate," he retorted.

"Whatever. You get my gist." I sighed. "Look, I'm not a doctor, nor do I claim to be one, but I don't have to be to know that you can't bring something back to life after it's dead."

Rick narrowed his eyes at me. "Viable organs are harvested from corpses every day. This isn't that much different." He glared. "You need to move past your own preconceived notions and narrow-mindedness. You claim to be a man of science, so are you denying what you experienced?"

While my ire demanded that I shout down this poser, I needed to rethink my thinking. Like it or not, he had a point. Sometimes the line between fantasy and fact could be razor thin.

Pulling the pad off my neck, I glanced at the holoimage of the boy, then stared at the oversized fob in my hand. As much as I wanted to tell him that what he'd described could not be done, I had felt the briefcase in Rodger's hand, touched Janet's waist, and "remembered" their future child. Those sorts of simulations could not be fabricated. I knew because we'd tried.

According to Arthur Conan Doyle's character Sherlock Holmes, once everything false had been eliminated then whatever remained, no matter how unlikely, had to be true. While not a scientific proof, I'd never once been able to find a counter example to his reasoning. By that logic, it meant Rick could, in fact, extract the memories from dead human brain tissue. My mind reeled at the notion. "No, I can't deny it."

He nodded and leaned back in his chair, the smugness returning to his expression.

Though I still couldn't wrap my head around the concept of memory extractions, I didn't need to. We'd been arguing semantics. Either he could or he couldn't do what he'd said, but either way, it didn't matter. He'd delivered an almost life-altering experience that we might be able to incorporate into our video games. That's what I needed to focus on.

I turned the fob over in my hand and stared at the extra circuitry. "It's one thing to see and hear what someone's remembered, but how did you know you'd captured their feelings?"

He pointed at me with one hand while the other made the flaming arc lighter slink and slither through his fingers. "Now *that's* a good question."

I held my breath and waited for his halitosis fumes to dissipate.

"Though I'd suspected we'd gotten more than just tactile," he said, "we had no way to know for sure. Feelings aren't projectable. They aren't measurable. They don't show up in graphs. We could see that there was metadata that came along with the images and sounds, but we had no idea what it was."

He took the fob and held it up. "This is not as efficient or as sophisticated as it could be, but your technology helped us fully realize all that we'd accomplished."

So help me if this disgusting slob puts my company down one more time, I'm going to knock his nasty teeth in.

I took a deep breath, trying to stifle my growing anger.

"Anyway," he continued, oblivious of my desire to help him into a new pair of dentures, "we were about to start the process of designing something similarly rudimentary when we discovered your company had already done most of the work for us. Plus, you've already developed the infrastructure and got the marketing in place, and though the hardware needs some improvements, it already supports the extra data."

Irritation and worry vied for the top spot in my heart. "Do you mind stepping out for a minute? I need to have a quick conversation with my tech lead."

Without saying a word, Rick dropped the fob onto the desk, stood, and stepped out of the sound silo.

I turned to Calvin. "Rick's off the charts weird. Are you absolutely sure we can trust him?"

"Come on, Jeff. You of all people should know that some of the smartest people in the world are also the most idiosyncratic."

I glanced at the short man outside our silo. He sat and stared at a huge holodisplay full of glowing schematics while he absently played with the flaming arc lighter.

"I don't know, Cal. This simulation—or extraction or whatever it is—is too good. Too complete. Something feels wrong."

He frowned. "Does something feel wrong or are you just pissed that they were able to solve a problem that we spent years trying to figure out?"

Damn Calvin and his inane ability to cut through the bull and get right to the heart of things. Even though I'd spent a good portion of the last hour being annoyed by Rick's apparent success, my friend's unflappable humility didn't let him get bogged down by such petty details. He put his heart and soul into everything he did, but if someone did it better, made a discovery he'd missed, or succeeded where he'd failed, it never bothered him. He celebrated their victory and admired their accomplishments, and he did it without malice or jealousy.

Be like Calvin. Get out of your own way.

I tried to separate my ego, distance myself from my dislike of Rick, and swallow my pride. A task I found only moderately easier than reversing the spin of the planet by using the power of my mind. "I don't know. Maybe."

"Maybe nothing." Calvin gave me his most endearing smile. "I know you, Jeff. And like it or not, you wear your heart on your sleeve. The two of you have been playing who's got the biggest data pipe since you met."

"They did something amazing," he continued, "and you feel left in the dust. But I can guarantee that's exactly how our competitors have felt since we opened our doors. Now let's really smoke them. Come on, this is the ticket to the big times. A merger with these guys would be a huge win for all of us."

I huffed out a breath. "I didn't know about any of this until an hour ago, so you'll have to excuse me if I'm not jumping up and down with excitement."

Calvin put his hand on my shoulder. "Look, I know it was a slap in the face for Ceos to steal our company. But our new dictator-on-steroids is keeping you on because she believes that you know how to make us the best in the business."

He grabbed the fob and held it up to my face. "*You* created MindLink. *You* created a whole new market. Just because the purse strings have changed hands doesn't mean our mission to make Virtual Adventures great has. *This* will take us to the next level."

Had anyone else tried to dump such a huge stinking pile of positive rationality on me, I probably would have throttled them. But Calvin's genuine enthusiasm and calmness didn't just mollify my anger; it made me feel silly for getting upset in the first place.

The tension in my shoulders relaxed, and the heat pumping through my veins cooled. Just like that, he'd broken my fever.

I had the sudden, irrational urge to wrap the bean pole of a man in a bear hug. Refraining from unconventional displays of public affection, I touched his shoulder and smiled. "Thanks, bro. You're right."

He held the fob out to me. "Now, tell me what you're thinking."

Having finally been broken out of my emotional rut, I took the little marvel we'd created and focused, logically working through the possibilities and the pitfalls. I glanced at the image of the ghost boy still floating above Rick's mobile. "The argument over extractions aside, I need to know if you understand how all of this works. I don't want to just take his word for it. I want someone I trust on the inside."

Calvin's smile grew. "It's complicated, but I feel like I understand it about as much as anyone can. Tell ya what, you and I can sit down later and go over it circuit by circuit."

"What about extractions on dead people?" I asked. "Do you believe that's even possible?"

His grin faltered, his face growing serious. "What I think you mean is—could he be lying, and is he actually breaking the law?"

"I'm sure you did your due diligence," I said. "But this is really important, so I have to ask."

He thought it over for a second. "From everything I've seen, Rick is telling the truth." He grimaced. "I've actually seen a video of an extraction—which, for the record, isn't something you'd ever see on family primetime."

"Pretty nasty?" I asked.

He curled his upper lip in disgust and nodded. "Remember how before cellular imagers, medical examiners used to have to cut people up to figure out how they'd died? Well, an extraction is not too far from that." He shuddered. "But I also got to review the resulting records."

"And?"

He shrugged. "It seems legit."

There was no one I trusted more than Calvin. If he believed it, I would too.

I motioned for Rick to rejoin us. As he entered the silo, I asked, "Are you able to access all of the thoughts and emotions of dead people?"

He fell back into the chair and shook his head. "Humans are not computers. What we feel, taste, touch, and remember isn't stored in a single part of the brain. It's distributed and very little is kept long-term. And what is there is often fragmented and overlaps with other memories."

"When Rodger touched Janet's waist, he had an image of her pregnant," I said. "Only that would have been years later. That's an example of an overlap?"

"Yes," he said. "The two memories occupy the same space because they are both about the same person and each is tied to a significant event."

"But the cars, buildings, and the crowd were gray and blurry while the images of meeting Janet were crystal clear. Why?"

He rolled the arc lighter over the back of his hand, catching it in his palm. "Some memories are more powerful than others."

Instead of elaborating, he sat there watching me. Getting information from this guy was like trying to pull hydrogen atoms from a binary stream. "What makes one stronger than another?"

"Emotions," he said flatly. "The higher the emotional state, the louder and clearer the memories are. Joy and excitement are helpful with recollection, but not as much as pain and stress."

I raised an eyebrow, uncomfortable with the light in his eyes when he spoke of pain and stress.

"If the donor dies under great duress—say, being buried alive or as the victim of long-term torture—we can extract a lot more memories, including those not related to their death," he said. "The more extreme and the longer they experience cruelty and violence, the more their brain is flooded with recollection hormones. The influx of hormones makes *all* of their memories clearer and more complete."

Cruelty and violence? What exactly has Calvin got us mixed up in?

He paused, and an odd, almost self-satisfied expression crossed his face. "I once did an extraction on a POW who had been in captivity for years. I got images spanning from the moment he bled out with his guts splashed all over the floor all the way back to when he was still sucking on his mommy's teat."

I shuddered. "Eh. That's gruesome."

Rick leaned back and smirked his mock smile. "Ordinarily, finding the perpetrator of something so heinous is difficult if not impossible. But because of my extraction, I could tell the powers that be exactly where to send our troops."

A glimmer of crazy blazed in the scientist's eyes as his smile turned sinister. "Those men were watching the video of themselves committing the murder when our robotic soldiers stormed in and slaughtered them and their entire village. Now, *that's* justice."

It may have been justice, but instead of looking appalled like a normal human being, Rick looked jubilant. Proud even.

Calvin had called him idiosyncratic. I called him warped, unfeeling, and narcissistic.

Cal had compared extractions to autopsies, but without having seen one, I didn't know what that entailed. I took a long breath, hesitant and afraid of the answer to my next question. "I know we talked about the legality of it, but *could* you do this on a live person? Just stick a probe in someone's head and begin downloading?"

Rick drummed the fingers of his free hand on the arm of the chair. "That's an interesting question. Probably. In fact, the fresher the tissue, the more information will still be intact, so it would most likely provide an even more complete extraction. But I'd never do it to a live person." He chuckled. "Well, at least not anyone I cared about."

Do I dare ask more?

Though I didn't know if I wanted him to answer, I needed to know as much as possible. "Why not?"

"Why do you think we call it an 'extraction?'" He arched his eyebrows. "The procedure is completely, physically destructive and requires chemically disintegrating the neural cellular walls."

"You melt their brain?" I asked, incredulous.

His sinister smile grew into a mean-boy-smirk. "Like I said, I wouldn't do it to anyone *I* cared about."

My gut gurgled unhappily as a wave of nausea rolled through me. I tried to not read anything into the comment. "Not for family primetime," Calvin had said. *No kidding.*

Did I really want to go into business with someone like this? Day after day of bad breath, derogatory comments, and sinister undertones. Idiosyncratic or evil, only time would tell.

Unfortunately, in this industry we didn't have the luxury of time. If I didn't jump on this, someone else would, and they would destroy my company in the process.

Ignoring the little voice in my head that screamed at me to stop and reconsider, I nodded. "Even though it sounds a little barbaric, having no way to do this on a live person may actually help us. We need to sit down and write up a plan."

"Cal," I said, "when we get back to the office, let's stop in and talk to legal and see if they agree with the loophole in the law. Public Relations too." I pulled out my mobile, expanded the keyboard, and started taking notes. "They'll certainly need a heads-up about a potential shit storm that could be coming our way. We can—"

"Jeff," Calvin said, "you need to talk to Tamara."

My fingers, which had been flying over the little keyboard, paused mid-stroke. *Oh, damn.*

"I thought your CEO was Ceos Wells," Rick said.

"She is," I replied.

He looked at me. "Well, then who's Tamara?"

Calvin glanced at him. "That's Jeff's girlfriend, who also happens to be a corporate lawyer, a privacy advocate, and the head of the local Anti-Virtualists chapter." He leaned in closer to me and whispered, "Though if you'd ever man up and ask her, she'd be your fiancée. How long have you been holding onto that little box? Three months?"

"Ssshhhh. Not now," I muttered and subtly elbowed him in the ribs.

Still keeping his voice conspiratorial, he held a hand to his mouth so only I could hear. "She's so smart and gorgeous, if you don't do it soon, I might switch teams and ask her myself."

"Not now!" I hissed.

A putrid wave of halitosis accompanied Rick's sharp bark of laughter. "You can't be serious." He pointed at me. "*You* are dating an Anti-V? You." He shook his head. "So tell me, when she organizes a rally or pickets a new product launch—trying to get your company shut down and you arrested—how awkward is the dinner conversation?"

I glared at him. "We do just fine. Just because most people can't talk civilly or find common ground on differing political views doesn't mean we can't."

"Differing political views?" he scoffed. "That's what you call it? She and her loonies don't just want limits on virtual reality; they'd have it completely abolished if they had their way." He folded his arms, studying me as if seeing me for the first time. "You've got cojones. I'll give you that."

I'd had enough of this buffoon's judgment. "Tamara and I work together. In fact, she and I wrote the VR limits bill together. It's called rational people who disagree finding common ground. She sees my point of view, and I see—"

"Jeff," Calvin said. He raised his eyebrows and gave me the slightest shake of his head.

What about this guy keeps putting me on the defensive?

I took a long breath, settling my blood pressure. "I'll talk to Tamara and get the Anti-V take."

Though I'd downplayed it to Rick and his mighty ego, a tremor of dread quaked through my bones at the thought of explaining to Tamara how we'd found a way to make VR even more addictive. Unless I presented it just right, she might literally kill me. I needed to be prepared for her to—

"What about Ceos?" Calvin interrupted my morose thoughts.

"Huh?" I blinked as he derailed me from my mental tracks. "Ceos? What about her?"

He smiled at me as though leading a small child through a crowded department store. "Do you think we should get her buy in?"

Back to business. *Focus, Jeff.*

While I still had the executive power to make this call without her, she and I didn't exactly see eye to eye on... anything. Perhaps by extending an olive branch, we could get past some of our bad blood and start building a civilized working relationship. Besides, even though she'd given me leeway to make purchases at my discretion, she should know about something this big.

"Good call. If we decide to move forward, we'll need to allocate some capital." I thought for a second. "She'll want to know about the potential legal and political problems we could be facing by using extractions, but I'm confident that she'll be okay with it because of the huge marketing possibilities."

I turned back to Rick. "I'll need to do a demo for Ceos."

Rick held up a hand. "Hold on a minute. Before we go any further, there are couple of things you and I need to talk about."

"Okay," I said. "Like what?"

He pointed at Calvin. "Things that are not meant for the ears of underlings."

My friend's face blanched, and two bright spots of color appeared high on his cheeks. "Oh. I…um. Okay, I can just step out while you two talk." He turned to go.

"No," I said, touching Cal's shoulder. I stepped up beside him. "You're not going anywhere."

I faced Rick. "Calvin has practically been there from Day One. My company wouldn't exist without him, and we," I motioned between myself and Rick, "wouldn't be here talking about a possible joint venture if it hadn't been for him." I pointed at Calvin. "He's just as much a part of VA as I am, and I couldn't begin to fathom a world where I'd make any sort of major decision without him."

Calvin's humble smile warmed my heart. He stood shoulder to shoulder with me and puffed out his nonexistent chest.

Rick's eyes blazed into mine. "This has nothing to do with development. It's strictly business."

"And?" I said.

He let out an exasperated breath and sighed. "Fine. Whatever."

His gaze moved between us, irritation flashing through his eyes. "Up until this point, our research has been funded by a private foundation. But times are tight, and management has lost interest in the forwarding of scientific research and the advancement of mankind. They're 'diversifying' their money. As such, they've discontinued support."

Suddenly, the pieces fell into place. Rick had told Calvin that they hadn't branched out because they only wanted to focus on science. While partially true, the real reason they'd reached out at all is because they'd gotten desperate. Their expenses had to be astronomical, and without time to find another source of income, they'd be forced into bankruptcy.

I studied Rick's sour expression. He could most certainly find another partner, but not quickly and not one with our infrastructure and resources. I might be able to turn this to our advantage during negotiations.

"How long do you have?" I asked.

Rick snorted as if the entire notion of money and finances annoyed him. "We have less than two weeks before they shut the power off and evict us from the premises. When they do that, all of what we've done will be lost. All of it."

CHAPTER FIVE

SANDY

Jesper glared down at me like a bovine with crushed nads. Nostrils flaring, the broken veins in his jaundiced eyes pulsed crimson as he squeezed my throat.

I forced myself to remain passive while asphyxiation clawed at my self-control and panic loomed like a feral cat awaiting its chance to tear me to shreds.

He wanted fear to overwhelm me. He wanted pain to cow me. He wanted threats of death to terrify me. He could want until hell froze over.

A broken man spills his secrets. A man of grit only spills his blood.

Just as black roses bloomed in my vision, threatening unconsciousness, he let go, cocked his arm, and smashed a rock-hard fist into my face.

I smiled at him as my sight began to clear. Though my arms and legs had been bound to the chair for the past forty-eight hours, I'd controlled this beast with alternating doses of apathy and indifference. He couldn't kill me. Not yet anyway. He needed something, and as long as he did, I would stay alive.

The blood in my mouth had so many sources—busted lip, missing teeth, smashed nose—it would take an army of monks a year to scribe all my leaking fluids and body aches. I spit coppery goo, a proprietary snot-blood concoction—*Snood, anyone?*—that I could take to market…if I survived.

Red saliva hit the dirty floor, splattering gore onto the boot-clad foot of my imprisoner.

Jesper's gaze fell to the shiny crimson droplets on the scuffed leather. Eyes blazing, he backhanded me across the face. My head whipped around at the impact.

As a distraction, I'd started making a mental list of the parts of me that hurt as a result of the torture delivered by this beast.

I scrolled down the *Slapped Cheek* column of my imaginary clipboard, adding a check mark next to *Jaws*, another next to *Teeth*, and oddly one next to *Lower Back*. This last one perplexed me. Maybe the twisting of my neck had some sort of chain reaction that had traveled along my spine and into my upper buttocks?

Interesting.

Flipping to the page titled *Things that Annoy Jesper*, which encompassed pretty much everything including birds singing, the sun shining, and any inkling of human emotion, I logged *Doesn't care for dirty boots*. I glanced at his footwear, reconsidering the wording.

Hmmm, not quite right.

Noting the crusted mud around the soles, I erased the entry and changed it to *Doesn't like other people making his boots dirty*.

The pain in my jaw and ribs had begun to get hot. Beading sweat dripped from my forehead.

Concentrating, I sent a signal to the Department of Homeland Security's surgically-implanted Endocrine Enhancement System to release another small dose of opiates. The little gizmo, simply known as The Gland, had been part of the DHS's operative "safety initiative program" and was something I'd fought to keep out of my body. If I'd let them, they would have stuck a hundred such little gadgets and whatnots inside of me, but I'd adamantly refused to let them turn me into a cyborg. And even though I'd hated losing that argument, in this instance, I was glad I had.

As hormones flooded my system, rounding off the worst of Jesper's brutalities, my internal thermostat began to drop. I gave him my most charming, though gap-toothed, smile. "Sorry about that. I was aiming for your ginormous melon-shaped head, but, you know, someone's been using my face as a punching bag. Ordinarily, I could have spit in your eye, but it's hard to get that kind of distance when half your teeth have been knocked out."

He raised his blood-caked knuckles and punched me in the abdomen.

I added to the list *Doesn't like having his head compared to a ginormous melon*. After mentally scrolling down the *Punched in the Gut* column, I made a tick next to *Knocked Wind Out of Me* and another by *Ruptured Spleen*.

The first time I'd added this item to the list, I'd laughed out loud. I had always been able to find amusement in the most absurd places. Harmony had repeatedly accused me of being warped, and over the years I'd been able to convince my bride that I'm not demented, just perpetually sarcastic as a result of the throngs of idiots that are drawn to me like flies to a pile of cow shit.

Not that I'm cow shit. Though in this metaphor, I suppose I am.

Maybe deep down this was what I really thought of myself? Perhaps I should seek counseling about my fecal-infused self-image? Would said counselor want to discuss my potty training days?

Regardless, at least Harmony had finally given up on trying to change me, concluding that all of my mental mess was just part of my charming personality.

I love that girl.

Unfortunately, I'd not had the time to convince Jesper that he should try and look at it from my perspective. I felt like we got off on the wrong foot. If we could have talked things over, my list of injuries and the resulting cross section of aches would have undoubtedly tickled his funny bone until he giggled like a school boy who'd farted during quiet reading time. In between pummelings, I'd tried to explain that I hadn't been laughing *at* him but laughing *with* him. Sadly, Jesper's lack of social sophistication prevented him from grasping my subtle witticisms.

I guess when you only speak rage and cruelty, some things get lost in translation.

I'd noted on the second page of my mental list that Jesper lacked a sense of humor and that I should avoid sharing jokes, quips, and amusing family stories with him unless I was looking for new and inventive ways of experiencing pain.

Hey, Jesper. Did you hear the one about the torturing asshole who attended a proctologists' convention?

Okay, maybe he wouldn't find that as funny as I had.

The huge man loomed over me, cracking his knuckles, a habit I found oddly annoying.

"Do you know that if you keep doing that, you'll eventually get arthritis in your joints?" I asked, trying to grin at him.

In response, he backhanded me across the face again. Our first inside joke and he had to go and get all pissy.

What a dick.

My mental pencil scratched across the surface of the stark white paper as I added *Caring and Sharing* to the list of things that annoy Jesper.

I had The Gland inject another happy packet into my bloodstream. Unfortunately, the chemicals had diminishing effects the more I used them. Like a junkie, my body needed ever-increasing levels to keep the pain at bay, but the thimble-sized dopehead had a very limited supply. I needed to pace myself.

He shoved the little table in front of me and pointed at the piece of paper on its surface.

I didn't need to read the blood-smattered form to know what the smudged ink said. But trying to be less annoying and more accommodating, I looked. *System Admission Code* followed by a blank line. I glanced back up at him. "You can keep on pointing at that all day, but I can't help you. I have no idea what you're talking about."

Sticking his face into mine, he snarled. The little hairs of his nostrils stuck so far out, they appeared to be trying to escape his nasty nasal passages and join their scattered mustachio brothers. "You work for the Research and Development of Psychological Warfare Department at the Pentagon. You illegally recorded a private conversation between two private citizens. You also created a false report for the Department of Defense with some less-than-flattering remarks about my colleagues. We were able to delete the report before anyone saw it. However, you made a copy, which you stored on your personal drive at the Pentagon. You're going to log on to the server and delete that report and the recording."

Because these Neanderthals had kidnapped me, I'd never actually gotten the chance to send that report. In fact, I'd never even told anyone about it. No one. How had this knuckle dragger come by this information? A worrisome anxiety settled in my bones. I'd underestimated these thugs yet again. I needed to find out everything they knew and report it back to HQ.

Attempting to cover my surprise and dismay, I laughed in his smug face. "You have been seriously misinformed, my friend. I'm just a simple insurance salesman. Now, if you and the missus want to take out a new home owner's policy, I'm your man."

He pulled back his fist, probably to punch my lights out again.

"Hold on, hold on, Jesper," I said.

He paused. "What?"

I had to swallow a thick clump of blood before I could talk. "Look, I don't know how to get into the Pentagon, but in the third-grade, Jimmy Mane and I had a secret handshake that would get you into our hidden fort. If you agree to let me go, I'll teach it to you."

∞ ∞ ∞ ∞

Some unknown time later, the cold water pouring over my head and running down my neck brought me back from blissful unconsciousness. "Are you ready to learn that handshake now?" I asked weakly.

He thumped my temple with a thick finger. "I know the government stuck security codes and memories into your brain." He pulled out a knife and wiped it across my cheek. "And I don't mind rooting around in your skull to find them. In fact, I think that would be kinda fun."

As part of the authentication process, an encrypted fob sent a series of codes and images implanted by the Pentagon's fun squad in my central cortex. Other than having the disconcerting knowledge that the government can make me crow like a rooster any time it wanted, I knew little about how the system worked. That Jesper understood the process, and claimed to know how to get past it, gave me pause.

"What I need to know," he continued, "is the code."

The last step in the authentication process, a sixteen-digit fob companion-cipher, was, perplexingly, what Jesper had been trying to beat out of me for two days.

I shook my head at the impatient buffalo. "The access code won't do you any good. There's too many layers of security."

He pushed his ugly bull-face into mine. "That's my problem."

I coughed. "Man, don't you ever brush your teeth? Your breath smells like you've been drinking squirrel splooge."

As he beat me, I added *Does not like his love for squirrel splooge commented on* to the *Annoys Jesper* list.

The brute—who should have been winded given his extracurricular endeavors but seemed as though he could do this sort of thing all day without breaking a sweat—stood and snarled down at me.

I raised my eyebrows, waiting to see what he would do next.

Jesper narrowed his eyes and snorted, a slow smile spreading across his lips.

Something about the grin chilled my bones more than anything he'd done to me so far.

He glanced over his shoulder. "Hey."

A steroid-laden freak in camo, carrying an assault weapon, entered from a side room. I'd seen him a couple of times before, but he usually disappeared after doing whatever mundane task the beast asked of him. "Yeah, boss?"

Jesper glared down at me. "Bring me the sonogram."

A shiver ran down my spine. The shit had just turned bad. Not that anything that had happened to me in the last couple of days would be turned into a tearjerker chick flick or anything, but things had gone from unpleasant to serious.

I'd figured these bastards would carry on this nonsense for several more days before they gave up and killed me or I managed to escape. As time went on and I drained The Gland, I would slowly be left to handle the pain on my own. The effects would be gradual, and I should be able to mentally take over where the hormones left off. But if they disabled the device, I'd be left completely on my own all at once.

I commanded it to dump all of its contents into my system.

Steroid Freak handed the hulking beast the sonogram.

Studying the small screen attached to the touchless wand, Jesper waved the cabled rod over my body. After a few minutes, it beeped, and a smirk formed on his buffalo-thick lips.

I rolled my eyes. "That's a standard diabetes control tablet."

Setting the medical instrument aside, he pulled out his knife and waved the blade in front of my face. The thug ripped open my pant leg. He sliced through my skin and began digging around in my thigh, sending waves of fire blazing through my body.

Metal clinked and Jesper's broken-capillary-filled eyes found mine. His smile turned sinister.

When he jammed a pair of needle-nosed pliers into the incision, a thick trail of blood gushed out of the wound and splattered to the floor, staining the dirty concrete. He yanked out the tiny drug lord, and I had to clench my jaw to keep from screaming.

The buffalo held up the gore-covered gizmo and grinned. "Now you should be a little more cooperative."

My breathing had grown ragged. Not even the drugs in my system could smother the inferno burning in my leg. "Congratulations. You just gave your hostage wacky blood sugar," I gasped.

Crimson gushed from the cut, so he used an arc lighter to cauterize it. The smell of seared flesh assaulted my nostrils while wave upon wave of agony crashed over me. Though I'd been able to weather this almost unbearable pain so far, as soon as the opioids wore off, that incision, along with a whole new batch of other indignities, would bring me to my knees.

He sneered down at me. "Now, we'll just give it a little time for the drugs to wear off. Then I think you'll be ready to have a real conversation."

Retreating to the furthest corner of my mind, I started putting up mental barriers. Up until now, I'd been largely sheltered from the pain. But soon it would be plowing into me with all the force and mercy of a runaway locomotive. The time had come to batten down the hatches and prepare for a full-on assault.

∞ ∞ ∞ ∞

The room had grown dark. Having exited stage left a few minutes before, Jesper and Steroid Freak had not yet reappeared.

I strained to listen, but nothing disturbed the stillness. I didn't know where they'd gone or why, but I couldn't pass up the opportunity.

Gathering my strength and preparing for a typhoon of pain, I took a deep lungful of air and pulled against my restraints. My throbbing joints screamed, the cuffs ripped at my raw skin, and the rattle of chain reverberated around the room. I pulled until I thought my veins would explode, but the bindings remained as secure as ever, and I slumped over.

Exhausted, I tried to relax and find someplace on my body, any place on it, that didn't hurt. My hair didn't ache, or, at least compared to the rest of me, it didn't.

Focus. Move your chai...chow...chi? Whatever. Become your hair. Be only your hair. I am my hair. I am...deluding myself if I think this is going to work.

I took a long, exasperated breath. Damned Jesper. Without the assistance of The Gland, I'd already started getting weaker, and the pain burned like a forest fire. Some agents got two Glands in case they were ever captured and their torturers cut one out. I'd fought so vehemently against getting the one that two had been out of the question.

In retrospect, that hadn't been the wisest decision of my life.

I had to find something to help lessen the pain burden on my battered body. I took stock of what I could do.

I'd kept my bare feet under the chair whenever the beast moved in front of me—Jesper had a habit of stomping on my toes with the heels of his boots if I left them in his way. I slid my feet back in front of me, cooling the bottoms on the chilly concrete. I couldn't remember when exactly, but at some point during the festivities, Jesper had removed the bright orange sneakers I'd nicked. He'd then burnt the soles of my feet with cigarettes and an arc lighter. The cold floor eased the heat radiating from my torched skin.

A bright light flared to life, shining directly in my face. I blinked against the brilliance, but even through closed eyes, the illumination pierced the thin membranes of my lids. My head already throbbed from Jesper's unique recipe of beating, starving, and dehydration. The glare pounded even more ice picks into my skull.

A hulking man stepped in front of me, eclipsing the light. Jesper lowered his buffalo-sized head until he'd leveled his gaze with mine. "Hello, prick."

Assaulted by the cancer rasp of his voice and his moonshine breath, I tried to laugh. "You still haven't gotten around to brushing your teeth, have you?" I held his gaze even though it made my eyes water. "Whatcha got up your sleeve this time, Jesper? Are you planning to tan me to death? Well, give me a Mai Tai and hand me some oil, but if you think I'm going to let you do my back, you're crazy."

Just the act of talking sapped what little energy reserves I had left. Though every cell in my body wanted to give in, wanted to fold and go to sleep, I fought the fatigue. I struggled to appear alert and ready for another round. If I showed the slightest bit of weakness, if the brute knew he had me on the ropes, if he knew that his efforts had nearly beaten me, I'd be lost for sure.

The man appraised me, and I prepared for another onslaught of torture. But, instead of hitting me, he shook his head and moved to the side, letting the light once again blaze against my skin.

As he strolled away, his whispered laugh drifted out of the ether. "No, just a change of pace. See, I realized that you and I could do this all day because you don't care about yourself. Even without drugs, you'll still be just as obstinate and uncooperative as ever."

A door opened, allowing a breeze to drift through the room and turn my wet clothes to ice. I began to shiver. "So, you've given up? Decided to let me go? It feels like I've known you for months, but this is the first intelligent decision I've ever seen you make." I tried to keep the rattle of my teeth out of my voice, but even I heard it.

The door slammed shut, and from beyond the brilliance, wheels—a cart or cabinet on castors—rolled over the concrete, squeaking again and again.

I tried to look around the damned light to see what new horrors approached, but the glare practically burned my retinas off.

The squeaking stopped just outside of my field of vision. Something thudded, and a man grunted.

Despite my exhaustion, my heart tripped. Now what nastiness had these thugs thought up?

Someone redirected the light to the ceiling, and I had to wait for my eyes to adjust to the sudden dimness. As the world materialized from the dark, my stomach dropped. I gasped. "Mike!"

My brother—gagged, blindfolded and tied to an office chair—had a few bruises on his cheeks and a cut on his forehead, but otherwise, he appeared alright.

"'andy?" He tried to talk around the cloth in his mouth.

Camo Guy smacked him across the face.

Rage and hate flooded my system. I'd signed up for this job. Knew the risks. But Jesper had stepped way over the line when he'd gone after my family. "You son of a bitch, where are you?"

A looming shadow arose out of the vapor.

I snarled at the beast. "This has nothing to do with him. Let him go."

Jesper grabbed my face in his huge paw. "Now we're getting somewhere. I knew I'd eventually find something you cared about." He shoved me so hard the chair almost tipped over.

"We're actually getting further and further away from what you want." I nodded toward his neck. "That scar on your throat. Someone tried to kill you once. You hurt my brother and I'll finish the job."

The king thug laughed. "You'll do no such thing. After we slowly kill your precious brother, there are other, less accessible people we'll go after."

I knew I shouldn't let him see me get angry. Knowing my weaknesses gave him somewhere to press, but my seething heart could not be contained. "You'll never get to them."

"We got your brother because he was easy," he said. "Your government didn't want to spend the money on an unlikely target, so there were no security drones around his house. No proximity monitors. But if you think they can protect the rest of your family, you're a fool."

He paused for several heartbeats as if thinking. "You know, I've seen pictures of your wife and daughter." He glanced back at Camo Guy. "Pretty, don't you think?" The second thug laughed as Jesper smirked at me. "Some guys might even be into young twin boys." He shrugged. "Who knows? Different strokes and all that. But the girls… Well, I'll bet they taste even better than they look."

Terror fed my roiling fury, and I yanked against my bindings. Never in my life had I wanted to kill someone as much as I wanted to kill this monster. "I'll slaughter every last one of you. Ask your boys that nabbed me. Ask them how well it worked out for them when they underestimated me. You'll never get what you want, and you'll die trying."

He smiled the evil grin of a hyena that had just cornered its prey. "They were simple muscle for hire. Stupid and weak. You did me a favor by thinning the herd. But I'll tell you what. If you cooperate, I'll leave your precious flowers alone, and I'll even consider letting little Mikey go."

I studied his smug face. He'd finally gotten to me. Gotten under my skin. Even worse, he knew it. "You and I both know you're lying. If I give you what you want, you'll just kill us anyway. How do I know you'll keep your word?"

"I guess you're just going to have to have faith. At the very least, you'll save your family." He glanced at Mike. "Well, what's left of it."

Camo Guy handed Jesper a mobile.

I shook my head. "We've been over this. You can't get into the system. There's too many layers of security."

He called over his shoulder at Camo. "Our esteemed guest still doesn't feel very optimistic. Help him feel more confident."

Camo Guy turned and disappeared into the gloom. He returned and headed toward my brother. The thug held a portable car charger in one hand, the cord from the small power jumper dangled from the other. The ends of the wires had been stripped of their shielding. Copper flashed and glinted like a monster's teeth.

I looked up at the big man. "You don't have to do that. They won't let me in, but we can try."

Jesper waggled a finger in my face. "The time for playing nice has passed. I don't want to leave any doubt in your mind as to what will happen if you keep procrastinating. Consider this a little preview."

From behind him, the distinct sizzle and pop of electricity shorting out via human flesh accompanied the horrific, muffled screams of my brother. The flying sparks fueled my rage and my resolve to kill him and everyone else responsible.

"Mike!" I yelled. But his shrieks overrode my voice. "Stop! Stop it now and I'll do what you want!"

Jesper narrowed his eyes, suspicion in his gaze, but waved a hand.

The electrocution ceased. The last of the sparks bounced across the concrete and dimmed. My brother's muffled cries quieted to heavy breathing.

The giant brute slipped a fob from his pocket and slapped it on my sensory tap. In my peripheral vision, it began to glow green.

I glared at the thug. "Move aside. I want to talk to my brother first."

He held up a finger. "You have one minute or he does another round with Old Sparky." He stepped out from between us.

Blood dripped from the corner of Mike's mouth, and burn marks dotted his arms and legs. "Mike, are you alright?"

The man I'd played with as a child and admired as an adult, pivoted his head at the sound of my voice.

I turned back to Jesper. "Take his blindfold and gag off."

The thug glared for several seconds before motioning to his goon. Camo Guy ripped the cloths off my brother's face.

Mike blinked and stretched his jaw. His chest heaved with huge gulps of air as he glanced at Jesper. "Sandy, what's this about?"

"The idiot squad here thinks I can help them hack into the Pentagon," I said.

Fear tinged my brother's eyes. "They think *you* have access to the Pentagon?" He looked at the buffalo. "You're wrong. He's nothing but a glorified paper pusher."

"Exactly," I said. "But he's got it in his giant, overripe melon that I can help him become a war monger or something."

Jesper poked me in the chest. "You have thirty seconds to say goodbye or help us."

I ignored the brute and focused on my brother. "I'm sorry you got caught up in all of this. I had no idea they even knew who you were."

Mike's exhausted, frightened smile broke my heart. "It's fine, brother. You always do the right thing, so do whatever it is you need to do. I understand."

My heart swelled. This man had stood by my side when I'd married my wife, fought alongside me during the war, and helped me lower our father into the ground when the old man lost his battle with cancer. He would sacrifice all to save me and those I loved. I nodded.

"Time's up," Jesper said. "What's it gonna be?"

I sighed and held my hand as high as the restraint would allow.

The huge thug grabbed my arm and pressed my palm against the mobile's screen. The device scanned an image of my hand and paused before bringing up the Pentagon's security menu. *Access Code.*

He expanded the keyboard and glowered at me.

I looked over at Mike. "I love you, bro."

Camo Guy pressed a long knife to my brother's throat.

Jesper grabbed my shirt. "Last time I ask before little Mikey here dies. Give it to me."

"I love you too," Mike said. He nodded. "Go on. Give it to him."

I took a deep breath and began to recite the code. Jesper typed along on the mobile's keyboard. After I finished, he set the device on the small table and stepped back as the fob on my temple turned from green to blue. A menu materialized above the mobile.

Jesper grinned and stepped up to the table. He chose *Search* and typed something on the keyboard. As soon as he pressed *Return*, the mobile detonated into a huge ball of flames.

The force of the explosion lifted me into the air, flinging me backwards. When I hit the floor, the chair broke apart, shattering into wooden fragments. I shook my head to try and clear it of the concussion as I untangled my chains from the bits of splinter.

Grabbing a sharp shard of wood, I stumbled to my feet, bracing for would-be attackers. I couldn't hear over the ringing in my ears, so I spun in a circle, trying to look everywhere at once.

But Jesper lay on the floor a few feet away. His shirt had been turned to smoldering embers, revealing his singed chest. The front of his face looked as though it had taken the bulk of the blast, the skin burnt and crispy with his brows and most of his hair gone.

My brother and Camo Guy lay together like tangled lovers. I ran to them. Tossing the thug aside, I cradled my brother's face. "Mike! Mike! Are you alright?"

His eyes fluttered open and he looked up at me. "Gawd, you can be so melodramatic sometimes."

Laughing with relief, I untied his hands. "You told me to do what I needed to. So, I did."

He pulled at the bindings on his feet. "What happened?"

I got the key from Camo Guy's pocket and unlocked the cuffs on my wrists. "There's an emergency signal I sent through the fob. Unless you type in a cancellation code, the system replies with a loopback pulse that detonates the power adapter in the mobile. It's an extreme measure of last resort that's supposed to kill everyone within a ten-foot radius. As you can imagine, I'd been hoping to not have to use it. But..."

"But then your brother messed up your plans." He frowned. "My head hurts like a bastard—and I'm not complaining to be alive—but if the explosion was supposed to kill us all, why are we still here?"

Shaking my head again, I glanced at the fallen brute on the other side of the room. "I don't understand either. I guess I'll have to talk to them about their security problems when I get back."

I glanced at the hallway entrance. "There are others here too. I can't hear so well right now, but I have no doubt they are headed our way. We need to get out of here."

I helped him to his feet. As I reached for my wooden makeshift weapon, movement caught the corner of my eye. I turned back in time to see Camo Guy headed toward me.

Mike shoved me aside, and the thug barreled into my brother instead.

The two men slammed to the floor. The thug raised his dagger and drove it into Mike's chest.

Screaming, I ran at him. The man tried to pull his knife free, but I got to him first and rammed the stake through his throat.

He wrapped his hands around the wood, staring at me as a river of red burbled through his fingers. He crumpled, and I shoved him aside.

When I turned, my heart cried out. My brother looked up at me as blood bubbled from his lips.

"Mike, hold on. I'll get some help." Before I could leave, he grabbed my wrist, his eyes imploring me to stay.

He tried to say something—what, I couldn't begin to imagine—but the ringing in my ears drowned out any words he may have been able to push past the blood pooling in his chest. I touched his face and held his hand as red spread like a blooming rose around the wicked steel.

I stared into his eyes, which held the exact same frightened, disbelieving expression I'd seen in my father's eyes during the last few seconds of his life. With my free hand, I ran my fingers through Mike's hair, trying to comfort him as he prepared for the unfathomable. "Don't be scared, baby brother. Dad's waiting for you."

Mike smiled. For a second, the years unwound. He was the boy I'd played with in the yard, the dorky teen that had crashed my car, and the man who beamed with pride as he held his newborn niece.

Then his smile faltered, and he shuddered. His weak grip relaxed, and as my brother died, his gaze turned glassy.

I closed his eyes as a tear slid down my cheek.

Over the buzzing in my ears, I thought I could make out the echo of storming feet. I wanted to stay and fight. I wanted to hurt them the way they'd hurt me. Kill them the way they'd just killed my brother. But I couldn't take them all. Couldn't stop them all. Remaining here would be suicide.

I gently lay my brother on the floor. "I'll come back for you, Mike. I promise." I studied his face one last time, then ran for the door. Bursting through, I sprinted across the field and into the dark forest that lay on the other side.

CHAPTER SIX

JEFF

I slammed the door behind me as I marched into the foyer of my condo. Stomping to the kitchen, I grumbled about the lack of foresight, imagination, and vision of my boss.

A soft voice floated down the hall. "Jeff? Is that you?"

I sighed. "Yeah, it's me."

Stockinged feet whispered against the hardwood.

Tamara, a goblet of wine in hand, glided into the room. With the live wallpaper, ceiling, and floor depicting the thick grass, lush ferns, and tall pines of "Green Valley," she could have been a fairy-tale princess and the commander in chief to an army of furry forest creatures ready to dance and dream with her about true love's kiss.

"Hey, baby," she said and then frowned. Tamara leaned against a "tree" while studying my face. "What's the matter?"

I let out a long breath. "Ceos. Sometimes I want to toss her off the top of the KOIN Tower. And that's on her good days. The rest of the time she *really* pisses me off."

Tamara's long thick braid swayed back and forth as she shook her head. "My poor tycoon. Relentlessly harassed by the playground bully."

"The bitch does own a controlling portion of my company," I said, folding my arms across my chest, "so there's a glimmer of truth to that."

She set her glass on the counter and stepped in front of me, placing her cool palms on my cheeks. "I'm sorry to be so insensitive. I couldn't begin to understand the frustrations of the rich and famous. Would you like to talk about it?"

I looked into her eyes, trying to gauge her seriousness. "Do you really want to know?"

"More than anything," she said and kissed me gently.

I took her hand, snatched her wine goblet, and led her down the hall. In the living room, I kicked off my shoes and we fell into the couch. Instead of taking her glass back, she picked up another goblet full of amber liquid waiting on the coffee table.

Tamara leaned back. She folded her long, muscular legs across my lap and took a sip as she looked at me expectantly.

She'd clearly been ready for me to come home and gripe about my life...again. While I appreciated her generosity, ever since Ceos took over, our conversations had become lopsided. Tamara had the patience of a saint, and I needed to be careful to never take advantage of her kindness.

I needed to push my problems aside and focus on her. "I'm always complaining about my boss. How about we start off with *you* telling me about *your* day?"

She cocked her head, her dark eyes lingering on my face. "Let's see. Well, today I spent most of my time researching the Positron Energy suit. I found a couple of glaring omissions and several fundamental flaws with the case against them. I'm pretty certain that by the end of the week, I should have the entire thing thrown out."

Though she'd said this as if commenting on a cloudy day, I had to stop and replay her words in my head. While Tamara focused primarily on Anti-Virtualism, my girlfriend's passions ranged from protecting personal privacy to fighting homelessness and hunger to protecting the Earth from irresponsible, abusive corporations. She usually tried to separate her professional and activism lives, but when she did take up the legal reins, she almost always sat on the plaintiff's side of the table.

"What? I thought you'd recused yourself from that case. Isn't having *you* fight the tree huggers a major conflict of interest?"

She shook her head. "After I researched these knuckleheads, I insisted on joining the case. I'm all for saving the planet, but not only are The Earthlings radical environmentalists, they're misguided hypocritical idiots that give those of us who are rational thinkers a bad rep. Groups like that need to be shut down because they do way more harm than good. So, no. It's not a conflict at all."

She tapped her cheek as though thinking. "That's the only highlight of my day." Reaching over, she touched my arm. "Now that you've done the good boyfriend thing, stop stalling and tell me what's going on." She took a demure sip and waited.

I considered trying to wave off the argument with my boss as inconsequential, but Tamara would have none of it. It would do no good to try and postpone the conversation further. "Ceos—"

"You know," she said, "lately a lot of our conversations have started this way. If you didn't hate her so much—and I weren't so incredibly captivating—I might be jealous."

I raised my eyebrows. "Don't tell me you're worried."

"About Ms. Hell on Wheels?" Tamara shook her head. "Not for my sake, but I'm concerned she's going to drive you into an early grave. After a day of working with Calvin and the rest of the geeks, you'd bore me to tears with your nerd stories, but at least you're happy."

"My stories aren't boring," I said. "They're just sometimes…technical."

Ignoring my argument, she continued, "But after you meet with Ceos… Well, I'm afraid one of these days you'll snap, and I'll have to come down to the police station and try to bail you out. Only, FYI, they don't release murder suspects."

While I wanted to be as cool under fire as Tamara and as unflappable as Calvin, Ceos and Rick chafed me like sand in my Jockeys. Maybe it wasn't the assholes in my life that caused me strife. Maybe, just maybe, it was my own personality flaws and utter lack of patience. If Tamara worried that I might someday kill Ceos—even if she was only half kidding—perhaps it was time for me to reevaluate who I thought I was and who I wanted to become.

Trying to make light of her comment, I raised my hand as though taking an oath. "I promise that I *probably* won't kill my boss…today."

She sighed. "Until the cops come to cart you away, I'll continue to be your psychiatrist. Carry on."

"The doctor is in," I said, smirking.

She made no reply.

The smile fell from my face. "The queen bee summoned me to her lair this afternoon."

Tamara raised her eyebrows. "I take it this wasn't to give you an award for a job well done."

"Hardly. Do you remember a few days ago when I told you about that company, Dencephalon?"

"Oh, yeah," she replied. "The one that Calvin found. The one with Dragon Breath Rick who had advanced something or other that you wanted to incorporate into your games."

"Right," I nodded. "Well, I did a demonstration for Ceos today."

"And?" she asked.

I let out a long breath. "Honestly, I thought partnering with them was a no-brainer. This technology will keep us dominating the market for at least a decade, which should have tickled her wallet bone. In fact, we've been using it to enhance the realism of the games we've been designing specifically for her, so I thought she'd be pleased. But after the demo, she flipped out. She said she would *never* invest a single dime to purchase this company. Never."

Tamara blinked. "What? I thought showing her this new immersive whatchamacallit was a formality. Why would she get upset about you doing your job?"

"I don't know for sure," I said. "She didn't really give me a good solid reason, but she went on and on about privacy groups and the Anti-Vs picketing and burning our company to the ground. I'm starting to wonder if it's because this idea came from me."

Tamara narrowed her eyes, staring hard as if she could read my thoughts. "Something doesn't add up. Ceos wouldn't have gone crazy just to spite you. She's hard, not petty. There has to be more to it than that. Jeff, what aren't you telling me?"

When I'd first told Tamara about my meeting with Rick and Calvin, I hadn't been able to adequately describe the experience of being Rodger Thornton. Of really, literally, knowing what it felt like to walk in his shoes and meet his future wife.

Also, since I hadn't fully believed Rick's story about being able to download a cadaver's memories, I'd seen no reason to tell her about the extraction process. But yesterday, after I'd seen a recording of one, I'd finally come to realize that Rick could, in fact, do the seemingly impossible.

Tamara still smiled at me, but her eyes had grown serious. The instincts of my cunning, tenacious lioness of a girlfriend had been pricked.

I could never hide the truth from her. She'd smelled the not-quite-deception on me as if it leached out of my pores.

Dread filled my gut. She wouldn't like this, not one bit.

I took a deep breath, resigning myself to the inevitable, and began. "The simulation that Dencephalon created is not actually a simulation. It's a download of someone's memories."

She cleared her throat and assumed her no-nonsense,

lawyerly demeanor. Though she remained calm and collected, a predator lurked beneath the mask of professionalism. "Please tell me they didn't turn on the fob's two-way communication."

"No," I said. "That's what I thought at first too. But they did find a loophole in the law."

"As a lawyer I would be very interested to know what it is that *they* found that *I* missed," Tamara said, folding her hands in her lap. "Alright, Jeff, start from the beginning. This time, do not leave anything out."

I took a deep breath and started with Calvin dragging me to Dencephalon a few days ago. I described being Rodger and holding Janet in my arms, the wind in my hair, and "remembering" our future child during Rick's demonstration.

Though her expression remained professionally passive, the small vein in her temple—the one that only flared up when she got really pissed—began to pulse. I wished I could've stopped, wished I could've changed the facts, if only just for her, but I barreled on, telling her everything.

I hadn't been entirely forthcoming during our earlier conversations, but I'd never lied to Tamara. Never sugar-coated how and what I did for a living and I wouldn't start now. When I described the extraction video I'd witnessed yesterday, I internally cringed as Tamara's lips formed a tight little slit while her eyes flared with anger.

"When I explained all of this to Ceos this afternoon," I continued, "she said that we may as well make a commercial about digging up grandpa and jamming probes into his skull." I shook my head. "But as long as it makes her money, she couldn't care less what anyone thought. That's when she told me about never investing a dime in the company and threw me out of her office."

I gulped down the last of my wine and fell silent, giving Tamara time to process.

She slowly shook her head. "You know, sometimes I don't think you know me or care about me at all." Her voice had the same quiet, calm foreboding of a pending cyclone.

"Tamara," I said, "this isn't about you. It's about the advancement of—"

"That's true." She nodded. "You didn't consider me, even a little bit, and that's part of your problem, Jeff. When we first started dating, you asked me to help you make morally responsible decisions when it comes to VR. But I guess that's only when those choices are easy."

She pointed at me. "In the end, you answer only to the god of money and 'progress.' Be damned about destroying civilization through electronic addiction as long as you can keep making your little pretend worlds more realistic. Be damned about violating the most fundamental of all human rights to keep our own thoughts and feelings private. No, as long as you gain a profit, then you see nothing morally wrong with ripping the emotions right out of someone's head. It's okay; there's a loophole in the law. Even worse, you want to make every private, intimate moment of our lives available for anyone to peruse at their leisure."

"We would never—"

A furious storm raged in her eyes, and she yanked her

legs off my lap. "Don't say you would never because that's exactly what you're trying to do. Only Ceos, of all people, saw the indecency in it when, for whatever reason, neither you nor Calvin could. I expect this kind of narrowmindedness from him, but you, Jeff? You? After all the time we've spent together. After all that we've talked about, none of it has made a bit of difference. None of it made you even have second thoughts on whether or not you *should* do something just because you *could*."

"Tamara, this technology is coming out one way or another. It's best if we control it—"

She slammed her heavy glass against the table. Amber liquid sloshed across the surface in a spatter pattern that oddly resembled blood. The sound of glass on wood reverberated around the room like a gunshot. "Damn it, Jeff. Is that the only way you see things? Have you not even tried to think of it any other way?"

"Yes… I mean no… I mean, I wanted to talk it all over with you, but I didn't believe Rick at first." My mouth seemed to have disconnected itself from my brain as meaningless words tumbled from it.

She stood like an enraged goddess and glared down at me. "You had a chance to tell me everything before you started moving forward, but now that time has passed. Right now, I can't even talk to you."

Tamara stormed out of the room. She stomped down the hall and, a few seconds later, stomped back. Rage blazing through her eyes, she gave me a cursory glance as she marched through the living room. "Don't wait up."

As she left the condo, she slammed the front door so

hard that the trees and shrubbery in the live wallpaper blurred for a few seconds. I sat alone in the middle of the forest as Typhoon Tamara moved on to wreak havoc on the rest of the world.

∞ ∞ ∞ ∞

Several hours later, I languished in a hammock beneath the shade of a huge umbrella. Ocean waves lapped the sandy shore, far-off seagulls squawked and bickered, and a salty breeze ruffled my shirt.

Tamara, wearing a vibrant blue two-piece and a huge floppy hat, swayed beside me as she demurely sipped from a tall glass of something red and slushy. She'd just returned from a swim, and in the twilight, her smooth chocolate skin glistened as if covered by thousands of tiny diamonds.

I'd thought her eyes were closed behind her huge round sunglasses, but a minx-like smile formed on her lips. "I can see you checking me out, you know?"

"You are just so good-looking, it's hard not to ogle," I replied.

She gazed at me over the top of her shades. "Ah, you only want to look? Too bad." As she reached over and touched my cheek, a dagger of pain ripped through my head. The world around me flickered, pixilated, and faded.

Bolting upright, I hunched over and squeezed my eyes shut, willing the chainsaw slicing through my temporal lobe to hurry along its way. Finally, the agony receded, and I blinked.

Tamara stood over me. Though she was as wet as she

had been in the beach simulation, she most certainly did not glisten. Loose strands of her hair had been plastered to her scalp, while large dark stains hung from her shirt's armpits and covered her chest.

Based on the telltale wrap lines still circling her wrists and forearms, she must have just finished punishing the boxing bag. Though not as good as being in the Mediterranean, at least I only had to deal with the stink of her sweat and not the business end of her gloves.

"Instead of trying to escape your problems through this nonsense," she held up the fob she'd pulled from my temple, "perhaps you should try and face them."

"You're the one that left," I said. "Not me." I pointed at her gym bag lying on the floor beside the bed. "Besides, you have your way of working through your stress, and I have mine."

For a second, the rage still lingered in her eyes, and I wondered if I *would* have to deal with the business end of her boxing gloves after all. Then, the fire went out and her shoulders slumped.

She set the fob on the nightstand, stripped off her sweaty shirt and shorts, and plopped down onto the bed next to me in just her underclothes. She remained quiet for several heartbeats as she soaked the pillows and sheets. "Look, I'm sorry I went off like I did. I probably should have stayed and worked it through."

Her words soothed my heart in a way the beach simulation never would. Now we could talk.

Despite our opposing ambitions and philosophical differences, nothing in the world meant as much to me as this sweat-soaked woman. I admired her passion and willingness to take a stand for the causes she believed in and her undying loyalty to the values she held dear. That she'd apologized to me, when every fiber of her being loathed VR, made me love her even more.

I took her hand. "I'm sorry I wasn't more forthcoming with the whole extraction thing. I just didn't believe Rick at first, or maybe I didn't *want* to believe him." I shook my head. "Either way I should have told you."

"I needed some time to think," she said quietly. "I'll be honest, Jeff. I don't like this. Not one bit. In fact, I can safely say I hate it. But, as much as every cell in me feels that this is wrong, as you pointed out, it's coming one way or another. I have to be realistic."

She sighed. "Once I got past being pissed and frustrated, I started to wonder if we could use this whatever-you-call-it for something a lot more practical than video games."

My heart broke a little. Deep in her soul she wanted nothing more than to make the world a better place. Part of me longed to hand this beautiful spirit the pureness and cleanliness of her dreams. Yet despite the impossibility of her envisioned utopia, she still found it within herself to compromise and find opportunity where others only saw limitations. "What are you thinking about?"

Her gaze found mine. "It's possible we could gain critical understanding and make huge leaps in mental health. It's also possible that we could finally level the playing field for civil and human rights. Imagine how quickly our bad behaviors would change if we could all experience the horrors of starvation or enslavement or being discriminated against because of our race, gender, or beliefs. This could be a powerful tool...if used properly. Mom always said to be patient and understanding of others because you can never truly know what it's like to be in someone else's shoes. Only with this, we can."

I'd only been trying to make my company better, but Tamara saw a way to improve humanity and solve some of the biggest problems that had been plaguing mankind for millennia. My ambitions looked cheap and petty in comparison.

"I hadn't thought of that," I admitted, "but you're absolutely right. If we take this on, I want to sit down with you and come up with ways to implement some of these ideas." I nodded as the possibilities formed in my head. "I think this might be a very powerful tool. Your mom was right. For a few minutes, I was Rodger. It felt as real as sitting here with you." I grinned. "Though, not nearly as sweaty."

She poked me in the ribs. "Watch it. I still have my boxing gloves."

Chuckling, I shook my head. "Okay, what else are you thinking?"

Her eyes grew serious and troubled. "Besides the disgustingness of the extraction process itself, I think it's the fake world part of it that really bothers me. You've already created a game that's more addictive than drugs and alcohol combined. People spend thousands of hours a year living false lives, talking to fake people, and ignoring their friends and family. Birth and marriage rates are lower now than they have been in centuries."

She shook her head. "This breakthrough you've discovered will make these worlds even more enticing. Those who have never tried it may be tempted. Those who are casual players will become addicted. Those who are addicted will become obsessed. I'm worried no one will ever come up for air. Pretty soon we may as well keep our bodies in pods while our minds traipse through the digital tulips."

"Yeah, I've thought about that too," I said. "We need to write up a new VR limits bill. The one we wrote before didn't have enough teeth to it. We've learned a few things now that we've lived with it for a few years. I think we need to put in more stringent time limits and consequences for violators."

I ran a hand through my hair. "Unfortunately, every time we add limitations to the game, some evil basement dweller creates a workaround just as quickly. Within seconds of a release, everyone can bypass the time restrictions."

"We will work harder to beat them then, but you need to know that people's lack of self-control is not your fault," she said. "Addicts are who they are. They will get their fix no matter what we do."

She hesitated. "There's something else that's bothering me."

"What's that?" I asked.

"You don't," she began, "have the right—legally, I

mean—to, as Ceos so poetically put it, jam probes into grandpa's head and start downloading. Each donor would need to give consent."

I had suspected we'd eventually get around to this aspect of the process. Fortunately, I'd spent a lot of time with Rick's legal advisor to make sure we weren't opening ourselves up to potential lawsuits. "I asked this very question and was told that in each case, permission was obtained from the next of kin or surviving spouse." I paused. "When we offer to provide copies of any memories we were able to obtain, as well as a fairly large sum of money, most people jump at the chance."

"Ugh," Tamara grunted, shaking her head. "The almighty dollar. I'd guessed as much, but I had to ask." She fell silent for several heartbeats. "Jeff, I don't know what it is, but something about this feels off."

I traced the back of her hand with my thumb. "I know it does. I've thought that since the minute I pulled up to Dencephalon's door. But if we don't buy this technology, someone else will. At least this way, we would get to be in control of it." I paused. "Well, we *would* be in control, except Ceos forbid it."

Tamara remained quiet for several seconds. "Sometimes when we talk about this stuff, I feel like I'm making a pact with the devil."

I frowned. "What does that mean?"

"Ceos," she said, "told you *she* wouldn't invest in Dencephalon."

I waited for the punch line.

Tamara pointed at me. "*You* buy the company, then

lease the rights to Adventures."

I sat up straight, my mind spinning as the pieces fell into place. "Yes, that's a brilliant idea." I rubbed a hand over my face. "Duh. Why hadn't I thought of that?"

"Well, geniuses *can* be pretty dumb."

"But capital…" I shook my head. "They're willing to let me buy them for pennies on the dollar, but still, the initial investment is a lot more than I have access to. It's a great idea, but without the money, there's nothing I can do."

"What if you get partners? You don't have to do it alone," she said.

I snorted. "If I try and get investors, Ceos will find out and shut the whole thing down. She knows everyone with money, and it'll get back to her."

Tamara fell quiet again, a thoughtful expression passing over her face. "Tell you what, I'll lend you the money."

I blinked. "But not even you have that much." I hesitated. "Do you?"

Tamara shrugged. "I invest well and may have forgotten to mention that I inherited a bit from my grandmother."

"We've never talked about it," I said, shaking my head. "Your financial worth isn't important to me. You are."

She ruffled my hair. "That's so sweet. Naive, but sweet."

I looked her in the eyes. "You should really think about this. It's a considerable amount of money."

She sighed. "Yes, I'm sure. The money isn't a problem. But you need to know that I'm going to hold you to your promise to write a new VR limits bill. This one will be based on that new what-do-you-call-it."

I thought for a minute. "*Total Immersion*. We'll call it *Total Immersion*."

"Fine," she said. "You will use part of this capital to pay for a study group, get a professional psychiatrist's opinion, and then we'll write it up together. Not only will you be required to have an addiction disclaimer on every subscription, but this bill has to be all the way through Congress before a single person logs on. Oh, and you get to help me present it to the Anti-V chapter."

I regarded her. "I don't know what to say."

"You don't know what to say?" She folded her arms. "We've been living together, own this apartment together, and now we're going into business together. It's about time you stop hemming and hawing and get that little box out of your nightstand."

Calvin. Damn it. I never should have told him. The guy could not keep a secret. As soon as I told him, he'd probably gone and blabbed it to half the free world.

"Oh, and before you go blaming Calvin, he never said a word." She smiled. "You aren't exactly difficult to read, Mr. Subtle."

Well, shit.

I slid open my nightstand drawer, reached inside, and pulled the small black box from the back. Jumping out of bed, I went around and got down on one knee beside her. "So, I haven't figured out exactly what to say."

She shook her head. "Pathetic. Just pathetic. How about, 'Tamara, you're passionate and beautiful—breathtaking really—and smart—brilliant actually. I'm already the luckiest man in the world just being with you. Will you marry me?'"

I grinned. "Are you leading the witness, counselor?"

"Let's call it a suggestion." Tamara touched my nose with the tip of her finger.

"Tamara, you're passionate and beautiful—breathtaking really—and…um what was the next part?" I looked up at the ceiling as if searching for the words.

She raised her eyebrows. "Smart. Brilliant."

Nodding, I continued. "Right. Right. You're smart. Brilliant actually. Just being in your presence makes me the luckiest man in the world." I looked deep into her dark eyes. "I love you and want to spend my life with you. Will you marry me?"

"That wasn't verbatim…but, I like your version better, so yes." Tamara squeezed my hands.

I leaned forward and kissed her.

She pulled back. "How did we go from fighting to me agreeing to lend you money to me agreeing to marry you?"

I smiled. "I'm marrying you for your beauty, passion, and intelligence. You're marrying me because I'm irresistibly charming."

She laughed and wrapped her arms around my neck. "Is that so? Well, since you can't seem to charm your business into being mega-successful, maybe I should run that for you? I'm sure that with my superior intellect, I could point out the mistakes you've made…aaaaah!"

No longer caring about her sweaty stank, I tickled her neck with breathy kisses. "You need to stop talking."

Tamara giggled and ran her hands through my hair.

"Oh, yeah? How you going to keep me from jabbering all night?"

I pulled back, smirking. "I have my ways."

And I kissed her again.

CHAPTER SEVEN

SANDY

Trees rose out of the nighttime fog like rusted prison bars. I pressed my back against the thick trunk of a pine as I clung to the rough bark. The jagged surface poked against my spine and dug deep into my muscles. Balancing precariously on the large, moss-covered roots, I tried to keep my feet out of the thick bed of pine needles and wet foliage covering the forest floor.

I yanked some leaves off a nearby sapling and swiped at the blood dripping from the twin puncture wounds on my calf. Heat and ice radiated from the bite in a streaming torrent of pain, as if a pranking forest gnome had seared my skin with a blow torch while also pouring liquid nitrogen on the injury. The expanding diameter of poison radiated from the epicenter in malignant waves, spreading not just out but down, deep into my flesh, feeding on the muscle like a parasite.

My thumping heart sporadically raced and knocked like a failing engine. New and exciting pains stabbed at my gut in places that I didn't realize could hurt.

The toxin, which now infiltrated my body, seemed to be playing "Pop Goes the Weasel" with my vital organs.

Lucky me.

Every wing flap and insect chirp in the forest echoed in my skull like an out of tune, out of control carousel. My mind raced, leaping from thought to thought, without settling on a single one for more than a millisecond.

I closed my eyes, trying to calm the chaos threatening to mentally rip me to shreds. If I couldn't get myself back under control, I might as well hand myself over to Jesper's thugs and be done with it.

My eyes flew open as something just beyond the safety of my tree root island slithered through the rotting flora. I strained, trying to see what new horror lurked in the dark, but the weak moonlight concealed the creature in pockets of shadows.

Things hid in the forest floor. Awful things. I hadn't known that before.

I hadn't known a lot of things before.

From the other side of the tree, a sharp snap sent a bolt of terror through my nerves and tore my attention away from the things that slithered. My stuttering heart paused then lurched.

Every muscle tensed as I focused on the surrounding sounds. My pounding pulse and ragged respiration roared like a truck-laden freeway in my ears as I tried to figure out this new source of horror…but then I knew.

Jesper.

Somehow he'd survived the explosion and now stalked me through the night. In a few seconds, he would shove his way through the bushes, and his cancerous voice would carry above the noise of the forest. "Come out. Stop fighting. You and I both know that you're going to lose. If you don't come out on your own, I can't guarantee you'll live. Do as you're told and I will take you someplace safe. Do as you're told and no one else in your family will have to die."

I waited for the poisonous lies and false promises, but no such proclamations came.

A breeze whispered through the Ponderosas, rustling the branches as if a restless spirit drifted through their pine-covered boughs. But something more substantial than wind stomped through the nearby brush, and I pressed deeper into the tree, trying to meld into the randomness of darkness and splinter. Hiding from the one man I couldn't seem to beat.

Tiny convulsions pricked my injured calf, but I willed it to relax. I couldn't afford for the twitches to morph into a full-on spasm.

After a minute, I tentatively flexed and stretched the aching limb, weighing my limited options. It might still carry my weight, but, then again, it might not. The muscle twisted again, warning of impending cantankerousness.

My gaze roamed the murky forest.

If Jesper had been tracking me and I attacked him, the element of surprise might help me get lucky. Except that every time I'd gone hand-to-hand with him, I'd lost. Perhaps, if I could find a large stick, I could exploit his injuries from the explosion. The blast had torched his hair and knocked the bison-sized brute unconscious. Surely, not even he had walked away from that unscathed.

A glimmer of hope broke through the darkness in my soul, and a smile creased my dry, cracked lips. But the grin faltered, and the flame died in a puff of reality's breath.

The large man with the jagged scar on his throat wouldn't be caught off guard, even if I had a bazooka and the combined luck of every Irishman on the planet. As though straight out of a demon's harem, Jesper couldn't be overpowered, blown up, shot, burned, or outrun. He didn't even carry a gun. A weapon would simply be redundant.

But if I couldn't fight, I had to run or risk being recaptured.

Twisting my neck until the tendons creaked, I scraped my cheek against the rough bark as I peered around the tree. My breath condensed in the cold night air, hindering my view as it misted in the darkness. Staring through my own man-made fog, I gazed deep into the hodgepodge of shadows.

I tried to make sense out of the patterns of randomly crisscrossing saplings and shrubbery, but only gray and black phantoms, as deep as eternity and forever as space, haunted the gaps in between moonbeams.

The brush rustled again. I expected the vague silhouette of the huge man to materialize from the gloom, so the emerging outline of what could have been a jaguar or a cougar perplexed me.

As I frowned and leaned forward to study the shape closer, my calf muscle twisted into the sharp spasm it had been promising. My heel slipped off its precarious purchase, plunging deep into the forest carpet. My foot landed on something hard, and when it rolled out from under me, a crushing pain ripped through my ankle.

As I fell, the back of my head thudded against the tree, then scraped and bumped its way down the harsh surface until I landed heavily on the large root. My filthy, ultra-thin, sweat-wicking running shirt had done nothing to protect me against Jesper's brutalities, and now, it did nothing to protect my ribs from the bark-claws raking my skin.

If I survive this ordeal, I will henceforth only work out in chainmail.

I slid my butt up onto the slick wood and yanked my feet out of the pine needle carpet. Wincing, I gingerly touched my ankle, which had already begun to swell.

My calf twitched again, and I had just started to massage the unhappy muscle when something rustled in the grass.

I froze.

It moved again. The sound, louder than before, echoed off the surrounding pines, making it impossible to triangulate the source.

My injured leg would never allow me to run, so I searched the immediate vicinity for anything with which to protect myself. Nothing. With no viable options, I turned my attention back to the forest floor. Another stabbing twitch knifed through my calf as if reminding me of the things lurking in that rotten, smoldering carpet. I hesitated.

I glanced around once more, but no alternatives presented themselves. I took a deep breath and plunged my hand beneath the surface of twigs and cones.

At first, only slimy leaves, prickling needles, and clammy earth slipped through my fingers. I'd almost given up when my hand smashed into something cold and hard. A rock. I gripped it and, with all my might, yanked it from the ground.

Victorious, I wobbled up onto my good leg. Sneering against would-be assailants, I wielded the makeshift weapon as if it contained all the power of Thor's hammer.

A snapping staccato drew my attention from the threats that had not yet materialized.

Confused, I scanned for the source of the rattling and clicking when a white-hot sting in the soft flesh between my thumb and forefinger snaked up my arm. Hissing, I clamped my injured hand to my belly.

The rock slipped from my grip, bounced off the top of my foot, and tumbled back into its birth beneath the straw. I cried out at the crushing pain while also cursing about the loss of my only means of protection. But when I reached for my foot, I froze mid-stoop as my gaze landed on the luminous insect clamped to the back of my hand.

Glimmering as though its cell walls emitted photons of light, the glint of its shiny black shell glowed in the gloom. About the size of a mouse, its girder-like hind legs had hooked into my flesh, gripping it tight. Wicked-looking front claws widened a slim tear in my skin.

A hallucination. It had to be.

I'd never even got to see what had bitten my calf. Maybe a snake or something man-made. Whatever it had been, the poison it sent pounding through my system must have conjured up this new terror from my subconscious.

The classes at the academy had warned about the power of mind-altering chemicals. No creature on Earth, living or dead, had ever looked like this. I had to focus. If I could reign in my imagination, I could will this thing away. I closed my eyes.

It isn't real. It isn't real.

I reopened my eyes. It hadn't disappeared, but instead of horrifying me, the odd insect enraptured my exhausted mind. The sensation that I'd inadvertently stumbled into Alice's wonderland of white rabbits and hookah-smoking caterpillars temporarily overrode my need to regain control of the world.

Fascinated by this mirage, I leaned in, staring at the clicking, chirping creature. Perplexity and awe kept my fright at bay.

It paused, falling silent. Pivoting its bulbous head, it directed its glowering gaze at me as though it too found me worthy of study. Not like a typical mindless drone, but examining me, as if the insect could read my thoughts. It chirped, and then cobra-quick, it sliced at my face with its claw.

I yanked back and, in disbelief that this drug-induced illusion had the audacity to attack me, explored the ravaged flesh at the tip of my nose. Perplexed, I rubbed my fingers together, which came away slick with hot blood.

That's one hell of a hallucination.

The creature cocked its head, chirping again. It sliced the hole in my hand even wider and thrust itself up to its shoulders under my skin.

Before I could stifle it, a small cry escaped my lips, and I grabbed the bristly legs and hard, almond-shaped body. I pulled.

The insect popped and clicked rapidly, protesting my efforts, but held firm.

With panic circling, ready to assume control of my emotions, I wriggled my fingers under the creature's body and grasped it as though preparing to throw a knuckleball. I yanked, but the vermin held tight to my flesh with stiff barbed legs. It snapped, rapid as a machine gun, as I pulled, but the giant bug burrowed itself deeper.

Rather than continue a losing battle, I slipped my hand out from under it, flipped my wrist, and compressed it under my palm. At first, it resisted, the staccato rap becoming a whirring blender with a spoon in it. The cacophony reverberated through my skull, rattling my bones and drilling into my teeth, but I carried on, pressing even harder.

Then the creature screamed, and its exoskeleton crunched. A cold gelatinous raw-egg goo squirted from between my fingers. The insect fell mercifully quiet.

I shook my injured hand and started yanking the thing out of me, ripping it to pieces in the process. As I pulled the body free, its head tore off and remained lodged beneath my skin.

Even though it had obviously died, its mandibles resumed biting and tearing, burrowing deeper inside of me.

Frantic, I dug at it, loathing the sickening way its jaws chewed at my flesh.

I tore harder, but my fingernails proved inadequate. Only a knife or scalpel could free me of the torturous insect.

The clicking started again in earnest, and I beat at the spot, trying to force the bug out of my flesh. Panicking, I began flailing my hand around, and before I could stop it, a frustrated scream erupted from my throat.

A responding roar echoed through the trees. My blood froze, and I stared around the forest.

Only silence greeted me.

My gaze roamed the darkness. Nothing had changed and nothing moved, but the hair on the nape of my neck stood on end. While I'd been focused on the bug, something had gotten close and now watched me with a palpable malevolence.

A slight mew, like the hungry purr of a cat, emanated quietly from the dark, and I peered into the inkiness.

A pinecone bounced a few feet away and understanding dawned. Slowly, I raised my gaze skyward. In the blackness of the tree boughs, two ember eyes stared down.

My mind hiccupped, as though stumbling over the impossibility of the creature leering down at me from the limb of the massive evergreen. Primal survival instincts overrode all logic and reasoning, and my sporadic heart began knocking with the intensity of a jackhammer.

Broken ankle or not, I sprang off the tree and began running blindly, sailing past trees and tearing through brush. Trampling the undergrowth, pine needles and leaves erupted in a wave around my bare feet.

The creature shrieked and began to give chase. The bellow, like nothing I'd ever heard on the Nature Channel, sounded part cougar, part lion, and part something straight from Hell.

My ankle bones ground together like broken glass, but every nerve in my body urged me to move faster. Nothing else existed except the creature leaping from tree limb to tree limb and my frantic need to outrun it.

I shoved through a grove of sticker bushes. Long sharp thorns tore at my face, gouged my cheeks, and ripped apart the tender soles of my burnt feet. Blood seeped down my neck from a thousand cuts, but I paid them no attention. I'd deal with the injuries at another time, a million miles from this awful place.

I glanced back over my shoulder. The beast leapt nimbly, and I caught a terrifying glimpse of it in the moonlight.

About the size of a large German shepherd, the creature's shiny, midnight-colored fur flashed in the lunar glow as if it and the insect shared a common bioluminescent ancestor. Thick shoulders and haunches launched its lean body through the air with trapeze-like ease while its gleaming chrome-colored claws grasped branches with the dexterity of an eagle.

The beast's thick bony head, sleek snout, and long silver canines looked modeled after something primal and prehistoric. As if the designers of this cougar-lion-hybrid had composed the blueprints based on a robotic, land-based version of the great white.

Even as it navigated the complex forest canopy, the creature's glimmering eyes, confident and predatory, never glanced away from its quarry.

Dread filled my heart as if Death had already wrapped its eternal black cape around my soul. I ran harder, pushing my respiratory and muscular systems to their explosive limits.

After sailing through an unusually long stretch of shadow, I came out the other side only to collide with a tree. As my face plowed into the trunk, nose crunching against the hard, unforgiving surface, pain reverberated through my head and down my spine. The air ruptured out of my throat, and when I tried to inhale, my lungs refused to cooperate.

I collapsed to the ground. After several attempts, my spasming diaphragm relented, and my chest filled with cool night air. Rolling to my side, I stared back the way I'd come.

The beast hopped down, landing on the ground near my feet.

My racing heart circulated the invading poison throughout my bloodstream, feeding the venom to every cell in my body. It ate at me. Dined on my flesh at a molecular level like I'd already died and lay decomposing beneath the dirt.

Not to be left out, the insect in my hand came back to life. Slithering beneath my skin, it burrowed deeper, seeking refuge in my bones.

Heavy and sluggish as though my muscles had been replaced with pea gravel, I tried to get up onto my hands and knees. My world spun, flowing in and out of focus. Dizzy and nauseated, I got one foot under myself. But my body gave out and I collapsed onto my back.

Through watery eyes, I could do nothing but watch as the creature approached.

With the glowing red irises of a demon and the cunning mercilessness of a velociraptor, the beast blew steam from its nostrils. Maybe both the insect and this cat-robot-thing would prove to be nothing but a figment of my imagination?

I shook my head, hoping to clear it away, but it still strutted around me, glowering and hungry. Appraising. Metal claws ticked against stone while its large paws moved through the leaves with an underlying whir of servos and the pump of hydraulics.

I stretched out my hand and grasped a rotten branch that lay nearby. As the creature continued to pace, I wriggled myself up to a sitting position and held the makeshift weapon above my head.

"Come on! Come get it!"

I only had bluster left. Jesper had beaten me almost to death. Poison, probably fatal, ravaged my system. But I refused to relent. Refused to just give up and die. If I pretended to not be defenseless, maybe some circuit somewhere in the creature would send it in search of easier prey.

It paused, tipping its head to the side, then chuffed as though laughing at my pathetic attempts to ward it away.

The cat-thing snarled, its eyes brightening to simmering amethyst as a small electric motor whirred to life.

The beast sprang, lithe, graceful, and deadly. Roaring, it landed on me and knocked the stick aside as its claws raked my battered body.

Up close, the fangs looked like they'd been cut from the blades of a jet engine. Garrote-thin and wicked, the razors could slice flesh like a guillotine.

As the creature tore chunks from my shoulder—the smell of hot electronics filling my nostrils—tears pricked my eyes. A slew of images drifted through my mind. My little Rachel, who'd just learned to walk, toddling toward me as I came home from work; the tenderness in Harmony's gaze as I pulled back her veil on our wedding day; the triumphant expressions on the twins' faces when they made it into little league; the brave way Mike had died trying to save us all.

The memories made my heart both sing with joy and weep with loss.

My wife had no way to know that she would become a widow, my children fatherless.

The beast clamped its jaws around my throat, tearing ligaments, muscles, and arteries, but I felt no more pain. The darkness, my final darkness, blissfully carried it away as blackness encroached on the edges of my vision.

I smiled at my last thought—of Harmony and her joyful happy face on the day I'd proposed—and then the world faded to nothing.

CHAPTER EIGHT

JEFF

Game Over
Thank you for playing *Treason*.
Be sure to visit the Total Immersion library for more great adventures.

~Virtual Adventures~
We don't augment reality. We supersede it.

I ripped the fob off my temple and tore the pad from the back of my neck. I wiped away sweat from my brow and a tear from my cheek.

As MindLink relinquished regulatory control of my respiratory, circulatory, and nervous systems, my heart began to thud, cold and heavy in my chest. Though the building's furnace kept the room comfortable, a frigid shiver ran through my body as if a malevolent phantom had injected nitroglycerin into my bones. I rubbed my arms to warm myself.

My calf twitched. My breath caught in my throat as I waited. When the muscle spasmed again, I rolled my chair back and yanked up my pant leg. But nothing oozed from twin puncture wounds. No heat radiated through my bloodstream as poison infected and ate my cells. I rotated my foot, but my ankle bones moved together as smooth and painless as greasy ball bearings.

I released my pant cuff as another feeling took root.

I don't belong here. This isn't where I'm supposed to be. Someone just murdered me.

No, that can't be right, because obviously I'm alive. I must have dreamt I'd died after I fell asleep in this office. Only I don't have an office. I work out of a cubicle in the Pentagon.

I reached over and picked up the small brass plaque sitting on the desk. *Jeff Braxton. Who's Jeff Braxton? I'm Sandy Frost. But for some reason I've been pretending to be Jeff Braxton...* My heart started to pound as I looked around the workspace.

"Mirror me," I commanded the mobile on the desk.

A holographic image flared to life, hovering just over the surface. Gray eyes. Dark hair. When I moved, the man in the mirror app moved too. Not Sandy Frost.

Pull yourself together. Jeff. Your name is Jeff Braxton, just like the plaque says.

No...that can't be right. I started to stand but stopped myself as the man in the holograph got up too. I paused then sat back down.

Look around you. This is your life. Your world. You belong here. You are not Sandy; you created Sandy. You created Virtual Adventures.

My mind reoriented itself, and the Sandy Frost—I-showed-up-to-school-in-my-underwear—feelings began to fade. I took several long deep breaths, calming my scattered thoughts and racing heart.

My stomach growled. When had I eaten last? I couldn't remember exactly. Had it been days or hours? Did I have breakfast with Tamara this morning, or had I drunk a meal from the vending machine at the Pentagon a week or so ago?

When my stomach gurgled again, I decided it didn't matter and slid open a drawer, retrieving a meal shake and some aspirin. I washed the pills down with a long pull of the chocolaty concoction while blotting perspiration from my neck and face with a rag.

Dropping the damp cloth into a drawer, I stared sightlessly ahead as I finished the chalky drink and absently rubbed the smooth skin between my thumb and forefinger.

Something just beneath the surface slithered, and goosebumps broke out over my back and scalp. I scratched at the spot harder. Just a few minutes before, a mouse-sized bug had been digging itself under my flesh.

Only it hadn't.

I hadn't been running through the trees, chased by some exotic wild cyborg sabretooth panther demon. I didn't have a daughter, twin boys, and a wife who would mourn my death after the steampunk nightmare killed me. I hadn't been starved and beaten and tortured.

Instead of being captured and held in some abandoned warehouse in an isolated part of the country, I'd practically spent the last six months in self-isolation, at this desk, playing and replaying *Treason*. Granted, my office sometimes felt like a prison, but it in no way bore a resemblance to the concrete chamber of horrors where my brother…Sandy's brother…had been killed.

But the more time I spent in the *Total Immersion* world, the more the real one felt less…real. As if the true universe lay not with Tamara and Calvin but with Harmony, Jesper, Mike, and Camo Guy.

In the game, the forest and its creatures had been real. Jesper and his thugs, real. The pain and fear had been real.

Death, real.

A tremoring quake ran through me, and I shook my head. Evaporating as quickly as boiling acetone, the cascading feelings and swirling confusion suddenly vanished. My world realigned and my memories—my true memories—reasserted themselves.

I breathed a sigh of relief and glanced at my DigiSleeve.

Shit. Twelve minutes. I'd finished playing twelve minutes ago. *Impossible. My sleeve must be wrong.* It couldn't have been more than two, perhaps three, minutes at the most.

I checked again, yet the facts had not changed. I'd been confused about my own damned identity for twelve full minutes. It had only been nine the last time I'd played and seven the time before that. It was taking longer and longer to reorient myself to the real world with every iteration.

There was a reason Tamara and I were putting stricter limits on the amount of time people were allowed to play. I could keep myself in check. But if others played so far over the legal limit, like my job required me to, they'd become addicts.

They didn't have my self-discipline. *They* lacked my ability to bring myself back. *They* lacked my self-control.

As I rubbed my temples, I took several long cleansing breaths. Maybe we'd gotten too good. Perhaps we'd made this world *too* realistic.

Rick, Calvin, and I had played God. We'd not only created and smashed galaxies, decreeing life and death on a whim, but also figured out how to dissect and strip apart the layers of the human psyche. After manipulating the memories and sensations we wanted, we churned it through the dark matter server, weaving these highly-manipulated living segments with our computer-generated ones. The newly-spawned universes were similar enough to our own that we couldn't even trust our intuition to tell the difference.

Perhaps, by storing, altering, and regurgitating the thoughts and feelings of our fellow men, we *had* crossed a line that we, as a species, never should have crossed. Emotions and feelings made us unique.

But if we could replicate and generate those, had we suddenly become obsolete or, at the very least, redundant?

I stared at the fob on my desk.

What would Tamara think if she plugged in and became Sandy? Though I'd left out the guilt and the… self-identity confusion that lingered after the game ended, I'd otherwise told her about it in intricate detail.

But a million words couldn't adequately describe *Total Immersion*. How this world absorbed and captivated its players. Lured them in with a seductress' charms. It bewitched its victims by allowing them to become anyone and do anything, far removed from the confines of reality.

Tamara's words echoed through my swirling, churning thoughts. "Those that have never tried it, may be tempted. Those that are casual players, will become addicted. Those that are addicted, will become obsessed. I'm worried no one will ever come up for air."

VR had become the new lifestyle of choice. Used as a substitute for human interaction, millions never left the comfort and safety of their homes. For others, it had become an alternative to travel. Why risk being attacked by terrorists or waste time and money on hotels, rental cars, and entrance fees, when a complete, exciting, and safe vacation could be had with a simple subscription to MindLink?

In the real world, knees and elbows ached when it rained. Unfettered paunches and sloppy health habits made walking hard and sexual encounters embarrassing and uncomfortable. Difficult relationships, brought on by short tempers and even shorter attention spans, devolved into quagmires of unhappiness. Family members pestered one another for money and bored each other with idiotic drama and internal squabbling.

But despite all the chaos and inconveniences, Tamara and the rest of the Anti-V's insisted that only real experiences, real life, could be the backbone of our society. We needed honesty, not falsification, if we were to grow as a species. To do less would be a threat to our survival.

To Tamara's point, after experiencing *Total Immersion*, would people even bother coming up for air, or would this become the catalyst to the decline of all humanity?

Really, Jeff? "The decline of all humanity?" Feeling a little melodramatic and self-important, are we? This is a frigging video game. Nothing more.

I rubbed my face. I needed to stop arguing morals and playing philosophical table tennis with myself.

The psychiatrist we'd hired had helped us incorporate time limit restrictions right into the MindLink fob, thus protecting the public from itself. Like the cigarette companies had done in the twentieth and twenty-first centuries, Virtual Adventures put a disclaimer on every subscription and contributed to a government-controlled program to assist those with VR addiction.

We'd done our due diligence and, as a socially responsible entity, could sell our product with a clear conscience. People paid good money for virtual reality, but they would pay a lot more for *Total Immersion*.

That was the true reality.

I shook off my misgivings. I had a job to do, a product to deliver, and a timeline to meet.

I picked up a notebook and flipped through it. My chicken-scratch scrawl covered the pages with random doodles, notes of story points, changes to imagery, and, of course, problems, bugs, and errors. Though it was the most sophisticated software system in the world, it still needed some work.

I turned to the next blank page, pen poised above the creamy surface and paused. After a minute, I snapped the cover closed. "Lexi, I need to talk to Calvin. Can you get him for me?"

"Hold please, Jeff. I will ring Mr. Reynolds," my digital assistant said.

My image in the mirror app vanished as Calvin's face, his hair sticking out in multi-colored spikes, took the place above my mobile. "Talk to me." He glanced in my direction, then returned his gaze to something off-screen, never breaking from his rapid typing.

I waited for him to give me his full attention, but after a minute, I gave up and started talking. "I just finished reviewing the last track in *Treason*."

He half-smiled. "Pretty intense, right?"

I flipped back to my checklist. "It is. I've run it in world-exploration mode as well as through every conceivable track in mission mode. But the endings where he makes it home to his wife or where he takes down Jesper, just don't have the same…I don't know. Oomph."

Pausing, I tried to put my feelings and thoughts into words. "I don't know exactly how to say it other than Sandy's death feels more 'real' than the other endings."

I glanced back at my notebook. "Anyway, I'm really impressed with how well you guys integrated the robot panther footage."

He smiled as he continued to type. "I had to send the crew back to the forest three times to shoot more. By the way, I think we're done. If you and Tamara are looking for a new pet, Lassie's here in my office, and the backup panther, Cujo, is in the shed behind the warehouse where we did the filming."

I shook my head. "Lassie? Cujo? You named the cats after a couple of dogs? I think that's some type of feline blasphemy."

Calvin shrugged. "The electrical mechanic named them. We all liked the irony, so they stuck. Anyway, if you think your girl would enjoy having a cat or two around the house—or you've got mice problems or you want to give them to her as a wedding gift—you can go get them."

"Somehow," I said, "I don't think a robotic demon-panther would be something Tamara would enjoy having curl up on her lap at night. In fact, it might be a little frightening. But thanks anyway."

He cut his eyes to me, then back to his work. "They're just standard zoo-model robotic black leopards. Little kids ride them when their parents are tired of hauling them around the park. You're telling me Tamara is afraid of something that wouldn't harm a two-year-old?"

"They *were* harmless," I said, "until your team modded them."

His smile grew to a smirk. "What? We just added glowing eyes…and some metal claws and teeth. Extra-thick metal skin. Jacked up their servos and overclocked their processors. Oh, and we may have removed the safety protocols…and cranked up the 'nasty' in their dispositions a few notches."

I moved down the list to the next bullet point. "Anyway, that jankiness we had earlier with the memories and feelings associated with Harmony and the kids, it looks like you guys finally got that smoothed out."

The spike-headed man-child nodded. "I hear a 'but' coming."

I sat back in my seat. "From a storyboard point of view, I think it's a wrap. But the only things left are the sensation adjustment settings. They still aren't right. I set them to almost zero and expected to feel no pain at all, but the bite on my calf and the rock landing on my foot still hurt like a bastard."

I rubbed a sudden itch between my thumb and finger. "Actually, everything hurt. A lot."

He paused in his typing for a heartbeat before resuming. "Yeah, we've been having trouble getting the sensory settings right. Unfortunately, there's no precedent for us to work from; it's all brand new. I uploaded a new version of the sensation levelers if you have time to run through the game again and see if there's any improvement—but trying to isolate and adjust each one is a bitch."

"This data…" He shook his head. "It's not like anything I've ever seen before, Jeff. Using software to filter out the layers is like trying to separate salt from ocean water using a coffee strainer and a vat of wishful thinking."

I leaned forward. "We've had this conversation before, but I feel like there's something you're not telling me."

Calvin's shoulders dropped, and he stopped typing. Slowly, he turned to face me. "I'll admit I don't understand it very well. The biometric stuff from Dencephalon is in that crazy 4D format, and even after they convert it to something MindLink understands, it's still insanely complex. And no matter how much time I spend digging through their code, I'm not making any progress on understanding it any better. It's incredibly frustrating. I don't like not knowing something, and maybe that's my problem..."

"But?" I asked.

He sighed. "But, it feels like there's just too much. I've pored over the metrics and measured the relays. This new data feed uses the fob's *entire* capacity during a simulation."

I rubbed my chin. "When we designed it, we overengineered it. We thought we were leaving a ton of extra capacity for future enhancements."

"Right," he said. "Even our most advanced games never began to touch the fob's limits."

I thought it over. "Don't forget, there are the memories too. Not in our wildest dreams had we even discussed including memories, so we never ran any preliminary boundary tests."

He frowned. "Yes, of course. Still..."

Calvin's unusual uncertainty struck the same something-is-off chord I'd felt when I'd first met Rick and the team. Some indefinable wrongness—like a dormant virus waiting for the right time to consume its host—tainted their product, their process, their people, and their motives.

Perhaps it had been Rick's willingness to violate and steal from the dead, or perhaps it had been the massive dark-matter server, or maybe it had been the graffiti vampire skull with the dripping blood that had roughed the hackles of my intuition.

A looming premonition of wrongness urged me, compelled me, to abandon the project. Tamara had sensed it too even though she'd never laid eyes on Rick or experienced *Total Immersion* firsthand. Despite that, she'd still helped fund the purchase of Dencephalon, and I'd kept myself from pulling out largely because neither of us had been able to reason out a logical explanation for our apprehension. "What is it specifically that's bothering you?"

The man-child shook his spike-covered head. "I think it's just too much. Everything you've said is true…technically. Yes, the simulation would require a lot of information. But I've spent months working with the team, and on the surface, they seem very open and honest about how things work. Only…"

"Only it feels like they're hiding something," I finished for him.

He ran a hand over his face. "Yes… No… I don't know. Gawd, I hate this touchy-feely stuff. That's what I have you for."

I arched an eyebrow at him. "Come on, Calvin. This is a safe place. You can share with the group."

He flipped me the bird, then stared at the ceiling as if the answers he sought had been scribed across the tiles above his head. "Look, I just feel like there's more information than there should be. It's like there's a bunch of metadata hitching along for the ride."

He shook his head. "Or maybe it's just me. I'm so used to completely understanding every aspect of our systems and our software, it bothers me that there are elements beyond my control. It's disconcerting."

I chuckled. "Well, I can certainly see how that would bother you. But, just an FYI, this is what it's like to be the rest of us. It's uncomfortable at first, but then you learn to trust the team you've hired to build it."

This did nothing to alleviate the turmoil in Calvin's eyes.

I pointed at him. "Do you trust them?"

He blew out a long breath. "Jeff, you know I don't trust anyone. Not even you."

"Touché," I said, smiling. "Alright, let's look at it another way. Should we pull the plug?"

His eyes flew open. "What?"

Folding my hands on the desk, I leaned forward. "We need to be able to trust the people we partner with. I've always had an odd feeling about them. But you vouched for Rick and the rest of those brainiacs, and I trust you. If you're uncertain about Dencephalon, if you think they are up to something, then we need to get out. We haven't released yet, so it's not too late."

"You'd really do that based on my word alone?" he asked.

"Yes," I said. "I got in it on your word alone, and I'd bail on it too."

He stared at me. "Jeff, you've personally invested millions. You could lose everything. Plus, the game is set for review with both *VR Monthly* and *VR Gaming World* next week. We'd eat industry shit if we cancelled the release."

He paused. "You'd really stop production based on my gut feeling?"

While I agreed with him on getting slammed by the industry, part of me would be relieved to cut Dencephalon loose. I longed to go back to when things had been simpler, when we controlled every aspect of our product, and we didn't spew as much moralistic ambiguity.

But even after reflecting on it for weeks, I still couldn't tell if I wanted to go back because I pined for the simple times of our start-up days—before Ceos and before we'd become a slave to the market—or if I wanted to go back because in some unknown way it felt as if this partnership might be poisoning my company.

"It would certainly hurt us in the market and financially as well," I said. "Not to mention that Ceos would probably feed me to her dragonfish once she found out that not only had I gone behind her back, but that I'd pulled out just before things got really profitable. To answer your question though, yes. If you said the word, we would delay and work around the clock until we could release without the extra sensory layers. It would hurt, but it's doable. The game would still be pretty kick-ass, just not what we'd originally hoped for."

"But after all the propaganda, we'd get eaten alive by the press." Calvin shook his head. "No. Let's move forward, Jeff. We're so close to having this thing out and not just owning the market but crushing it. I'm proud as shit of what we've done." He paused. "I think my ego doesn't like not knowing everything."

A mixture of relief and disappointment vied for the top spot in my heart. "Are you sure?"

Calvin nodded. "Yes, let's go. We have the reviewers coming, and I want to blow them off the map. On another topic..." He hesitated again.

I waited, studying his face. "What is it, Calvin?"

"There was something else I wanted to talk to you about." He furrowed his brow as if trying to find the right words.

Having no idea what could be on his mind, I sat back and motioned with my hand. "You and I have never minced words. So, let's have it."

He took a deep breath. "Well, I noticed that your online hours are triple the legal limit. And I'm not even talking about the new ones that you, Tamara, and that psychiatrist came up with for *Total Immersion*, but the older, less-strict limits."

"Yes," I said. "I've had a lot of testing to do. We all have. But, rest assured, I'm the one that helped establish the old and new congressional guidelines, so I'm very aware of when I've had too much."

He nodded. "Okay. But not even the developers have logged a quarter of the hours you have. When they start pushing their limits, I make them unplug and test using the imagers and the sound silos. In fact, I disable their fobs to take away the temptation of plugging back in."

I kept my face passive. "Yes, and I'm glad you do that. We have to keep our liability low and protect the team."

"I'm just saying," he continued, "it's time for you to unplug too."

I gave him my most reassuring smile. "Sound silos give me migraines. Besides, someone needs to test the new sensory controls you just uploaded, and that can't be done unplugged. You've got enough on your plate. Focus on getting ready for next week's demo and stop worrying about me."

"I am focused, Jeff, but you need to back down a bit. We really don't know how addictive *Total Immersion* is nor do we know the long-term psychological effects it could have. You said it yourself, you put the limitations in place for a reason."

He had a point, but we couldn't sit on the brink of launching the most advanced product in the world only to release it with defects. It had to be perfect. I studied Calvin's uncharacteristically concerned face. I needed him working, not worrying. "You're starting to sound like Tamara, but I take your point. I'll back off."

Calvin stared at me for a heartbeat. "If you don't, you know that legally I'll have to disable your account or I could be held liable."

I held up my hand. "Scout's honor."

He hesitated again and I prepared for him to continue his lecture. Instead, he nodded, told me to have a good night, and signed off.

I leaned back in my chair, the old leather and wood protesting under my weight. Sometimes the squeak of my chair accompanied me when I slept, its complaints at holding my bulk the soundtrack to the work dream I never escaped.

Reaching into my pocket, I slid out a small disk. I held the hacker extension I'd printed that morning between my thumb and forefinger, examining it from all angles.

This simple little bit of circuitry that bypassed the system limits could be the undoing of all humanity…or it could just be that the hackers understood the true meaning of freedom—ironically, better than I, the Anti-V's, or the government ever could.

Picking up the fob from my desk, I snapped the extension over the sensory tap interface. When I touched the expanded device against my temple, it snicked snuggly into place.

In the corner of my eye, the fob began to glow green.

"See, Calvin. No need for you to worry about me going over my limit anymore."

I placed the pad on my neck and started *Total Immersion* on my mobile. I folded my hands on my lap and leaned back in my chair as the ominous opening music of *Treason* began again.

CHAPTER NINE

JEFF

Light rain, driven by the cold northern wind tapped against my office window. I leaned back in my chair, letting my mind relax after the intense day of testing.

The building swayed slightly as heavy gusts shoved it this way and that on its giant foundational springs—an architectural requirement as the Northwest prepared its infrastructure for The Big One. The supposed doomsday earthquake that would turn valley vistas to oceanfront viewing when the disaster heaved the western Cascade Mountains into the sea.

The new mayor had promised that, in addition to more earthquake readiness and to make Portland even weirder, he also wanted to make the city nighttime beautiful. As a result, he and the rest of his cronies had passed a long series of ordinances, one of which extended the no-manual driving zone several kilometers past the city limits.

A sister bill had banned the littering of all non-structural lighting, such as those produced by auto headlamps since computers didn't need to see to navigate after all. The ban hadn't stopped Portlanders from grand self-expression though. Personalized pictorials and animations, ranging from playful cats to spaceships to advertisements, danced, flew, and promoted across the live metal skins of the autos prowling the boulevards, turning the streets into a living quilt.

Neon-colored bridges, connected by self-illuminating asphalt roadways and glimmering skywalks, glowed in the darkness. Underwater lights, running deep down the center of the river, glimmered like ember-filled dragon eggs. The black water, which had always divided the city into two, now beckoned for all to come unify in peace and harmony…

Or some such nonsense.

At the time the bills had started going through unhindered one after the other, I'd wondered why we'd paid these monkeys ridiculous sums of money to make our lives more inconvenient. But from my corner office thirty stories in the air, the city looked as though it had been painted by a futuristic maestro wielding fire-injected acrylics to turn the landscape into his own personal canvas.

Perhaps, the mayor and his cronies hadn't been as wasteful as I'd originally thought.

Feet propped up on a barrel-shaped stool, I rocked back and forth to the gentle sway of the building. Sometimes I changed the virtual window on my office wall to "Malibu Beach" or "London Heights," but this evening, the blustery Portland weather perfectly accompanied the squeak of leather and the creaky, tired hinges of my old desk chair.

The computer pinged and Lexi's voice broke my reverie. "Tamara is calling. Would you like to answer, or should I take a message?"

I rolled around to face my desk. "I'll take it."

Tamara's smiling face materialized above my mobile. "Hey, fiancé. How's my big shot corporate tycoon?"

An answering grin tugged at the corners of my lips. "Hey, baby. Oh, you know, ruling the city's minions from my high-rise as always."

She took a long sip off a bottle of water. "It must be exhausting brainwashing the masses and counting your gold coins all day."

"You have no idea," I said. "People can be so stubborn. I work really hard to rid them of their individuality, but some refuse to give in and become part of my lemming army." I chuckled. "You just get done at the office?"

Signs and buildings blurred past in the background of my wife-to-be as her auto drove her down the freeway. She grimaced and shook her head. "No. I needed to hit the gym before I left."

"Uh oh," I said. "Rough day?"

Tamara rolled her eyes. "Let's just say, if you go crazy on Ceos someday, I may just end up in an adjoining cell."

"What happened?" I asked.

"Mitch botched the Positron Energy case," she huffed and began a convoluted story involving mouthfuls of legalese. As "affidavit," "exculpatory evidence," and "litigation" rolled over my brain like tsunamis, I tried to remain focused and engaged, even though my mind continuously wandered back to the *Treason* universe.

Her nostrils flared as she wrapped up her tale of Malpractice Mitch. "Sarah saw how pissed I was, so she agreed to let me punish her on the racquetball court for a while."

"Is she still alive?" I asked, only half-kidding.

Tamara shrugged. "She knew what she was in for. Besides, she can mostly hold her own. Anyway, I'm headed home now. Gonna get a hot shower, slip into my comfies, and drown my sorrows in a glass of Merlot. What's up with you?"

I leaned forward, and my chair squawked. "I'm done for the night. I think if I had to run through the game just one more time, I'd go completely insane. If I hear that damned intro music again, I may just fling myself out the window."

"You know your window isn't real, right? It's just live wallpaper set to look like a window." She smiled. "Though it would be amusing to see you try. I'll wait if you want."

I cocked my head. "You really know how to suck the melodramatics out of a self-pity party."

"Oh, sorry. Right, right." Tamara assumed a mock-serious expression and tsked. "My poor baby, you should definitely avoid flinging yourself out the window, fake or otherwise. At least for tonight. As your betrothed, I'd feel obligated to come stand around while the police scraped you off the pavement. But I just finished working out, so I'd have to go home, get cleaned up, then come back. I'm already tired, and it takes a lot of effort to look sad and pathetic while remaining dazzlingly beautiful. Besides, the rain would mess up my makeup, which would spoil my hot widow vibe."

Nice. This is the woman I'd asked to marry me. Or had she somehow finagled me into asking her? My recollection of the events leading up to my proposal had grown fuzzy.

Her expression turned for-real serious. "I know you want your game to be perfect, but you haven't gone over your hours have you? We put those limits there to protect everyone, which includes you. You can't sacrifice your sanity for a VR game. That would be a tremendous waste."

I rolled my eyes. "Between you and Calvin, I'm very aware of the limits. As I keep telling everyone, I'm the one who suggested putting them in place to begin with."

Her gaze sharpened as she studied my face. I'd hated being on the receiving end of her cross-examination. "Jeff, you're avoiding my question."

Yes, I avoided it on purpose. Of course, I should have known I could never get away with not answering. I'd been at least quadruple the legal limit when Calvin called me on it, but the hacker extension fooled MindLink into thinking I'd switched to an imager and sound silo. When I shut it down this evening, I'd purposefully avoided checking to see how many hours I'd put in. A lot... A whole lot.

But, nothing untoward had happened. My mind, while tired, had not suffered any adverse effects from VR exposure. I'd avoided cowering in a corner, drooling on myself, and sucking my thumb. I didn't have a burning desire to hide away in a cave, and I certainly had no urge to return to the *Treason* universe.

Everyone needed to cool their jets because I was just fine and dandy. "I've gone over some, but Calvin caught it and made me unplug."

Please don't ask if I mean I went over the old limits or the new ones.

She regarded me, a flicker of doubt and suspicion clouding her dark eyes. "Okay, well, you need to be safe. I don't want to get married to a vegetable."

I smiled. "I promise, you won't be marrying any produce. Though, I may become a bean pole. It's been so long since I ate, I think my body is trying to ingest itself."

"A victim of overindulging on your own brilliance—potential suicide by becoming an asphalt pancake and now the possibility of starving to death." She frowned. "Hmmm. Being a game designer seemed like such a safe, albeit boring, occupation."

My spongy brain sputtered and failed to produce a snappy comeback. So I went for her stomach as a distraction. "So, I'm going to order some Szechuan beef on the way home. You hungry?"

Her eyes lit up. "Starving."

"Okay, I'll get a double then," I said. "Heading out in a few minutes."

Tamara took another sip of water. "Let the car drive you and have a beer on your way home. All the cool kids travel hands-free."

I smiled. "I'm sure they do, but the car's manual controls were expensive, and I almost never get a chance to use them."

She shook her head. "There aren't road signs anymore. It's a wonder you even know how to get home."

"GPS," I said, shrugging.

Amusement danced in her eyes. "Sometimes I wonder if you were born in the wrong century, darling. Your company makes the most advanced video games on the planet, yet you reject modern conveniences, like getting to enjoy a fermented beverage on your commute home after a rough day. It was geeks like you who *invented* digital chauffeurs. Besides, I don't see the point of buying insurance for the 'privilege' of driving. It's not a privilege at all, but an avoidable nuisance."

I sighed. "Well, since almost all the roads are mandatory auto-control anyway, you may have a point."

Tamara lifted her bottle of water into the air. "When your car is driving you home, raise a toast to laziness and government oversight, sweetheart. For they are the future."

I laughed long and loud.

Her smile grew. "Anyway, I'm holding you up. I'll be waiting for my man to bring me my dinner, so don't be long. I love you."

"Love you back." I ended the call and spun my chair around to stare out the window a little longer.

I didn't like my less-than-forthcoming part of the conversation with Tamara, but she'd had enough to deal with without having to worry about me too. I reached over, clicked the live wallpaper, and turned off the window.

Taking a deep breath, I got up and slipped on my long coat. "I'm headed home, Lexi."

"Good night, sir."

I exited my office, pausing in the entryway. "Looks like I'm last to leave again tonight."

My digital assistant turned off the lights behind me. "You are, Jeff. But, I've noticed this is your usual behavior during the weeks leading up to a release. Other than fatigue and trouble sleeping, your physical health does not seem to be overly affected by the extra hours. However, my observations suggest that stress is mentally exhausting you. Might I recommend taking a vacation after *Treason* goes live?"

A vacation? Under Ceos' watch? I snorted a laugh and started toward the elevators. Halfway down the hall, the rattling of a keyboard halted my progress, and I turned back to the open office. Though littered with chairs, desks, and computers, the work area remained as dark and lonely as the bottom of the ocean.

Only the click of keystrokes broke the eternal stillness.

I glanced over my shoulder at the awaiting car Lexi had summoned on my behalf. I considered ignoring the anomaly, which would probably turn out to be Calvin or one of the other developers trying to get a few last-minute tweaks in on the software before the reviews tomorrow. I could either go home to Tamara's warm embrace and dinner or satisfy my curiosity about who still toiled at this late hour.

My stomach growled as I glanced at my DigiSleeve. "Lexi, I thought no one else was here?"

"That is correct, Jeff," she said. "As you stated earlier, you are the last to leave tonight."

The keyboard clicking continued, and I frowned. "Are you sure? Can you double-check? Maybe someone forgot their proximity badge?"

My digital assistant paused for a moment. "I have completed an infrared sweep of the building. Other than you, there are no other occupants on this floor. However, on the second floor, there is a cleaning crew consisting of—"

"Then who's typing?" I interrupted.

My digital assistant did not respond.

"Lexi?"

"Yes, Jeff?" she replied promptly.

I ground my teeth together. "I asked you who was typing?"

Again, Lexi remained silent.

We'd spent months working out the bugs in our software, yet my digital assistant's designers had evidently not felt the need for such prudence. I cursed under my breath about the ineptitude of my own industry.

"I'm sorry," Lexi said. "I didn't catch that. Is there anything else I can do for you?"

I rolled my eyes. "No, thank you."

Unable to quell my growing unease, I started wading into the rows of desks and cubicles, following the incessant typing. The tapping of the keyboard grew louder as I weaved among the empty workspaces. When I neared the far wall, the clicking stopped. I stopped too. When the typing resumed, it seemed to have moved to the opposite side of the room.

"What the?" I had almost been on top of my rogue worker…at least I thought I had. Maybe sound waves in an empty office bounced oddly off the empty furniture? Though my theories were weak, no other explanations presented themselves.

I re-triangulated, turned, and jogged down the next row. But as I passed empty cubicle after empty cubicle, no one lingered in the desks. When I came to the corner where the outer walls met, I paused again.

As though thwarting my efforts to find the perpetrator, the lone typist seemed to shift to the center of the floor.

Abandoning all subtlety, I ran. As I neared the middle of the large space, the ticking fell silent and I halted. Spinning in a circle, I ran my gaze over the dark shadows of office equipment.

"Lexi." When my digital assistant didn't reply, I cleared my throat and tried again. "Lexi."

"Yes, Jeff?"

"Please turn on the office lights. All of them." Nothing happened. "Lexi?"

"Yes, Jeff?" My digital assistant's voice, chipper and obedient, grated on my nerves.

"Please turn on all the office lights." Again, I waited, and again, nothing happened.

A sudden cold draft chilled my skin, causing waves of gooseflesh to break out over my body. I strained to hear, but in the absolute stillness my inhalations and exhalations echoed in my ears as loud as a freeway.

I gazed over the large space, searching the hodgepodge of sharp angles and office paraphernalia, but nothing moved. I closed my eyes and rubbed my temples. When I opened them again, an elongated version of my own shadow, cast by a soft light from behind me, stretched from my feet to the top of the wall.

My breath caught and I spun around. A small lamp and holographic monitor illuminated a previously empty desk.

A man in a military uniform, four flashing and glinting gold stars on each shoulder and a quilt of medals tacked to his chest, stared at the floating graphics and text. His eyes wobbled as he read.

Pain suddenly pressed against my forehead as if an infection had been set loose in my sinuses. I started to double over but froze when the name of this stranger materialized in my mind like a flashing sign. "General McKenzie? You are General McKenzie, right?"

He held up a finger while his other hand typed some more. He read over the display one last time and nodded. He closed the extended keyboards on his mobile, slipping it into the breast pocket of his uniform. "Hello, son."

The pain and pressure pounding on my skull eased as I stared at the squatter. "You didn't answer my question."

The man folded his hands with military precision and leaned forward. "I don't have the patience to answer something that you already know the answer to. If that's the way you are going to play this, you're wasting my time."

My head began to throb as more images fell into place. The general receiving a recognition certificate before a military audience. The general describing terrorist threats to our country. The general's wrath as he argued with those that disagreed with him. The general's betrayal…

"Sir…" I hesitated. "What are you doing here?"

He regarded me with sharp, intelligent brown eyes. "The question isn't what I'm doing here; the question is what are *you* doing here?"

I shook my head. "I own this company."

When he sat back, his chair made the exact same squeak and pop as my own. "Do you? Are you certain of that, son? By my measure, it's someone else that's in charge."

I nodded. "Well, yes. Okay, technically someone else owns the controlling shares of the corporation, but I still run things."

He shook his head. "Are you sure about that? You just said that you own the company, but now you're backpedaling. I want to be absolutely certain that you understand the facts."

"Yes," I said. "I'm certain."

He gave a slight, curt nod. "I'm glad we have that straightened out. You seemed very confused."

"Sir," I said, "I'll admit, I am very confused. I know you, but I don't know why or how. You're General McKenzie of the Air and Space Coalition. We've worked together…only that's impossible because we've never met until just now."

He arched an eyebrow. "You and I have accomplished a lot together."

Another wave of pain crashed into my head. I groaned and rubbed my temples until the worst of it passed. I took several deep breaths. "Okay, let's say that's true. Why are you here?"

The general's lips narrowed to a hard slit. "Son, don't you think you should have all the facts before you start an investigation on me? Betraying our government is a very serious allegation. I know things, secrets, that would make you scamper back home to your momma. So, before you go making accusations, maybe you need to understand that you don't have all the information."

My mind spun as if I'd slipped into some alternate vortex. This general, who couldn't possibly be here, maddeningly spoke in twisted riddles. Despite that, a clang of truth reverberated through his words. Something resonated, though I couldn't recall exactly what, as if we'd had this conversation before. "Sir, I haven't started any investigations on you."

"Just like you," he pointed at me, "I'm looking out for the greater good of our country. You can't persecute me just because I'm not afraid of making the tough decisions. Someone has to face reality. Someone has to be the adult."

I ran my hand down my face. My fingers came away wet with sweat. "General, I'm not even in the military. I couldn't investigate you even if I wanted to."

He slammed his palm against the desk, the lamp rattling from the impact. The smack of skin on wood sent daggers of agony into my forehead. "Don't lie to me! You can hide from the things that go boo in the night, but don't *ever* hide from the truth."

The throb behind my eyes ebbed and flowed as I tried to connect the pieces of this random puzzle. "General, I—"

He refolded his hands and glared at me. "I've never betrayed our country, son. And I never will." He leaned forward. "Can you say the same? Before you proceed, before you go making a mess and a mockery of everything and everyone I hold dear, I suggest you think twice about what you're about to do."

Before I could answer, he reached over and snapped off the light. The ache in my head vanished as the room plummeted into darkness.

My heart hammering, I stared at the aura left behind by the general. As it too faded, the overhead lights came on, assaulting my eyes with an onslaught of brilliance. I spun around, but no one occupied any of the desks. "Lexi, where did General McKenzie go?"

Lexi's digital voice contained a trace of perplexity. "I'm sorry, Jeff. I don't know a General McKenzie. As we discussed earlier, you are the only one here. You asked me to turn the lights on, so I did." She paused. "I am registering elevated blood pressure, heart rate, and skin temperature. Do you feel you are in danger? Shall I call security?"

I hesitated before answering. "No. I'm fine."

"Are you sure? Your rapid breathing and the strain in your voice indicate—"

"No," I snapped. "I'm fine. Please turn out the lights and bring the car around."

"Very well, sir."

The room dimmed as I made my way out. When I passed my office door, I stopped and turned back, surveying the large space. I half expected the rattle of the keyboard to begin once again, but only a tomb-like silence greeted me.

A dream. It had to be a dream. Lexi said that there's no one else here. My assistant may have a few bugs in her, but no way would she get that wrong.

I shuddered and stepped into the awaiting elevator. The doors began to slide closed, but just before they shut off my view of the office, another stab of pain shot through my forehead, and the light at the general's desk snapped on.

My heart lurched as the doors sealed me inside and the car started slowly dropping to the ground floor.

∞ ∞ ∞ ∞

All the way home, I'd debated telling Tamara about my encounter with the non-existent general. If I did, her questions might lead her to press me again about the number of hours I'd been testing while plugged in.

I'd gotten away with fudging the truth on our call, but in person, anything less than full disclosure would activate my bride-to-be's lawyer intuition. She would see the deception in my eyes and hear it in my voice. I didn't want to even consider the paths the conversation might take from there.

Even though we hadn't yet swapped vows, we'd still committed to pledging our lives, faithfully and truthfully, to one another. So rather than lie to the woman I loved, I planned to hold onto this little secret. Despite our promises to be open and forthcoming, I still needed to protect her from the dangers of my occupation and the sacrifices I had to make to be successful.

As I pulled into the driveway, a delivery drone lifted off the front porch. Lights flashing, it sailed away into the night sky where it became another random dot among the stars. Still tussling with the morality and obligation of full disclosure, I stooped on the steps to pick up the Chinese food left by the little robot.

Entering the foyer, I kicked off my shoes and hung my coat on the wall rack. "Tamara, I'm home."

"In here," came the reply from down the hall.

I stopped by the kitchen, got plates and silverware, and headed to the back of the house. She sat on the couch, a glass of red wine in her hand and her extended mobile in her lap. "Hey, baby."

I'd never once found a room that had not been enriched by Tamara's beauty. Though I'd made a concerted effort to nonchalantly hide that just the sight of her makes my pulse race, I thought she knew it all the same.

That my acting skills were not up to concealing even a fraction of my attraction to her had never been a topic of debate with us. She'd never called me on my bluff nor provided clues to help me improve wrangling my emotions. In fact, judging by the gleam in her eyes and the catlike smile that always tugged at her lips, I believe she found my efforts both endearing and part of the irresistibility of my charm.

Or maybe I was just flattering myself.

As I gave her a peck on the lips, I caught a sweet whiff of her wine-kissed breath and her mango-strawberry shampoo. "Hey, yourself. How are you doing?"

She took another sip from her goblet. "I'm completely spent." Though she smiled, the usual spark in her eyes had been overshadowed by sadness.

"What's wrong, honey?" I asked.

Tamara sighed as she ran her fingers through her damp hair. "I made the mistake of turning on the evening news. Did you know that more people have gone missing?"

"You mean the government employee kidnappings?" I asked. "I had no idea. With all that's been going on, I've been a little out of touch with the rest of the world. I just assumed that by now they'd have figured out who was doing it. How many have been taken?"

She furrowed her brows. "I'm not sure. About two dozen in all, I think. But this is either a copycat or the same people that hit England last year, France before that, and Germany before that. The disappearances in those countries went on for months, and then they suddenly stopped, only to start again somewhere else."

"So now it's our turn," I said.

My fiancée nodded. "Yes. They say there's no consistent connection between any of them other than they all work high up in different government agencies. These people are being snatched from their homes—in malls, and grocery stores, usually in broad daylight—and then a week or so later, their cremated remains are mailed back to their families."

She shuddered. "It's beyond repulsive, and the authorities don't seem any closer to solving the case than they were when they started a few years ago. None of the agencies are saying anything. Evidently mum is the word of the century, but the rumor on the street is that it's a new type of terrorist attack, though no one has any idea who's behind it."

I shook my head. "If it is, it's the most random attack ever."

Tamara shuddered. "Anyway, I couldn't handle watching anymore, so I tried to focus on my work. Except that

I haven't been able to find another chink in the Positron lawsuit. I've gone over it line by line. Though it's better than the news, it's still pure drudgery and about as mind-numbing as an all-day ice cream headache. Except I don't get any ice cream chocolaty goodness, just the excitement that more unhappiness awaits me in the morning…and the next morning…and the next."

I chuckled. "Well, the good news is that while there are a ton of calories in chocolate ice cream, there are none in drudgery and unhappiness."

"Speaking of calories…" She snatched one of the takeout containers from my hand, broke the seal, and inhaled deeply of the rich fried rice aroma emanating from the vacuum insulated hotbox. Tamara rolled her eyes back and smiled happily. "I prefer to get mine from cheap takeout."

I took the container back and started setting up the smorgasbord on the coffee table. "Only the finest of cuisine, for us. This is how we high rollers eat."

Her mobile slid from her lap, and I caught a glimpse of the screen. "Hmmm, that's the oddest legal document I've ever seen. I'm not a lawyer so you'll have to forgive my lack of understanding, but that looks suspiciously more like gossip and fodder than legalese."

She turned it off and tossed it onto the couch. "I'm just letting my subconscious ponder the finer details of the case, while I direct my attention to more…lighthearted topics. I learned in law school that it's good to let your mind ruminate on complex issues."

I snatched up her mobile and flipped it back on. "So, law school taught you that it's good for your mind when you read about a prehistoric bat boy undisclosed sources say they found deep in an African jungle?"

She giggled. "Maybe. Besides, I was all into my work like a good kid when that Rick Tieg guy stopped by and broke my concentration."

She couldn't have surprised me more had she said that old Saint Nick himself had dropped in and unloaded a sack full of toys. "He did? Why?"

"I take it you didn't know he was coming?" she asked.

Shaking my head, I said, "I never would have invited him here, especially not when you're here by yourself."

"He said he wanted to drop off a 'golden' fob for tomorrow's demonstration." She gestured to a small box on the table. "I know you have to work with him and he's brilliant and all that, but there's something about him that really bothers me."

Him stopping by our home aside, a dissertation on the man couldn't adequately describe all of his idiosyncrasies. "Yeah, he's really intense…and stuff."

Tamara nodded. "Yes. Exactly. And stuff. He creeps me out in a 'I'm going to eat your liver with some fava beans and a nice chianti' sort of way. We had this stilted conversation with these weird pauses and his breath… You told me about it, but damn." She curled her lip in disgust. "And the whole time he played with his lit arc lighter while I felt like he was feeling me up with his eyes." She shuddered again.

The thought of Dragon Breath Rick in *my* living room with *my* fiancée made my blood boil. Tamara could undoubtedly kick his ass if she needed to, and while the image of her pounding his face like an old boxing bag gave me a glimmer of amusement, I hated that he'd made her uncomfortable. "Did you feel threatened?"

"Not exactly." She thought it over for a minute. "It's just…just…"

"Something you can't put your finger on," I finished for her.

Tamara pointed. "Exactly." She glanced back at the table and scratched her chin. "Don't you already have a bunch of those fobs?"

I nodded. "So weird. He came all the way across town to give me one when he knows we have dozens staged for the presentation. It's possible he made some more mods to it and wants me to see what he's done."

"Jeff, he's a super genius." She shrugged. "There's no way you could predict what's going through his head. Maybe he just wanted a reason to come see you so the two of you could talk about tomorrow."

While technically plausible, none of these explanations rang true in my heart. If he wanted to talk, he could have called or messaged me at any time. I never take my DigiSleeve off. This felt more…personal or something. As if dropping off the fob had been a cover-up for some other ulterior motive. Though what that motive could be, I didn't have the foggiest idea.

"He will *not* be stopping by our house unannounced again," I said. "Ever. I have to deal with him at work, but coming here crosses the line. I know he's kind of an introvert's introvert, and I think part of it is he's just so out of touch with reality that he's unaware of the social rules. I will remind him of them tomorrow."

Tamara touched my cheek. "My hero." She slid her hand down my neck, grabbed my arm, and started shaking it. "Forget about that for now, I'm starving. Please serve us dinner, or I'm going to stuff my face into a container and start chowing down like an animal."

Brushing away my misgivings, I began to scoop food onto our plates.

Tamara sniffed. A look of apprehensive confusion crossed her face. "So, baby. While I appreciate you bringing me dinner, I have to wonder if maybe you're trying to get out of marrying me by killing me instead."

"What do you mean?" I asked.

She picked up a plate. "Shrimp."

I shook my head. "What? We always…" Stopping myself, I stared.

She put a hand on her hip. "We always what?"

We didn't "always" do anything that involved shrimp, except avoid it.

A turning point in Tamara's childhood had been the evening a trace amount of shellfish had found its way into her mother's dinner. The woman's implanted EpiGland either malfunctioned or the dosage had been inadequate to compensate for her body's reaction. When her throat sealed shut, she'd succumbed to a full-on seizure, cracking her skull so hard on a table leg that she'd splattered her ten-year-old daughter with blood and left behind bits of bone. By the time the medical drone had swooped into the restaurant a few seconds later, the seizure had ended, but so had Tamara's mom's life.

Because of this, I'd always gone to great lengths to use my DigiSleeve's allergen scanner on every morsel of food I gave to Tamara, searching for telltale bits of poisonous shellfish.

While she could take care of herself, this small service had been one of the few ways I'd been able to help protect her and show her how much she meant to me. Despite years of habitual scanning, this evening I hadn't even activated the DigiSleeve program, and for a few heartbeats, I had actually believed that this had been our favorite go-to meal.

I sat down heavily, staring at the plate. If Tamara had eaten the food I'd dished up for her, she would have... Ugh. I didn't want to think of it.

I glanced up at her. Concern, hurt, and misgiving lingered in her eyes. She'd been thinking of it too. I hated that I'd let her down. Hated that I'd hurt her. She'd always implicitly trusted me, but this betrayal—accidental or not—had damaged her confidence in me.

Just then, I understood I could never tell her about the meeting with the general that hadn't been there. Something inside of me was out of alignment—this incident, yet another example of that off-ness.

Until I'd sorted that something out, I needed to keep my mouth shut. I'd just hurt the woman I loved, but if I didn't focus and get my head on straight, I might do it again. Only next time, we may not be so lucky.

"I'm sorry, baby," I said. "Lexi must have misheard me. And that's not the first time tonight she's gotten something wrong. Damn digital assistant is full of bugs. When I served us, I wasn't paying attention. I'm really tired, and to be honest, my mind hasn't left the office yet. We have the game reviewers coming in tomorrow, and I have…"

Secrets.

The general said that we all had secrets but discovering his would make me cry for my momma. Not his exact words, but something along those lines.

It's true. I had a growing list of secrets too. Maybe I'd underestimated the effects of too much VR exposure? Consumed by the world of spies and terrorists, I'd become a victim of my own overactive imagination. Could too much *Total Immersion* cause hallucinations and confusion? I didn't think so, and as far as I knew, the control group never exhibited any symptoms.

Perhaps these weird happenings had nothing to do with the game. Maybe, overcome by exhaustion, I'd simply gone to sleep at my desk and had the mother of all dreams.

I could almost make myself believe the lies. Almost.

I scraped the food back into the containers. "Lexi, please place a double order of Szechuan beef. I'll pay the extra for the express delivery."

My digital assistant paused. "Your order has been placed, Jeff. The food should arrive in about five minutes."

Getting a fresh plate, I dished Tamara some fried rice, scanned it for any traces of deadly shellfish, and handed it to her. "Here. This should tide you over until the rest of it arrives."

My fiancée furrowed her brow, the concern in her eyes deepening to worry. "You started to say something a minute ago. You have…what? Please finish your thought."

I took a long deep breath. "I'm sorry. I have to focus and be present. My mind is a million miles away. That's all."

Pain still lingered in her eyes, but her gaze softened, though only a little. "That's obvious."

Trying as hard as I could to act nonchalant, I poured myself a glass of wine and sat back. "So, how exactly did Mitch muck up your case?"

CHAPTER TEN

JEFF

VR Monthly's entourage filled half of the small auditorium and *Virtually Real* filled the other half. While Rick remained on stage, completing the equipment setup, Calvin and I chatted up the familiar faces and introduced ourselves to the new ones.

These groups, as part of the standard operating geek procedure, decimated the donut and muffin spread we'd laid out for them. Serious gamers, such as those attending our demonstration today, did not represent the fittest members of society.

A sinewy man in a tweed coat and bow tie glowered at us as we made our rounds. Not only did he not approach, but by skulking in the back of the room behind the crowd, he remained almost unreachable. Unlike the rest of the gamers, he neither socialized nor partook of the pastries. The bottom arch of his tie exactly matched the scowl that pulled at his lips and dug deep lines of disconsolation into his face.

While I shook hands and talked with the journalists, he glared at me with a palpable hatred. Not understanding the man's hostility, but determined to decipher the mystery, I started wading through the mishmash of pasty gamers toward the back of the crowd.

But before I could get even part of the way down the aisle, Calvin grabbed my shoulder. "Jeff, it's time. We need to get in place."

I didn't want to start the presentation late, but curiosity urged me to confront the tweed coat man anyway. I glanced at my DigiSleeve. Damn. Only six minutes until show time. "Hey, Calvin. Who is that?"

He followed my gaze. "You mean the anachronism that fancies himself an eighteenth-century London law professor?"

"Yes," I said. "He's not one of the usuals, and he's not one of ours."

Calvin shrugged. "I don't know. He must be new to one of the magazines. There's always a lot of turnover in those places."

"Yeah, maybe. I just hope he's not one of Ceos' drones."

Like everything else we'd done surrounding our latest technology, we'd locked this demo down, making it an invitation-only affair to prevent one of Ceos' minions or anyone else from getting a sneak peek at our game. Even in our marketing paraphernalia, we'd purposely played down the tactile, emotional, and memories elements of the game. Word of mouth would be our biggest advocates.

But if Ceos found out what we'd been up to before the reviews and money started rolling in… Ugh, I didn't want to even think about what her reaction might be. "I really need to find out who he is."

"No one got past security that we hadn't invited, so I don't think you need to worry." Calvin motioned for me to follow. "Come on. You can solve the case of the mysterious gamer after the presentation."

Despite my lingering unease, I trailed behind him toward the front of the room.

"He's probably unhappy because he has to wear such an ugly coat," Calvin said as he glanced back and grimaced. "Maybe he lost a bet or something?"

I forced a laugh. "I suppose so." As we mounted the stage, I slipped behind the side curtain, out of sight of the audience. "Rick, are we good to go?"

He looked over at me then nodded his head to the huge holodisplay before him. Various graphs and monitors wove, spun, and blipped like EKGs on steroids as the computer monitored millions of system health points. "We're ready. The communication sockets are solid."

He pointed to another graph. "The storyboard and sensory relays are synchronized. Individual server and overall system health is at a hundred percent, boss."

I gazed across the vast array of reports. "Okay, great."

"Did you get the little gift I left for you at your house last night?" he asked.

I nodded. "Yes."

I'd been trying to find time to launch into a lecture on personal boundaries—instead of sleeping last night, I'd lain awake, rehearsing and rehashing my spiel and the resulting conversation in my head—but I could practically feel Calvin's eyes burning into my back, urging me to hurry.

Rick smirked. "Your fiancée is really pretty."

An angry bed of white-hot coals stoked my heart. I considered going off on him anyway, bad timing or not, but I held myself in check. There would be time for that after the demonstration.

When I hesitated, Rick raised his eyebrows and nodded toward the stage. "I've got things handled from a technical point of view, so you two worry about the meat sacks."

Ugh. Over and over, Rick had proven his technical genius, but the lack of regard he had for our customers, and people in general, bothered me. I'd tried to brush it off as the introvert's eccentricities and complete absence of social skills, but something about it disturbed my bones. He waved his fingers, indicating for me to move along.

I huffed and walked away. As I took my stool next to Calvin, I glanced over at the man behind the curtain. Rick's gaze found mine, and though he gave me a thumbs-up, he smirked as if he'd hidden a moldy sardine in my pocket and couldn't wait for me to find it.

"Everything okay?" Calvin asked.

I considered telling him about Rick's latest shenanigan, but my friend already listened to more than enough of my griping. I needed to rise above petty belly aching. I had a job to do. A lot of people depended on me to really sell this thing, and I couldn't do that distracted.

Focus. Rise up and forget about it...for now.

"Yeah, no problem," I said quietly. Swallowing my misgivings and shoving down deep my disdain for the man,

I redirected my attention to the chubby sharks dining on sugary treats and expensive coffee, trying to gauge the group's mood. Leaning into Calvin, I whispered, "So, how do you think this'll go?"

He grinned and rubbed his palms together. "I think we're going to blow their socks off."

Immeasurably intelligent and unconventional even for a Portlander, Calvin had a childlike enthusiasm for anything that stoked his passion. I glanced at his Christmas morning grin and bright eyes and completely forgot about Rick. My heart swelled with brotherly love for this man-child, who nine days out of ten wore a different colored hairstyle and swore by the healing powers of maple bacon donuts.

By trusting his keen insights and sharp instincts, the two of us had built this company out of dream, dust, and sweat into an industry leader. If he thought we'd woo these reviewers, I had no choice but to agree with him. If all went well, we would rock the house, and hopefully the world. I touched his shoulder and smiled back. "Yeah, me too."

He waggled his eyebrows and continued to rub his hands together.

Chuckling, I turned my attention to my DigiSleeve and messaged Tamara. *The demonstration is about to start.*

Almost immediately, she replied. *Good luck. Go forth controlling the feeble minds of the masses. Give them the tools they need to purge themselves of their individuality, morals, and social skills. I know you can do it. I'll go rally the Anti-Vs, so we can picket your company tonight.*

Nothing quite like the woman I loved supporting my entrepreneurial endeavors.

Calvin tapped my shoulder and grinned. "Showtime."

Nodding, I stood and strolled to center stage. The crowd grew quiet as they found their seats. "Good afternoon, everyone. On behalf of Virtual Adventures, I welcome you all. You are part of a very elite group who, other than the engineers and executives of Virtual Adventures, will be the first to get to experience the absolute latest in gaming."

A *Virtually* guy, donut grasped in his chubby fingers, raised his hand. "Come on, Jeff. I read all the mumbo-jumbo about your supposed new technology, but no matter what spin you put on it, we're here so you can convince us to sell a million new MindLink subscriptions to our readers. Or you want our followers to upgrade to 'platinum' or you've got some other fancy way to pilfer the contents of their pockets."

Several audience members nodded in agreement.

"I looked over the preview of your new game," he continued, "and there's not a thing new about the synopsis. In fact, it smells like a hundred other games I've already tried and already beat. We can all read between the lines. You figured out how to make the grass a little greener, the blood a little redder, the explosions a little louder, and now you're trying to pass it off as revolutionary when in reality, none of us will be able to tell the difference. I almost didn't come because, from what I can tell, there's nothing unique about it."

A murmur rose from the crowd as they glanced at one another and nodded.

I smiled at the rotund man. "You always break the ice the same way, Lucas. Every couple of demos you threaten to not come, but we all know you'd fight a pack of demons for the free Voodoo Donuts."

A light chuckle drifted through the auditorium. Laughing, Lucas shoved the last of a cereal-covered chocolate pastry into his mouth and waved at me to carry on.

I glanced around at the audience. "Free donuts aside, this really is like nothing you've ever experienced. Sure, you've seen the demo footage and read the whitepapers, but the question everyone wants answered is, 'How does that translate to reality, or, in our case, *virtual* reality?'"

Leaning forward, I stage-whispered, "Well, let me show you."

I clapped my hands together. The room plummeted into darkness and a sizzling electric guitar came to life, filling the air with a staccato riff.

The fob Rick had dropped off the night before, slid into my palm. I counted, letting the music wash over the crowd, and then with a subtle flip of my wrist, I launched the little marvel of technology out over the audience.

The device flew. A spotlight blazed to life, tracking its progress as it sailed through the air. The rhythm section joined the guitar in a crashing cacophony just as the fob reached the apex of its arch, and its forward momentum halted as though grabbed by an invisible giant.

Already tumbling end-over-end, the golden trinket began to gyrate until it became a blur. Seemingly energized by the cascading waves of rock 'n' roll, it rose toward the ceiling.

The audience, straining their necks to watch, gawked and awed. As the pulsing, spinning fob reached its zenith, it paused, lording over all who gazed upon it while the drums and bass shook the building as though an army of blacksmiths forged thunder by striking hammer to anvil. The tiny blazing sun flashed and glinted like an ancient orb summoned by a disco-themed alien race.

I held up my arms. "Ladies and gentlemen, I'm proud to introduce *Total Immersion*, the final evolutionary step in virtual reality."

I allowed the audience to stare at their new man-made deity for several heartbeats before clapping my hands together again. The spotlight snapped off as neon strips in the floor came to life up and down the aisles, casting a sunrise blush around the room.

Along the sides of the small auditorium, an army of glowing-rhinestone-tuxedoed waiters marched in from the back. As they paraded around the large space, their footfalls landing in time with the music, the flecks of silver and gold in their outfits flashed and glinted like the scales of brook trout.

The servers carried ornate, luminescent trays upon which sat several boxes whose swirling, whirling purple surfaces resembled the floor-bound storm of the dark matter server. On each lid *Total Immersion by Virtual Adventures* flashed in neon, and just below that, our gilded logo morphed from the infinity symbol to a human chromosome to a vector atom and back again in a never-ending cycle.

The waiters delivered a box to every press member, then vanished as quickly as they'd appeared. Lucas' eyes bugged above his chubby cheeks as he flipped open the hinged lid and stared down at the golden, over-sized fob laying in a bed of glimmering silver-infused navy velvet.

While we'd distracted the audience with their new toys, I nodded to Rick, who still crouched behind the stage curtain. He redirected the electromagnetic suspender, and the fob sailed across the room, settling gently in my hand.

Calvin leaned over toward me. "Weren't those the guys from that restaurant where you met Ceos? The Brine and Pimps or whatever?"

I laughed. "It's Brins de Printemps, and, yes, some of them were willing to moonlight for me. Being a waiter at the most stick-up-your-ass French joint in town doesn't pay as well as you might think. Besides, it seemed apropos to nip something from a place Ceos loves, considering that was where she told me she stole my company."

He shook his head. "Not only are you going behind Ceos' back with Dencephalon, but now you've stolen the waiters from her favorite restaurant too. You've got big brass balls, man. I'll give you that."

"Technically, I didn't steal anything," I said. "This is a free market, and they can work for whomever they please. Ceos of all people should be able to understand that. Besides, I think they fit in well with the presentation, don't you?"

"Yeah," he said just loud enough to be heard above the music. "They looked amazing. I just don't know if it's a good idea to give the middle finger to the most powerful person on the planet."

Irritation threatened to overcome my presentation façade. I needed to focus, and Calvin, for whatever reason, had chosen this minute to lecture me on business relations and protocol. I swallowed down a thick glob of bitter bile, just as I'd had to swallow down my pride again and again over the last year.

Without so much as a warning, my investors—many of whom I'd considered friends—had sold out when Ceos went in waving a fistful of dollars and unsubstantiated accusations that I'd been incapable of adequately managing the financials and running a corporation. I didn't need Tamara's lawyerly degree to know that, though slimy and underhanded, I would never be able to legally undo her treachery.

Fine. Whatever. Business, as they say, is business. I'd tried to make my peace with losing control of my dream while also reidentifying myself and finding my new place in this new world.

No longer Jeff Braxton, CEO, I still ran our massively expanding technology division. Unlike Calvin, who dedicated sixteen hours a day to managing and coding our flagship product, I never had time to get my knuckles greasy. He'd kept himself grounded, doing the thing he loved most while I'd had to give it up to run operations.

Now, I floated in a no-man's-land in the middle of the corporation, neither slinging code nor guiding management. But regardless of who actually flipped the bits or steered the ship, Calvin and the four other product managers reported to *me*, not Ceos, and I sure as hell didn't need to check in with our overlord for every decision, big or small, that I made.

On paper I only owned forty-two percent of the stock to Ceos' fifty-two—Calvin held the remaining shares—but

Virtual Adventures would *always* be my company. *Always.* And I would do with it whatever I thought best.

"Look, I'm not giving her the finger," I said out of the side of my mouth while trying to keep my expression neutral for the audience. "Even though I'm not at the helm anymore, I still want our company to be amazing. I've never lost sight of that goal. If borrowing some waiters helps us succeed, then that's what I'm going to do. In fact, you could even say that I'm doing this for Ceos…even if she doesn't know it yet."

Calvin smiled. "It's been nice knowing you. You can say it's for her all you want, but the bitch is going to turn your nuts into doorknockers. Your family jewels, which she'll have bronzed then nailed to the entrance of her lair, will serve as a warning to anyone who even considers double-crossing her."

Done trying to justify my choices to Calvin or anyone else, I said, "She can kiss my ass." I stepped forward on the stage. Back to business. Time to forget about Calvin, Rick, Ceos, and everything that had happened this past year. Our moment had arrived, and I wanted to savor every second of it.

As I neared the lip of the platform, the stage lights slowly came back to life, and the music quieted to background ambiance. I smiled as the audience gawked at their boxes. Many members of the press talked excitedly while holding up their golden fobs, turning them this way and that.

Lucas looked up at me. "Okay, you have our attention. But pretty trinkets do not an outstanding game make."

Smiling, I held up my hands until the audience settled down. "My outspoken friend has a point. I could stand up here and yammer at you all day about breakthroughs and geeky 'mumbo-jumbo.'" I did the air quotes and pointed at Lucas.

He laughed and waved at me again.

"But why should I *tell* you about it? Why not put my money where my mouth is and *show* you?"

I touched the golden fob to the sensory tap in my temple. It snicked into place, the cool metal warming as it powered itself from my body. "Your fobs have already been preset into one of five groups. Instead of having an avatar or a Virtual Adventures engineer be your host, we have something extra special in store for you."

I paused as I gazed around the room, letting the audience wonder for a few seconds.

Smiling, I continued. "You may have heard the rumors that Virtual Adventures is expanding its entertainment options from video games to interactive shows. Imagine being able to participate in—and in some cases *star in*—cooking shows, late night comedy, and family sitcoms all from the comfort of your living room. Well, today, we have brought in a few of the future hosts of our new lineup, who, aside from me, will be your *Total Immersion* guides."

I glanced down at the outspoken chubby man. "We drew straws, and I lost. So, Lucas, you're in my group."

The crowd chuckled again.

Already having my neckpad in place, I slipped on a pair of sunglasses. "Please, join me."

Several audience members whooped, and one by one, they slid pads onto the backs of their necks, slipped on their glasses, and attached their fobs. Clicks resounded around the auditorium as the little computers grabbed hold of their new owner's sensory tap.

The room glowed green, illuminated by the legion of fobs drawing power from their hosts.

Lucas looked around at his silent colleagues, an odd uncertainty tinging his eyes. Finally, he took a deep breath, glanced at me, nodded, then attached his fob. It magnetically gripped his temple and began to glimmer green. The journalist slipped on his glasses and relaxed into his seat.

I glanced over at Rick. He smirked and gave me another thumbs-up. Though I had no reason to be frightened, my heart lurched all the same. I had the sudden urge to rip the fob off my head and scream at the roomful of people to do the same.

But before I could begin to make a move that would decimate not only the demo, but my career as well, the room faded from green to blue as MindLink turned the auditorium into a single neural network.

Then the world went black.

CHAPTER ELEVEN

JEFF

Opening my eyes, I stood in a pure white chamber with my preselected audience members around me. Each player's name floated in a bubble above their avatar.

Lucas, rather than his natural rotund figure, had the broad shoulders and the gruff exterior of a Minotaur Viking. Leslie, a willowy woman in the black body suit of a ninja, stood next to him. She flexed her long, sinewy muscles as she looked around.

One man represented himself as a griffin, two others as elves, another as a vampire. The mishmash of mythological creatures looked like a Tolkien party crashing a George R.R. Martin family reunion.

"Before we begin," I said, "we have a little bit of set up to do. Lexi?"

A dot of light appeared just above the floor. The speck grew, erupting into a flaming circle of lightning. Twisting and snapping with fiery electric arches, the circle began to rise.

The body of my digital assistant formed in its wake as though being constructed out of raw electrons. As the last of Lexi appeared, the circle shrunk to a pinprick just above her head. It flashed, streaking out in all directions, fading back to the nothingness from which it arose.

Someone from the group whispered, "The girl knows how to make an entrance."

My digital assistant faced the small entourage. "Good afternoon. My name is Lexi, and I will be guiding you through the *Total Immersion* calibration process."

Lucas held up his hand. "Hold on. I thought we were here for a demonstration, not to be calibrated."

"I can understand your caution," Lexi said. "However, this is a completely non-invasive process that will allow the updated MindLink neckpad to measure and synchronize itself with the physical movement inputs traveling along your spinal column. These signals will be redirected to *Total Immersion* and allow you full control over your avatar. While your body safely naps back in the real world, you get to have an immersive adventure in this one."

Lexi held her arms above her head. "Please follow me as we perform some simple movements."

The press members warily looked at one another, then each raised their hands over their heads.

"Very good. Now march in place." Lexi demonstrated, swinging her arms and pumping her knees. The audience tried to follow, but for many, their knees and elbows flew about as if drunk marionettes had taken control of their bodies.

"This is totally normal," Lexi said. "Please continue so the system can finish its calibration."

The group obliged, and their movements grew more fluid and natural.

My digital assistant halted. "Very good. Now, last, please look in all directions with your eyes only. Keep your head still." She demonstrated and again everyone did as they had been told.

"Your personal calibration settings have been saved," Lexi said, smiling. "Unless you find your avatars behaving awkwardly, you will not have to perform these setup steps again. Thank you all very much and enjoy your *Total Immersion* experience." The ball of light reappeared above her head. It flattened out to the pulsing lightning circle. As it traveled down her body, Lexi disappeared.

I turned to the group. "I appreciate your patience as we get things set up. I handpicked each of you from the groups because I only wanted the best of the best to be part of my clan."

Leslie cocked her head. "We're part of your clan now, are we, Jeff? Well, Chief, what are we going to be doing here? Fighting ghosts? So far, other than your DA's disappearing act, you haven't shown us much of anything."

I spun around slowly, inspecting the blank walls surrounding us. I turned back to the group and smiled. "You've got a point. This doesn't look like Avalon, and we don't look like much of a clan. Let's do something about that. First, let's make this world a little more interesting."

I raised up my arms and the walls and floor fell away. Beneath our feet, thick grass sprang to life creating a vast rolling green meadow. Around us, trees and rock-covered mountains erupted from the ground, turning the field into a long valley. An ocean of sky replaced the bare nothingness overhead and the sun blazed to life.

The group stared, but I didn't give them time to take it all in. "But things are quiet. Too quiet, don't you think?" I gestured and the rumbling of thunder echoed through the valley as a giant mountain exploded out of a nearby hill, rising until it towered thirty stories above us.

From the side of the newly-formed mountain, water began to trickle. The stream grew, became a roiling torrent and, shoving aside the rocks at the base of the cliff, formed a crystal-blue lagoon. A thin river cut through the valley, sweeping away the grass in its path and flowing down the gently sloping floor.

The water bubbled and burbled over its rock bed like a happy baby. In the distance, the land fell away into earth, a beach forming in the vacancy. Waves lapped at the shore as seagulls squawked and squalled at one another.

Everyone turned in circles, their eyes huge and round as millennia of geological anomalies forged around them in seconds.

I waved my hands like a magician summoning a rabbit from a hat. "Let's add a little zing for your sniffer."

Next to the lagoon, a small tent camp complete with stone-encircled fire pit arose from the ground between a pair of old oak trees. The tang of ocean drifted through the air, mixing with the acrid smoke of burning wood and hot ash.

"Our world is looking better and smelling better," I said, "but we don't *look* like a clan. How about some new outfits?"

I clapped my hands and battle armor instantly materialized over my group's bodies. They gawked at the cycling infinity, chromosome, and vector atom Virtual Adventures crests blazing on their breastplates. Warrior boots, leg and arm leather, helmets and shields completed the ensembles. As one, they grinned, their fierce gazes holding mine.

I placed my hands behind my back. "We now look like a fighting unit, but things feel a little…flat. It's as if we can't feel anything at all. How about we take care of that too?"

When I pointed at the sun, suddenly its warmth wrapped around my body like an electric blanket. The crowd gasped. I whistled, and a girl carrying a huge basket stepped out of the tent. She made her way around the circle, handing each person a loaf of bread as a cool breeze graced my skin and tussled my hair.

An elf's eyes, already overly large, grew even bigger. "I can feel the sun and the wind! And the bread! It's hot!" She took a bite. "Not only can I taste it, but I can feel it as I chew. It's like it's melting on my tongue."

The others took bites of their bread and began to jabber among themselves.

I let them savor their food for a minute before taking the lead once again. "I'm glad you are enjoying yourselves, but did you really come here to eat bread, no matter how delicious, and hang out in a meadow?" I shook my head. "No. We are people of action and adventure."

They stared at me as I threw my hands into the air. "Let's add ten tons of excitement then."

A roar, accompanied by the beat of tremendous wings, ripped across the tranquil terrain. My clan turned, staring at the mountain as a spiked dragon rocketed up from behind the tree-covered peak. A collective gasp echoed through the crowd.

The huge creature flew in a circle above our heads, casting us in its shadow when it passed in front of the sun. The beast came about, banking into a steep aerial slide toward the valley floor. Swooping low, its great blue-green belly flashed over our heads.

Soaring up into a sharp arc, it sailed high through the troposphere and turned, racing over the mountaintops. The creature of dream and nightmare, myth and legend, fantasy and lore dove again, following the gentle curve of the hillside. At the last second it gave a tremendous flap of its wings, pulling itself up short and landing on the cliff above us. The ground rumbled and rocks fell, as its huge clawed feet tore at the earth.

The giant lizard screamed in rage, spitting a long stream of fire through the air. The flames torched the surrounding forest, turning pine and leaves into ash in an instant. The beast unleashed another torrent of fire against a massive tree, shredding the bark from its surface, and stripping it of its needles and branches. Releasing a thunderous shriek, it whipped its massive, spiked tail, pulverizing the base of the trunk. As the huge pine fell, the ground beneath our feet tremored and shook.

I turned to my group. "Don't just stand there. We're in danger. Protect the clan!"

The vampire held up her empty hands. "With what?"

"Oh, I forgot." I pointed at each of them in turn. As I did so a weapon—a sword, bow and laser-tipped arrows, glowing meteor-sling—materialized in their hands, completing their warrior outfits.

The dragon launched itself into the air again, raining down flaming breath upon me and my people. Covering ourselves with our shields, we waited for the beast to pass. I gripped my sword, the heavy metal cool in my grasp. As the beast came about, arrows and rock-slings flew. I waited and, at the last second, leapt, swiping my sword across the creature's belly.

It roared and landed, ripping the ground apart with its huge talons. Dirt and rocks rained down, peppering our armor. The dragon's horned head turned this way and that as my clan charged. With a flip of its tail, it launched the vampire through the air. She landed in the grass on the far side of the meadow. Staggering to her feet, she shook her head and charged again.

Nostrils flaring, the beast roared fire and we held our shields up to ward off the attack. Heat blasted around me as flames licked the edges of the metal. "Lucas!"

He turned to me from behind his shield.

I pointed. "There's an enchanted wand by that rock. Charm the dragon before it chars us."

He followed my gaze, and as soon as the creature's breath died down, he dove. Somersaulting past the boulder, he grabbed the wand and sprang to his feet. Raising the slender rod, he flicked the tip, casting a huge bolt of lightning into the dragon's face.

My clan stared as the beast bellowed in rage and pawed the ground. Slowly, its angry rampage eased to a simmer, then it lowered its head, laying its chin on the ground.

Everyone hesitated before standing, tense and ready should the creature decide to strike again.

Without prompting, Lucas ran and jumped onto the beast's back. He grabbed onto its neck. "Fly, you bastard, fly."

The dragon looked back at him with huge, yellow-slitted eyes. It crouched and leapt into the air. Lucas yelled and laughed as it flew.

Together, rider and beast soared above the mountain range, tracing the waterfall back to the lagoon, where the beast pulled up, aiming for the sky. Its tremendous wings beat the air, and it grazed the tops of the trees. Raising their fists and weapons above their heads, my clan roared with approval. Lucas and the dragon flew beyond the meadow, out over the rolling ocean. They finally circled back and landed in the field.

Eyes wide, face exuberant, Lucas jumped off the mythological creature's neck. "I've tamed the beast. Who's next?"

They each took a turn soaring through the air on the now-docile dragon. After the last of my clan finished their ride, I turned to it. "Go now. Go home and never come here again." The huge creature flared its nostrils, looked around once more at the group, crouched, and launched itself. All attention remained fixed on it as it disappeared into the sunset.

"It seems that night is upon us," I said. "Come, sit around the fire."

We wandered back to the camp. Happy-faced, my people took seats around the stone circle. The flames crackled, creating a bright bloom in the darkening landscape. A bubble of heat emanated from the fire, driving away the chill left in the wake of the setting sun.

"As you have seen, we are not alone." I gestured to the tent. "Let us now be joined by some old acquaintances."

A middle-aged man and woman in peasant clothing emerged, joining the young girl with the basket. The man smiled. "Thank you all for saving us from the beast. Tonight, we celebrate!" He picked up a barrel and, placing it on a stump, began to fill cups of ale from a wooden spigot while his wife handed them out.

Several of my clan drank thirstily while others just held their cups, staring at the world around them.

"Do you not like beer?" I asked one of the non-drinkers.

The elf shook her head. "It's not my thing. I prefer wine."

I smiled. "Oh, okay." I pointed at her mug, and the liquid turned from amber to deep red.

Her eyes widened and she took a sip. "It's delicious and exactly the right temperature."

The vampire stopped the woman handing out the mugs. "Hey, I know you." She looked at the rest of the woman's family. "I know all of you."

The elf leapt to her feet and ran up to the husband. "Yes. Down at the dock. We got a ride from you to Davenport."

Everyone gawked then started talking all at once.

"We had to help you with the boat."

"The journey took days."

"We ran out of food, but you showed us how to catch fish."

"Then there was the terrible storm. We almost lost the boat…but we managed to keep her afloat."

The two elves in our party turned to each other. "I love you," they said in unison.

They remained fixated on one another. "But, how's that possible? I remember knowing you my whole life, but I know we just met an hour ago."

The vampire stared at the peasant girl. "You're like a daughter to me. I was there when you were born. I…I held you in my arms."

Lucas turned to me. "I…we remember these people. We feel too. They're our family and we love them. But how? That's not possible. We've never done any of that. We've never even met these people before."

I smiled and held out my arms. "My friends, welcome to *Total Immersion*."

∞ ∞ ∞ ∞

An hour later, I opened my eyes to reality, and a brief flash of vertigo struck me. The transition from the virtual world to the real one often came with some turbulence.

The audience members stood, stretching and removing their fobs. The blue lights on the little devices went dark as the hosts removed them from their sensory taps. The crowd talked amongst themselves, the ruckus growing louder as each player woke.

After the last one removed their fob, I returned to center stage. "Thank you all for coming today."

At first, no one said anything. The room fell eerily quiet. Suddenly, the audience leapt to its feet as it erupted in applause and cheers. I stared, dumbstruck by the response. I'd expected people to enjoy themselves, but never before had I heard of such a reaction.

Lucas clapped his hands over his head and whistled.

As my heart leapt with excitement, Calvin double-high-fived me. I glanced back at Rick. He gave me a smug, self-satisfied grin. Unsure what to make of the expression, I returned my attention to the audience.

The ruckus quieted to a rumble as I started to speak. "Take your new fobs and neckpads with you. While we were fighting dragons and hanging with our clan, our team has been busy adding *Total Immersion* to your Virtual Adventures menu. Our first title, *Treason*, is waiting for you. Though we've had fun this afternoon, as my grandfather used to say, you ain't seen nothing yet. Thank you all for coming and have an adventurous night."

The crowd applauded again and began talking animatedly amongst themselves as they dispersed.

Despite the joy in my soul and my floating-above-the-clouds mood, I leapt off the stage and headed toward the back of the auditorium, determined to talk to the guy in the tweed jacket. I started up the aisle but stopped halfway.

The London Law professor had disappeared. I turned around, my gaze finding Calvin's. I jerked my head to the side to indicate the empty last row. His eyes swept the back of the room. He looked and shrugged.

I needed to find out who our mystery visitor had been, and I needed to do it soon.

CHAPTER TWELVE

JEFF

The cork exploded out of the champagne bottle. It flew across the room and smashed into my Portland Petals baseball pennant, knocking it off the wall.

Calvin and I gawked as the banner fluttered to the floor. We turned to each other and erupted with laughter.

As foam spurted from the bottle, I tried to fill our plastic cups. But mostly I made a mess, splashing froth and bubbles on the floor, on my desk, and over Calvin's rail-thin arm and bony fingers.

I finally managed to fill our cups and lifted mine into the air. "A toast. To us. You and I took this thing from my garage and built an empire. We've worked our asses off, beat the crap out of our competition because they suck, and now we own the market."

Calvin laughed. "I don't think you're supposed to put others down when you toast. Pretty sure that's a rule or something."

I stopped mid-sip. "Really? Oh, I had no idea. Okay, how about this?" I held my cup up to his. "We've worked our asses off, beat the crap out of our competition because they couldn't code themselves out of Hello World One-Oh-One, and sent the losers home crying to their mommies. And now we own the market."

My friend doubled over with laughter and had to set his cup down to keep from spilling even more on the carpet. "Oh, that's much better. Total class all the way."

The sweet champagne didn't taste nearly as sweet as the victory that danced through my blood. I looked once again at the headline from *Virtually Real*.

Virtual Adventures Redefines VR
By Lucas Sanborn
Virtually Real
Let me be frank: There simply are no words that can fully capture the awesome magnitude by which Virtual Adventures' new Total Immersion system rocks. I've been a gamer for nearly forty years, and never in all that time…

I reread the article and then pointed at the text hovering above my mobile. "I've already set the wallpaper in the lobby to include this review. Now when people come to visit, it's the first thing they'll see when they step off the elevator."

Calvin shook his head. "Forget the wall. I'm getting it tattooed on my bicep." He flexed.

"Not sure if there's room," I said, squeezing his arm. "That's a pretty small space."

He raised his cup to mine. "Kiss my ass."

I clinked, plastic-to-plastic. "And you mine."

My DigiSleeve pinged. When I glanced at my arm, my heart leapt. "It's a message from Leslie at *Monthly*."

One fantastic review from a well-respected magazine would be good, but I needed more, a lot more, if I expected Ceos to back down on her original decision to not support Dencephalon. I needed to prove that not only had I been correct in acquiring and using their technology, but more important, that she would be receiving a king's ransom as a result.

We'd shown the world what we'd been doing. The proverbial cat—or in our case, robotic demon panther—had been let out of the bag. I just hoped we'd done enough. If not, then as Calvin had said, Ceos might be using my jewels as door knockers.

Calvin finished his drink in one long gulp and tossed his cup into the trash. "All right. Let's see what she has to say."

I set my cup on the desk, my nerves drawing up as taut as a pair of asymptotically tightly-coupled program interfaces. "Lexi, can you show us Leslie's message please."

Lucas' review faded, replaced with the message from Leslie.

Jeff, our article comes out in a few days, but I wanted to let you know that your new game is better than multiple orgasms on a Sunday afternoon during the Super Bowl while eating pizza. We've never been unanimous on ANYTHING, not ever, but the entire Monthly team wants to bear your children. Go buy a private jet or take a trip to the moon, then get to work on the next title, because I've already finished Treason…twice, and am anxiously awaiting the next game. I know my readers will be too.

My whole body relaxed as my soul sighed with relief. We'd done it. We'd beaten the odds again. We'd taken a huge gamble, putting everything on the line, and won. I still had to face Ceos and get her blessing, but after all of this, that should be nothing more than a formality.

I hope.

Calvin's eyes had grown huge and round as he read. "I don't even know what to do. We've been working on this for so long, and now it's just…" He shrugged. "Done."

I nodded. "I know, it's a little like the day after Christmas." We fell silent for a moment, and then something else occurred to me. "Hey, one of the reviewers said that he'd seen a hack online for the new fob. Do you think you could look into it? Find out who did it and take it down."

Calvin studied my face, a frown gracing his lips. "Um. Sure. But you know that as soon as I do, two more will take its place."

"I know," I said. "But I want to look proactive. Besides, it's weird how we haven't even released the schematics yet but there's already a hack on the market. It makes me wonder if it came from inside the company."

Calvin looked on the verge of saying something when Lexi broke in. "Jeff?" My digital assistant's face replaced the glowing note.

"Yes, Lexi?" I said.

Though devoid of actual emotions, Lexi could, on occasion, weave feeling into the tone by which she told me things. The designers of digital assistants, however, seemed focused on negativity. While the delivery of good news had only the slightest of upward tones, bad news came in the same somber, world-ending timbre as a doctor who'd failed to save a child's life and was now faced with telling the parents. "Ms. Wells would like to see you. Immediately."

"Uh-oh," Calvin said. "The evil queen is bidding you to her chambers. What does this summons mean for our hero? Knighting for a job well done or beheading for secretive dastardly deeds?"

I plunked down into my chair as my heart started to race. The time had come. Ceos knew, or at least she knew enough. Undoubtedly, the old harpy would chew my ass out for going behind her back, but even she would have to recognize the greatness of what we'd accomplished and marvel at the soon-to-be fat bottom line.

"You've been spending too much time working with the story board team," I said. "Their drama is starting to rub off on you."

Calvin shrugged. "Maybe. Do you think your summons is about the review?"

"I don't know," I said. "Probably. But the queen mum could want anything." I thought it over for a minute. "Yeah. It almost certainly has to do with Lucas' article."

He snapped his fingers. "You know, it probably has nothing to do with you going behind her back to buy Dencephalon and leasing the rights back to Virtual Adventures after she told you not to. More likely, she's confessing that she's fallen madly in love with you and wants to buy your soul... Oh, wait, she already owns that too."

Shaking my head, I shooed him away. "Go on. I have adulting to do."

He turned and bounded toward the door. "Ooooh, well, adulting. I'll let you get to it then."

As he practically skipped from the room, I swiveled around in my chair to face my digital assistant. "What's this about, Lexi?"

"There's no agenda provided, Jeff," she informed me unhelpfully. "She only said to come to her office right away."

"Of course there wasn't," I replied. Ceos' request for my presence wasn't really a request at all but an edict that I drop everything and scamper to her lair posthaste.

Ceos Wells—the owner of every parent company of every parent company of every major network, satellite, and communications institute on the planet—didn't care about her subjects' schedules or obligations. She didn't even care if they were having open heart surgery. The shrew expected everyone from paupers to presidents to always be at her beck and call. And they should not only come precisely when she'd commanded but arrive prepared for anything.

While I felt somewhat confident I'd survive unscathed, I could never predict how Ceos would react. I resisted protectively covering my crotch as I wondered if my family jewels would, in fact, be hanging on her door by the end of the day. On the surface the notion seemed preposterous, but Ceos…

"Okay, Lexi, let her know I'll be there in a bit."

Calvin popped his head back through the door. His green and orange spiked hair made him look like a hippie puffer fish. "Have you started adulting yet?"

I spun in my chair, raising my eyebrows at him. "Doesn't it look like it? Actually, I was about to head over to talk to the evil queen. What do you need?"

He came bounding into the room. "I almost forgot. This is for our fearless leader." He set one of the new, oversized fobs and a neckpad on my desk. "Tell her the next story she asked for is available now."

"What does she need a new neckpad for?" I asked. "She has at least two already."

"Rick said that because of her disabilities, he made a new one that should work much better with her damaged spine." He shrugged. "I don't really know, and I didn't have time to look at the changes he made to it."

As far as I knew, Ceos had never had any trouble with the standard model. Perplexed, I picked up the pad. There didn't seem to be anything different about it. Why would Rick take it upon himself to create one specially for her? What, for that matter, did he even know about her disability? Was this just another eccentricity of an introvert's introvert?

Perhaps with his medical background, he really did have something revolutionary to offer her. "Huh."

Calvin waited in the doorway. "Everything okay?"

I scratched my chin. "Yeah. It's nothing. Go on. You've got stuff to do."

The man-child smiled at me, turned, and practically skipped out of the room.

I flipped the pad over in my hand again, but I still couldn't see anything unique about it. Taking a deep breath, I got up, popped it and the fob into my bag, and started for the door. Time to face the queen.

∞ ∞ ∞ ∞

As I once again sat in Ceos' lobby waiting to be summoned, I reread the review from Lucas. ...*There simply are no words that can fully capture the awesome magnitude*... Though I remained calmly sitting on the couch, inside I jumped up and down like a three-year-old on espresso-laced gummy bears.

We could be successful beyond anything I'd dared to dream. We sat in a position to own the entire entertainment market. No one could compete with us, and no one could stop us.

No one.

Finishing Lucas' review, I started to reread Leslie's message when the sudden sense of being watched niggled at the back of my mind, distracting me from her words. I glanced around and at first didn't see anyone. I almost disregarded the sensation as an overactive imagination when my gaze landed on Ceos and her chrome and silver wheelchair parked in the doorway.

The slightest of smiles crossed her razor-thin lips as though she'd caught me red-handed looking at pornography.

Though I tried to hide it, the mere sight of her sent a cold shudder through my body.

Before her plane had been shot down by terrorists, claiming not only her beauty but her husband and three sons as well, Ceos Wells had rivaled the grandest of duchesses and the most elegant of English princesses. But now, only the faintest shadow of the previously regal, striking figure remained. This shriveled, chair-bound scarecrow more closely resembled an embalmed carcass rather than a member of the royal court.

While physically decimating, such a life-altering event might have softened the hardest of hearts, inspired gratefulness for the gift of survival, or incited self-reflection, self-introspection, and self-evolution. But in the ensuing years, the darkness in her soul had not only grown blacker, it had metastasized.

She'd become meaner, more demanding, and had flexed her financial and political powers like Hades wielding his bident. This woman lorded over Wall Street, held the financial world by the short hairs, and sent the most politically influential members of the world scampering.

"Come along, Jeffrey. This won't take long." She spun and wheeled into her office.

Inwardly I groaned, but dutifully stood and followed her into her lair. The door slid silently shut behind me. I started to sit, but Ceos held up a twisted hand. "Don't," she said.

Standing by her desk, I waited. I'd been on the receiving end of her lectures before. Actually, every time we got together, the conversation flowed in only one direction. She gave. I received. But an electric tension permeated the air that hadn't been there since that first time we'd met, when she'd told me she'd stolen my company.

Gearing up my emotional blast shield, I prepared to play defense against another of Ceos' wraths. "Okay."

She faced the window overlooking the city, keeping her back to me. "I've gotten to this position in life because I know what I'm doing. I've built more than an empire. In fact, I *own* more empires than you could begin to count."

Great. Here we go with another "Ceos is awesome and Jeff is an incompetent dolt" lecture.

"My instincts," she continued, "told me to leave you in charge of Virtual Adventures because you'd created it. You'd nurtured it from an idea to a corporation. Albeit, one that was doomed to fail because you lack the foresight, creativity, and the expertise to run a successful operation. But I believed in you and thought that somewhere in all that ignorance lay the passion to create something truly amazing without taking shortcuts."

I refrained from making a snide comment, though several danced on the tip of my tongue and begged to be let loose.

She paused and took a long breath. "My instincts about how hard you'd work proved accurate. Unfortunately, I hadn't anticipated how incredibly unfit you are to run anything more complicated than a lemonade stand."

I frowned. "Ceos, I—"

"No, Jeffrey," she said, holding up a crooked finger. "You don't get to talk. Your actions have done all the talking for you."

She turned her chair around. "See, someone brought to my attention the little demonstration you had a couple of weeks ago. Perplexed by the features you bragged about, I had them dig a little deeper. Surely, there was some kind of misunderstanding or, for marketing purposes, you were simply exaggerating. But do you know what my source discovered? They found that the very corporation I forbade you from buying, you did, in fact, purchase."

The London law professor guy. It had to be. Damn it. We should have been more careful.

Taking a deep breath, I began the argument I'd been preparing for since the day I'd laid down my first dollar for Rick and his flying nerd monkeys. "You said *you'd* never invest in Dencephalon, so I purchased it with my own money. Not a single penny of Adventures' capital was used in the acquisition." While it had sounded logical, reasonable even, in my head, my own argument now felt weak and inadequate.

"Semantics," she scoffed. "At the end of the day, I don't care who owns what. The reasons I gave you for not purchasing it still apply."

Her gaze bore into mine. "Have you not been watching the news? Surely, your fiancée has been bragging about how the privacy groups have been starting riots and just this morning shut down city hall. And do you know why? Because the police are extending the use of scatter cameras."

Her nostrils flared as though she might begin breathing fire at any second. "You already can't take a dump without one of them filming you. So what if they add a few more so they can see me wipe too? But these privacy fools are all lathered up and ready to march and picket at a moment's notice. Can you imagine what'll happen when they find out you're desecrating the dead?"

I shook my head. "Ceos, we—"

She cut me off, blazing ahead with her lecture. "We are about to become the whipping post for everything that's wrong in the world. Those mindless lemmings will crush your pathetic little dream like a roach because someone with a bullhorn and a vlog told them to."

"No," I said. "I talked to Tamara about this. She—"

Fire raged in Ceos' malevolent eyes. "I hardly think that anyone's going to take the soon-to-be-wife of a greedy and unscrupulous CTO seriously. There's no way you can argue that she's not going to be a direct beneficiary of this game's success. Just like yours, her pocketbook will be thick at the expense of millions."

Her argument that Tamara had become corrupt perplexed me. Several times over the course of our business arrangement, Ceos had told me to get Tamara's take on the Anti-V view. I mentally brushed away Ceos' concerns because when she saw the profits to be made, she'd squelch the naysayers.

"Ceos," I said, "we stand to make hundreds of millions of—"

The super-mogul thumped her chair with a twisted hand. "Spare me your high school economics lesson. If you understood anything, you'd know it isn't just about the money."

I shook my head, unsure I'd heard her correctly. Ceos *only* cared about the money. Trillions of bucks *literally* stopped with her.

Ceos let out a long breath. "I'm an objective woman. Willing to admit when I make a mistake."

Uh-huh. On the surface, her words may have sounded reasonable, but I doubted this sudden conversation shift would be my salvation. Most likely, she was gearing up to put yet another nail in my coffin.

"So," she continued, "after our little meeting last year, I, evidently unlike you, did a little digging on your new acquisition. I wondered if I was being closed-minded, so I brought in the best of the best in both psychology and physiology."

She leaned forward. "Guess what? Based on their studies, they came to an unambiguous and inescapable conclusion. The integration of memories and feelings into your games will become so addictive in such a short amount of time, that it'll make the world's narcotics problems look like a preference for sweet over salty."

"Come on, Ms. Wells," I said, "it isn't that bad. We had a study group and even brought in our own professional—"

"Not that bad?" she said. "Do you know that *you* spent four times the legal limit playing the game?"

Guilt slammed into me like a speeding truck. I'd misled everyone on just how much time I'd spent testing *Total Immersion*. If only she knew by how much, she—probably with Tamara's and Calvin's blessings—would have me tossed out the window. "Ceos, I was testing. This is all new technology, and we were having problems—"

Ceos glared at me. "Jeffrey, even you don't know you're an addict."

"No, I am not," I said.

She took a deep breath. "The Anti-V's and privacy groups, and now the Department of Health and Human Services, are going to tear us apart."

"Ms. Wells, we drafted a new VR bill and integrated those limits right into—"

Ceos rolled her eyes. "Damn it, Jeffrey. You're so good at giving lip service about being socially conscious, but you don't have the foggiest idea how to be globally responsible."

I threw my hands up in the air. "So, what do you propose?"

She pointed a gnarled finger at me. "I'm beginning damage control immediately, starting with you. As of right now, you are going on administrative leave."

I glared at her and shook my head. "No. That's not going to work. I'm the face that started with nothing but a dream and gave the world the most advanced virtual reality system ever created." I jerked my thumb back at my chest. "Me. I am the quintessential American Dream."

"Stop yapping like a poodle or you're going to make my ears bleed," she said, waving her hand dismissively. "You're nothing more than a quintessential wet dream, and I don't have the time nor the patience for your masturbatory self-aggrandizing. Falsely inflated accomplishments might help you sleep at night, but they aren't worth the oxygen you waste to spew them."

My brain stymied as I searched for a comeback. Any comeback.

But, before I could reply, she leaned forward on her elbows. "Behind all your 'success,' you have a dirty little secret. Until I took over, your company was on the verge of collapse under the weight of your own lazy, idiotic ineptitude. The world that's supposedly so grateful to you for your invention was about to find out you're nothing but a fraud."

I ground my teeth together. "Each is entitled to their own opinion."

"That isn't an opinion, Jeffrey," Ceos said, folding her skeletal hands together. Through her paper-thin skin, the atrophied muscles of her arms twisted and slithered around her reedy bones like the coils of a snake. "But I didn't bring you here to debate the highs and lows of your failures. While I can't legally take away your shares, I can take away your executive powers. Since you won't go on leave willingly, as of this instant, you are no longer a managing member of this company."

My head felt as if it had been detached from my body and now floated somewhere up near the ceiling. Someplace, in another world, I heard myself say, "What? No. I've got this. I'm—"

"You don't have anything." She zipped her chair across the floor. "Calvin will take your place until a competent replacement can be found. I'll tell the privacy groups when they come for blood that you are entirely responsible. You not only went behind my back but also lied to me and everyone else in the company about what you were up to."

"No, Ceos. I—"

"We won't be completely free of the stains of you," she snarled, "but it'll give the world a sacrificial lamb to slaughter. Not even Tamara will be able to defend your sorry ass. Before she even begins her opening arguments, the press will have already tried and convicted you."

Ceos continued to bear down on me, forcing me toward the door. "The first thing Calvin will do in his new position is pull the plug on this abomination of yours. You can tell Rick, if that's his real name, that the deal is off. I don't care if it bankrupts you. I don't care if you lose your home. I don't care if you lose that lawyer fiancée of yours. I don't care if you have a heart attack and die. You deserve it and more. You went against my direct orders after I trusted you."

I bumped into the door, and the room suddenly seemed devoid of oxygen. The air contained no sustenance by which to keep me alive. Ceos would get her wish. I would die right here in her office with her watching as I asphyxiated.

The super-mogul stopped inches from my shins. "Now, go home. But don't you dare talk to anyone or I'll sue your ass so hard, the courts will garnish your great-grandchildren's wages. I will handle all external communication. You are to say nothing. Is that clear?"

My entire body had gone numb while my lungs screamed for air. Unable to speak, I nodded and started to reach for the side button that would open the door when she stopped me. "Jeffrey."

I looked at her but didn't say anything.

She held out a gnarled hand. "I believe Calvin gave you something for me."

Pushing aside her overwhelming, sickening hypocrisy, I dug into my pocket. I retrieved the over-sized fob and neckpad, dropping them into her palm.

She hit the button and the door slid open, giving me a good case of rug burn. One of the panels smacked the back of my head as it whipped past. With my *former* boss inches away and nothing to lean against, I fell back, stumbling across the threshold and into the waiting room. I filled my chest with the cool, humid air.

Ceos snarled. "Now, get out. If you ever come back, I'll have you arrested." She slapped the button again and the door shot out of the wall, sealing the entrance to her lair.

Standing in the lobby, I stared at wood as thick and formidable as a drawbridge. I turned and, without looking back, slogged my way across the lobby and into the waiting elevator. Climbing aboard, I, like my career, sank to the bottom.

CHAPTER THIRTEEN

JEFF

I slammed my fist against the dashboard as the auto drove me out of the parking lot. "Son of a bitch."

Rain thrummed against the roof and splattered across the windshield, falling from a depressing gray sky. The foul weather mimicking my foul mood.

I'd known that buying Dencephalon would be a risk, but not buying it would have been riskier. I'd hoped that Ceos would have recognized her own shortsightedness when she found out the number of pre-release reservations for *Treason*, but evidently she had been too mired in her own opinions to remove her blinders.

Taking a deep breath, I massaged the back of my neck, trying to ease the ache beating through my skull. The car turned down Broadway, heading toward the edge of the city. "Lexi."

My digital assistant's irritatingly chirpy voice echoed through the small space. "Yes, Jeff?"

"Take me to Twenty-Fifth and Lovejoy," I said.

She hesitated. "Jeff, you've never been to this location before. Are you sure this is the correct address?"

I rubbed my forehead, perplexed by my impulsiveness and questioning my own sanity. I had no idea what had made me change directions. I also had no idea what lay at this destination. However, I did know I didn't feel like debating with a computer. "Yes. Please take me there."

The car turned left and left again, heading into downtown. Neither my digital assistant nor I commented on my sudden erratic behavior as the auto navigated the city's busy streets. The car pulled out of traffic and slid in next to the curb in front of an unmarked steel door.

Unlike most other businesses in the city, which had raised their entrances to skybridge level, the owners of this establishment had left this one on the street. Grimy, dirt-caked concrete walls flanked the entrance. Heavy-duty bolts held thick bands of crisscrossing iron to the surface as though it had been designed to ward off an army of robotic death zombies.

I stepped out onto the sodden sidewalk. Two stories above, pedestrians meandered casually along the skywalk while cyclists on blade bikes flew down the twisting, turning mag rails that interlaced the entire city. But no one looked at me as I stared in every direction, trying to find some sort of clue as to what had possessed me to come here.

Though I couldn't explain why, the iron door seemed to beckon me. I strolled up to it, trying the handle. It didn't budge. *Maybe I should forget this whole thing. Get back in the car and just go home.* That would be the smart thing, the rational thing, to do.

But a small pad jutting out from the wall caught my attention. Before I had a chance to reconsider, I traced my finger in a star pattern over the surface. The door clicked, and when I tried the handle again, it turned.

With a mixture of surprise and apprehension, I almost let the door close. But having just been fired from the company I'd created from nothing, my veins flowed with righteous indignation and anger, propelling me recklessly forward into the unknown.

I pulled the medieval-like, iron barrier open, and a wave of heavy metal music, as thick as a maple syrup tsunami, enveloped me. As I crossed the threshold, the frantic beat of the bass and drums assaulted me, rattling my ribcage and vibrating my teeth.

I let the door close behind me and paused in the entrance.

As my eyes adjusted to the gloom, I began wading through a sea of small tables full of leather-clad, anorexic patrons. A man with thick eyeliner and an angry mob of violent tattoos sat at the bar, a flaming orange, yellow, and brown layered drink in front of him. He stared at the liquid as though it held the secrets to the universe within its murky depths.

Swiping a menu on the bar top, I clicked on House Pint and confirmed the payment on my mobile. *Thank you. Your order will be ready momentarily.* A slot in front of me opened, and a tall dark mug with a perfect foam head rose from the depths of the counter.

I sighed. Not only was I at a place I'd never been for reasons I did not understand, but now I had ordered a beer—which I hated—on purpose. Staring at the beverage, I took another resigning breath and picked it up.

Turning around on the stool, I looked out over the corpse-still crowd. Everyone, like my tattooed friend, stared into their drinks while the heavy metal music thrummed like a squad of wrestling demons.

A man in a military uniform came in through the door. He paused for a few seconds, then marched along the side wall toward the back of the bar. The brass stars on his blazer flashed and winked in the weak light.

Though his face remained obscured in dreary bar shadow, something about his posture and the squared-off shape of his head and shoulders struck me as familiar. The gloom, however, concealed his features, making identification impossible.

As the man neared the back wall, he walked under a sputtering light and glanced over his shoulder.

My body jerked in surprise, and I bolted up from my seat.

General McKenzie halted as he scanned the crowd. For a heartbeat, the general's eyes found mine. But no recognition flashed in his gaze. He moved on and paused to glance around one last time before he slipped through a crystal beaded curtain on the far wall.

I moved through the bar, wading past the tables and comatose patrons. Though I loathed the idea of another encounter with the ghost that had roamed through my office and haunted my dreams, I nevertheless followed the general, parting the long strands of beads where he'd disappeared. As I stuck my head through the sparkling curtain, my ears popped painfully, but the thrumming beat and screaming guitars faded to muted white noise.

I breathed a sigh of relief. I'd never been grateful for a sound silo before, but my heart filled with a deep affection for this one. Any more exposure to the Satan's Symphony, or the Devil's Dissonance, or whatever they were called would have ruptured my eardrums and melted my brain like Rick performing an extraction on me.

The small room—which at one time may have been an office or a modest conference hall before the bar owners redecorated it in ghetto refuge—contained only a smattering of mangy tables. Confusingly, though not surprisingly, the general did not linger among the few sleepy customers sprawled about like wasted alley cats.

"Jeff?"

I jerked back at the voice that originated at my elbow. I'd been so preoccupied looking for the general that I'd failed to notice the lone occupant of the table nearest to me.

I blinked. "Lucas? What are you doing here?"

He gave me a pained smile as he took a sip from the twin of the heavy mug in my hand. "Funny, I was going to ask you the same thing."

Frowning, I pushed into the room and sat across from the game reviewer.

The rotund man wiped a pearl of condensation off the side of his mug. "He's not here."

I stared at him over my beer. "Who?"

He raised his eyebrows. "General McKenzie. That's who you're looking for, isn't it?"

I couldn't have been more surprised had he dumped his brew over my head. "What? You've seen him?"

The dim, yellow light exacerbated his pallid complexion and made his hound dog brown eyes look sunken and jaundiced. He nodded. "Three times now. Once at work, once at home, and just now."

Lucas pointed at the strings of beads sectioning off the entrance to the room. "He poked his head through the curtain just like you did. He looked around and left. I thought I was going crazy, but then you came in. I could see by the expression on your face that you'd seen him too."

I tried to make sense of my swirling, whirling thoughts. Given time and distance from my encounter with the military man, I'd reasoned that a combination of a lack of sleep and an overwhelming abundance of stress had led to me hallucinating or dreaming the general to life. Either one reasonably accounted for my meeting with someone that, per Lexi, hadn't been there.

But Lucas had seen the general too, and unfortunately, my explanation did not account for two of us experiencing the same phenomenon. By proving my hallucination theory to be false, it followed that General McKenzie had to be real.

Yet, Lexi had not detected his presence. I'd attributed her mistake to a bug in her programming, but now I wondered if I'd been too quick to throw her makers under the bus.

So, what could Lucas and I see that my digital assistant could not? Perhaps we'd each been visited by a ghost? I almost dismissed the preposterous notion without giving it any consideration at all.

Once again, deferring to Mr. Sir Arthur Doyle's infallible Mr. Holmes...

But paranormal encounters only happened in children's books. Not in a bar, not at home, and certainly not at work. Yet, the disheveled man studying me had also seen the specter. Something had put that miserable expression on his face. If not a ghost, then what?

I watched my drinking companion lethargically sip his beer. He didn't even bother to wipe off the obligatory foam mustache. "You look terrible," I informed him.

Lucas shrugged. "The life of a game reviewer. I spend a lot more time in the virtual world than the real one. I'll admit, it can be overwhelming from time to time. Then, of course, thinking that you're nuts because you're seeing someone that isn't really there... Only now there are two of us that are nuts..."

I looked around, but no one lingered near enough to overhear our conversation. "Have you talked to him?"

He nodded. "Yes, but I really don't understand what we talked about. Something about me starting an investigation on him and secrets and something about my mom." He rubbed his hand through his thinning hair. "He said some other stuff, but I missed it because my head hurt so bad. The little I do remember made no sense whatsoever."

My breath caught in my throat. Part of me rejoiced that I hadn't gone crazy, but the other part of me cringed that

I might have to seriously reexamine my belief in the ever after. "He and I had a similar conversation, and all the while I thought my head was going to explode." I paused. "Do you think he followed you here?"

Lucas shook his head. "I can't be sure of anything anymore, but I don't think so." The chubby man laughed dryly. "Hell, I've never even been to this place before. In fact, until about twenty minutes ago, I didn't even know it existed. Whatever compelled me to walk here from my office also told me the right pattern to open the door."

He glanced at the cracked ceiling and the stained walls. "Man, this place is a dive. I cannot imagine why there's even a lock on the door."

Ordinarily, I might have been appalled that his revelation didn't surprise me, but compared to being haunted by a ghost general, the two of us finding the same bar barely rated. I shrugged and took my first sip of the beer. Though I loathed most alcoholic beverages other than wine, this one flowed as smooth and creamy as warm syrup down my arid throat. The bubbles tickled my taste buds in a pleasant way I'd never imagined.

"Same. I was headed home, and before I realized what I was doing, I told the car to take me here. At the time, I didn't even know there was a *here*."

"Let me guess," he said, pointing at my mug, "House Pint?"

I nodded. "Yes."

He sat back in his seat. "So, two guys who've never been here before suddenly show up at the same time.

They both see a general that's not there and order the exact same drink. What the hell is going on?"

"I don't know," I said, "but I'm getting out of here. I'm grateful that awful music is so much quieter in this room, but I think the silo's giving me a headache."

"Your head is hurting too?" he asked.

"Like a bitch," I said, "and I'm not waiting around to see if it's the noise cancellation that's causing it or our ghost." I started to stand, but he reached across the table and grabbed my arm.

"Wait."

What little color the man had in his cheeks drained as he stared over my shoulder.

I slowly turned around.

A short bullish man, with long shaggy hair and huge biceps stood in the entrance. He glanced our way, then headed to the table furthest from us. He plopped down into a seat.

I braced for the crash of splintering wood as the chair collapsed from his bulk, but to my amazement, it held.

Something in the corner of my eye drew my attention from the newcomer, and I glanced back to the entrance. My heart seized. Though he'd shed the star-studded uniform, the unmistakable face of the general lingered just beyond the beaded curtain. He pushed through, making a beeline for the brute and sat down opposite him.

The men huddled together, starting a quiet conversation.

Lucas' face had gone white. "Jeff, what is this? Who are those guys? Isn't that General McKenzie?"

I swallowed and nodded. "Yes. I think so."

"How can I possibly know his name?" His frown deepened. "But the very first time we met, I somehow already knew him."

He glanced around the dingy room. "Kinda like how I knew about this place and how to get in. I've been wracking my brain but cannot get my mind wrapped around it. It sounds like you are having the exact same thing happen. What could *we* possibly have in common, Jeff? What do we both know or do that would make us hallucinate the same things?"

My stomach lurched as the seemingly random pieces fell into place. It wasn't a ghost, but the answer might be even worse. "Are you sure you want to know?"

He sat forward in his seat. "Wait. You know? Of course I want to know."

"I think," I said, letting out a long breath, "that it's *Treason*."

"What? As in your game? There's no General McKenzie in *Treason*..." He blinked. "Wait. So, you're saying he's not actually there?" He tipped his head toward the military man. "Except, neither of us is playing the game, and yet we both see him all the same."

He scratched his chin. "No, no. That makes no sense. Even if our visions are from your game, he's not in a single scene..." He paused, squinting his eyes and rubbing his head. "Actually, what you're saying is true, though I'll be damned if I know why. He's in there somehow. But... how?"

I shook my head. "I have no idea."

General McKenzie and his companion glanced over at us.

Lucas smiled and waved at the men, then turned back to me. "I knew I knew the name and the face from somewhere."

His visible relief at finding the answer melted like snow in July. "But that only raises more questions. You think this guy is from your game, yet why are we both seeing him right now? Why, for that matter, are we here at this bar? Is there something wrong with the game? Did it inject something into our brains? Are we going to get cancer or something worse or are we just going crazy?"

"Jeff, what the hell did you do?" he asked.

I held up my hands. "I don't have the answers to any of your questions. I only just now realized how I knew the general." I hesitated. "Lucas, honestly, I figured that I'd played the game so much that it scrambled my brain a little. I assumed that the exhaustion and stress, from deadlines and Ceos, had caused my hallucinating the general. I didn't have any idea that anyone else suffered too."

He furrowed his brow. "How much did you go over?"

I'd not told Tamara, or Ceos, or Calvin, or anyone the truth, and I had a lie ready for the game reviewer too. But as I looked at Lucas' ashen face and sullen, bloodshot eyes, my heart broke. This man had paid a steep price because of my shortsightedness.

If I'd done my homework as Ceos had or listened when she'd said to not buy Dencephalon, then my friend wouldn't be sitting here in this dive. He wouldn't be suffering from visions or fearing for his sanity. Even if he'd broken every limit rule ever written, even if he'd hacked the system, Lucas didn't deserve to suffer. At the very least he deserved an honest answer.

I took a long, deep breath. "I don't know for sure. But by my estimate, I'd say that for about a month, I was playing around ten times the legal limit."

I expected him to be surprised and start lecturing me on the dangers of too much VR. That, even with the older version sans tactile simulation and memories, the chances of confusion and mixed-thoughts exponentially increased with every extra hour of play time. Instead, he looked down at his hands.

"Lucas, did you use an extension to bypass the limits?"

He let out a long sigh and nodded. "I may have gone over…a bit."

I tried to capture his eyes, but he looked away.

"How much?" I asked.

Evidently, he found the dirty, cracked ceiling tiles very fascinating because he looked up. "Does it matter?"

"Lucas," I said. "How much?"

He looked down. His sad eyes found mine, and he rubbed his forehead. "At least twenty times the legal limit. Maybe more."

I leaned back. Lucas hadn't wanted to admit to his overindulgence any more than I had. Since he hadn't read me the riot act, I let him off the hook as well. "Of the dozens of reviewers and developers, we are the only two that I know of who have played that much."

"Has anyone else reported visions or knowing people they shouldn't?" he asked.

I shook my head. "No. It's only been good reviews. Otherwise, all has been quiet on the western front."

He leaned forward. "But once the game goes live, we won't be the only ones. You and I both know that everyone will print extenders, and once they start playing, we're going to have a world full of...visionaries."

Ceos had been right after all. Even Lucas knew better than I did.

Maybe instead of barreling ahead, I should have started with "whether we should" not "how can we?" *Damned impulsiveness.* My tendency to leap without looking had just bitten me squarely in the bum once again, costing me my company and maybe even my sanity.

"Jeff," he said, "we have to tell people. This thing is dangerous."

"Actually, we don't," I said, absently rubbing condensation from my mug. "Ceos fired me and pulled the plug on the entire *Total Immersion* project this afternoon."

He started. "Seriously?"

"Yep," I said. "As of about a half hour ago, I am gainfully unemployed. I guess it's a blessing in disguise."

Before he could reply, the two men, who must have finished with their conversation, got up and crossed the room to our table. The general's companion, who looked roughly like a Clydesdale in both his face and his size, stared down at us. "Excuse me."

General McKenzie studied Lucas while the Clydesdale stared at me.

Lucas scowled. "Yes?"

The general leaned over, pressing his knuckles against the table. "Are you Lucas Sanborn?"

The game reviewer narrowed his eyes. "Are *you* General McKenzie?"

The military man furrowed his brows and glanced at the Clydesdale. "No."

"Then I'm not Lucas Sanborn."

The general glanced again at the Clydesdale and jerked his head to the side. The huge man came around and picked Lucas up by the front of his shirt. He stuck his huge horse's head into my rotund friend's face. "That's funny, you look just like him."

Lucas held the big man's gaze. "Are you sure? How can you see clearly with your eyes all tearing up like that?"

The big man snarled. "What are you talking a—"

Suddenly, the Clydesdale's body went rigid and he began to shake. His eyes rolled back, and when his mouth slammed shut, his teeth snapped together like a rat trap. He dropped Lucas and, falling to the floor, writhed about as if having a seizure.

The general charged, slamming into Lucas' abdomen. The two men fell to the floor. The general rolled on top of the reviewer's generous belly, pulled back his fist, and hit my friend in the face. Blood splattered across the grimy linoleum.

I grabbed a chair and swung for home field.

The seat connected with the side of the general's head. The man grunted, toppling to the side. He rolled over, wobbling up onto his hands and knees, while glaring at me.

Lucas stuck a small box against the general's neck and pressed a button. Like the Clydesdale, the military man went rigid and fell to the floor. He foamed at the mouth like a rabid dog while his arms and legs flailed and spasmed.

I reached down and hauled Lucas to his feet. "Come on. We need to get out of here."

"You don't need to tell me twice," he said.

Lucas wiped blood from his cheeks as he stumbled alongside me. I pulled him through the beaded curtain where the blast of demon metal music assaulted us anew. Ignoring the daggers of pain hacking at my skull, I half-dragged him toward the front of the bar. Even the leather-clad, makeup-wearing, coma-induced patrons glanced up as we bumped tables and chairs out of our way.

"Lexi."

I could barely hear my digital assistant's voice over the throng of grinding guitars. "Yes, Jeff?"

"Bring the car around," I yelled.

"Are you in danger? I'm reading elevated blood pressure and extreme heart rate. Your voice sounds stressed, and someone from your location has alerted the police to an altercation."

Fine time to worry about my well-being. "Just do it."

Slamming through the fire exit, we barreled out into the fading twilight and the sweet patter of evening rain. I pulled Lucas across the sidewalk to the street's edge.

As my car came to a stop in front of us, the door flew open, and I dove inside. Reaching back, I grabbed my friend by the shirt. "Get in here, Lucas." I yanked the big man into the vehicle.

He landed on top of me with a grunt.

"Go, Lexi," I yelled. "Take us home."

The door closed, and the car pulled away from the curb.

I wrestled Lucas' girth into the passenger seat and popped my head up in time to see the general and the Clydesdale charge out onto the sidewalk.

The horse pointed at us.

I waved at them as the duo dwindled into the distance. Sighing, I turned around and leaned back against the headrest.

Lucas pulled himself up in his seat and, wincing, rubbed his nose.

I turned to face him. "What did you do to those guys?"

He opened his hand, revealing the capsule-shaped tube in his palm. A cone-like disk stuck out at the tip, with a slim button on the side.

I gaped. "How the hell did you get your hands on a Sonic Boom?"

"I know people," he said, shrugging.

"I thought those were only used by burglars to break unbreakable jewelry cases, shatter windows, and that sort of stuff."

He held it up between two fingers. "The sound waves it creates are, as you said, designed to break glass. But it can also be used to cause a temporary paralysis. Like the name says, it causes a sonic boom in your nervous system."

"I've never seen someone paralyzed by sound waves before," I remarked, amazed.

He aimed the little device at my stomach. "Would you like me to show you how it works?"

"No. No." I held up my hands. "I saw it, and that's good enough for me. Why are you even carrying such a thing?"

He rolled his eyes. "Really? I'm a fat, out of shape video game reviewer who lives in a bad part of the city and, present company aside, publicly decimates just about every game that's out there. I have millions of followers and almost as many enemies."

Shaking my head, I glanced over at him. "I really had no idea being a reviewer was such a dangerous job. I figured you just got to play the latest games all day and raked in big bags of money."

Lucas guffawed. "Yeah, that's what I thought too when I started this business."

The car slowed and pulled in against the curb.

I stared around at the unfamiliar business district. "Lexi, why did we stop?"

My digital assistant's perky voice filled the small compartment. "I'm sorry for the delay, Jeff. However, the police have ordered us to pull over."

I blinked. "What? Why?"

"There was an incident at the drinking establishment you and Mr. Sanborn just vacated," she said. "The police wish to question Mr. Sanborn." A bulletin materialized above the dashboard.

Lucas' eyes went wide. "No. We can't do that. We have to get out of here."

"What for?" I asked. "It's not a problem. We'll just tell the police what happened. Those men attacked you, and you defended yourself. It's that simple. I'm sure there are scatter cameras all over that place that can corroborate our—"

He grabbed the front of my shirt. "No, Jeff. We can't let the police take me in. They will turn me over to the general and his lackey."

I tried to fit the odd pieces of the puzzle together, but the picture they formed didn't make any sense. "I don't understand. How do you know this?"

"Please, Jeff," he pleaded. "Order Lexi to drive."

"I'm sorry, Lucas," I said. "She won't do it. I can't make her ignore a police bulletin. What's this all about?"

He glanced around at the dozen micro scatter cameras embedded in the interior of the car. In times of emergency or police action, the vehicle automatically streamed the feeds to the authorities. They would be listening to every word we said. Monitoring our every action. These recordings could be used to save us in the case of an emergency or prosecute us in the event we'd committed a crime.

"I can't..." He reached over and tried the door handle, but it refused to open. "Shit."

I touched his shoulder. "Lucas, just tell me what's going on."

He looked out the back window. All the cars behind us had also pulled over to the curb. In the distance, several uniformed men ran down the sidewalk in our direction. Behind them, drones flew above the street.

"Look, we only have a few seconds before they get here," he said. "Jeff, promise me you will *never* play that game again."

I stared at his frightened face. "What are you talking about?"

He glanced back once more and grabbed my arm. "*Treason*. Don't play it, and for God's sake, do not release it. *Ever*."

"I don't understand." I shook my head. "I told you that Ceos pulled the plug on the whole thing."

Lucas' huge eyes stared into mine. "There are secrets embedded in the software. Those memories are more than just memories."

Someone shouted. A man pointed, directing several uniformed men toward us.

Lucas grimaced. "Sorry, Jeff."

"Sorry for wh—" My words faltered when Lucas pressed the Sonic Boom to my waist and pulled the trigger.

My entire body went rigid, and my head slammed into the side of the car. Somewhere, in another universe, glass shattered. Someone grunted and heaved like a wild boar rooting out grubs.

The car began to move again and everything faded.

∞ ∞ ∞ ∞

"Jeff? Jeff?" A familiar voice floated up from the fog. "Jeff?"

I cracked open my eyes. A school of stars swam in a sea of ink. Night had overcome the day. I slowly sat up, rubbing my temples.

The car had parked in its customary spot in front of my house. I shivered as a cool breeze drifted in through the fragmented remains of the passenger window. My head felt as though it had been encased in concrete and then dropped from a thirty-story balcony.

"Lexi?"

"Yes, Jeff. It's me. We've arrived home."

Tiny glass crumbles littered the empty passenger seat. "Where's Lucas?"

"Mr. Sanborn is no longer in the vehicle."

Sighing, I started to look around, but an unhappy wave of dizziness and nausea forced me to temper my efforts. "Yes, thank you, Captain Obvious. Where is he?"

Her irritating, fact-focused voice grated on my nerves. "I do not know his whereabouts." She paused. "I can find no recent public records either."

I gently massaged the throbbing, twisted muscles in my neck. "What does that mean?"

"He has neither been arrested nor is he in the hospital."

Taking a deep breath, I tried not to let her get under my skin. "Then where is he?"

"I'm sorry, Jeff. All I know is that he exited the vehicle through the window. The authorities tracked him as long as they could with my external cameras. However, once he was out of range, I proceeded to carry out your last given order, which was to take you home."

"I don't understand." I slowly shook my head. "I thought they wanted to question us about the fight at the bar."

The police bulletin rematerialized above the dashboard. The sudden brightness pierced my brain like a whaling spear, and I scrunched my eyes shut to keep my head from exploding. "The police were only interested in talking to Mr. Sanborn. Since he was no longer within the car—and you were not an accessory to his escape—there was no need to delay. So I took you home."

I stretched my arms, flexing them experimentally. My back and abdomen muscles ached, probably because I'd had some kind of seizure when Lucas jammed the Sonic Boom into my ribs. "Why are we here? I thought you were supposed to take me to the hospital if I got hurt?"

The bulletin vanished, and a Digital Doctor report took its place above the dash. "When your body spasmed, you hit your head on the door. I contacted the hospital and reported your injuries. The prescribed treatment, as long as your heart rate and respiration remain normal, for both a Sonic Boom encounter as well as a cranial impact, is eight hundred milligrams of ibuprofen and several hours of rest."

I took a long breath and, trying not to move any more than necessary, reached down into my briefcase and pulled out my handheld med dispenser. I chose the type and dosage, then pressed Confirm. A small gray square slid out, and I slipped the paper ibuprofen under my tongue. My stomach quivered, promising future unhappiness if I didn't do something to quell its discomfort, so I took two doses of anti-nausea strips as well.

As the pain killers started to do their magic, the last conversation I'd had with Lucas came back to me. What did *Treason* have to do with what had happened at the bar?

What had he meant when he said the software had secrets embedded in it?

That chaotic, frantic conversation had created so many more questions than it had answered.

Lexi opened the car door. "Are you ready to go in now? Tamara should be home soon."

I shook my head. "No. Take me to the office, Lexi."

"Sir?"

"I have some research to do."

CHAPTER FOURTEEN

JEFF

A small circle of light from the desk lamp lit up the small work area in the lab. Nothing, save for the quiet hum of servers, broke the silence.

I scrolled through another page of *Treason* notes—storyboard ideas, bugs, memory and sensory overlays, graphics data. I'd seen it all a thousand times before, but now, I scoured the archives with fresh eyes and a new perspective. However, no matter how many times I read and re-read the pages, I couldn't find anything that would cause hallucinations or sudden knowledge.

Leaning back in the chair, I stared at the folders spread across the massive holodisplay. They laid out the process from beginning to end…almost.

The raw, unprocessed tactile and memory files should have been here with the rest of the sensory data, but no matter where I looked, I couldn't find them. Maybe they'd been stored on their own cluster? I moved out of the standard MindLink directory and started searching through the auxiliary folders.

"Excuse me. What are you doing?" The voice came from over my shoulder.

I swung around in the chair. Calvin, his hair standing straight up in a rainbow-colored Mohawk, stood in the entrance to the lab. He cocked his head.

"Jeff? What are you doing here at," he checked his DigiSleeve, "almost ten at night?"

"I could ask you that same question," I replied.

He waltzed across the floor and leaned up against the desk. "Man, you know I don't have a life. With Drake being out of town for another week, no one's there to keep my bed warm at night. Other than him, I've got no family, no friends, and no life. I live and breathe this place. You've got a gorgeous girl at home, so again, I ask, what are you doing here?"

I nodded my head toward the display. "I'm looking for the extractor files for *Treason*. Where are they?"

He furrowed his brow. "What do you mean?"

"The raw dumps," I said. "The very first day I went to Dencephalon, you and Rick wowed me with the love story of Rodger Thornton. Well, I'm looking for the Sandy equivalents."

He contorted his thin lips into a confused smile. "What do you need those for?"

For a moment, I considered telling him about seeing General McKenzie, about the bar, about Lucas and me getting into a fight with two ghosts, about the police, and about Lucas' dire warning to not release the game. But the more I thought it over, the more ridiculous it seemed. "How about for right this minute, you just humor me?"

He stared at me for a heartbeat, then nodded and stepped up to the terminal. "Well, the problem you're having is that you're looking in the wrong place."

"What do you mean?" I asked. "I'm logged on to the main Dencephalon server. They should be here somewhere."

He shook his head. "You're looking on the live gaming partition. What you're talking about are the raw, unprocessed files, which are on their own storage array." He opened a command window and started typing.

I stared at him, surprised. "I didn't know that. How come I've never seen the raw data before?"

"Jeff," he said, raising his eyebrows and looking at me as if the answer had been scrawled across the desk, "you're busy running five divisions. It hardly seemed necessary, and since you never asked to see the raw files, I never showed them to you."

Calvin continued to type. "I don't make it a habit of granting permission to anything unless someone specifically has a need to see it. It's called 'security.'" He typed some more. "There. I've given you read access to the files. No offense, but I can't think of any reason for you to modify them."

I nodded. "Yeah, that should be fine."

"It's just a precaution," Calvin said and stepped aside.

Resuming control of the keyboard, I listed the contents of the main directory. *United States, England, France, Germany, Switzerland, Russia, Egypt, Australia.*

I paused. Something about the list struck me as familiar. A conversation or something pinged the faintest of bells in the back of my mind.

Unfortunately, I didn't have time to think through the connection so I clicked on the *United States* directory and scanned the contents of the *Sandy* folder. A long menu of sequentially numbered files filled the holodisplay. I opened the summary page for the first one.

Subject(s): Sandy Frost
Extractor: Richard Tieg
Approximate Age: 46
Memory Donor: Lincoln Grey

Lincoln Grey. Like the list of countries, this name also sounded familiar. I wouldn't bet the farm on it—hell, with the weirdness of my memories as of late, I wouldn't bet a cup of coffee on it—but something about the name rang a bell.

Maybe we'd had a discussion about the files sometime during the past year and I was just too dumb to remember it. Trying to not get distracted, I let the thought go for now and continued scanning.

File Size: 34 Petabytes

My mouth dropped open. "That is huge."

"Right?" Calvin said, smiling. "It's about the same size as two hundred Libraries of Congress. Like I told you, massive stuff."

I returned to the holodisplay and checked the subject's names for each entry. Sandy. Sandy and Harmony. Sandy and Jesper.

Calvin touched my arm. "Okay, I need to stop you now. What are you looking for?"

When I hesitated, he waved at the display. "Look, there's a ton of information here. If you tried to sort through it all by yourself, it would take years. I've practically been living in these files for the past ten months, so let me help you."

When I didn't reply, he folded his scrawny arms. "Jeff, I don't know what's going on, but you can trust me."

With everything that had happened, it would be beneficial to have the help of someone with intimate knowledge of the system. Calvin had been in charge of every step of the process and would know exactly where to begin.

My "leap before I looked" approach to life had gotten me into a heap of trouble as of late, and I couldn't find what I needed without him. To do that, he would have to know…everything.

I had to trust someone, so why not Calvin? "Okay, well, things have been a little insane as of late, but the first thing I need to tell you is that I lied to you."

He blinked. "Pardon?"

I took a deep breath. "Do you remember when you found out that I'd played way over the time limit?"

"Yes." He nodded. "And you said you'd stop."

I shrugged. "Yeah, well, I didn't. I'd found an extension online and…"

"Used it to bypass your own restrictions," he finished for me.

"Yes," I said.

He scratched the back of his head as he digested the information. "Okay, since this seems to be confession time,

I'll let you know that even though I didn't know, I still knew. But you're a big boy. I did what I did to protect you, but I can't do much more than that." He paused. "So, why are you telling me this now?"

"Other than feeling like a complete shmuck that I lied to my friend? It ties in to what's been going on the last few days."

He smiled. "Fortunately, I'm not one to hold a grudge. Alright, now that we have the touchy-feely stuff out of the way, let's have the rest of it."

Nodding, I began my story, starting with the hallucination of General McKenzie. For now, I skipped the part about Ceos firing me and pulling the plug on *Total Immersion*. That news would devastate him and needed to be delivered gently.

Calvin sat on the desk, listening intently. He didn't interrupt until I got to the part about Lucas taking down the Clydesdale.

He laughed. "What? Don't get me wrong, Lucas is a nice guy and all, but he's not exactly Olympic boxing material, if you know what I mean. I wonder how he got his hands on a Sonic Boom? I'm pretty sure those are illegal except at construction sites."

"I think you're right," I said. "He told me he uses it for personal protection, and based on what I saw, I don't doubt it. But there's more."

He chuckled. "Of course there is."

Calvin didn't stop me again until I told him about Lucas' warning to not release *Treason*. "What? That's nonsense. There's nothing hitching a ride on our game. That's completely preposterous."

I raised my eyebrows. "Is it?"

He stared at me for a heartbeat, as if trying to judge my sincerity. "You can't be serious. Yes, of course it is. Jeff, you can't possibly be taking any of what he said seriously. It's totally insane. And we don't have a lot of time to go proving that he's crazy and our game is benign. We need to get it out. I don't know if you've noticed, but we have over thirty million preorders. Thirty *million*."

I sighed. "Believe me, I'm very aware. But there's something else you need to know."

"What? What is it? I can see on your face that there's something bad you're not telling me." He stared at me, waiting.

"Ceos," I said. "She fired me and pulled the plug on the entire *Total Immersion* project."

Calvin leapt up so fast that he stumbled, falling to his knees. He bounced back up like a rubber ball and landed on his feet this time. "What? No, she can't do that."

"She can, and she did," I said. "In fact, you're never going to guess who's in charge now."

"Who?" he asked. Anger radiated off him in waves.

I put my hand on his shoulder. "You."

His mouth dropped open and his eyes went huge. "Excuse me?"

"You are, Cal." I nodded. "It's probably only temporary, but, I admit, you're the perfect choice."

"Jeff, I don't want to be in charge." He began pacing. "That's your job. We're a team. Besides, I hate meetings. Hell, I hate people, and your job is almost all politics." He spun around. "How did she even find out?"

"I think we were right about the London law professor guy," I said. "I don't know for sure, but I think he was a spy."

Calvin shook his head. "There's just no way to stop the release. It's too far along. The game automatically goes live at 6:00 a.m. sharp. That's in less than," he glanced at his DigiSleeve, "eight hours from now. Plus, all the preorders have been processed. We're either going to have to start handing out refunds, somehow cripple the game to not deliver memories and sensations, or delay. No matter which of those options you choose, we'll be crucified. This will kill us. If we do this, it'll be the end of the company."

"Actually," I said, "it's whichever of those options *you* choose. You're in charge now, remember?"

Calvin rolled his eyes.

I sighed. "That being said, you're right. No matter what you choose, it'll probably kill the company. But if the game's dangerous, if Lucas is right and something else is hitching a ride along the stream, we have to protect the public."

"The game's not dangerous." He pointed at my chest with a stick-like finger. "Remember, I warned you about being connected to *Total Immersion* too much, and you promised to use an imager and sound silo. Only you didn't. No. You and Lucas overindulged like starving pigs at an all-you-can eat buffet. Mental exhaustion is what caused your hallucinations. Not some phantom data."

I looked the man-child in the eyes. "Mental exhaustion? That doesn't explain both of us knowing someone not in the game, the bar, the code to get in, the police, all of it."

"I don't know. I can't explain it." He put his hands on his non-existent hips. "But I can tell you it's not *Total Immersion*."

I returned my attention to the long list of files. "Well, I'm going to put in some due diligence and see if I can find anything. You might be right, but I need to know."

He slapped the top of the desk. "Fine, Jeff. It's a wild goose chase. However, you are the owner of Dencephalon and the CTO of Virtual, but I want to warn you that reviewing the files in their raw state is much more powerful than the game. We filter out lot of extraneous stuff. If you use the fob, I can't guarantee you won't have even more visions. You can connect for a little while, but then you need to use an imager and sound silo."

"Okay. Noted." I glanced at him. "Now will you help me search, or do I need to spend a year trying to figure this out?"

Calvin sighed. "Okay, what are we looking for?"

I knew my friend would defend his baby, just like I knew he'd eventually concede and help me. The warring alliances inside of him would almost certainly drive him crazy, but I had to push him anyway.

"I want a list of files with both General McKenzie and the Clydesdale in them. If we can find out what they were up to, hopefully it'll give us a clue as to why the police took Lucas."

"Here. Let me do it." Calvin stepped up next to the keyboard. "Remember, the names in the game have all been changed. So, what we need to do is cross-reference the processed files with their sources."

I slid the keyboard over to him. Calvin began typing like a demon. Pages of text flew past at a blinding rate. In all the years since he and I had slogged through the first version of MindLink, he hadn't lost his touch. Calvin slapped a key and pointed. "There. These are the ones we want."

"General Hudson?" I asked.

He nodded. "General McKenzie's real name is General Hudson."

I clicked on the file. "Lincoln Grey, General Hudson, Unknown Man. Unknown? How could they not know his name?"

Calvin shrugged. "Either Lincoln didn't know it, or Rick couldn't access that part of his memories."

Picking up an oversized fob, I pressed it to the sensory tap in my temple and slid a game controlling pad onto the back of my neck.

"Turn the safeties off," I instructed him.

He hesitated. "But if things get too exciting, the system won't be able to regulate your heart rate and breathing. More importantly, if he gets hurt or killed, you could die. Your body won't be able to tell the difference between virtually getting stabbed in the heart or hit by a bus and physically getting stabbed in the heart or hit by a bus. We call them 'safeties' for a reason."

"Cal, I might be responsible for putting millions of people in danger. Me. I don't have time to play it safe. I need to know as much as I can as fast as possible, and I can't do that if the system is dampening sensations or filtering out thoughts."

Calvin did not look happy. "We don't know that anyone's in danger."

"We don't *not* know it either." I tried to give him a reassuring smile. "Don't worry. I'll use the safe word if I need to abort.

He grimaced. "Fine, but I want my objection noted."

I started MindLink. "Done."

Time to become Mr. Lincoln Grey. My world faded to black.

CHAPTER FIFTEEN

LINCOLN

I sat at my desk, flipping through the list of reports on the mobile.

Populace Mental Destabilization Post-Terrorist Attack
Kidnap and Murder of Senator Harold Green
Terrorist Sympathizers and Coalitions
9/11 Presidential Speech
18 Month Post-Traumatic Stress Census
Potential Vulnerabilities and Targets of the United States

I sat there and wondered what to read—thriller, horror, drama, or bedtime snoozer. As I mulled over my amazing, oh-so-entertaining options, I picked up the stained foam cup, took a sip of the cold black sludge, and wondered what went best with gravel-strained coffee.

Then the answer hit me—the dramatic life of terrorists doing what terrorists do best...killing.

I chose *9/11 Presidential Speech* and the tablet paused. As GovLink accessed hidden memories from deep inside my brain—probably something to do with my mother—I typed in an access code, then pressed my hand against the mobile's screen. It scanned my palm and paused again.

Everything around me turned fuzzy as if my world had been dropped under water. A message materialized over my blurry universe. "This is a Classified Top Secret document. Do you agree to frequent full body cavity searches by Hulga Giant-Fingers the Hun and concede to henceforth have sex only with monkeys?"

Of course I do, especially if chimps—like the baboons that make me ask for permission to read a document I wrote—are involved.

I selected the I Love Having My Orifices Violated button on the screen. After another brief pause, the report replaced the menu overlaying my underwater universe.

Scrolling through the pages, I scanned the contents.

A Top Secret watermark covered the tightly written text that listed what I believed to be our country's greatest vulnerabilities. Thousands of man-hours and billions of dollars had gone into an effort to predict and protect our country against the next attack. But the most powerful computers, the most dedicated agents, and the most stringent security systems had been unable to keep the president, the First Lady, or the Speaker of the House safe.

We'd prepared for chemical and biological warfare, giant fireballs, and legions of missiles. But we hadn't thought to inoculate the First Lady against the two dozen self-replicating microbots that, during a pre-inauguration charity event, had been slipped into her drink. The little bastards had drilled into her bones and lay dormant for years.

I started the embedded video of the president's 9/11 anniversary speech. The man with the silver hair and sharp eyes began to speak about freedom from tyranny and fear, about liberty and justice.

I paused the video as the refined woman standing beside him, looking both proud and fascinated, suddenly frowned, her hand sliding up to a slight bulge in her neck.

In the analysis of her remains and the subsequent investigation, doctors had ascertained that the microbots had used the woman's own flesh as the raw material to reproduce. As newly created bots joined in the fray and fed upon the First Lady's soft tissue, each one created hundreds of copies of itself, thus increasing the swarm's rate of replication exponentially.

I resumed the video.

She cried out only once before her body melted into the podium as if her blood had been replaced with hydrochloric acid.

A cloud, as thick and black as tire smoke, erupted from the puddle of flesh that had, just seconds before, been one of the most elegant women to ever grace the White House. The mass hovered, growing in both size and density. Before the agents surrounding the stage had a chance to react, the swarm descended upon the leader of the free world.

I paused the video again just as the Speaker of the House, who'd been standing behind the president, began to swat at the invading microbes. He too fell under attack.

Instead of studying the two men who, at this point, literally had seconds to live, I scanned the crowd. Confusion, terror, and fear universally etched on each spectator's face, save for one man in the third row.

He too stared at the scene before him, but rather than horror, his expression remained neutral. He stood rigid while those around him had already begun to flee.

I zoomed in on his face. The slightest of grins tugged at the corners of his lips. In the ensuing investigation, it had been argued that the man had been in shock. That he hadn't been smiling, he'd just had an odd reaction to the events unfolding before him.

The irrelevant debate over whether or not he'd smiled had been quickly forgotten when it had been discovered that the man in the third row had been a nobody. The divorced father of two from Iowa—who worked as a sales clerk at a home store during the week and played video games with his kids on the weekend—had no political ties, no trips out of the country, and no odd movements of money in or out of his accounts.

He could not have been more vanilla. Had he survived, he might have been able to answer their burning questions, but his demise had left the FBI, CIA, and Homeland Security scratching their collective heads.

The scatter cameras around the stadium rendered the images in full spectrum, ultra-high definition three-dimensional. I pivoted around to see the events unfold, as the entire world had watched on that horrific day, from every conceivable angle while the swarm devoured the flesh from the leaders' bodies.

Unlike with the First Lady, the black mass worked from the outside in, turning the men's skin and muscle to gelatin in an instant. Agents that tried to help immediately fell under attack, becoming victims as well.

Only seconds after it had started, the cloud rose off the president and the Speaker. What little of the men remained dribbled down the platform and pooled onto the stage.

Suddenly the cloud exploded in all directions, attacking the audience in the risers. The crowd—already fleeing in horror—screamed, trampling one another and stumbling over their seats. As the fog enveloped the throng, cries of terror turned into shrieks of pain. In their attempts to elude the ineludible, several of the spectators had leapt over the bannister, falling the twenty feet to the concrete floor.

The man in the third row slowly spun. Surveying the torrential sea of pandemonium roiling around him, he neither fled nor did he appear to be under attack from the microbots. He looked about once more and then—as if hearing the pop of a starter's pistol—sprang forward, leaping over the backs of chairs, and sailed over the railing.

Thousands of scatter cameras captured the final sprint of his life, and hundreds recorded him jumping. But only one had been at the proper angle to capture his swan dive into the concrete far below the bleachers. At the very instant he made impact with the ground, the writhing, swirling black cloud flashed into a puff of gray smoke.

While one group had investigated everyone else in the crowd, I'd been assigned an entire team dedicated to ripping the third-row man's life apart. We'd looked for patterns, potential suspects, collaborators, enablers, and the control source for the microbes. We'd scanned his body at a molecular level, melted his bones, and even studied his DNA in our efforts to find clues.

But months of work had only led to a few false leads. Ultimately, we'd found nothing.

Several hate and extremists' groups had claimed responsibility, but each had been discounted. Despite millions of investigative man-hours, the perpetrators of the president's murder still had not answered for their crimes.

Of the four thousand men, women, and children that had been present at the speech, thirty-eight—including the First Lady and the commander in chief—had been killed, with hundreds more injured. But nothing compared to the psychological damage inflicted upon the nation.

As had happened after the attacks on Philadelphia two decades earlier, hundreds of thousands signed up for the military. Though no investigations had uncovered an incontrovertible perpetrator, a "highly probable" target had been chosen.

The government, with the blessing of its allied nations, had launched nuclear weapons against the island nation of Yomi, deep in the Celtic Sea, obliterating the small country from the face of the Earth. A subsequent witch hunt for sympathizers and corroborators had begun in earnest. The People had gotten the revenge they so needed to end the horrors that ate at their nerves the way the microbes had gorged on the First Lady's flesh, and the government had used the opportunity to capitalize on its leader's death.

Someone, the man from the third row perhaps, had declared war against our country. Seven years later, we still didn't *really* know who.

I opened the blueprint of the stadium. As far as horrific events go, the plan had been brilliantly executed. No metal detector in the world could have found the microbes slumbering within the First Lady, nor would she have even been aware of her own infection.

The bots had been designed to elude all but the most sophisticated and potent anti-nano inoculations. Before the president had taken office, I'd tried to warn Congress that our preventative measures had become stale and that eventually someone would figure out a way around them.

I bet they wished they'd listened to me.

Studying the map, I tried to calculate how the attack could have been done better. How it could have had a bigger impact. How it could have been seen by more cameras. Killed more people.

After the president's death, the Pentagon switched me from defense to offense, making it my full-time job to figure out how to murder Americans. I had not only been tasked with finding ways to kill them but also terrorize, infect, and cripple them, as well as bring down their infrastructure.

Over and over, I'd drawn up plans that included the technology needed, the manpower required, and the optimum time to execute. The big brains of the Pentagon and Homeland Security were then tasked with figuring out how to stop the scenarios I'd created.

I flipped to the latest proposal created by the most ingenious strategists and warmongers on Earth. I almost laughed. They had no idea what I, or anyone else, could dream up.

"Lincoln."

I switched my visual focus. The document turned fuzzy and everything else became clear.

When I saw who stood before me, I sighed and thought my safety word. *Melody*. The stadium, the blood, and the death all faded. The proposed plan to protect our nation also faded.

I opened my eyes and turned my attention to the tall man with pepper-gray hair, four stars on each shoulder, and an axhandle sized stick of self-righteousness shoved snuggly up his butt.

"Hello, General Hudson."

He gave me a curt nod. "I'm here to see if you have completed your evaluation of the DOD's proposal."

I reached under my desk and pulled out a soda. Popping the top, I leaned back in my chair. "General, you can't be serious."

He narrowed his eyes. "I'm completely serious, son. Are you saying you found flaws in the plan?"

I took a sip. Carbonated beverages had gone out of vogue years ago, but I still knew where to lay my hands on some. The fizz felt so good going down my throat I could almost forget about the feebleminded barreling our country toward the edge of doom. "Well, if your goal is to get not only the president killed but everyone around him, then I think it's a brilliant plan."

The general's nostrils flared, but he otherwise gave no indication that I'd just insulted his brainchild. "Please explain."

Taking a deep breath, I set the can down. "You and the

rest of the geniuses at the Department of Defense want to use an EMP."

"Correct," he said. "At the first sign of a nanotechnology threat, we release an EMP to disable all electronic devices, which would include the microbots. Had we done this seven years ago, we not only would have saved the president's life, but we'd have had the evidence we needed to catch the perpetrators. The offensive would start with a single burst—"

I held up my hand to stop him. "Yes, yes. I read the report. You'd unleash your electromagnetic pulse ray gun and destroy the tiny little robots. And as the paid antagonist of this scene, I completely agree with you."

He furrowed his hairy eyebrows. "I don't understand."

I picked up my cola. "Let's say I'm Mr. Third Row and I wanted to inflict severe damage and trauma against the great devil. I'd go down to the five and dime black market and pick up the cheapest bots money could buy. I'd let them loose on your little shindig, and in response, you'd set off your ray gun. Time to celebrate, you destroyed the tiny robots. Unfortunately, everyone with a pacemaker, neural implant, or artificial organ also just dropped dead. While the crowd is going crazy, because half the population just croaked right before their eyes, I'd swoop in old-school style and do my business."

The general's face had gone flush and his eyes blazed. "My men could stop you."

I laughed. "General, your boys in blue are running around with their thumbs up their asses because they can't talk to each other. Remember? Your ray gun crushed their coms too. They also can't protect themselves because you zapped their pulse guns. Oh, and let's not forget that most of them are having seizures because their GovLink fobs exploded and liquefied their brains."

He clenched and unclenched his fists as if he'd like nothing better than to sock me in the eye.

I do so enjoy bringing out the best in people.

I couldn't help myself. To add to his ire, just because I'm a self-proclaimed ass, I made a "mind-blown" hand gesture. "Blam."

Hudson's fists balled up into a permanent clench, more puckered than his butthole.

"My guys, on the other hand," I jerked my thumb back to my chest, "don't have the latest gadgets. Their automatic weapons, knives, and clubs are completely unaffected by your ray gun. They have free reign to take over the place with good old-fashioned brute force. To answer your question, it sounds like a great plan…if you hate this country."

The general's face turned crimson. "That would only be the case if they knew about our plan. Otherwise, it'll work just fine."

"Sir," I said, "with all due respect, I vehemently disagree. Homeland Security is a sieve. Someone will talk, and word will spread."

"I don't care what you agree or disagree with," he said, glaring down at me. "I'm presenting my plan to the congressional committee this afternoon."

I leaned forward. "And I'll be submitting my report to them as well."

General Hudson regarded me. "I'm tired of your meddling and derisive attitude, son. If you think we can't find someone better qualified to poke holes in our security, think again. I may not have been the one that hired you, but I can fire you."

I held his gaze. "Well, then go ahead and do it. But your idle threats won't make me compromise my opinion. I refuse to bow to your idiocy. It was that kind of thinking that got the president killed, and I won't be part of it. But until I'm standing in the unemployment line, I'm doing my job and won't let assholes like you intimidate me."

"You may as well start packing," he said, shaking his head.

I shrugged.

He grabbed my government-issued mobile. "Consider yourself on notice." He pivoted and marched away. The sharp tick of his military shoes rapped on the floor as he stormed down the hall. After boarding the elevator, he turned and sneered at me.

As soon as the doors closed, I pulled out another mobile and linked it to my fob. I completed the security routine to establish a connection to the CIA's investigation server and waited. The ocular viewer flashed *Connection Established*.

I linked up the auditory and visual feed from the general's embedded fob. At a certain rank in his military career, the GovLink fob, as per regulations, had ceased to be an option and, in the name of national security, had become a permanent fixture. Implanted just beneath the skin of high-ranking officials, it could neither be felt nor tampered with.

Due to the Sensory Privacy Act, an undisclosed tap

could only be executed through an inter-agency investigation. My security clearance made such permissions a mere formality. By design, General Hudson would be unaware that I now piggybacked on the signals from his fob.

I started the sensory recorder on my workstation, and my world changed from office to elevator. If anything came of the investigation, I would turn the recording, along with my report, in to the oversight committee.

The elevator indicator dropped until the small car reached the ground floor. Out on the street, he summoned his auto and ordered it to take him across town, where he disembarked.

The military man walked several blocks and slunk into an alley. In the dark space between two buildings, he banged on a rusted door. He paused, then did it again.

The door opened, though no one stood in the entrance, and the general walked through.

When the door slammed shut behind him, the room plummeted into darkness. What had he gotten himself into?

"Hello?" he said.

Nothing. Suddenly, the general grunted. The sound of shuffling resonated throughout the room. Whomever or whatever General Hudson had gotten mixed up with did not treat visitors gently.

The lights came on, and he blinked against the harsh rays. His eyes adjusted, and there before him stood a man with giant biceps, a thick chest, and a head as large as a horse's.

"Hello, General," said the Clydesdale.

CHAPTER SIXTEEN

JEFF

A brief flash of vertigo rocked the room and I blinked. The Clydesdale's huge face faded as I returned to the computer lab of Virtual Adventures.

Calvin watched me expectantly. "Jeff?"

I shook my head while a million thoughts swirled about, each ping-ponging for dominance and attention.

He touched my shoulder. "Jeff, are you okay?"

"You were monitoring on the viewer, right?" I asked.

He nodded.

Rubbing my forehead, I sat back in my chair. "The man Lucas and I saw with the general…"

"You mean the guy you call the Clydesdale?" he asked.

"Yeah, him."

"What about him?" he asked.

"I think we just witnessed a secret meeting between him and the general," I said.

Calvin sat on the desk, remaining quiet for a minute. "So, those two are in cahoots… But we don't even know who this guy is, nor do we know the significance of his meeting with some general."

I stared at the ceiling while the various pieces of the puzzle spun around and around inside my head like cows trapped in a tornado. "Well, first of all, it means that I'm not going crazy. There really was…or is…something going on with the general and the horse guy."

He chuckled. "Congratulations. You're not entirely insane."

I nodded, then paused. Within the chaotic storm of thoughts and emotions, a significant association lingered just out of my mental grasp. As the notion balanced precariously on the edge of my consciousness, I relaxed, trying to not get in the way while my mind reached for the connection between two seemingly unrelated pieces of information. With an almost audible clunk, the thoughts resolved.

My breath caught in my throat. "Calvin, you said you watched the playback on the monitor."

He frowned. "Yeah, what about it?" He stared at my face. "Jeff, you're as white as a ghost."

I turned back to the display. "Yes. Yes. Pull up the footage of the president's speech." My heart hammered, and a huge drop of sweat rolled down my back.

Calvin stepped up next to me and began typing. "Okay, got it. What are we looking for?"

"Start from the beginning, but only roll forward a few frames at a time," I instructed him.

The visual feed of Lincoln's memories halted and jerked in small increments.

"Stop," I said. "Go back."

He typed something, and the footage slid back several seconds. "Okay. But this is just the audience, Jeff. I don't know what—"

I pointed. "There."

He stared. "Where?"

I got right up in front of the holodisplay. The First Lady's hand had just started to reach for the bulge in her neck, but I looked past her at the throng of spectators watching the president give his final speech, all unaware that they had just lived their last few seconds of innocence.

"Focus on that person." I pointed—not at the president, the First Lady, or the Speaker of the House but to an audience member, a man, high up in the bleachers.

Cal zoomed in on the face, and his breath hitched. "Is that…"

"Yes," I said, plopping onto the desk. "It's the Clydesdale."

He stepped away from the keyboard and slowly started to pace the room, glancing randomly at the display. "That cannot be a coincidence, but I'll admit I'm completely confused. We just watched Lincoln discover that the general was meeting with this horse guy."

As he collected his thoughts, Calvin began to wear a path in the floor. "And *you* were able to pick him out of the crowd. But Lincoln, who was supposedly some kind of counterterrorism specialist, or something, missed it."

Calvin stopped and put his hands on his hips. "I don't mean any offense by this, but if *you* made the connection, shouldn't *he* have also been able to put the pieces together?

I mean, you might have just made a huge breakthrough in the president's murder, but it's weird that he missed it."

My nerves tingled, and my mind raced. "Lincoln didn't miss it if he'd never seen the Clydesdale before. If this was the first time he'd seen him, then maybe he did put the pieces together. Maybe that memory is in a later file." I turned my attention back to the terminal, closed the MindLink monitor, and started scrolling through the contents of the directory. "How can I tell the order of the memories?"

Calvin scratched the side of his head. "Huh?"

I scanned through the pages of text in front of me, searching for a pattern. "I want to find the files that contain the next set of Lincoln's memories. Maybe he made the connection but died before he had a chance to tell anyone. Or maybe the general's still under investigation. Either way, we won't know until we find the next file."

"That's a good idea, but I don't think it's possible." Calvin shook his head. "Our brains aren't like a computer where things are stored chronologically."

He pointed at the display. "These files are just raw downloads of randomly segmented data. The only way to find the next set of memories is to go through every one of them and try to piece the events together by hand, which may or may not even be there. Sometimes the thoughts are complete, and other times, parts of them are lost before we can get to them."

I stared at the thousands of entries. "But I thought Dencephalon went through them all?"

"No," he said, "not the way you mean. What you're talking about is an overarching contextual evaluation, which I don't believe is possible, not even for Rick and his fleet of super-brains. At least not yet."

I frowned. "But surely someone else made some of the same connections we did. They aren't that hard to see."

"I don't disagree with you," he said, "but the problem is, no one actually looks at the raw memories."

I rubbed the back of my neck as I tried to put the pieces together. "That doesn't make any sense. Why wouldn't anyone review the files?"

"Because we don't need to," he replied. "There are hundreds of thousands of hours of recordings, but the dark matter server finds and strips out the pieces we need for the game. The memories themselves are stored in a completely random order. So unless you're trying to make a documentary about this guy's life, there's no reason to create a chronological sequence of events."

Sighing, I leaned against the desk. "Damn. It'll take months to go through it all." I paused. "But that still leaves a huge elephant in the room. The Clydesdale and general aside, do you understand the significance of what we've discovered?"

He frowned. "I guess not. I can see by your face that I'm missing something obvious though."

"This guy," I said, "is legit."

Calvin squinted. "I don't…" His eyes suddenly flew open. "Oh, you mean he really was a…"

I nodded. "Yes. We created a game about a high-level government official going rogue. Only we used a real high-level government official's memories to do it. He really *did* work for the Department of Homeland Security. He really *was* some super analyst that reviewed the presidential assassination that led to the war. He may have even been a super-ninja like in the game."

Cocking his head, Calvin put his hands on his hips. "Okay, but so what?"

I threw my hands up. "What do you mean 'So what?' We have this guy's memories, and he really is a high-placed official and has…had…access to top secret documents."

"Well," he said, "that certainly helps things seem more authentic, don't you think?"

I took Calvin's place and began to pace the floor. "Of course, it makes it seem more authentic because it *is* authentic. This guy's the real deal. How did we even get access to his memories? It seems like the government would have balked at him being a donor. He's not some normal everyday shmuck. He had access to things that the knee-busters in the Pentagon would never want us to see."

Calvin glanced at the holodisplay. "I don't know how they get the memories they do, but since these people are dead, we don't exactly have to do background checks on them. All the usual rules of access don't apply because they are, you know, dead."

"It seems—" I began, but Lexi interrupted my train of thought.

"Calvin?"

He rubbed his forehead. "Yes, Lexi?"

My digital assistant's voice echoed around the room. "Tamara is trying to get a hold of you. She says that it's urgent."

"Why would Tamara be trying to get in touch with you?" I asked.

He shrugged. "Haven't the foggiest. Let's ask her, shall we? Put her on, Lexi." He set his mobile on the desk, and my fiancée's face materialized above it. "Hey, Tamara."

Her eyes were huge and round. "Calvin, I'm looking for Jeff."

Calvin glanced at me, and I stepped up next to him. "Hey, baby. What's up?"

"Jeff! Thank god," she said, breathing a huge sigh of relief. "I've been looking all over for you."

I nodded. "Yes, it's been a hell of an afternoon. There was an…incident. I didn't want to be disturbed while I researched it, so I told Lexi to put me in private mode."

An odd expression passed over her face. "You didn't go see Ceos this afternoon, did you?"

A double-tipped sword of perplexity and fear pierced my heart. Something about the ominous tone in her voice gave me pause. "Yes. She and I had a meeting. But I—"

She held up her hand. "Jeff, stop. Don't say another word."

My pulse tripped and then started to race. Tamara had just gone lawyer. Maybe this had something to do with the Lucas episode earlier today? But she'd asked if I'd seen Ceos. Maybe the bitch had put a warrant out for my arrest after all. "Tamara, I don't understand. What's going on?"

When someone out of the mobile's field of vision said something, she glanced to her left. She nodded several times and turned back to me. "Okay, do exactly as I tell you to. First, I need to know where you are."

I looked at Calvin. He shrugged his bony shoulders.

"Sure. Okay," I said. "I'll do whatever you say. I'm at the office."

She nodded. "Go downstairs and wait in front of the building. You are to go unarmed. A car will meet you."

I blinked. "What? I don't even own any weapons. Tamara, what's this about?"

"I only told you to go unarmed because, as your lawyer, I'm required to ensure the safety of you and everyone you interact with." Though she maintained a professional expression, fear lingered in her eyes. "Do not take so much as a bread knife with you. Do you understand?"

"Sure. Um. Okay." I nodded. "Yes, I understand and will do as you say, but who am I waiting for?"

She took a deep breath. "Jeff, the police are on their way to pick you up. Go with them willingly, but do not say anything. Not 'Hello.' Not 'How are you doing?' Nothing. They will take you to the local precinct. I will meet you there in," she checked her DigiSleeve, "about twenty minutes. If you cooperate, then you are simply going in for questioning. If you don't, you will be arrested as a suspect."

I did a double take. "A suspect? For what?"

Tamara stared at me. "Jeff, Ceos was murdered this afternoon."

CHAPTER SEVENTEEN

JEFF

The police station smelled of shoe polish and stale coffee.

I sat in a small room on a hard, plastic seat created by the same legion of terrors who had invented waterboarding and the IRS. Instead of being created for rest and relaxation, the chair seemed to have been designed specifically to annoy the nerves in my butt. After just a few minutes in the torturous piece of furniture, my cheeks tingled with numbness as though poked and pricked by a mild electric current flowing through my jean grommets. I tried rocking back and forth to alleviate the discomfort, but no amount of shifting or swapping my weight from side to side soothed my indignant derriere.

Unable to withstand it any longer, I slid the chair back, perching on the edge. The plastic lip bit into my skin, but in comparison, the mild discomfort felt like a full-bottom rubdown from the most talented masseuse in the universe.

The cops had confiscated my mobile and DigiSleeve, leaving me no way to contact the outside world. The bare metal table, which looked turn of the century—not this century but the previous one—had scratches and random doodles etched into its grimy surface.

Raynard was here.
Bacon is the only kind of pig I like.
All who go forth are dumed.

The intellect went on and on. Some of the proverbs even included little hand-drawn graphics to assist readers' understanding of the brilliant absurdities and authority-loving commentary. The click of an old-fashioned clock echoed in the space as men and women in blue roamed back and forth on the other side of the windowed wall.

The last few hours had felt as unreal and disconnected as a nightmare. The police believed that someone had murdered Ceos. While I'd often dreamt of killing her, now that it had purportedly happened, my brain seemed to have gone into an odd state of denial and refused to entertain a world without the terror from the lair.

I glanced around the small interrogation room, amazed that just this morning Calvin and I had been celebrating. Now I could possibly spend the night in jail or even end up in Torpor Prison.

Given my tumultuous relationship with my boss, had I been in the police's position, I might have suspected me too. But scatter cameras and Ceos' own digital assistant would have recorded me leaving her office with her still alive. By now they must have already seen the footage and read the logs. Given that, I couldn't fathom why they would even consider me tangentially involved.

Tamara approached the desk sergeant who pointed to me. She made a beeline for the small room, and a uniformed officer let her inside.

I stood as she entered. "Hey, baby. Fancy running into you here."

She raised her eyebrows but didn't reply as she took the opposite seat. Tamara set her tablet in front of me. *Agreement for Employment of Legal Counsel* scrolled across the top of the page. "Don't say anything until you've signed this."

I skimmed the legalese, stopping at the line marked *Client Signature*. I smiled at her. "Are you sure you're the best lawyer for me? Maybe I should shop around? I've heard you're expensive."

Tamara narrowed her eyes. "Are you seriously going to make jokes at a time like this?"

"These guys have got nothing," I said, shrugging. "It's no big deal." *Did I really just say that being hauled in as a murder suspect was no big deal?* My own reaction baffled me. It's as if my thoughts weren't my own.

Tamara looked as surprised as I felt. She reached over, grabbed the tablet, and stood. "Well, it sounds like you've got this under control then. I'll just take my twenty years of legal experience and leave your dumb ass in here to rot in a cell alongside the drug addicts and serial killers. Besides convincing the police to question you instead of taking you into custody on murder charges, I guess I haven't been able to do much. But you go right ahead and convince them this is 'no big deal.' I'm sure that you and some half-wit public defender will do a bang-up job."

Get your shit together, Jeff. Stop acting like an idiot. I gently took her hand, preventing her from turning and leaving. "You're right. I'm sorry."

Though irritation flashed in her eyes, she paused as though waiting for me to say something more profound.

That's not enough, dummy. Damage control. Stat!

"I'm just having trouble taking any of this seriously," I said, shaking my head and trying to sound as pathetic as humanly possible. "The day was crazy already, and this…" I looked around the interrogation room, "is off the charts insanity. I'm so overwhelmed I don't even know what I'm saying, but I'm grateful you're here. I need your expertise. I need *you* to represent me."

I slid my hand down and tried to take the tablet, but she wouldn't release her death grip on the little device. "Please, Tamara," I said.

Finally, she let it go.

I breathed a sigh of relief as I pressed my thumb to the signature line and handed the tablet back. *No more jokes. No more anything. Do exactly as she says and don't mess up.* "I feel like I'm in a dream, and at any minute, I'm going to wake up and things will be back to normal."

The anger left her eyes. She took her seat again, glanced at the signature, added her own, and stowed the tablet in her bag.

Tamara sat straight in her chair staring at me. "Look, Jeff. I know you're in shock, or this seems like a nightmare, or whatever, but you could be in real trouble. We only have a couple of minutes before the detective comes in to question you. Here's the deal, I'm assuming these bozos are leaping to unsubstantiated conclusions and that you're innocent. In spite of some of the things we've discussed over the past year, I know you were just expressing your frustrations and would never actually do any of the things you talked about."

She hesitated. "I'm sure the evidence they have is completely circumstantial and explainable."

I paused, studying Tamara's face. Though she'd said she believed me to be innocent, something about her words—or the uncertainty in her eyes—said she also believed it was at least *possible* that I had committed murder.

Wow.

I didn't know if the lawyer in her just naturally mistrusted her clients or if my relentless joking about throwing Ceos off the KOIN Tower had been the source of her unspoken suspicions. Either way, I needed to alleviate her concerns.

She had to not just believe me but believe *in* me. She *could* defend a guilty client—I'd seen her do it a hundred times—but it would be a lot easier for her to protect an innocent one.

"Tamara," I said, shaking my head, "there is no evidence because I didn't do anything. There are some other things, unrelated to this, that happened today that I need to tell you about, but I did not hurt Ceos."

"Good," she said, nodding. "Then we don't have anything to worry about. I wish we had more time to prepare, but the detective is coming. Tell the truth, but only answer the questions he asks you. Do *not* elaborate. Also, only answer if I give you the go ahead. Understand?"

I nodded.

The door opened and the same man who had driven me to the station strolled in. Tamara moved to the seat next to me.

The officer took her chair. "Good afternoon. I'm Detective Mires, and I'll be asking you a few questions. If you answer completely and truthfully, you may be walking out of here tonight."

I did my best to put on a fearless, slightly bored demeanor. I would *not* let this guy get under my skin. If Ceos really had been murdered, there would be a ton of pressure on the police to find and arrest a suspect. Just because they were in a hurry didn't mean they'd be pinning this on me.

"Detective," I said by way of greeting.

He pulled out a tablet. With thick, calloused thumbs he scrolled and clicked on the small screen. "Let's start off with a few easy questions. You worked for Ms. Wells?"

"Yes," I said. "She is the primary stock holder in Virtual Adventures, so I report to her."

Tamara tapped my arm and shook her head.

Damn.

Right out of the gate I'd already made a mistake. This did not bode well for the rest of the conversation. I reminded myself to *only* answer the questions he asked. I had to remain calm and in control.

I'd think of this as a super-efficient algorithm to help me focus. The smaller and tighter the code—or in my case, the smaller the number of words—the less likely it would get corrupted and arrested by the system admins.

He typed something on his pad. "And how long have you been in business with Ms. Wells?"

I folded my hands on the table and looked at Tamara who nodded.

Single, small string answer. "About eighteen months."

He waited, and when I didn't continue, he glanced back down at his tablet. "According to the recording of the conversation with your lawyer from earlier today, you went to see Ms. Wells this afternoon."

When I didn't reply to his statement, he stared at me expectantly.

"I believe my client is waiting for a question, Detective," Tamara said.

He glanced at her, then returned his focus to me. "Did you go see Ms. Wells this afternoon?"

Boolean question. Boolean reply. "Yes," I said.

He again waited, not saying anything. The silence spun out, but I did not elaborate.

"Please tell me what happened this afternoon," he said.

Tamara touched my arm for me to wait. "Can you be more specific, Detective?"

Detective Mires glanced at Tamara again, then refocused his attention on me. "Sure. Why did you go see Ms. Wells this afternoon?"

I kept my hands folded neatly on the desk to help prevent myself from fidgeting. I didn't understand why it seemed so difficult to act natural. "Because Ms. Wells had summoned me."

"And why did she do that?"

I didn't want to answer this question, though I'd suspected he'd ask. I just wished I'd had time to talk to Tamara beforehand. Keeping my face as neutral as possible, I said, "To fire me."

If my proclamation surprised my lawyer or the detective, neither of them showed it. It suddenly dawned on me that each of them already knew. No wonder Tamara had been suspicious.

Ceos' digital assistant must have recorded the conversation, which the police would have been able to subpoena. I thought back over the meeting and tried to recall the details of what we'd talked about. Aside from being fired, everything else blurred together into a mishmash.

He glanced down at his notes. "When you finished with your meeting, she was alive?"

I considered making a smart remark but reeled in my sarcasm and nodded. *Boolean question. Boolean reply.* "Yes."

He scrolled backwards on his tablet. "Did you give Ms. Wells anything?"

"Yes," I said.

The detective raised his eyebrows. "And what was it you gave to her?"

I said, "A new fob and neckpad."

Detective Mires looked at me expectantly as if my reply had been insufficient. *Sorry, Detective, that was a scalar function question. If you want more, you'll have to request it.*

"We found two other similar pads in her desk drawer, as well as one of these." He selected a picture on his tablet. "Is this a fob?"

"It is," I said, resisting the urge to tell him about it being an older design.

"I see," he said. "If she had one of these fobs already, why would she need a new one? Was her old one broken?"

I paused for a second, crafting my sentences concisely. "One of her games was ready. It required an updated version of the fob."

He nodded. "Tell me about this game."

I glanced at Tamara, who also nodded. "Ms. Wells is wheelchair bound, with no hope of ever regaining the use of her legs or any feeling below the waist. She also has very limited use of her hands and arms. She wanted to be able to go rock climbing and hiking again, so she had us create an outdoor adventure simulation for her."

"So, it wasn't a 'game' in the traditional shoot 'em up sense?" he asked.

I shook my head. "No. It was more of a pseudo-activity type adventure."

He no longer referenced his notes. "I see. And you were one of the developers for this pseudo-activity type adventure?"

I shook my head again. "No."

"What part, if any, did you play in the creation of her 'game?'" he asked.

I counted slowly in my head, giving my mind time to formulate the thoughts completely. "I drew up the basic storyboard with Ms. Wells and assisted with quality assurance, but the actual coding was done by my team."

Tamara broke in. "Detective, I don't really understand the relevance of this line of questioning."

He turned to her. "It's relevant, Counselor, because we believe *your* client used this game to murder Ms. Wells."

CHAPTER EIGHTEEN

JEFF

I jumped to my feet. "What? No. That's completely asinine. It's impossible to use a video game to kill anyone." I glared at him. "This is *exactly* what I'd suspected. You've got nothing. There's no evidence to corroborate your accusations, but you need someone to take the rap."

I pointed at him. "*You* need to show you're making progress solving the murder of the most powerful person on the planet. And if you don't get something soon, the media, the mayor, and hell, the whole damned world will chew you apart."

Jerking my thumb back to my chest, I said, "You will *not* use me as a scapegoat. If you don't have any better evidence than this, you will cease this line of questioning immediately and release me, or I'm sending your name and badge number to Homeland. You don't get to go dragging a federal agent in on trumped-up charges without serious ramifications, Detective Mires. End this now, or by tomorrow morning, it will be your career that has been ended."

I huffed and puffed like I'd run up several flights of stairs. Drops of sweat rolled down my forehead, but victory and righteous indignation marched through my veins. I'd be out of here in minutes. Time to leave this nonsense behind.

In unison, he and Tamara blinked, looked at one another, then stared up at me with their mouths open.

The detective scratched the side of his head. "Um... So, who, Mr. Federal Agent, exactly are you going to call in Homeland?"

I ground my teeth together. "Are you seriously going to push me to take this to..."

Suddenly, my mouth went dry, and my brain hiccupped. The man had a valid question. Confusion and a slight case of vertigo spun my world as if I'd gotten swept up in Dorothy's tornado. Once again, my own behavior baffled even me.

Had I really just claimed to be a federal agent? Who did I think I knew in Homeland Security? I'd never even *been* to DC. Why had I gone off on the detective like that? Round and round the questions circled like vultures.

Shaking my head and running a hand down my wet face, I said lamely, "Um... never mind."

He cocked his head, but even Detective Mires had no reply to my insane outburst.

Tamara reached up and touched my arm. "Detective, give us a couple of minutes, would you?"

He nodded. "Yeah. I think that's a good idea." He glanced at me. "In fact, I'll give you five. Counselor, you need to get your client under control." As he closed the door behind him, the unmistakable *snick* of the lock resonated.

Tamara turned to me. "Jeff, what the hell is going on? Are you trying to get thrown in jail? Don't make threats that you can't back up. In fact, don't make threats at all."

It felt as if the room had been transported to the deck of a ship caught in swollen seas. I rocked slightly to the side, caught myself, then fell back into my seat. My stomach turned, and for an awful moment, I thought I might lose my lunch.

"Are you okay?" Tamara asked. "You're white as a ghost and sweating." Concern covered her face as she laid her cool hands over mine. "You're a lot more overwhelmed by all of this than I thought. Jeff, you need to calm down. If you don't, you may have a panic attack or something."

I closed my eyes and took several deep breaths. While I wanted to pass off my tirade as stress-induced, it felt as if something inside of me had broken loose. A live electrical cable writhed and slithered in my brain, shorting out synapses and triggering irrational outbursts. I needed to hold my mess together, but terrifyingly, I couldn't predict when the next jolt of electricity would set me off. At the rate I'd been going, I might end up in the insane asylum instead of behind bars.

One thing at a time, Jeff. Focus. Just answer their questions and try not to go crazy…again.

After a few seconds, the world slowly righted itself, and I opened my eyes. "I think I'm okay now."

I took another long breath and faced Tamara. "Look, the bottom line is there's no way to kill anyone with our games. We have protocols and safeties and backup protocols and safeties and backups to the backups."

"I know all of this," she said. "You've talked about it dozens of times over the years. But what I want to know is if it's *possible* they somehow failed."

I shook my head. "No. No way. If the system senses there's a problem with the health monitoring and regulation modules, then it alerts us and shuts the whole thing down."

"You're sure the safeties can't fail?" she asked. "I'm not trying to goad you or question your capabilities, but the detective is going to try and make you seem incompetent at best and premeditative at worst."

As I forced myself to think through the familiar technical aspects of the system, a comforting calmness began to settle over my frayed nerves. I felt more relaxed. More in control. More…me.

Tamara touched my face. "Jeff, I need to know if there's any way that she could have been hurt using your game. Please think hard."

My internal thermostat had finally dropped back into normal operating parameters, letting me clearly mull over every detail of the application, the servers, and the protocols.

I shook my head. "No. I can't come up with anything. Our user base has logged over a billion hours of play time, and as far as I know, no one has ever had anything even remotely similar to this happen to them."

She glanced out the window, but the detective was nowhere in sight. "Okay. I believe you, but right now the police *think* it was used to kill her."

"Tamara, I told you that's not possible—"

She held up a finger, stopping me. "Yes, I know. Let's go off the assumption that somehow someone figured out a way to do it. We need to show that it wasn't you. Can you do that?"

"Yeah," I said. "That shouldn't be too hard. The system has tons of logs. We should be able to do an analysis and see exactly what happened."

"Okay. That's what I needed to know." Tamara raised her eyebrows. "Hey, no more federal agent stuff, no more threats, and no more outbursts. Got it?"

I nodded.

The door opened, and the detective strolled in. He plunked back down into the seat across from me. "So, have you got your story straight?"

Tamara turned to face him. "There is no 'story,' Detective. Just facts."

He held up his hands, a fake smile gracing his lips. "Glad to hear it. That'll make things much simpler. Usually people come in here and lie to me. I can't tell you what a huge relief it is to know that the three of us will only be dealing with facts."

He waved a finger at me. "Speaking of which, let's review the sequence of events. You and Ms. Wells had a fight this afternoon that led to you getting fired."

I glanced at Tamara who gave me a brief nod. "Actually, we had a philosophical disagreement about technology."

He flipped through the notes on his tablet. "I'd say you had more than a disagreement. Didn't she expressly forbid you from using Dencephalon, yet you went behind her back and did so anyway?"

I stared at him. How had this buffoon gotten that information? I studied his face. He knew a lot more than he was letting on. Heeding Tamara's advice to not lie, I proceeded cautiously. "Actually, you've got your facts a little mixed up."

Detective Mires leaned forward. "Oh, well then why don't you enlighten me?"

I leaned in too. "She forbid me from using Virtual Adventures' capital to *buy* the company. I bought Dencephalon with my own money and leased the technology to Virtual. It's something that happens all the time in the tech industry."

"Bending the rules happens all the time?" He shook his head. "Well, that's good to know."

"I did what was best for my company," I said.

He pointed at me. "You did what was best for *you*. You knew that if Ms. Wells found out, she'd shut you down. Maybe you'd hoped she'd change her mind, but you hadn't counted on her firing you. So not only are you out on the street, but now you've spent your life savings on a company that, without the windfall of a new game, is about to drive you bankrupt. But her death prevents all of that. It keeps your job, saves your company, and adds a lot of money to your personal account. That sounds like motive to me. A lot of it, in fact."

I leaned in further, narrowing my eyes. "That sounds like wild speculation to me. A lot of it, in fact."

"Detective," Tamara broke in, holding up her hands, "all of the inner workings of Virtual Adventures aside, it's not possible to harm anyone with this game."

The heavy man leaned back in his seat. "So I've heard, Counselor. I'll admit that even though your client has a history of breaking the rules and doing whatever he wants, it doesn't prove that he killed Ms. Wells. However." When he double-tapped the table, a digital folder appeared on the desktop. He flipped it open, revealing a document inside. "I have your client's fingerprints on the murder weapon." He slid the report across to my lawyer.

Tamara pulled the document to her and expanded it. "Yes, this report purports that Jeff's fingerprints are on the fob, but again, it's not a murder weapon. As I said before, you cannot kill with this game."

The detective pulled out another document and pretended to read it over. "I'm glad we aren't arguing over the chain of evidence. I have another report here stating that you were developing a new, heightened version of virtual reality. I read the reviews, and I must admit, it sounds quite intense. What do you call it?"

I sighed. The detective liked playing around. I had no idea where he planned to go with this, but I hoped he did so soon because most of my patience had already slipped away. "It's called *Total Immersion*."

He snapped his fingers. "Right. Right. *Total Immersion*. But to play it takes more than just sticking a—what-ya-call it? Fob?—on your temple, right?"

"Yes," I said. "There's a neckpad that goes with it. But that's not new. It's been around since the first version of our first game."

He put the report back into the file folder. "I see. And what does that do?"

I glanced at Tamara. She nodded again, so I redirected my attention back to the officer. "The fob delivers the virtual reality experience by overriding the user's senses. I don't know if you recall from elementary school, but that means sight, smell, taste, hearing, and touch."

Tamara slugged me under the table. Her eyes blazed a warning she did not vocalize.

Oops. I'd resorted to my brand-new friend sarcasm again. Not the greatest of times to discover a new talent. But after I'd claimed to be a federal agent and threatened to call Homeland Security, this slipup barely blipped on my insanity radar.

"Anyway," I continued, "our minds have difficulty telling the difference between reality and virtual reality. Because of this, our bodies react to the stimuli in the game. Players can experience an increased heart rate, increased breathing, and heightened levels of adrenaline—the same as if they'd been exposed to an actual fight or flight situation. The system takes a baseline reading on our body's rhythms, and besides controlling the player's avatar, it uses the pad to keep things regulated during a session."

The detective scratched his head. "It sounds very complicated, but basically the neckpad is a virtual joystick and a safety of sorts."

I nodded. "In Ms. Wells' case, she wanted to hike, climb, and run again. She wasn't into first-person shooter games."

"Right. Right," he said. "So, forgive me for my ignorance, because I may have missed something. But you said that there's no way for the user to come to harm while playing the game?"

I nodded again.

"But," he said, "you just told me that the neckpad is controlling the player's heart rate and breathing. I'm no doctor, but as I recall from school, those are both pretty important. What if there's a malfunction?"

He seemed to be taking the conversation in the same direction that Tamara had just a few minutes ago. Oddly, the sense of familiarity made me nervous and even more cautious. I didn't want to unwittingly step in a trap. "There are a ton of safety protocols. If the system detects any sort of abnormalities within itself or if the user is having an adverse reaction to the game, it automatically shuts down. Even if the pad failed and the system didn't abort, the worst that would happen is she'd hyperventilate. If she passed out, again, the system would have detected that and shut down."

"Hmmm." He picked up the report again. "So, let me ask you a hypothetical. Is it possible to shut these protocols off? Say the user was reacting poorly or maybe their blood pressure spiked. Can these so-called safeties be disabled?"

I shook my head. "No. Even if someone wanted to do that, they're so ingrained in the program, I don't even know where they'd start."

He swiped the digital folder. Flipping past the report, he pulled out several photos, arranging them in an arch in front of us.

In the first few, Ceos leaned forward, held up by the safety strap around her chest. A dried river of blood trailed from her nose down the front of her shirt. Blood pooled in her ears and dripped from her thin lips. While I'd dealt with death in the virtual world all the time, seeing it on the face of someone I knew felt raw and slightly unreal.

He enlarged one of the images until her face filled half the table. The photographer, perhaps going for a dramatic pose, had gotten a front facial shot. Ceos' lifeless blue eyes stared accusingly. Even in death, they still roiled with malice.

I gazed at the dead woman's face.

Societal rules dictated that we only speak fondly of, and remember the good times spent with, the dearly departed. But try as I might, I could find no sympathy or love in my heart for Ceos. From our first meeting—the day she'd told me she'd stolen my company—to the day she'd died, she'd only shown me cruelty and callousness.

Though I hadn't killed her, given that she'd treated everyone the same way, it wouldn't have surprised me if someone else had. "It looks like she died of some kind of ruptured aneurysm or a hemorrhage. Like you, I'm no doctor, but based on her physical health, that seems most likely. What I don't understand is why you think it was our software that killed her."

He swiped his arm across the desk, clearing the surface. He pulled a file out of the folder, sailing it across the table. It stopped in front of me.

He glared. "Go on, watch."

I hesitated. This smelled like a trap, though I couldn't begin to imagine what lay in wait for me.

Tamara asked, "What is this?"

Detective Mires interlaced his fingers and leaned on his elbows. "This is the MindLink playback recording. Specifically, Ms. Wells' just a few minutes before she died."

I glanced at Tamara and after she nodded, I clicked *Play*.

The video began, breaking into three familiar windows. The first showed Ceos' vitals, all of which appeared normal. The second window showed the MindLink settings and the commands sent to her nervous system to override her body's natural reactions to stimuli. She'd set her pain and sensation levels to a *moderate*. Enough to feel a little pain, spinning, and so forth, but not enough to be debilitating.

The third window showed the game play. Ceos, her pre-accident beauty and health restored, pounded a piton into a rough rock wall. She ran a rope through the loop, securing herself, and glanced down. The forest looked like match sticks hundreds of feet below. Ceos gazed around at the brilliance of the day as the wind caressed her jacket.

I shook my head. "I don't understand what this has to do with—"

Detective Mires' eyes remained fixated on the scene before us. He pointed a thick finger. "Wait for it. We're almost there."

Ceos turned back to the wall and grasped a small outcropping. She pulled herself up over the edge of the slight rock jettison and came face-to-face with a snake.

Her heart rate monitor instantly shot into the red zone. In the override window, instead of countering her physical reactions, the system did nothing, allowing the woman's heart and breathing to race.

I stared in surprise. Before I thought to stop myself, I said, "What the hell? That shouldn't be possible. The system should have never allowed her heart to—"

Tamara touched my arm and shook her head.

Right. Don't say anything.

The snake reared back, revealing the hood of a cobra. It wavered to-and-fro as it hissed.

I didn't need to review the storyboard to know that there were no snakes in Ceos' game. She hated them and had insisted on the most realistic simulation possible…minus snakes. How did a cobra end up in her game?

Ceos tried to lower herself away from the reptile but moved too late. The snake sprang forward, biting her in the cheek. Screaming, she let go of the rope and grabbed onto the cobra. As she began to fall, the serpent fell with her.

"Mavin," she yelled. The cobra writhed and lashed, hissing and biting as she struggled to pull it free. "Mavin," Ceos screamed again.

I glanced at the settings window and, with horror, realized that the pain and sensation levels had all been set to *maximum*. Each of her vital markers peaked at the very top of their thresholds, yet the system did nothing to calm her galloping heart and spasming muscles.

None of that should have been possible. The pain settings would have only changed if Ceos herself had set them, but that could only be done vocally.

Never in a million years should the system have kept going with her health monitors spiked. Never.

My own heart raced, and cold dread filled my gut.

Ceos fell past the piton she'd just hammered into place. The rope caught her, snagging her up tight, and she dangled from the small loop as she continued to wrestle with the snake. The creature seemed to have gotten caught in her climbing gear.

She screamed in agony as it bit her over and over. Ceos growled and yanked the reptile free. Swinging it around by the tail, she began to beat it against the rocks. Time and again the thump of the snake's head rebounded against the granite while her ragged breathing played over the speakers. When the reptile went limp at last, she threw it and began to weep.

"Mavin," she said through her tears.

A small stone hit her in the face, and she glanced up. The piton, evidently jarred loose by the commotion, hung precariously from its hole in the rock. "Mavin!"

I had a sudden premonition of what was about to happen. I wanted to shout out, to stop the game, to prevent the inevitable. But the horrific video played on.

Ceos looked around and down. She tried to slip her foot onto a small outcropping, but before she could gain purchase, the stake popped out. She screamed as she fell.

The rope caught again, and she thudded against the wall. She took a deep breath and looked up just in time to see the next piton pull free. Three more times she fell, and each time, the stake came out.

She growled as she hung from the last one. "Jeffrey, you bastard, you will pay for this."

The piton slipped and Ceos fell. The vitals monitor yelled its silent warning as the woman plummeted toward the jagged granite teeth at the bottom of the canyon. Ceos screamed "Mavin!" one last time before colliding with the rocks.

Game Over flashed across the screen and Ceos' vitals went flat.

My stomach roiled, and a sickening numbness spread over my whole body. If this could happen once, it could happen again. There must be a bug someplace deep in the *Total Immersion* program. We missed something, and because of that, Ceos had died. But I'd logged hundreds of hours, as had our test group and magazine reviewers, and no one had been hurt. Something didn't add up.

The detective tapped the table and the video flew back into his folder. "Tell me, who or what is Mavin?" Smug satisfaction lit up his eyes. He already knew the answer to this question too.

"That was the name of her oldest son," I replied.

"I see," he said. "So why did she keep saying his name?"

I let out a long breath. "That was her safety word. As soon as a player says their word, the game is supposed to end immediately."

"Yet," he said, pausing for effect, "in spite of saying this word multiple times, the game did not stop. I ask you again, is it possible to shut the safety protocols off?"

I shook my head. "No. It's not possible. Those are inherent features of the MindLink servers. It's not something that can be programmed or changed in the game itself."

"Then how do you explain everything that just happened to Ms. Wells?" he asked.

I shook my head. "I can't."

"Hmmm." He scrolled through his notes again. "Did you just say the game runs on the server? You need a mobile to play, so I assumed that it ran on that."

"No," I said. "The mobile app is just an interface which tunnels to the server cluster. The user's directionals are sent over the wire, and the game is streamed pre-rendered."

He chuckled. "Clusters. Directionals. Streamed. I really have no idea what any of this means. However, I do understand enough to know that the 'game' runs on computers that Virtual Adventures controls. That means that it's possible to meddle with them. Maybe even shut off a safety or two."

"No," I said. "It's not possible. No one in my company would do that."

He cocked his head. "I wasn't blaming anyone in your company."

Tamara leaned forward. "Detective, are you accusing my client of disabling these protocols? He didn't even work on the project except peripherally."

"I don't need to blame him," he answered as he turned to me. "I have an affidavit that says you were not only the lead developer on the project but you wouldn't allow anyone else access. That you, despite everyone's objections, insisted on handling the safety protocols yourself."

I leapt to my feet so fast my chair clattered to the floor. "That's a lie. I barely worked on the project. Who said that?"

The detective pulled another document out of the folder and slid it across the table. Tamara caught it and flipped it around so we could read it.

I stared unbelieving. "Rick? No, there's no way he'd…" My mind faltered as I recalled the conversation I'd had with him earlier. "Fiancée." I turned to Tamara. "He called you my fiancée."

She frowned. "Did you tell him?"

"No. I only told Calvin. Yet, when he and I were talking at the reviewers' exhibition, he didn't call you my girlfriend. He called you my fiancée. Do you know who else called you that but also had no way of knowing? Ceos."

Tamara pulled out her tablet and started scrolling. She looked up at me. "You're right. It's here in the transcript of your conversation with her. How could she have known?"

I scoffed and, after righting my chair, sat back down. "She said she made it her business to know."

Tamara rolled her eyes. "Yeah, that's helpful."

"Right? Well, that's Ceos for you."

"Wait," she said, holding up a finger. "Do you remember that night Rick stopped by our house unannounced?"

As realization sank in and the pieces fell into place, rage flooded my system. "Shit. I'll bet there are scatter cameras in our living room. If he got the right kind, they could pick up any conversation from anywhere in the house."

"But why?" Tamara asked. "Why spy on us?"

"It had to be for Ceos," I said. "That's how she knew about the demo and how she knew about us being engaged. I'd just assumed she had moles everywhere, but it was Rick all along. He may have been trying to get me fired or," I glanced at the detective, "blamed for her murder."

I turned my attention back to Tamara. "That's the only thing that makes sense."

She frowned. "But you were business partners and you saved his company. Why would he do that?"

I shook my head. "I have no idea."

The detective glared back and forth between us. "Okay, your little dating game thing is all really interesting, but it's not relevant to my investigation. Not only did you create the program, but you delivered the fob personally to Ms. Wells. Do you deny these accusations?"

I shoved the document back across the table. "You're damned right I deny it."

He narrowed his eyes at me. "You're saying you didn't give the fob to Ms. Wells?"

The detective had craftily been setting up another trap. If I didn't take a moment and catch my wits, I'd fall right into it.

I took a long breath, slowing the rapid flow of thoughts fluttering through my mind like panicked birds. "Calvin handed me the fob and neckpad. He asked me to deliver them since I was going to see Ms. Wells anyway. I asked him who'd given them to him, and he said that *Rick* had. When I asked him why she needed a new set, he said he didn't know. Just that Rick had asked him to have me give them to her."

"You admit to giving her the fob then? I have you on record of this?" He leaned forward, eager to get a win.

I counted slowly to three before answering. "Yes. I delivered the fob, which Calvin had given to me, which *Rick* had given to him."

"In my experience," he said slowly, "the owner of the fingerprints on the murder weapon is usually the murderer."

I glared at him, ready to give him a tongue lashing about the ineptitude of the police and him in particular, but Tamara broke in before I could get started. "Detective Mires, have you completed the investigation? Has your cyber team looked at the logs to see who did what? My understanding is that the system contains thousands of records and will tell you exactly who did it."

He double-tapped the folder. It and the documents vanished from the table top. "We have forensic teams working on that now. Unlike you, Mr. Tieg has been more than cooperative and provided us remote access to your servers."

I scoffed. "I'll bet."

Tamara glanced in my direction but did not reprimand me this time.

"It's too early in the process for any substantial leads," he said. "But we're working on it."

She stood. "Then without solid evidence other than an uncorroborated statement from a potentially unreliable witness, you don't have anything, and we are free to go."

The police officer made no move to stop her but raised his hand. "Hold on a second. Your client is now under investigation and, I believe, a flight risk. Thanks to the new streamlined regulations, I'm allowed to track him." He reached into his pocket and pulled out a tracker band. He held out a hand. "Wrist please."

I looked at Tamara.

She scowled. "Yes, technically Portland law now gives him the right. Though I have to say, it feels like you're abusing your power. I'll be filing a motion about you overstepping your authority and your flagrant harassment of this citizen."

"Oh," he said. "I know you mean business since you used the word 'flagrant.'" He pointed at me. "Now give me your arm."

I held out my hand, and the detective snapped the tracker band around my wrist. Though it looked like a thin bracelet, it had an embedded circuit that remained in constant communication with the city server.

"If your client tries to run, I'll find and arrest him." Detective Mires smiled smugly. "None of your fancy tricks will stop me either." He raised a finger. "Also, you should know that even though you're his lawyer, you're also engaged to your client. If he runs and somehow eludes us, I suspect that you'll most likely go with him."

"Are you just babbling, or are you trying to make a point?" she asked.

Now who's getting sarcastic?

He reached into his pocket and pulled out a second band. "They make a lady's version too."

Tamara glared at him but held out her hand. After he clicked it into place, she put a hand on her hip. "Detective, you need to return my client's personal property."

He held her gaze for a moment before reaching under the desk and pulling out my mobile and DigiSleeve from a bag. He handed them to me. "I expect I'll be collecting those again soon."

Tamara did not reply. She turned and strutted away. I followed her to the door.

As we filed out, he called after us. "I'll be in touch, Counselor."

She turned back. "I look forward to it, Detective. And I look forward to having your badge." She pivoted on her heels and marched through the sea of desks and out the front door.

As I followed her toward the front of the building, we passed a desk marked D. Mires. Three tiny bags of pinhead-sized scatter cameras sat in the corner.

Get one of those.

I didn't know why the thought popped into my head, but after all that had happened, it would take a lot more than a rogue notion to surprise me. As subtle as a pickpocket, I palmed one of the little bags. While I didn't know what I'd need it for, intuition told me it might come in handy.

CHAPTER NINETEEN

JEFF

I stopped on the police station steps as the door closed behind me. "Tamara." When she didn't turn around, I called to her again. "Tamara."

She whirled on me. "Don't say a word, Jeff. Not a single word."

"We need to talk," I said.

"Not out here we don't."

I looked around the deserted street. "Tamara, it's the middle of the night, and there's not another soul for miles."

She put her hands on her slim hips. "Are you really so naïve?"

When I didn't answer, she motioned at the buildings around us. "Scatter cameras. They're everywhere and they're recording everything we're saying right now. It doesn't matter if we're covered under attorney-client privilege if you start spilling your guts to the entire damned world. We need to go someplace private, which apparently isn't our home thanks to Rick the Prick."

Ugh. Of course. I'd been so focused on the detective that I'd forgotten. I moved down the steps until I stood in front of her and lowered my voice to a whisper. "I didn't do this. You have to believe me."

"You don't get it, do you?" she hissed. "It doesn't matter if I believe you or not. The richest person in the world was just killed, and that detective in there," she pointed at the station, "is building a case against *you*."

She held up her wrist, her bracelets jingling and jangling. "We already have trackers on us. If that son of a bitch gets a single whiff of a slipup, he'll put you under house arrest, and he'll be free to have a fob embedded in your skull. Then he and every other asshole at the precinct can see what you're doing every second of every day. We'll have no privacy. None. On top of that, everything we say and do can be used in court. I don't want to live like that, Jeff."

In all our years together, I'd wondered if, at some point, I'd push Tamara's love for me too far. Though we'd worked hard to move past our many philosophical and moral differences, my being charged with murder might be her breaking point. She'd stood by me in the interrogation room, but pain, anger, and embarrassment had all lingered in her eyes. The sanctity of her home had been spoiled, her own integrity questioned, and her fiancé had made the police's most wanted list.

I took a long, deep breath, trying to figure a way out of this mess. No matter how hard I clung to it, my world had been spiraling out of control for a while now—my company, my career, my mind, potentially my freedom, and now my relationship with Tamara. It all seemed to be slipping from my fingers.

To survive, I had to take control. This would be the murder case to end all murder cases, tried by the media long before it ever made it to the courtroom. My destiny wouldn't be decided on fact and evidence but by popularity and public opinion.

I could either slink away and hide, or, since the world watched us anyway, I could use the publicity to take control and give the people the show they wanted.

I continued down the steps to the sidewalk, slipping past my future wife. "Lexi," I said into my DigiSleeve. "Please bring the car around."

"Where are you going?" Tamara called after me.

I turned back, aware not just of the police cameras but of the local and national news cameras as well, all recording our every word. "If the police are going to be so narrow-minded as to only focus on me, then I'm going to do their jobs for them."

She trailed after me. "What does that mean?"

When the auto pulled up to the curb, I opened the door for her. "It means that we'll have to figure out who really killed Ceos and why."

She climbed in and I followed, settling into my seat. "Lexi, take us to my office."

Tamara frowned. "Why are we going there?"

"Like I told you, we need to find out who really did this and why." I opened the small bag of dots I'd taken from the police station, pulled one of the pinhead-sized specks out, and dropped it into my shirt pocket.

Tamara pointed. "Wait. What is that?"

"What? This?" I asked, holding up the little baggie. "Scatter cameras."

"Okay, yes. I can see that. But where did you get them?" she asked.

"Detective Mires' desk," I replied.

Tamara did a double take. "What? You stole those... from the police. Oh, my gawd, Jeff. You are determined to go to jail, aren't you? Why the hell did you do that?"

I shrugged. "I'm not sure yet. They just seemed like they might come in handy. Don't worry, they won't activate as long as we don't take them out. The bag has magnetic fibers woven into the plastic, which keeps the cameras turned off until—"

"Yes, yes. I know." She pointed at my shirt. "But you put one in your pocket. That one *is* live."

"It is," I confirmed. "But they're non-networked. They only record. They don't broadcast. If we have a conversation with Rick where he incriminates himself or if we need proof of what we've been doing to solve the police's case for them, I want to have it all documented."

She took the bag of dots and studied it. "Jeff, you can't know that Detective Mires isn't watching and listening right this minute."

I nodded. "I do know, and he's not."

"How?" she asked. Fear and uncertainty lingered in her dark eyes.

"The Electronics Communications Privacy Act, Amendment Four specifies that all networked micro, aka 'scatter,' cameras have a transmission designation." I held the bag up. "See, no lines or other markings. These are plain gray. Hence, they are the non-networked, passive recorders."

Tamara shook her head. "Do I even know you anymore?"

Good question. I didn't reply as I shoved the bag into my back pocket.

She remained quiet for a minute and then glanced at me. "You think there are clues in your office?"

I nodded. "Yes. I think that's the only place I'm going to find any answers. Plus, I'd love to ask Rick why he told the police that I'd created Ceos' game even though he knew I had nothing to do with it."

My fiancée growled. "And I'd like to ask him why he put cameras in my house."

The car pulled away from the curb, and we headed back to Virtual Adventures.

∞ ∞ ∞ ∞

On the way over, I repeated my confession about running over on my VR time limits. This time, I left nothing out.

Though Tamara didn't interrupt me, the vein in her temple pulsed, and a simmering anger built in her eyes.

Since she already knew that Ceos had fired me, I skipped that part but told her about meeting Lucas in the bar I'd never been to and seeing the general that wasn't there.

At last I finished my tale, but she remained quiet. Even after the car pulled in front of the sidewalk and we entered the building, my fiancée didn't utter a single word. As we rode the elevator in silence to the thirtieth floor, I gave her time to process.

Finally, the doors slid open, and Tamara let out a long breath. "What do you hope to find here?"

I led the way to the server room. "When you called, Calvin and I were reviewing the raw Lincoln Grey files."

She frowned. "Who's Lincoln Grey?"

"He's the donor of the memories that we used in *Treason*," I said. "He's Sandy Frost."

She shook her head. "I don't understand what that means."

I logged back in to Dencephalon's server and pulled up the menu. I pointed at the display. "When the extractor downloads the memories from a cadaver, the files are processed and converted into a format that's compatible with the MindLink server. There's a cleansing process that strips them of extraneous information and another that will go through and swap out names and other identifying characteristics to protect the donor's and their family's privacy. In this case, Lincoln got renamed to Sandy."

Tamara moved up beside me. "These are all of Lincoln's memories? Moments with his kids. Private time with his wife. Work and family. Pain and joy. His whole life is here in nice, neat little packages. Every thought and feeling he'd ever experienced available for you to peruse, pick through, use, and manipulate in any way you see fit."

Though we'd discussed this very thing on several occasions, talking about it and seeing the entire breadth of a man's life splayed open for anyone to view at their leisure were two very different things. I wanted to tell her that we hadn't violated Lincoln's privacy. That we'd respected his memories and his life, but at that moment, I couldn't help but see the vulgarity in what we'd done. "Yes."

She took the keyboard from me, changed to the parent folder, and started to browse. "There are hundreds of people here."

She selected *Rosalie Leads*. Tears pricked the corners of her eyes as she read the metadata on each of the dozen files. "Mom, dad, brother. High school boyfriend. Wedding day. Wedding night. Birth of first son, George. George diagnosed with leukemia. George's death... These are more than just random thoughts and feelings, Jeff. These are the most intimate moments of her life."

I nodded. "Yes, I know. Rick told me that usually only the most poignant memories, the ones associated with a high emotional state, are retained long-term." I looked over the files. "I hadn't realized just how significant that was until now."

She examined the list and pointed to the file labeled *Extraction*. "Show me."

"Show you what?"

She stared at me for a heartbeat. "Show me the extraction process. That's what's in this file, right? I'm sure that Legal makes you record each one. I know I would. I want to see how this is done."

I wanted to wrap Tamara in my arms and shield her from all of this. Of everything on this server, she'd picked one of the files that would cut to the bone the hardest. I shook my head. "Tamara, I don't think that's a good idea."

"Now!" she said, smacking the desk. "Or I swear, Jeff, I'll bring the holy hell of the Anti-V's down upon you. The fire and brimstone Ceos dumped on you will feel like a summer breeze compared to the hurricane I'll stir up."

Roiling, raging fury stormed behind her eyes. Guilt slammed into me, squeezing my heart and sucking the air from the room. My actions, my deceptions, had hurt the woman I loved. I couldn't do anything to repair the damage other than do what she'd asked.

Turning back to the display, I opened the file. "You're right. Every extraction is documented." I glanced at her. "We record it to prove that the donor was treated with respect."

"Yes, yes." She rolled her hand through the air. "And people say that lawyers are the leeches of society. Now show me how you violated this woman."

I sighed and started the recording. Rosalie lay on an autopsy table, her body covered in a white sheet. Her long dark hair hung down like a curtain.

Tamara's breath caught. "She's not much older than I am."

I paused the video and opened her bio. "She died in her sleep of an undiagnosed heart defect. One in a million chance. You're right. She was only thirty-four." Closing the file, I resumed the video.

Rick, in a long lab coat, gently lifted her hair. He pressed a small drill to the base of her skull. I cringed as the tool whirred to life and began boring through bone. He inserted a long steel wire and a thin tube through the hole, then repeated the process several more times around her head.

Tamara pointed at the display. "What's happening here?"

I hesitated, but when she raised her eyebrows, the vein in her temple pulsed more forcefully. "He's inserting the wire into the locations in her head where the memories are stored."

"But what's the tube for?"

"Remember, we talked about this," I said quietly. "Human memories are sealed and have to be chemically released. The tube delivers a protein-based solution that breaks apart the membranes, which frees the information. The data's only available for a nanosecond. The wire sends a mild current through the resulting material to record the signal."

Her nostrils flared, but she did not comment.

Rick connected the wires to a tablet and the tubes to a bag of blue fluid. Once he opened a valve, the liquid began to flow, and the woman's head started leaking. Not just blue, but small chunks of white and gray also poured out of the holes. Running down the gutters of the table, her essence, or what remained of it, drained into a bucket.

Her life and memories flashed across the tiny screen—a child's smiling face, a bride in white, an old man sitting on a bench—this woman's life turned digital and stored in an easy-access data repository.

Tamara stared at the display. "He's melting her brain. Literally."

My stomach had gotten queasy. I wanted to tell her that the simple procedure respected the donor. That it only *sounded* barbaric. But as Rick turned off the tablet and began to pull out the wires and tubes coated in gore, I could not formulate the words to make the argument. I couldn't make any words at all.

As the video ended, Tamara put her hands on her hips. "I don't care if they are dead. These are people, and you're intruding on their most intimate thoughts and feelings. This process is disgusting. They may have signed a consent form, but they've got no voice to stop you."

I turned back to her and placed my hands on her shoulders. "Honey, I know you find this completely outrageous. But I explained the process to you before we purchased Dencephalon. You and I agreed that the technology was inevitable and that, of all the people in the world, you said you trusted me the most."

"I know I did," she said, pushing my hands away. "And it's not fair to change my mind. Though, you didn't tell me the truth about the extractions, and you lied to me about going over your limits. That's not fair, so maybe that makes us even."

Her eyes found mine. "But now that I've seen it, I want you to know I can't let this go. I can't live with this." She pointed at the display. "This is repulsive."

I can't live with this.

Though she'd meant my use of extracted memories for video games, I couldn't help but wonder if her words had a double meaning.

I'd forced myself to gloss over the awfulness of the process. The indecency of it. I'd told myself to focus on the big picture, getting our games to market and beating the competition.

Ceos had tried to tell me and may have died for her efforts. Tamara had seen it too and called me out. No matter how much I wanted to, I couldn't deny it now either.

She appraised me. "You think so too. I can see it in your face. You thought that by ignoring it, you could pretend like it was no big deal."

My head sagged to my chest. "Yes, you're right. I saw it once but likened it to buying a steak at the store. I don't have to look the cow in the eyes before it becomes my dinner."

"Jeff," she said, "this is wrong, and you know it. It's not just about the desecration of the person's body but about being able to see their innermost thoughts and feelings. You've taken everything that's sacred and sold it to the world for the price of a game subscription. That's a violation."

"Yes, okay, I see your point." I looked at her. "But that's not why we're here, and we're running out of time."

"I have one more question before we get back to saving your ass," she said.

I couldn't imagine what else she wanted to know.

"How many extractors are there?" she asked. "When I was looking through the files, I only noticed Rick's name. How many people are out there desecrating the dead?"

I shook my head. "I don't know. It never occurred to me to ask." I turned back to the keyboard and ran a search on the files. "Unless everyone logs in as Rick, it doesn't look like anyone else on his team performs the procedure. He's the sole extractor." I paused. "Is that significant?"

She appraised me for a second. "I'm not sure. It seems so, but I don't know why yet. Anyway," she motioned toward the holodisplay, "what do we need to do?"

I turned back to the computer. "I need to finish going through the Lincoln files."

Tamara furrowed her brow. "Why?"

"Because of Lucas' warning," I said. I checked my DigiSleeve. "We have about four hours before the game goes live. If Lucas is right, we need to pull the plug."

She folded her arms. "We don't have time for that. You need to start finding the evidence that will keep you out of jail."

I turned to her. "I know it seems like a wild goose chase, but the public may be at risk. I can't let anyone else get hurt. Please help me."

She stared at me for several heartbeats. Finally, she nodded.

I turned back to the holodisplay and exited out of Rosalie's folder. Returning to Lincoln's, I began to scroll through the list.

"Jeff, I'm a little confused," Tamara said.

"About what?"

She indicated the display. "When we were in Rosalie's folder, there were maybe a dozen files. But in Lincoln's, there are hundreds, probably more. What's the difference?"

I scratched my head. Did that matter? Did a clue hide not just in the files themselves but in the quantity of them as well? If it did, I didn't understand the significance of it. "Well, from what I was told, only the most poignant memories, the ones tied to strong emotional connections, will be readable. We slough off a lot of the randomness in life, so none of that should be in our long-term memories."

"Okay," she said. "And not to be sexist or anything, but women generally are more connected to their emotions than men. Given that, shouldn't there be more files for her? However, *he* has significantly more. By a rough guess, I'd say at least ten times as many."

I shook my head. "I don't know. According to his bio, he was off the charts intelligent. Maybe he remembers more than the average person?"

"Jeff!" Calvin came barreling into the room.

He didn't slow down and practically knocked me off my feet as he threw his arms around me in an awkward hug.

Embracing Calvin felt like cuddling with a wooden support beam, but I wrapped my arms around him and patted him on the back.

He let go and nearly stabbed me in the eye with his pointy hair while also stepping on my foot. My friend almost fell, but I caught him.

"Thank god. What happened? Did you get arrested? Did Ceos really get murdered?" He didn't even seem to notice his close encounter with the floor. He just stared at me with huge, round eyes before blinking and turning, as if seeing the woman standing next to me for the first time.

"Oh, hi, Tamara." The man-child looked unsure of how to greet her. He moved forward, gave her a stiff-arm hug, and then stepped back, looking relieved to have the unusual display of emotion out of the way.

Tamara smiled. "Hi, Calvin."

I held up my wrist, showing him my tracking band. "My bling, courtesy of the Portland Police Department."

"Classy," he remarked. "So, Ceos?"

"The police think she was murdered," I said.

His mouth dropped open, and he started to say something but stopped. He looked at me for a minute, the question obvious on his lips, though he seemed incapable of asking it.

Shaking my head, I smiled. "No, Calvin. I didn't kill her."

He released a long breath. "I didn't think so, but still… She sure gave you enough reason to. No offense, but I might have suspected you too." He paused. "But if you didn't do it, who did?"

I considered telling him my suspicions about Rick. But I didn't have any proof, and the police had already made enough unsubstantiated accusations for one day.

"I don't know," I said. "She wasn't exactly the nicest person. I'd guess there is a long line of people who would have paid big money to have her killed. But the detective that interrogated me thinks that whoever it was used *Total Immersion* to do it."

He looked back and forth between me and Tamara. "What? Um, no. That's completely impossible."

He, like Tamara, thought I might have done it. According to those closest to me, I was apparently capable of murder. I pushed my feelings aside and pointed at him. "That's what I keep saying."

"Anyone who says that has no idea what they're talking about." He huffed. "Anyway, I'm glad you're back because I found something you'll find interesting." His gaze stopped on Tamara's face. "Um, I'm glad you're here too."

I touched his shoulder. "Calvin. What do you have for us?"

He turned to the holodisplay. Opening a new window, he began to type. A sealed schematic flashed on the display, but as he continued to pound away on the keyboard, it turned to encrypted gibberish and then revealed its contents.

"Isn't that the schematic for the fob?" I asked.

Calvin grinned. "Sort of. It's the hacked version with the limits removed. But that's not the interesting part." He scrolled to the bottom and pointed. "Look."

I leaned in, and my mouth dropped open. "What? Seriously?"

Tamara stared at each of us in turn. "What are you looking at?"

Calvin and I exchanged a glance. "Every schematics file," I said, "contains the originating name of the server that created it. Think of it as an unalterable digital signature."

"Okay, so this one is significant then?" she asked.

"I'll say," Calvin said. "It's one of ours."

"What?" she said.

Rick. It had to be. He'd been spying on me and Tamara and reporting information back to Ceos, and now we'd discovered that he'd created an unlimited version of the fob. I nodded. "Someone created the hacked version of the fob right here in Virtual Adventures."

Tamara's eyes grew wide as she stared at me. I could tell she'd probably been thinking the same thing I had been.

"But why?" she asked.

"That's the million-dollar question," I said, pointing at her.

"I checked out the extension file too," Calvin said.

"Let me guess, it also came from here."

He nodded. "Yep."

My mind spun. Those files were available weeks before *Total Immersion's* scheduled release date. Why would anyone from *here* want people to be able to bypass the limits? It made no sense.

I turned back to the holodisplay, closed the schematic, and returned to the list of files. "Well, that makes it all the more important that we crack this."

Tamara frowned. "Jeff, can you sort the files by name?"

"Sure," I said. After typing the command, the text scrolled down the display.

She looked at me. "Do you see what's missing?"

"I do," I said, "but that doesn't make sense either."

Calvin stepped up next to me. "What's not here?"

"Lincoln's extraction file," I said.

He frowned. "It has to be. It's a legal requirement."

With all that had been going on, it didn't surprise me that something had been either deleted or cleverly hidden. Shrugging, I indicated the list. "I know, but it's not there."

"Maybe it's in the last file," he said. "It could be that they just didn't label it."

I sighed. "Well, a lot of good that's going to do us. There's no way to find it in all of this."

My friend leaned closer to the display and paused, his hands hovering over the keyboard. "Actually, while you were having donuts and yukking it up with the local fuzz, I think I may have come up with a way."

He pecked out a couple of letters, hesitated, then started again. The pace of his typing increased as a smile formed on his lips. While his fingers blurred over the keyboard, he explained, "You know how we can cross-reference the source files with the game files? Well, we might be able to pull enough of a timeline from those to order these."

As the mad scientist worked, I gave Tamara a brief overview of the Lincoln file I'd been looking at when she'd called.

She scratched the side of her head. "Lincoln was a contractor or something for the government?"

I nodded. "It appears so. In fact, at the very end of his last memory, he'd just tapped into General Hudson's fob feed. The general was meeting with some guy in an old abandoned warehouse, but we ran out of file before we found out why."

"Got it!" Calvin whooped. "These are the next set of memory files, in their approximate order."

I fist bumped my friend. "Let's see what we've got."

I clicked the fob to my temple, slid a pad onto my neck, and, selecting the next item on the list, started MindLink. Time to get back into Lincoln's head.

CHAPTER TWENTY

LINCOLN

Through General Hudson's eyes, I stared into the unhappy face of the man with huge biceps and an even huger head. "Evan, we've got a problem."

He regarded Hudson. "I'll bet you do."

"No," the general said. "*We* do."

The large man pulled up a chair, flipped it around, and sat in it backwards. He rested his obscenely immense arms on the back of it and stared. "Oh, do *we* now? And what problem would that be?"

"Lincoln Grey."

I started. *Me?* Though the general and I didn't see eye to eye most of the time, I had no idea I'd gotten under his skin so deeply. I studied the huge man's face. *Who is this Evan guy, and why does he seem familiar? Evan? Have I heard of that name before?* I couldn't recall.

Evan cocked his head. "I thought you'd said that he wouldn't be a problem."

The general put his hands on his hips. "Well, it seems that your EMP plan didn't fool him as well as you thought it would. He figured it out. All of it. It's like he's read your playbook page-by-page."

Evan's small, hard eyes peered out from under a thick forehead and even thicker eyebrows. "The best plans can be ruined by a poor presentation. Your inadequacies are starting to become a hindrance."

Huh. Well, I've got news for the both of you. No matter how you dressed that pig, I wasn't going to kiss it. But why even bother trying to pass off Evan's idiotic plan as his own? Hudson had to have known I'd kill it.

General Hudson leapt to his feet, knocking his chair over backwards. "How dare you imply that this is my fault. I told you he'd never go for it, and now he's going to submit a report to the congressional committee. Do you know how bad that makes me look? Those idiots love nitpicking the military to death, and because of you, they're going to have a field day at my expense."

The huge man glared. "You'd best watch your tone."

He got right into Evan's face. "Watch *my* tone? No, I don't need to watch *my* tone. You need me, not the other way around. Because of *me*, your king—your father—was able to do things he otherwise never would have even dreamed about. Because of me, his cause was advanced by decades in just a few years. I'm the one that trades favors with senators and congressmen whenever any of you snap your fingers. I'm the one that got your dad access to the First Lady long before she stepped foot into the White House. It was my idea to plant that decoy in the third row during the assassination."

My stomach lurched. Could this conversation be for real? We'd turned over every rock trying to find out how the First Lady had gotten infected and found nothing. Yet, the general had known all along. It seemed completely impossible.

"That was all *me*," the general said, jerking his thumb back to his chest. "Those morons in the FBI, CIA, and Homeland still have their heads crammed up their butts trying to figure out why and how that guy killed the president."

Evan glared at him. "You seem to be forgetting that the real keys to the operation were getting the bots and turning that family man into a human drone. That and everything else was all my *father's* doing."

"You 'royals' are always taking credit for our successes but sloughing the failures onto everyone else. I told him who to call for the bots, and let's be honest, he didn't do jack to that guy except kidnap him, which any two-bit thug could have pulled off. It was that brain doctor of his that turned Mr. Third Row into a puppet."

The man from the third row had been a decoy. No wonder we hadn't found anything on him. But how? How did a "brain doctor" make someone their puppet?

Evan's face flushed with anger. "Your task was to do more than get my father the tools he needed and hide his involvement. You were supposed to have your people in the UN vote to retaliate against the target my father gave you."

"This again?" Hudson rolled his eyes.

"Yes, this again. You—"

Hudson cut him off. "I tried, but I can only control so much. Did your father not think there'd be a formal investigation? Did he not think that everyone from the CIA to the FBI to Homeland would ignore me and dig and dig? That's what they do. The king of your two-bit country and a few of his radical friends murdered the president for Christ's sake. They couldn't trace it to my people, but your dad didn't take the precautions I told him to."

He paused. "Besides, no one noticed or cared if a few insignificant people got removed from the gene pool."

Evan gripped the back of the chair so hard, it bleached the color from the skin on his knuckles. "Yomi was my country. Those 'insignificant' people had nothing to do with what happened to your president."

Hudson shrugged. "Your dad used to say we're at war. News flash! There's collateral damage in war."

"Those were *my* people. *My family*. They were already victims of a world that had cast them aside like garbage, and now they're all dead. Granted, my father and I didn't agree on a lot of things. I foolishly thought we could bring about awareness through peaceful means within the law, while he believed that only something as radical as the president's assassination would get everyone's attention and bring about change. The loss of one man was supposed to give voice and life to hundreds of thousands. It was supposed to be a message that would change the world."

The general stared into Evan's eyes. "Didn't work out exactly the way he'd planned, did it? The ones he gave voice to are nothing but ash. Now that you've taken the reigns of what's left of your daddy's organization and his fortune, maybe you should heed that lesson. If you don't want to pay, then maybe you shouldn't play."

The fury in Evan's eyes changed to a hateful dark determination. "You have no idea just how high of a price the world is going to pay for what it has done. I was in the bleachers the day the president was murdered. Saw it with my own eyes. I believed in my father's ideals, but I thought his use of violence, his methods, were too extreme. Now I know he wasn't extreme enough."

Something about the malignant confidence in the tone of his voice sent a cold shiver over the surface of my skin and a tremor through my heart.

Either Hudson didn't notice the shift in Evan or he didn't care. Hudson said, "Your father and I created an alliance because our needs aligned. Out of my respect for him, I've extended that cooperation to you and your organization. Your..."

"White Raven."

"Yes, that. Your White Raven. But you need to remember your place. I'm the one who pulls the right strings at the right times to make it all work."

Our people did this. No question about it. I shook my head. We'd focused our efforts on external groups when we should have been looking within our own ranks. Our own people had helped kill the president. I never would have believed it.

Clearly, the general and 'his people' had wanted the president out, though I couldn't begin to fathom why. And then, armed with our outrage and our need to strike back, we'd killed millions in the nuclear strike and millions more when our robots and tanks rolled in. But in our haste and our hatred we'd inadvertently created a terrorist cell hellbent on murder. We'd played right into the general's hands. He'd eliminated the president, and we'd eliminated his accomplice.

My stomach roiled. At the time, rumors had flown around about the small country's innocence, but we, as a nation, had jumped the gun in an attempt to satiate our unquenchable thirst for retribution. Maybe we should have slowed down and only punished those responsible instead of obliterating an entire nation for the actions of a few.

Evan pointed. "You think you're in a position of power and that we need you? We don't. You are replaceable."

Glowering, the general held his gaze. "Maybe it's time for us to part ways then. I worked with your father, but you and I, I just don't see it. Not long term."

The big man shook his head. "You know it doesn't work like that. We don't just shake hands and then you go retire to a beach somewhere. That's not how we operate. Once you're in, you're in. And if you try to leave anyway, we'll find you and toss you into a pit so deep and dark it'll make Hell look like a four-star resort."

"Because I know what you people are capable of, I've prepared a few 'assurances' of my own," the general said. "If something happens to me, this whole operation will get shut down before you have a chance to say boo."

Evan growled. "Is that so?"

Hudson nodded.

"Well, I wouldn't worry about what'll happen to White Raven." The large man leaned back. "We're creating an empire that will last a thousand years. Besides, by the time whatever you have gets out, everything you think you know will have been wiped clean. You'll just look like a desperate man trying to save his own ass."

"What empire?" Hudson asked, shaking his head. "That's complete insanity. You've got nothing left to fight for. Take your billions and go retire. Live a life of luxury. No one is hunting you. No one is looking for you."

"We are carrying on my father's legacy," Evan replied. "Except now we're more...focused. Instead of trying to clean up the world, my brother and I will rule it."

Hudson scoffed. "You are completely delusional. Whatever. Live in your dream land. Just remember, I *will* take you down if I have to."

"About that," Evan said, holding up a finger. "Just one piece of advice before you even consider doing anything rash. Remember that we always have a backup plan."

The general hesitated. "What sort of backup plan?"

"Normally," the big man said, leaning forward on his elbows. "I don't share this sort of information, but since I'm in a generous mood, I'll fill you in. But just this once. Listen carefully." He smirked. "You're only alive because you're useful. But once you cease your usefulness, you'll find yourself under a dirt carpet, and there won't be anyone around to protect your pretty little daughter and her family anymore. With you out of the way, I'm sure that my men would enjoy sampling her, her girls, and probably even her husband."

The general snarled and leapt forward, but someone grabbed him from behind. "You bastard. Don't you dare lay a finger on them."

"What do you think?" the big man asked, his focus directed at the person restraining the general. "Would you like to sample something young and supple?"

A cancerous-sounding snort echoed around the room. "I'd love to."

General Hudson struggled to get free, but the person holding him didn't let go.

The huge man nodded. "After we're done with them, if they survive, I'm sure they'd fetch a fair price. There are markets for pretty girls and boys. Hell, I've heard they even have on-the-job training."

The general tried to lunge again, but again, someone kept him restrained.

"Now here's what's going to happen," Evan said. "You're going to march back to your little office. You're going to stand in front of the committee, and if they hand you your ass, you're going to thank them profusely. And then you'll scamper away with your tail tucked between your legs." He folded his hands in his lap. "You used to be somebody, but now you're nothing more than a political puppet. *My* puppet. And you'll do what you're told."

The treasonous military man snorted. "And what about Lincoln Grey?"

Evan smiled. "He's no longer your problem. Since you can't handle some simple contractor, I'll take care of him. For now, do as I say, then wait for further instructions."

I tried to make sense of all this information. What should I do with it? I couldn't trust anyone in the Pentagon; Evan and Hudson had said that others within the ranks had been in on the assassination. I couldn't even be sure White Raven hadn't infiltrated other levels of the government.

I took a deep breath. First things first—I had to get the facts straight. If I went out with a bullhorn and a script of accusations, this entire thing would become a witch hunt. Everyone would suspect everyone, and it would be chaos.

But I'd have to be quick and quiet since I'd have Evan and his goons on my trail. He'd said he was going to "handle" me. *Others have tried and failed, my friend.* While I dodged White Raven thugs, I'd spend every free minute digging out the truth. One week—tops—and I'd bury Evan, Hudson, and everyone else involved.

Shaking his head, the general huffed. "Fine. Whatever." The man holding him shoved him, and he stumbled toward the door.

"Oh, and General?"

He turned.

Evan smirked. "Don't forget what I said or else…" He pointed back into the room.

The other man—the one that had been restraining him, the one with the voice so raspy it sounded as though he'd done a couple rounds with throat cancer—stepped forward. Though his face remained hidden in shadow, the light flashed on a smirk-shaped scar running around the base of his throat.

The world went dark.

CHAPTER TWENTY-ONE

JEFF

I yanked the fob off my temple. My ragged breath came out in gasps and rasps, as if someone had slipped a garrote around my throat.

Tamara put a hand on my shoulder. "Jeff! Jeff, are you alright?"

Calvin, as pale as a morgue sheet, fell into a chair.

I shook my head as my mind spun. "No, I don't think I am."

It felt as though I'd swallowed a bag of sand. The implications of that one memory, if it proved true... I scanned through the other titles.

Tamara watched as I worked. "I don't understand. What happened? Why did it just end, and who were those guys?"

"Hold on." Not bothering with the fob this time, I chose a file from further down the list. The holodisplay came to life. The sound of a vehicle crunching over gravel echoed through the lab.

On the imager, a sliver of sunlight slipped past the edge of a trunk lid, slicing through the small chamber of darkness beneath. Brakes squeaked as the car stopped. The hatch opened, and two thugs stared down. Lincoln's feet shot out of the back of the car, grabbed one of the goons around the neck, and slammed his face into the edge of the trunk.

Calvin's eyes lingered on the display, and he shook his head. "No. That's not possible."

I stopped the playback and started another. A tropical storm of water splashed over the imager. When it cleared, I paused the video. We all stared at the display, and Jesper's snarling face stared back.

My body started to shake so hard I had to hold onto the desk to keep from falling over. I looked at Tamara. I didn't even know where to start. "It's not a game."

She frowned. "What do you mean?"

I took a long breath and wiped my brow. "*Treason*. I helped write the storyboard for it. Well, I thought I did anyway. We created Sandy, a genetically enhanced contractor who worked for the government. We made up the man named Jesper who captures and then tries to break him. All of that. Only, these," I pointed at the display, "are Lincoln's *real* memories. He really is that guy."

She shook her head. "Are you sure there wasn't just some mix up in the processing? You said it's really complicated. Is there a way to verify?"

The tiniest flame of hope lit in my soul. Maybe something *had* happened during the conversion process. It didn't seem out of the realm of probabilities. I closed the file and opened the last one on the list.

"Come on! Come get it!" blared from the speaker.

My heart sank, and the small light of hope extinguished just as surely as Lincoln's life would end, bloody and gruesome. I'd heard Sandy say those words a million times as I ran through the game. The midnight black robot panther chuffed a laugh, sending a shiver running down my spine. It snarled, and its eyes grew bright as it crouched.

Tamara sucked in a sharp breath. "That's the cat from your game." She screamed and almost fell over the chair as the creature jumped straight toward us.

As it landed, it raked its claws over the doomed man's body. Blood gushed, and the beast bellowed triumphantly. It opened its mouth. Razor sharp teeth flashed and glinted in the moonlight for a heartbeat before it clamped its jaws around Lincoln's throat.

I resisted grabbing my own throat. While I'd felt the beast kill me a hundred times when I'd run through *Treason's* tracks, knowing that Lincoln really had been kidnapped, tortured, and murdered like this made my soul weep.

Who had done this? And why, for God's sake? Why?

Tamara gagged. "Jeff, oh my god. That's awful. Why are we watching this?"

While I wanted nothing more than to shut the video off and end the horror, I forced myself to let it roll. I took a long breath, trying to keep my knees steady and my heart from breaking. "Hold on. In the game, this is where we end it."

She furrowed her brow. "But it says there's still two minutes of footage left."

My eyes dropped to the status bar. "Exactly."

Suddenly, the lights came on and someone yelled, "Cut." The shuffling of leaves and underbrush grew louder, and a man said, "Aus." As the creature released Lincoln's neck, blood dripped from its muzzle.

The same man said, "Heir." The panther looked up and padded away. Lincoln gurgled and gasped as he stared into the trees above him.

"It sounds like he's blowing bubbles," Tamara said.

Calvin's complexion had gone from white to green. "He's choking. On his own blood."

A man's face appeared in the display.

"Rick!" Calvin said.

A second face joined him.

"Who's that?" Tamara asked.

I frowned. "I know that blue hair, but I can't quite place the name."

"That's Stephen," Calvin said, pointing. "He's the brain surgeon that Rick stole away from the hospital. But where's the third person?"

Tamara looked at him. "What third person?"

Calvin rubbed his neck. "Rick always says that three is the perfect working unit. He's got this whole long speech about it."

Another person joined the group leering down at Lincoln, and the three of us gasped in unison.

In the holodisplay, Evan's ugly, Clydesdale face grinned. "Hello, 'Sandy.' I'll be assisting these gentlemen in the extraction process today. Don't worry, this will be over soon."

Rick held a drill above Lincoln's face. He pulled the trigger a couple of times, revving the motor, and smiled.

Horrific bubbling and gasping filled the room. My heart felt as if it would explode out of my chest, and my stomach tried to reject the shake I'd had for lunch that afternoon. I swallowed down my bile as Rick pressed the button again.

The tool disappeared off the edge of the display. As the grinding of bone and the churn of gears filled the lab, Lincoln began screaming. He gurgled and sputtered in earnest while he tried to move his arms to ward off his assailant, but the other two men held him down.

Tamara started to cry. "Stop it. Just turn it off."

I stopped the video and wiped the sweat from my face. I looked over just in time to see Calvin vomit into the trash can. After he finished, I handed him a bottle of water. He took a long swallow and then sat back on the desk, his pallid, sickened expression reflecting the anguish I felt.

"Oh my gawd," I said. "So many things to process. Rick and this horse guy murdered Lincoln for his memories. But why torture him?"

Tamara swallowed. "Isn't it obvious?"

Calvin and I stared at her.

She took a long breath. "I don't know about the rest of it, but that part makes sense."

I glanced at Calvin, who shook his head.

"I don't see the connection," I said.

Tamara stepped up to the holodisplay and closed the video. She listed the contents of the folder and pointed. "Remember how we discussed there being so many Lincoln files? You said that the most poignant, emotionally-tied memories are the ones that can be read best by Rick's little probes."

I nodded, her point becoming clear. "Right. He also said that people who suffer through traumatic events might even remember everything. I think he used prisoners of war as an example. He created this whole scene so he could get Lincoln to remember as much as possible. But why? We didn't need it for the game. We had more than enough material."

Calvin rubbed the back of his neck. "It wasn't for us. We were just his tools, or his cover, or something. You saw the documents Lincoln had access to. Rick, or the Clydesdale, or someone wanted that information." He stood. "Instead of trying to hack into the Pentagon and risk getting caught, they simply kidnapped Lincoln and used our stage to steal his memories."

Tamara's eyes suddenly got huge, and she turned back to the display. Changing out of Lincoln's folder, she listed the names in the parent directory. Moving up one level, she scanned the list of countries, chose one, and listed its contents too.

She dropped her hands from the keyboard, and her shoulders slumped as she slowly turned around. "Jeff. These names. I know them."

I frowned. "How?"

She took a long breath. "From the news."

Suddenly it clicked. I remembered where I'd heard Lincoln's name before. "These are the people that have gone missing."

Tamara nodded.

Calvin shook his head. "No. No, that's not possible."

A huge tear ran down Tamara's cheek. "They've been kidnapping and murdering people to steal their memories."

"What are we going to do?" Calvin asked.

I stepped up next to Tamara and took the keyboard. "The world needs to know that there's a group called White Raven and that this Evan guy is not only responsible for killing the president but for all the kidnappings. They also need to know about Hudson and how the Pentagon has been infiltrated. In the recording, Lincoln hadn't told anyone because he didn't know who he could trust. Well, I have no such misgivings."

Pounding away on the keyboard, I pulled up several of Lincoln's memory files. Placing start and stop markers in each, I began configuring a conversion program.

"What are you doing?" Tamara asked.

"I'm converting some of Lincoln's memories to standard holo format," I said. "Not everything, just some of the fragments we've viewed. The results will be uploaded to a public server. The world has to know what they're facing and who the real enemy is."

As I continued to type, Calvin glanced at me. "But you've purposely limited the memory and allocated very little system resources. If you don't give it more, the conversion will take a week."

I nodded. "I know. But if it's a huge drain on the server, the system monitor may detect it and either alert Rick or shut it down automatically. I gave it its own thread pool, so it should remain incognito. As long as it runs quietly in the background, they probably won't notice it until it's too late."

"Good plan," he replied.

I closed that window and opened a new one. "Now that that's done, I'm going to pull the plug on *Treason*. I don't know what else Rick's been up to, but I'm not going to let it happen."

I looked over at my fiancée. "For the record. I will *never* use the memories of someone treated like that. Never. In fact, I can never, in good conscience, use anyone's memories again."

She nodded slowly but didn't reply.

Calvin came up beside me and checked his DigiSleeve. "There's no time to cancel the release. Even if you try, the system won't let you because it's too far along."

Continuing to pound away on the keys, I remained focused.

He cocked his head. "You're not on the game node; you're in the main server. What are you doing?" He paused. "Oh, smart. You're going to delete the system kernel, aren't you?"

"There can't be a game release if there's no game server to run it," I said.

He nodded. "Yep, that'll stop it alright."

Suddenly the screen went blank and dread filled my gut.

Tamara turned to me. "Did you do it? Did you delete the kernel thingy?"

Calvin and I looked at each other. I shook my head. "No. Someone cut off my access before I could. I've been locked out of the system."

"Well, of course we locked you out. We have a game release this morning. We mustn't disappoint the nerds dying to escape reality." The loathsome voice came from over my shoulder.

The three of us turned around.

Rick tsked. "We can't delay. That would be very bad for the bottom line."

Rage flooded my veins, driving the nausea from my system. "You bastard."

Without pausing to think, I bent at the waist and charged, driving my shoulder into his stomach. He let out a whoosh of air and fell over backwards. I used my body weight to pin him down and pulled my fist back, ready to drive it into his face.

Tamara screamed. "Jeff, look out!"

Someone caught my arm and yanked me up by the back of the shirt. Jesper, his nasty face covered in burn scars, smirked in satisfaction as his block-sized fist came around and connected with my nose.

CHAPTER TWENTY-TWO

JEFF

Water so cold it must have come from a glacier cascaded down my head, splashed over my shoulders, and ran down my back. I awoke to a pounding headache and the taste of blood in my mouth. My world spun like a lunatic's merry-go-round, and my stomach churned. I closed my eyes and tried to shake off the dizziness.

My shoulders throbbed, and when I tried to pull my hands from behind my back, they jerked short, tied together by a rough rope. The harder I pulled, the more the bindings dug into my skin.

As I wiggled trying to get free, my fingers brushed up against the back of my jeans and plastic crinkled. At first, I couldn't recall what I'd stuffed back there, but then the fog cleared enough for me to think.

"Welcome back, beautiful." I didn't need to look up to see who mocked me. I'd heard that raspy baritone a thousand times when I ran through the tracks of *Treason*.

I slowly opened my eyes. My pupils burned as they grew accustomed to the dim light. The huge grimy, concrete room. The muted sun filtering in through filthy windows. The dank, musty smell. I knew it all.

I swallowed, trying to wet my parched throat. "Where's Tamara? Where's Calvin?"

Jesper got in front of me. "Awwww, do you miss your ménage à trois? It's so touching the way your lovers bring out the passion in you, beautiful."

Staring into his nasty face, I winced. "Man, I thought you were ugly in the game, but in real, you make a gargoyle look like a prom queen."

He backhanded my face.

My world reeled and spun. My unstable stomach started to churn, and the pressure in my gut shoved itself into my throat. I slipped the small bag from my back pocket, using my gagging and retching to cover the crinkle of plastic.

My abdomen spasmed, and instead of trying to relax my body, I squeezed every muscle in my torso. I aimed my projectile vomiting toward the big man, who skittered back to avoid the spray. Evidently, even Jesper had limits.

At the same time, I emptied the contents of the small bag. Wracking heaves pounded my body, covering the sound of the pinhead-sized scatter cameras bouncing across the concrete floor. My stomach muscles ached with convulsions until, at last, my heaving subsided.

He smirked. "You're a weak little thing. Pathetic. Just pathetic." He stepped around and behind me, tipped the chair back onto its hind legs, and dragged me away from the mess.

"Afraid to get your shiny shoes dirty, Jesper? If you weren't such a lowlife, I'd say you were trying to make your mommy proud." I chuckled. "What am I saying? Your mommy probably took one look at your hideousness and tossed you into a dumpster."

He sneered as he yanked back his fist to hit me in the face again. I couldn't fathom what had made me provoke the monster. Here I sat, bound and helpless in the middle of an abandoned warehouse, about to be beaten and tortured, and doomed to die.

I should have been terrified. But all I could feel was irritation and animosity. The huge brute didn't scare me. He *annoyed* me.

My irrational thoughts and feelings echoed the sentiments I'd had back in the interrogation room with Detective Mires. Just like with Jesper, I'd threatened, poked, and prodded the policeman who'd wanted nothing more than to send me to prison.

In the car, Tamara had asked if she even knew me anymore. I began to wonder that myself.

Just as his fist began its arc toward my face, a voice from across the room stopped him.

"Hold on, Jesper. Give the man a minute to breathe. There'll be time enough for that."

I looked up, staring deep into the shadows.

A short, thick-chested man with graying hair stepped forward into the dingy light. "Hello, Jeff."

I shouldn't have been surprised. Everything that had happened had all centered on this man and his treachery. "Rick? What the hell?" My voice barely above a whisper.

He nodded to Jesper. "Give the man a drink."

Jesper lowered his fist. He pulled an old dented canteen from his belt and shoved it against my lips. He didn't wait until I opened my mouth before he started pouring. Most of the contents dribbled onto my lap, not that it mattered since my clothes were sodden from his earlier dousing. I did manage to catch a few sips before he yanked it away.

Rick shrugged. "Sorry about the nausea. Like most of the patients we deal with, the meds we have available are a little…expired." He smirked at his own joke.

I shivered, though not just from the wet, freezing clothes but from a chill that radiated deep in my heart. "Meds? What meds?"

"You've been on some heavy-duty tranquilizers for," he checked his DigiSleeve, "about three days now."

My breath caught. "The game…"

"Good news!" he said, giving me his mock smile. "It went live just as planned. I've been checking the rankings, and it's number one. Off the charts sales. Congratulations."

I glared at him. "I'm sure that it fulfills some awful plan of yours." I took a long breath. "Where's Tamara and Calvin?"

"All in good time. Please, just be patient."

In this situation, old Jeff might have succumbed to panic. But, if I gave in and let fear overwhelm me, I'd be no good to them or myself. I needed to stop questioning myself and who I'd become. I needed to survive to win.

I needed to play the game.

Shoving down the mental images of my fiancée's and friend's mangled bodies, I focused on my anger. My hate. My rage. Those would carry me through. "I don't understand any of this."

The scientist shook his head. "You don't? Surely that can't be. After all, this was your creation."

My world started spinning again as another wave of dizziness struck. My teeth chattered, and I took several long deep breaths and things slowly righted themselves. "I *thought* this was my creation. All of this." I looked around the cavernous space. "Sandy, the panther, and especially him." I nodded toward Jesper. "It was all supposed to be fictional."

Jesper stuck his scarred face in mine. "Want me to show you how real I am?" Spittle flew from his cracked lips, and his alcohol-laden breath washed over me as hot and toxic as Napalm.

"Let him be," Rick said.

The giant snorted like a bull and moved a few feet away.

"Rick, I don't understand. How did you… How could this have…" I shook my head, unsure of a way to even properly formulate the question.

Rick shrugged. "You do recall that I asked you to allow one of my people to be on the storyboard team?"

I had a vague recollection of this conversation. "I think you said it was to help align the game with the donor's memories." At the time, it had seemed logical, but I should have paid more attention. I should have paid more attention to a lot of things. "Only they did a lot more than *help*, didn't they?"

"Let's just say that Stephen is a wizard at manipulating both the hardware and the software of the human brain," he said. "And, let's be honest, a three-year-old could run mental laps around your storyboard drama queens."

When Rick moved closer, his sour breath washed over me like a sewage tsunami. "I kept waiting for you to put the pieces together. All those times you played the game, what were you at? Twenty times the legal limit? Fifty? I kept thinking that at any minute you'd realize that there's no way to fabricate things so…authentically, without them actually being authentic."

He nodded at Jesper. "We had a plan in place when and if that happened. But, like the addict you are, you just kept on playing and being blind to reality."

I stared back into his smug expression. "Yes, of course I knew that some of the imagery was real. We had a film crew that recorded the woods and the panther. It made things so much simpler. But Lincoln… I thought you just used his memories to enhance the story. That's what you said. But then…"

Rick turned and ambled across the room.

I took a deep breath, grateful to be out of the choking fumes of his halitosis.

He rolled a small, portable cart up next to me. "But then you saw his final memory file."

The image of the men standing over Lincoln and the echoes of the drill sent a shiver down my spine. "Yes. Why did you do that to him? You didn't even have the mercy to let him die first. You took his memories while he was still alive. That was disgusting."

"The ends justify the means," he said cryptically.

"What ends? What are you trying to accomplish? You and your terrorist goons have already murdered the president and millions of other people. What else could you possibly want, and what has any of this got to do with my company?"

Rick loomed over me. "Are you serious? Do you really not see? Could you possibly be that naïve?"

That was the second time someone had called me naïve. Tamara had been the first, back on the police station steps. Maybe I really was completely, utterly oblivious to the world around me.

When I didn't answer, a slow smile creased the corners of his lips. "You really don't know, do you?"

He turned and locked the wheels of the cart, then sat on the edge of it as though he hadn't kidnapped his boss and coworkers or been partially responsible for the genocide of an entire country. He pulled out his arc lighter, flicked it to life, and began to weave it in between his fingers. Just the two of us shooting the breeze on a Sunday afternoon while his feet dangled like a child's and he absently played with an electric flame.

Cognizant of the scatter camera in my pocket and the ones I'd dumped on the floor, I shook my head. "Why don't you tell me?"

He glanced at Jesper. "I suppose we have a few minutes. Besides," he shrugged, "I guess he won't be around to tell anyone anyway."

The huge man chuckled and rested his hands on his thick belt.

"See," Rick began, "the little bit you know about is just the beginning. There's a much larger plan in place, and *you* provided the solution to a problem we'd been trying to figure out for years. In fact, I can honestly say that none of what we're about to accomplish could have been done without you."

"I know you love the sound of your own voice," I said, "but really, are you going to get down to it, or are you going to bore me to death with pointless yammering?"

He palmed the arc lighter and pointed. "Do you want to have a conversation, or should we just skip the 'boring' stuff and get to the part where you die?"

Taking a deep breath, I nodded. "Go ahead. Enlighten me."

His eyes appraised me before continuing. "First, you got Dencephalon for a song."

I started. "What? No. I *saved* your company. You were almost bankrupt because your investors pulled out." When he raised his eyebrows and smirked, I suddenly understood yet another way I'd been played for a fool. "Only, you didn't have investors who just pulled the plug because Dencephalon is only a front for something else."

He shrugged. "We needed you to believe that we were on the verge of losing everything. Otherwise, you might have taken longer to look around and kick the tires, so to speak. You may have started to wonder why you could afford a company that had trillions in infrastructure, so we helped you focus on your pathetic need to be the hero. You needed to save not just us but your own ass as well."

"But I checked your financials," I said, shaking my head. "You really did only have a few weeks of operating money left."

"We figured out how to pull memories from corpses," he replied. "How hard do you think it is for us to stage some paperwork? Also, how incredibly convenient that you and your little girlfriend—excuse me, fiancée—had just enough capital to buy us."

I closed my eyes for a few seconds, trying to settle my stomach back to a gentle rumble. Whatever they'd given me had done a number on my digestive system. "But there was no way for you to know that Ceos would forbid me from using Virtual Adventures' money or that I would go behind her back. You couldn't know that Tamara would help me."

Rick chuckled. "Actually, it was a pretty solid bet. As I mentioned, Stephen is a master at manipulating and *predicting* human behavior."

Something about the blue-haired son of a B had struck me as off from the instant I'd laid eyes on him. But I'd allowed my desire to build an empire bury my intuition about Dencephalon, about Rick, about all of it. "But why, for God's sake, did you do all of this?"

He extinguished the lighter, slipped it into his pocket, and folded his arms. "Like you, we too have a product. While it's amazing and brilliant and does exactly what we need, it does us no good sitting on some server in a warehouse. What we lacked was distribution. You wanted to add a few tear-jerker moments and some feelings to an otherwise uninspiring way to pass the day, so we paired up to create what you business people call 'synergy.'"

He leaned forward and tapped my chest. "I have to admit, I'm impressed. You created a delivery system that puts FedEx, UPS, and the Global Postal Service to shame."

The entire time we'd been partners, he'd been using me for some ulterior motive. But despite buckets of his self-aggrandizing, I still didn't know why. "What product? What are you delivering?"

He raised his hands in the air. "A better world."

I needed to keep him talking. To spill whatever plans I'd inadvertently helped him accomplish. But the man's riddles and vague answers had provided almost no new insights. "And how exactly are you going to do that? Through White Raven?"

He pointed at me. "Exactly."

"But what is the purpose of Raven?" I asked. "What do you want?"

"We," he said thoughtfully, "are giving the human race exactly what it deserves." For the first time since I'd met him, true passion fire blazed in his eyes. "And even though you don't know it, you helped create something bigger, better, and more meaningful than another useless gaming system. You helped birth Osiris."

I had no idea what he meant, and I didn't have the patience to try and unravel more of his nonsensical yammering. "Rick," I said, sighing, "if that's really your name, I don't know where you get your delusions, but let me give you a little reality check. Ceos said that she was going to shut the game down. Now that order may have gotten postponed a little because, ya know, you killed her. But I can guarantee that her drones are making it happen. Probably sooner rather than later. Whatever this plan is, whatever this 'Osiris' is, it's about to be put on hold. Permanently."

He snapped his fingers. "I forgot. You've been taking an extended cat nap and haven't heard the even better news."

Dread filled my stomach, exacerbating the nausea. "What better news?"

"Well," he said, "since you murdered Ceos—"

"I did no such thing," I snarled. "The police only have me as a suspect because I was one of the last people to see her alive. And, of course, you lied to them. If they knew the truth, you'd be behind bars right now."

He waved a hand. "The truth is nothing more than what we believe to be real. If the police and everyone else believes that I killed her, then it must be true. If, on the other hand, they have the evidence that makes them think that you did it, then that must be true. History was written by the victors who believed they knew the truth. It's called 'his story' for a reason. But we can leave such philosophical discussions for a later time. We need to get back to the topic at hand."

"After you murdered Ceos," he continued, "an emergency board meeting was convened to handle her many financial endeavors. They decided that they wanted to distance themselves from Virtual Adventures. In fact, they were planning on closing it down. Immediately."

I frowned. "Were?"

"Yep." He nodded. "But don't worry. I stopped them from destroying all of our hard work. All our…synergy."

My throat had gotten even drier. "How?"

"Well, it's a little funny if you think about it," he said, though no amusement lingered in his expression. "They were willing to sell me Adventures for pennies on the dollar, and I just happened to be in a position to purchase it."

I rolled my eyes. "Come on. Now I know you're just making shit up. The emergency board can't do anything unless every participating member is present. Every member includes me and Calvin. I don't know what you did with Cal, but since you locked me up, I haven't exactly been available to cast my vote."

He slowly shook his head. "Jeff, as per your own bylaws, anyone under criminal investigation who is not actively cooperating with the police forfeits their right to be on the board. You, by cutting your tracker band and fleeing the city, are now a fugitive and no longer eligible to empty the board's trash bins. Calvin's association—and suspected collaboration—with you, allowed the rest of us to act as your proxies. The board was so thrilled to unload that huge stain on their portfolio, they sold Ceos' shares to me for almost nothing. Because Calvin was unable to attend the meeting, he still retains his shares. But don't worry, he'll be dealt with soon enough."

I traced my fingers over my bare wrist. The bastards had cut off the tracker band, probably back at the office, and then carted me out into the middle of nothing where the police wouldn't be able to find me.

"Also," he continued, "you should know that as the controlling owner of Virtual Adventures, it's my civic duty to help the police wrap up their investigation. As such, I negotiated a deal to help them apprehend Ceos' killer by providing them with all the system logs."

Detective Mires had said that his cyber team had already begun to dig into VA's records because Rick had given him access.

I could not breathe. My throat felt as if someone had stuffed it full of cotton. Rage and hate flowed through my veins. I'd never loathed anyone, not even Ceos, as much as I loathed this man. "No doubt everything was changed to put the blame on me."

Rick shrugged. "I'm letting the police run their investigation. As a concerned citizen, I only want to see justice done. But," he scratched his chin, "I think that Detective Mires did say the evidence looked compelling."

I wanted to scream in frustration. "But why keep me alive? Why didn't you just frame me after I 'committed suicide' or had an 'accident?' Obviously you're not above murdering in cold blood. It would have been much simpler. What else could you possibly want from me?"

"I'm glad you asked." He hopped off the cart, pulled a mobile from his pocket, slid out the extension screen, and held it before me. The top of the form read *Sale of Stock Authorization*, beneath that sat several tightly scripted paragraphs, and under that a line waited for my digital signature.

"First," he said, "I need you to sell your shares of VA stock to an investor that has, shall we say, a personal interest in the company's well-being. Your asking price for forty-seven percent of the company is one US dollar."

I laughed in his face. "And why would I ever agree to something so preposterous?"

He gave the briefest of nods to Jesper who stepped around behind me. The big man lifted up the back of my shirt and pressed a small knife against the base of my spine.

Rick leaned in. His horrific breath, bouquet of rotting corpse, made my nose hairs curl. "Here's what's going to happen. I'm going to ask you to enter your authorization code and sign the sale. Every time you hesitate or refuse, Jesper is going to stick a blade between two of your vertebrae. He'll start at the bottom and work his way up."

He shook his head. "I just hope you agree before we get to the parts that interfere with your hand and arm movements."

I snarled. "You bastard, you know even if I do sign, it'll never stand up in court. It's not legal to force someone to sell under duress."

"That's a future problem for the lawyers," he said.

Jesper pressed the knife harder against my lower back.

I stared at my former business partner.

Rick narrowed his eyes. "So, what's it gonna be, Jeff? Are you going to sign, or do we start draining spinal fluid?"

I glared at the murderous asshole. I couldn't begin to fathom for what purpose White Raven wanted my shares of Virtual stock other than it had something to do with the distribution nonsense Rick had been yammering about. But even if I refused, they would just kill me and get it anyway from my estate.

Only through the law did I have a chance to stop them, and I could only do that if I survived. "I can't sign. You have me tied up."

His mock grin reappeared. "Don't worry. Even in these difficult circumstances, I can be accommodating." He pressed a button on the mobile. "There, you see? I put it in verbal mode to help you with your…limitations."

Huffing a long breath, I began reciting my authorization code. When I finished, the mobile thought for a moment. *Sale Complete* flashed across the screen.

Rick snapped the mobile shut. He fished out a dollar from his jeans, held the bill in front of my face, then stuffed it into the breast pocket of my shirt.

For a horrifying second, I wondered if he'd find the hidden scatter camera. But when he smiled and put his hands on his hips, I let out a silent sigh of relief.

"There," he said, "that completes the deal."

Jesper came around and stood in front of me, slipping the knife into the sheath on his belt. As he folded his arms, a smug smile tugged at his buffalo lips.

"I gave you what you wanted," I said. "Now, let me, Tamara, and Calvin go."

Rick waved a finger back and forth. "Not so fast. The sale of your company and the delivery system were trivial matters. You still have a very important part to play in all of this. Don't you see?"

"No," I said. "I don't see at all. What are you talking about?"

Rick cocked his head. "You don't?" He took a deep, exasperated breath. "Well, please tell me you've at least figured out that I'm the one who released the hacked fob and the extension that will negate that ridiculous VR restrictions bill you and Tamara just put through."

My breath caught in my throat. "Oh, you released it…because you wanted me to find it. You knew that I'd go way over the limit during my testing, then you'd do to me what you're doing to the rest of the world right now. But why?"

"Think on it for a moment."

My body trembled as the pieces began to fall into place. Lincoln's memories. "Mine and Lucas' ability to get into the bar and us knowing about the general."

He rolled his hand forward. "Keep going. You're almost there."

"Both of us played way beyond the legal limit. We knew things that we shouldn't have known. But how?" Then realization dawned. "Metadata. The game inserts more into our heads than just some random memories and feelings. That's what Lucas' warning meant."

He turned to Jesper. "The man is taking it to the fences." He pointed at me. "Right you are. You experienced what I call 'memory bleed.' Unfortunately, our brains are not segmented into water-tight compartments. So, when you cram one part full, it tends to bleed over into the others around it."

He knocked on my head. "Things got a little jostled around because some of the game memories intermingled with real ones. For instance, the general's name got mucked up, but for the most part, I think we got those bugs straightened out."

I glanced at the floor. "But, I only have a few random memories. Nothing significant. You and your terrorist group are probably hoping I can give you my country's nuclear launch codes or harm them in some way. Only, I don't know anything. Even if I were willing, I don't have the slightest idea how to cripple our government."

"You don't know what you know," he said.

I tried to glean meaning out of the nonsensical words but failed. "Rick, you already have all of Lincoln's, and a lot of other people's, memories. It makes no sense that you would go through the hassle of injecting all that stuff into my head."

"Lincoln, in his original form, was a bit…" he glanced at Jesper, "difficult to manage and completely unwilling to cooperate. So, we elected for an alternate option. It pays to be flexible, you know?"

"The system downloads Lincoln's memories into every player's head?" I said, thinking about all the subscriptions we'd sold since *Treason's* launch announcement. "Why would you need a million Lincoln Grey's? How could that possibly be of help to you?"

He chuckled. "As amusing as that would be, it doesn't work like that. We get to pick and choose what we download and into whom. Think of it as the ultimate player customization. We needed Lincoln first and because we're a little pressed for time, we thought you were the only choice we had. Except we got a bonus we hadn't expected when we released the hacked fob. We got a backup. A plan B. You know, just in case something went wrong."

"What are you talking about?"

"After your little demonstration, your buddy Lucas found it too." He shook his head sadly. "You're a virtual reality drunk, but that guy's a junkie."

I looked around. "Lucas? Where is he?"

Rick glanced over his shoulder. "Hey! Bring our guest his friend."

From the back of the room, a man grunted. A minute later, General Hudson marched out, carrying a sheet-wrapped bundle over his shoulder. He tossed it onto the floor in front of me. Smirking, he undid the tie-straps holding it closed.

I gasped. Lucas, or what remained of him, lay at my feet.

CHAPTER TWENTY-THREE

JEFF

I stared at the man on the floor. "Lucas!"

His arms lay bent at odd angles, bruises covered his face, and blood drenched his shirt. I searched for signs of life, but his chest didn't move and his eyes remained fixed and glassy. I glared at Rick. "You bastards. What did you do to him?"

"Mr. Sanborn decided he was incapable of cooperating with us," he said. "The general and I tried to reason with him. Jesper tried motivating him into seeing things our way, but clearly, he refused."

He walked over to the dead man and picked up something that had slid out of the sheet. Holding up Lucas' Sonic Boom, he frowned. After turning the odd-looking, unmarked device over in his hand, he glanced at Jesper, who also looked mystified. The general provided no new insights, so Rick set it on the lower shelf of the cart and turned back to me.

A dark river of pure hatred flowed through my heart. Lucas may have been a self-absorbed, introverted prick, but he'd never hurt anyone—well, not physically anyway. He trash-talked gaming companies until they lost millions, but he certainly didn't deserve to die. "What do you want, Rick? Obviously, you brought me here for something."

"See? That's what I like about you." He turned to General Hudson and then to Jesper. "Didn't I tell you he'd get right to the point? He's a just-the-facts sort of guy."

Neither the huge oaf nor the treasonous military man said anything.

Rick walked around to the front of the cart and unlocked the wheels. "You are going to finish what your friend Lucas wasn't able to get done."

"And what was that?" I asked, putting as much sarcasm into the words as possible.

Ignoring the derision in my voice, he continued. "See, the general and Mr. Grey were more than acquaintances; they were coworkers. And—"

"Hardly," I laughed. "The general and some giant-armed buffoon named Evan killed the president."

The scatter camera in my pocket couldn't see through the fabric of my shirt, but it could record sound. Since Jesper had practically dragged me to the opposite side of the room after I'd tried to puke on him, I didn't know if the cameras I'd dumped on the floor could capture images from the scene.

Even if these goons killed me, I wanted to supply the police as many verbal cues as possible. I might even be able to provoke the pompous idiots into admitting their own guilt. My lawyer future-spouse would be proud.

"General Hudson," I said, turning to him, "you are a roach. The country needs to know what you did and then hang your ass from the highest tree. Millions died because the blame was pinned on some backwater country we'd never even heard of before. We nuked them until there was nothing but ashes left, but the whole time, it was you."

The military man snarled. "Watch your mouth, son. You have no idea what you're talking about. Our nation is in the shitter, and I'm the only one trying to turn it around. Because of my sacrifices, you get to sleep warm and cozy at night. If you knew the things that I know, you'd never stop shaking."

I scoffed. "You can call it whatever you want, Hudson. Patriotism, or self-sacrifice, or whatever lets you justify your treason. You're supposed to be the protector of the country, but instead you turned out to be exactly what we needed to be protected from. You're a disgrace. Lincoln figured out what you'd been up to and was going to turn you in. He died doing what you'd been hired to do."

I turned to the rotund scientist. "Maybe you should reevaluate who you choose to work with, Rick." Then I shook my head. "What am I saying? You tortured then killed Lincoln in cold blood. Lucas is dead because of you. You helped this son of a bitch with the presidential assassination. The two of you are runts from the same nasty little litter of piglets, and if I get a chance, I'll take the bacon from your asses and fry it for breakfast."

A part of me marveled at my own hubris—at my inner-strength and willingness to focus on revealing to the world the true nature of these two pieces of trash, even at my own peril. I didn't know when exactly I'd gotten so brazen, but I didn't fight it. Didn't question it. I had little to no chance of making it out of this alive, but a little extra pain would be worth it if I could take a couple treasonous bastards down with me.

Besides, I rather enjoyed watching these guys lose their mess.

Rick stared at me, anger brewing in his eyes. "You sure are willing to throw a lot of accusations around but aren't willing to own up to your own sins." He shook his head. "So typical. Let me point to the plank in *your* eye."

"What are you talking about?" I asked. "I've never killed anyone."

He thumped my chest. "No, I suppose not directly. But for a few bucks, you didn't mind being the dealer for millions of junkies, like your friend Lucas here. Marriage rates down. Human interaction down. Depression rates through the roof. Don't you think it's ironic and a tad hypocritical that you are accusing us of killing people, but you're nothing but a cancer sucking out the life of anyone willing to plunk down a few bucks for a subscription."

I nodded slowly. "We all have our sins. Though I prefer capitalism and entrepreneurship while you favor murder, mayhem, and the destruction of society."

Rick stared at me for another heartbeat, then he smiled sardonically and patted me on the shoulder. "You're a lot bolder than I thought."

"And you are a lot more of a weasel than I thought," I replied.

He huffed a forced laugh and stood up straight. "Anyway, as you pointed out, Mr. Grey had grown suspicious of General Hudson's allegiances. The good general thought he'd had your *Treason* star on a short leash, but evidently not short enough. Despite Mr. Grey's lack of assistance, we were finally able to remove all traces of his report and the evidence he'd documented from the Homeland server. But imagine our surprise when we saw in his memories that he'd kept copies of both his report and his recording of a particularly sensitive conversation. If either of those were to get out, there could be serious lingering consequences."

I briefly wondered if they'd discovered my conversion program too. If and when it finished and this "sensitive" conversation became public…

Wouldn't they be surprised to have victory snatched away a week or so after they'd done their touchdown dance. "Lingering consequences? That's the understatement of the year."

He took a breath. Clearly I'd stretched his patience, and I'd happily continue to make it as thin as possible for as long as I could.

"You know the recording I'm talking about," he said. "Good. That's helpful. What we need you to do, that Mr. Sanborn was incapable of, is access Lincoln's personal drive at the Pentagon and delete the investigation files and the recording. It's simple really. A trivial task."

"So many things…" I began. "Let's pretend like I'm willing to help you. I'm not, but for argument's sake, let's say I am. What makes you think that I'll even be able to access the files? I'm a game designer, not some hacker."

He smiled. "For argument's sake? Sure. As impressive as they are, we don't need your computer skills. All that we need has already been downloaded into your head."

I glared at him. "Round and round we go. What exactly hitched along for the ride when I played? You've never even answered that most fundamental question."

"Basically," he said, "everything that Lincoln Grey was is now stored in your subconscious. Initially, we thought we'd only need to do a subset of his memories, but you played so much that we were able to download everything."

Could that be true? Could he have used the Virtual Adventures system to stick stuff into my brain without my knowledge? I looked up into his smug, satisfied face. He sure believed so.

If that huge list of files Tamara, Calvin, and I had been going through in the lab now lived someplace in my head, it was no wonder I'd been having hallucinations and other…incidents. "Your theory then, as you said earlier, is that I don't know what I know."

Rick nodded. "Still one of the smartest guys I've ever met. Not the smartest, but right up there."

"Okay," I said, "let's keep on with the charade and pretend that what you're saying is true. Let's say you can turn me into Lincoln and I can delete these files. What's my motivation? Obviously, no matter what I do, I'm going to wind up dead, wrapped in a sheet, and tossed in some ditch. So why would I cooperate and betray my country the way General Schmuck did?"

His patented playground-bully grin tugged up the corners of his lips. "I'm glad you asked. Jesper?"

The huge man disappeared into a side room. A minute later, he emerged with a bundle in his arms. Gagged, with her hands tied in front of her and her feet bound, Tamara wiggled and twisted, but Jesper barely seemed to notice her thrashing.

My heart began to hammer, and my guts filled with lead. Tamara. I'd found the gumption to sacrifice myself in order to take these guys down, but Tamara…

Even if it cost me everything, I had to find a way to save her.

He strolled across the room and dropped her into a chair. Pointing a callused finger in her face, he said, "Be a good girl and stay."

I breathed a sigh of relief as I took her in. She appeared frightened but otherwise unharmed. A brief flare of hope lit up in me. Maybe they'd missed her tracker band? Perhaps Detective Mires and his posse would be here any moment?

The bindings mostly covered her wrists, but because of the rope, I couldn't tell one way or the other. Then I remembered that, according to my captors, we'd been gone for three days. Since the police hadn't already busted up this party, Rick's goons must have found it.

"Let her go," I said. "She doesn't have anything to do with this."

He chuckled. "I don't care if she's the Pope. She's part of my leverage. For you, probably the most important part."

"No." I shook my head. "No, you can't do anything to her. Do whatever you want with me, but leave her alone."

Rick put his hands on either arm of my chair and stared into my face. "That's completely up to you. Do as I say, and maybe we'll drug her back up and drop her off on your front porch. Don't and...well, let's just say that my friend knows about a thousand ways to make your fiancée long for death. He can get especially creative with women."

Before I had a chance to stop and consider the consequences, I rocked forward, my forehead connecting with the killer's nose. Unfortunately, my position in the chair, and my weakness from having been drugged up for several days, prevented me from hitting him hard enough to shove a sliver of bone into his brain.

Mystified by my own actions and this sudden discovery of the heretofore-unknown ability to strike, I was probably even more surprised than Rick. More of the "memory bleed" the madman had boasted about?

Rick stumbled back, glaring at me while holding his nose. It gave me a bit of satisfaction to see a drop of blood slip between his fingers.

He glanced at Jesper and nodded.

The beast strolled over to Tamara and punched her in the face.

She screamed as the big man grabbed her by the chin and put one hand on top of her head. He only needed to twist, and he'd rip her head clean off her neck.

Tears pricked her huge, round eyes, and she sobbed through the gag.

"No!" I shouted. "Don't."

My heart crumbled at the thought of anything happening to her. I wished I could take it back. All of it. Go back to the day I met Rick and got us involved in any of this. I'd undo everything.

But there are no takebacks. No do-overs. While it had been Rick that had lit the match, I'd laid the kindling and poured the kerosene. Me.

Tamara would most likely die because of my actions. My selfishness. I'd wanted to make my company great, and I'd thought I understood the price.

I had been wrong.

I looked at her. "I'm so sorry, honey."

Rick stepped between us. "You do anything else and she dies. You so much as sneeze and Jesper will yank off her head and set it in your lap. Is that clear?"

I narrowed my eyes, wishing with every fiber in me that he would just keel over and die. Finally, I nodded. "Fine."

The madman appraised me for several heartbeats before taking a long breath. "In spite of the somewhat strenuous circumstances, I think we can still work together."

He set a mobile on the top shelf of the cart, then held up one of the golden fobs we'd used in the demonstration about a million years ago. "It's poetic that we'll use this, don't you think? Granted, I'm not going to make it fly or anything, but we can still put on a good show."

I watched the murdering psychopath as he twirled the golden trinket. My mind raced as I tried to come up with some way out of this mess. "What are you going to do?"

"It's time for you to become Lincoln Grey," he said. "All of his memories are in your head. You may not know it, but they're all there. We just need to coax them out."

I needed to keep him talking. The longer he blathered, the more time I had to think. "I see. And what exactly does this do?"

"We don't have time to go into the technical aspects of how it works," he said, "but the long and short of it is that it wipes out your memories and replaces them with the ones we downloaded into your brain. All in all, it's a pretty simple concept."

I shook my head. "You can't. There's just no way it works like that."

He smirked. "Actually, I can, and it does. If you think that you've got a soul or that God will protect you, then you're deluding yourself. We aren't anything except the sum of our experiences and a bit of biology. Of course, you won't entirely be Lincoln. Not even taking his memories while he was alive would give us enough to do that. You'll be a shell of the man, but you'll get the essence of him."

He rolled the cart in front of me.

Terror seeped into my bones. Dying didn't scare me, losing myself didn't scare me, but what would they do to Tamara after they'd gotten their way and none of me remained to protect her?

I needed to fight as long as I could.

When Rick reached over to put the fob against my temple, I leaned as far from him as possible. He tried to hold my head with one hand, but I turned and bit his wrist.

He yanked his hand back. "Ouch! Damn it. This is going to happen, so you may as well make it easier on yourself."

When he moved to connect the fob again, I tried to bite him again. Rick barely got his fingers out of the way as my teeth snapped together. He called over his shoulder. "Come help me with this."

Jesper still had his hands on Tamara's chin and forehead. "What about her?"

"Forget about her and get over here and help me with him," he growled. "She's not going anywhere."

The huge man released my fiancée and came around behind me. He grabbed my head in his huge tennis racket-sized hands, holding me as Rick clicked the fob to my temple. It snicked snuggly into place, and for a brief instant, I saw the repulsive device through Tamara's eyes.

Millions of people had given themselves up for a little while to live another life. To be someone else. Until this instant, I'd never seen the true vulgarity of what I'd created. No wonder Tamara had fought it so vehemently. Unfortunately, my new insight came far too late.

"You bastard. You'll never get away with this," I snarled.

Rick chuckled. "Just so you're aware, we underestimated Lincoln the first time around and he damn near blew Jesper up. I've disabled the feedback loop he overloaded, so don't even try."

He paused and laughed again. "Why am I telling you this? In a minute, you're not going to remember anything."

He had me. Tamara and I locked eyes and I saw her pain. Saw her anguish. I had to save her. But how?

Jesper shoved my head hard as he let go.

My gaze passed the second shelf of the cart, and suddenly my heart gave a tremendous, hopeful thump. I had no way to know if it was even possible, but I needed to deliver a message to Lincoln. No other options remained.

He could save her.

I focused deep within myself, associating the shelf with my most emotional memory—connecting the two.

The killer turned back to me. "Goodbye, Jeff. It's been a pleasure."

I looked at my fiancée one last time. "I love you, Tamara. I always will."

A large tear rolled down her cheek. While the gag prevented her from saying anything, I could see the love, affection, and tenderness in her eyes. I'd disappointed her a hundred times over the years; we'd fought and disagreed. But the root of "us," the fundamental thing that had made us "us" had always been respect, friendship, and love.

No matter how they hurt me or tortured me, or even if he wiped my mind, Rick could never take that away. He could never take away the life we'd experienced or the bonds we'd created.

Even if Jeff Braxton no longer resided in this body, my heart and soul would always belong to her.

"Touching," Rick said as he hit a key on the mobile.

My world went black.

CHAPTER TWENTY-FOUR

LINCOLN

The universe spun in a dizzying kaleidoscope of images, memories, and sensations. Peddling my new bike the day I turned twelve. My heart hammering in my throat as a car sped out of a side street and came within a few inches of ending my young life. Me lifting Melody's veil and kissing my new wife. The difficult birth of our daughter, and a few years later, the births of our gen-mod twin boys. My years in the military fighting the war. My retirement as a soldier, which led to the job at the security firm that led to the one at the Pentagon.

The black panther stalking me through the trees. My death...

Blurry images and thoughts burbled through my mind in a frantic array of colors and flashing scenes. Disorientation whirled my mental cosmos as if someone had dumped the drawers of my mental filing cabinet out onto the floor.

The index cards of my life swirled around in an agitated vortex of confusion.

I took a deep breath and focused on calming my frazzled nerves. Separating my body from my mind, I kept the two affixed to one another through the thinnest of ribbons. My heartbeat slowed. My nerves settled as the last few months of my life started regaining their order.

While my mind sorted itself out, I noticed something odd about my body. Something off. Out of kilter.

But the jumbled mess in my head, rattling around like the Marley Brothers in search of Ebenezer Scrooge, made understanding those differences impossible. Perhaps once things settled down, I could focus and figure out what had happened.

Inhaling musty, dank air, I opened my eyes. Back. Somehow, I'd come back to the cement room. Back to the place of pain. Back to the place where my brother had died. Back to the place where the huge man had almost broken me.

Back again.

I looked around. The giant lug with the raspy voice and scar on his throat watched me. The mental list, *Things that Annoy Jesper*, floated through my mind like a toy boat on a cloudy tub of bubbles.

General Hudson, the traitorous son of a bitch, watched me too. Next to him, an oddly familiar, short stocky man peered at me like an unusual and interesting species of insect.

I looked at the lot. "Oh, an asshole convention and me with no toilet paper." My voice sounded foreign to my ears.

I forced myself to focus. Forced myself to wade out of a mental fog so thick it would have made Scotland jealous.

The newcomer folded his arms. "Who are you?"

I stared at him. "I know who the freak I am, but what I can't figure out is how I know you."

General Hudson pushed past him. "Come on, we don't have time for this nonsense."

The familiar man touched the general's shoulder. "Patience. It will take a little while for his mind to re-order things. If we try and rush the process, we could ruin everything."

I nodded. "Yeah. What he said."

The newcomer turned and looked into my eyes as though searching for the Ark of the Covenant. "My name's Rick."

Thoughts swirled and eddied around my head, then an image formed in my mind. I gasped. "You. Now I know how I know you. You drilled into my skull."

He pursed his lips. "We had to perform a procedure on you. Unfortunately, I was forced to act quickly."

Something about his words rang false, but I couldn't wrap my flitting, skipping mind around it. Across the room, a bound and gagged woman watched us with huge dark eyes.

"Who's that?" I asked.

Rick glanced back. "Don't worry about her; she's only here to observe."

Her terrified face registered in my heart. Love for her bubbled up from deep within me though I couldn't recall her name. Images of us kissing, me asking her to marry me, and us making love skimmed through my head. But none of those memories made any sense.

Other than Melody, I'd never proposed to anyone. I'd never dated anyone that even remotely looked like this poor woman. "She's observing? Looks like she's not exactly here voluntarily."

Rick shifted to the side, breaking our eye contact. "I know that you're a little confused right now, and that's perfectly normal. You've suffered a severe trauma. What you need to do is rest. I want you to close your eyes for a few minutes. Can you do that?"

Though part of me hated him for the "procedure" he'd done to me, another part grabbed onto the life raft of his words, desperate for any salvation from the mental stormy sea. I nodded and did as he'd instructed.

As voices around me talked in muted tones, I sensed the pieces of my life beginning to order themselves. They fell neatly into place, refilling my mental filing cabinet.

An unknown amount of time later, someone spoke into my ear. "Time to wake up."

I opened my eyes and found myself staring into Rick's face.

He removed a glimmering, gold-colored fob from my temple and replaced it with a standard GovLink model. "General Hudson is going to guide you through what you need to do next."

The general stepped in front of me. "I'm going to link you to the Pentagon's server. Once you're connected, log on to your personal account. From there, I'll guide you to some files that must be deleted. This is a matter of national security, son."

My eyes drifted from the general to Rick. Anger suddenly flared in my heart. This man had killed me. Drilled into my head and done something awful. I specifically recalled dying, so it made no sense how I could be remembering any of this.

But the sudden rage pumping through my veins didn't care. *National security*. The general had betrayed our country and had teamed up with a murdering terrorist organization. Somehow, I doubted his intentions were anything but nefarious.

The general snapped his fingers in my face. "Right here. Pay attention."

I glanced back to the woman. Tamara. Her name was Tamara. Love for her and a memory of me asking her to marry me bubbled to the surface of my mind again, followed immediately by another thought. At first it seemed like just another random image from the primordial soup in my head until my gaze dropped to the second shelf of the small cart.

Something about it rang deep in my heart. *But what?* The thought came and went, but I couldn't immediately grasp it. I looked at the bound girl, the cart, the girl, and the cart once more, and then it clicked.

Though I had no idea where it had originated from, I had a plan that might just get us out of this fix.

General Hudson pointed at Tamara. "Jesper, I think our friend needs a little motivation. Can you assist with that?"

The huge man smirked and strolled over to the bound woman, grabbing her head in his ginormous hands. He'd done this before... Someone had told me he would rip off her head and put it in my lap if I didn't cooperate.

Damn, I wish I could make sense of this mess in my brain.

The general grabbed my cheeks and narrowed his eyes. "Now, unless you feel like explaining to her family why her corpse has no head, I suggest you cooperate."

I needed the general to believe I'd do what he wanted. Glaring at the military man, I said, "Fine. Just don't hurt her."

He shoved my face, stood, turned to the cart, and clicked a few buttons on the mobile lying on the top shelf. A holodisplay flared to life above it. The general folded his arms and leered at me. "Go ahead, but don't try anything. I'll be monitoring."

I started to focus on the fob, but on a hunch, I instead directed my attention to the mobile. "Mirror me," I commanded.

The display instantly morphed, showing a strange man bound to a chair. Unfamiliar wide gray eyes stared back at me from a filthy, battered, and bruised face.

At first, the image confused me. The camera must have been redirecting a feed from somewhere else. But when I moved, the holographic man moved too.

My pulse quickened as I glanced down. The small scar just above my wrist—the one I'd had since my tenth birthday when my hand had gotten slammed in the car door—had disappeared. In its place lay a smattering of freckles over smooth, unblemished skin.

Except, I didn't have freckles. Not a single one.

I looked back up at the man in the holodisplay, refusing to believe the vision before me. Yet I could not deny the truth of what I was seeing.

As the implications of the facts dawned, my heart started hammering, and my throat sealed itself off. I fruitlessly yanked on my bindings while wheezing in air that no longer seemed to contain oxygen. Blackness encroached as I suffocated.

The general cursed. "He's going to send himself into shock."

"I told you not to rush him," Rick snapped. He stepped around the general and squatted down in front of me. "Calm down. Follow me."

He took a long deep breath in, then let it out slowly.

At first, the panic threatened to overcome me, but I stared at him, concentrating and matching his pace. The looming terror slowly abated, replaced by sorrow and loss.

He spoke gently. "The procedure we had to do was… drastic, I admit. But it was the only way to save you."

"What…what did you do to me?" I asked.

He stared into my eyes. Quiet and soothing, he said, "We transplanted the contents of your mind into another body."

I shook my head. "How? What body?"

He gripped the back of my neck gently. In some other universe, I registered that his breath would kill small woodland animals, but that hardly mattered at the moment.

He dropped his voice even more, as if sharing a secret. "The procedure is incredibly complicated. We can discuss that later, but the man's name was Jeff Braxton. He had an accident and was brain-dead. I know it's a lot to take in, but we saved you."

Something deep inside cried out that he was lying, that I couldn't trust him, but he continued before I had a chance to think it through.

"Now," he said in his smooth, confidential voice, "I need you to help the general. A lot of lives, including the life of the woman in this room, depend on you concentrating and getting the job done. I know you can do it."

I swallowed, glanced at Tamara, then back at Rick and gave the briefest of nods. The plan. Focus on the plan.

He patted my shoulder, stood, and stepped back.

The general glared at me, but I ignored him as I took another long breath and turned my focus inward, mentally activating the fob and beginning the connection sequence. The concrete room and all its occupants turned underwater blurry as the status from the Pentagon server overlaid it.

Establishing a connection... Connection complete. Authorizing...

A gentle vibration rattled through my skull as the fob retrieved something from my memories.

The general set a corpse's hand—a bloody stump cut off at the wrist—onto a mobile screen. Though it probably should have horrified me, given the magnitude of everything that had happened in the last few minutes, the dead flesh barely blipped my emotion radar.

The mobile scanned the palm and fingerprints, then prompted for a security code. The general tossed the hand aside and typed something on the small screen.

Access granted.

General Hudson turned back to me. "Now connect to Lincoln's personal server."

I requested access.

Connecting... Authenticating... Access Granted.

"Now find the investigation files," he instructed me.

I began moving through the directory structure.

"There," he said. "The files should be in that folder."

The *GH Investigation* directory contained a vaguely familiar series of reports and documents.

What are these? Obviously, I put them here, but what for? Irritation flared as I reached for memories that hadn't yet reasserted themselves.

"Delete them," he said.

At first, I hesitated, but an image of Tamara's headless corpse floated through my mind, so I did as he'd told me.

"Okay, now there's a video sub-directory."

I moved to that folder. It contained only a single file.

General Hudson Collaboration with Evan White of the Terrorist Cell White Raven.

"Good. Now, delete it," he instructed me.

Shit. Shit. Shit.

So that was what this was about. I must have figured out what he'd been doing and started putting together a formal investigation. He was having me destroy evidence. If I deleted this file too, he'd get away with murdering the president, collaborating with terrorists, and Lord only knew what else. But if I didn't, he'd kill Tamara.

More blood spilled for this treasonous asshole.

I thought for a few seconds. Could I do anything that wouldn't show on the general's monitor? Maybe if I pushed something off the edge of the ocular display, he wouldn't be able to see it either.

I opened the messenger app, careful to keep it out of the main window.

General Hudson turned and leaned in. "I said, delete the file. Do it now or your girlfriend dies."

I mentally dictated a short message, silently praying my hasty words made sense, and sent it. Letting the foreground connection to the Pentagon go blurry, I changed my focus to the traitorous military man standing in front of me.

Anger-filled, dark brown irises floated in a cesspool of bloodshot yellow. He cocked his head and started to say something when my eyes rolled back, my jaws snapped together, and my body went stiff. I thrust my legs out, kicking the general in the stomach.

He fell back and landed on his butt. The air in his lungs erupted in a whoosh.

I started convulsing and thrusting so hard that the chair cracked.

Rick leapt back. "Damn it. He's having a seizure. Give him some room."

Jesper ran forward, but my murderer held out an arm, stopping him.

My feet flailed, kicking the cart and knocking everything off its shelves. The chair collapsed as I continued to writhe. My body landed on the pile of splinters. Freed from the furniture's restraints, I rolled across the floor.

Rick grabbed the cart and yanked it back as I bucked and kicked. A few feet away, the men stood gaping.

The convulsions settled, and I lay still, save for the heaving of my chest as I sucked in roomfuls of air. I cracked one eye open just enough to see.

Jesper started to move toward me, but Rick grabbed his arm again. "Hold on. What's that beeping?"

The three of them looked at one another as pulses pinged quietly every few seconds. They stared in all directions as the sound ricocheted around the cavernous space. The beeping quickened for a few seconds, then quickened again.

Just as the pulse turned into a steady hum, Jesper pointed at me. "It's coming from him. I think he's got something."

Too late, asshole.

I smiled and kicked out with my foot. The Sonic Boom slid across the floor, stopping right in the middle of the three men.

They stared down, and, in perfect unison, their jaws dropped open. They each started to twist away as if to run, but before they'd taken a single step, the device blared. The Murderous Three flew in all directions as if God himself had swatted them aside. They skittered across the floor like stones skipping across a pond.

I stumbled clumsily to my feet, preparing myself for one or more of them to attack, though I didn't have the foggiest idea what I could do with my hands tied behind my back. Fortunately, I didn't need to improvise a defense. The men lay unmoving.

Half stumbling, I approached the bound woman. "Tamara, you need to untie me." I turned around, giving her access to my hands.

She strained forward and loosened the knots binding my wrists. I pulled free, then undid her restraints.

She removed her gag. "Jeff. Oh, Jeff." She stood and fell against me. Wrapping her arms around my waist, she pressed her cheek against my chest.

I stroked her hair.

She pulled back, staring into my face. "Jeff, are you okay?"

At first, I shook my head, but we didn't have time to discuss the implications of the scrambling that the general and Rick had just done to my brain. I had no idea how temporary or long-lasting the effects would be, but ultimately, it didn't matter if we didn't get away from the goons.

The Sonic Boom would only render them unconscious for a few minutes. When they woke, they would have the mother of all headaches and want to deliver some major payback.

I slowly nodded. "Yes... I'm okay."

Concern and sadness crossed her face. "Oh, my god. What did they do to you?" She touched my cheek and frowned. "Jeff? Something's different about you."

From his corner of the room, Jesper groaned. I glanced at him, then took Tamara's hand. "We can talk about that later. Right now, we have to get out of here."

The two of us ran.

CHAPTER TWENTY-FIVE

LINCOLN

Pushing through the side entrance, Tamara and I almost fell into the courtyard. Just beyond a weed-covered field lay a forest. She started toward it, but I stopped her as I stared at the dark grove of trees.

Tamara frowned and looked back over my shoulder, but no one pursued us. Yet. "What is it?"

I glanced at the woods. "If we go in there, we'll die. There are traps. A lot of them."

"Then what do we do?" she asked, glancing back again.

I looked around for a car or some other way of escaping. Nothing.

The shed.

I looked at Tamara. "What?"

She returned my gaze. "What, what?"

"Did you say something?"

She cocked her head. "Yes, I asked what we are supposed to do."

Go to the shed.

I spun but could see no one else. I suddenly realized that I hadn't heard the voice through my ears. It seemed to be coming from within my head. *Jeff?*

Yes. Do as I say. Go to the shed.

I didn't know if I'd gone completely crazy or if the man that used to occupy this body still rattled around in my skull someplace. In the end, it didn't matter since I couldn't come up with any better alternatives.

"Over there." I led Tamara by the hand to the building.

As I pulled open the door, she stopped me. "If we hide in here, they'll find us for sure."

"We aren't hiding," I said, "and I don't think we'll be here very long."

I tugged her inside. On the floor sat a large rectangular box covered in a thick black pelt. Following Jeff's instructions, I ran my fingers through the rough hair until I found a small lever. I pressed it, and a back panel popped open to reveal a keypad.

"Well, I'll be," I muttered.

Tamara, who'd been staring through a crack in the door, glanced at me. "Do you have any idea what you're doing?"

"I sure hope so," I replied. As Jeff talked, I started typing.

Tamara's eyes grew huge. "Is that some kind of bomb?"

I shook my head as I clicked the panel closed. "No." I stood and, after checking to make sure no one waited for us, pulled her out of the shed.

"Then what were you doing?" she asked.

"Hopefully saving our lives. I'll explain later. Right now we need to hurry." We ran for the parking lot, but as we neared the back of the building, the door flew open. Jesper and his men spilled out, followed by the general.

The huge, scarred man pointed at us. "There they are."

Bullets and laser bolts ripped apart the ground around our feet. I leapt behind a wall, yanking Tamara with me.

"Don't kill him. We need him," the general shouted. "You can kill the girl, but we need him alive."

Tamara scoffed. "Nice."

"Yeah," I said. "He was a real prince to work with too." I took her hand again. "Come on. This way."

We scrambled up onto the loading dock and through a back entrance. As I slammed it shut and slapped the lock into place, one of Jesper's men must have shot at the door. A small bulge suddenly poked out from the surface.

Tamara's eyes found mine for a second, and then, as one, we turned and hurried down a dark hallway.

We came to a crossing corridor and stopped. I listened for pursuers. Nothing. For now, this part of the building remained deserted. I led her past a series of abandoned offices and into a large empty warehouse.

I pointed to a door on the far wall. "There."

She looked. "Are you sure?"

I jerked my thumb over my shoulder. "Not entirely, but I do know that the general and his marauding band of assholes are back there."

She nodded. "Good point."

Together, we started running across the cavernous room. When we reached the center, a shot as loud as a cannon echoed around the space.

Tamara and I skidded to a stop. Slowly we turned around to find Jesper with a rifle leveled at us. A dozen of his men aimed their guns in our direction.

The general strolled in and beckoned us to return. "Come on back. You had a chance, but now you've run out."

When I hesitated, Jesper shot the ceiling again. "The next one goes into your girlfriend."

"Oh, didn't you hear?" General Hudson smirked. "They're engaged to be married. Well that's not quite right. Jeff's engaged to be married. Lincoln's already hitched. But you're kind of both men now, aren't you? Is that considered polygamy or schizophrenia?"

He frowned. "Wow, your life is really complicated. Anyway, come on. Don't make me ask twice."

Tamara and I glanced at each other and began to trudge back.

As we marched, she whispered, "Now would be a really good time for that plan of yours."

"Just wait a minute," I whispered back, hoping desperately that I could actually deliver on my promise.

She took my hand. "Well, we're running out of time."

Since we'd come within earshot of the general and his men, I didn't reply.

Jesper waved the gun for us to go back through the door when somewhere off in the distance a beast, straight from my worst nightmare, roared.

Rick glanced over his shoulder and smirked. "Hold on. Let's wait for our company to join us."

The roar echoed again, this time from the hall. Jesper's men glanced at one another, grins on their lips and knowing looks in their eyes.

Tamara squeezed my hand. "Is that the…"

I met her gaze. I wanted to tell her that everything would be okay. That soon we'd be out of this mess and would get to talk everything through as we drank cold beers and watched the sun set. Or, if I'd messed up, soon we'd both be dead. With the hodgepodge swirling around in my head, it could go either way.

"What did you do?" I asked the general.

He shrugged. "We didn't want to take a chance on losing you again, so we called in one of your old friends for help."

From down the hall, the clomping of metal on stone echoed through the cavern. Tamara's hand slid up my arm. She whispered, "Let's run."

Jesper waved his gun. "You aren't going anywhere."

She glared at General Hudson. "Why not? You're just going to kill us like you did Lucas, Ceos, and all those other people."

The rattling, scraping of steel grew louder, and Tamara, always the fighter, let go of me and stepped forward, hitting the general in the chest. "I saw the files. You are responsible for all those disappearances they've been talking about on the news."

He shoved her back. "It wasn't just me, sweetheart, but yeah, guilty as charged."

"You assassinated the president," she raged. "You've been murdering people and snatching them from their families for no reason. You're at war not only with your own country but with the entire world."

The general glared at her. "I'm fighting for the greater good."

"You're a coward," she said, shaking her head. "You listened to people speak gibberish about this or blather about that, and you bought it like a feebleminded imbecile. Then you turned on your own country. Leading hundreds of thousands to the slaughter. I don't care how you justify it, their blood is on your hands."

Hell's pet cat appeared in the doorway. Glimmering orbs shone from its huge head. As it snarled, its guillotine teeth flashed in the light. My heart beat so hard in my chest, I thought it might break through my sternum.

General Hudson glanced back at Tamara and smirked. "Actually, your blood will be on his."

She found my hand again, and, in unison, we moved back.

The panther stepped into the room, its metal claws scratching the grimy concrete. As it made its way into the space, it turned its gaze on each of us. The aroma of hot electronics and hydraulic oil filled the air.

"Call it off, General," I said. "Last warning. You'll regret it if you don't."

The panther stared around the room. It tilted its head back and bellowed. Leaping forward, it landed in front of us. Huge steel claws raked the concrete, digging narrow trenches into the floor. It walked toward us with the litheness of a housecat, belying its enormous size. The beast stopped, its face only inches from mine.

Jeff's voice again resonated from deep in my head. *Okay, time to test our theory.*

Wait. What? You don't know if this will work? I asked.

It should.

I sighed. *Great. Just great. Okay, tell me what to do.*

Jeff spoke quickly.

Instead of pulling away from the mechanical creature, I leaned in even closer and whispered. "Oben, oben, neider, neider, links, recht, links, recht."

The panther's eyes flashed blue and then returned to their normal amethyst color. While my attention remained fixed on the mechanical demon staring at me, in the corner of the room, Rick slipped out of the room and ran down the hall. I wanted to stop him, but I had my hands full at the moment.

I assumed an authoritative tone. "Anhalten." I pointed at Tamara. "Wache."

The panther paused, looked at Tamara, then backed up a couple of steps.

"What are you waiting for? Get them," the general shouted.

I shook my head and smiled. "No, I don't think so."

When the beast turned around, its glowering gaze landed on the general. One of Jesper's men grabbed Tamara and pressed his gun against her temple. "Call it off or the girl dies."

The creature's tail snaked out in a blur of motion and flipped the man's gun into the air. We all stared up at the flying weapon while the panther stabbed the man in the temple with the blade-tipped end of its tail. The thug slumped to the floor.

Tamara glanced down at the fallen man, then jumped back next to me.

"Obviously, we can't trust any of these guys," I said to her.

She nodded. "Obviously."

I waved my arm over the lot of Jesper's men. "Apport."

The beast spun around and crouched. It sprang into the air, roaring with a primal fury. It landed on top of the closest soldier, raking the man's face with its steel claws.

As the man died, another soldier shot it. The bullet pinged off its steel hide, and the beast snarled. The desperate soldier shot again just as the cat darted forward and clomped its huge jaws around the man's gun hand. Clamping down, it yanked its head to the side.

Blood flowed from the stump, splashing over the beast's mandibles and splattering across the floor in an arc.

The man screamed and clutched his severed limb. The panther raked its huge claws across the poor bastard's throat. His screams turned to gurgles, and he collapsed to the floor.

It looked up, staring at each of the soldiers in turn. Tamara and I dove to the side as the squad began to fire. The gunshots reverberated through the huge chamber.

Razor claws raked over the closest soldier's face. The panther pivoted and lashed out at another man while it pierced a third through the chest with its tail.

As the soldiers fell, one man broke from the group, sprinting for the door. The creature bellowed and leapt. It landed on the sprinter's shoulders, grabbed the man's head in its mouth, and clamped down. The man's skull exploded like a ripe melon under a car tire.

The creature pivoted and leapt onto the next soldier. Screaming, the rest of the unit fled in all directions, but one by one, the beast ripped and slashed them apart until the entire squad lay in pools of their own blood.

Finally, the creature turned to Jesper and the general, backing them into a corner. The general tried to slip behind the thug, but Jesper grabbed the treasonous-military man and held him up like a shield.

"Bleib," I told the panther. It glanced at me, then paced in front of them, whipping and flexing its tail in the air.

The general wiggled in the big man's grasp. "What are you doing? You're supposed to protect me. That was the deal."

Jesper raised him higher. "The deal's off." He looked at the panther. "Come on! Come get what you want."

The panther roared.

A pulse gun snapped. Jesper dropped the military man and stared at the circle of red in his gut.

The general turned and shot him again.

The front of Jesper's shirt and the skin on his chest vaporized in a spray of ashen skin. He froze as a bubble of blood popped from his lips. The big man fell back and slid down the wall leaving a trail of crimson on the cinderblock surface.

The panther's claws clicked on the floor as it paced back and forth. The general turned and faced it. He threw away his gun and held up his hands. "I surrender."

The creature leaned forward and screamed in his face.

The general snarled back. "I said I surrender, but if you're going to kill me, then just do it."

Tamara and I skirted the bodies littering the floor and stood beside the panther's shoulder. "I should have it kill you. You're responsible for the deaths of millions."

"You make me sick," Tamara spat.

From down the hall, the sound of boots on concrete echoed.

I glanced in the direction of the door. "The cavalry is here."

Tamara frowned. "Who is it?"

"Detective Mires and his brood," I said.

Her eyes flew open wide. "What?" She held up her wrist. "These bastards cut my tracker band off too. How did they find us?"

I shrugged. "While I was logged onto the Pentagon's server, I slipped a message to the detective to let him know where we are."

"You have no idea what you've done," General Hudson snarled.

She looked at him, then at the door, then at me. "You can still get your revenge, you know." She motioned her head to the panther. "Let it kill him. I won't say a word."

I stared at her. "I thought you were all about love and peace and harmony?"

She glared at the general. "Some pieces of filth are not redeemable."

"No," I said, "he's way more valuable alive. He'll spend the rest of his life answering questions and cooling his heels in a federal penitentiary." I turned to the panther. "Sitz."

"I—" she started, but the general interrupted her.

"You have no idea what you're doing," the general screamed. "I'm a humanitarian and a hero. One of the few who's willing to do what needs to be done to save the world."

Tamara glared at him. "Go to hell."

We turned and started to walk away. "Tamara, I need to tell you something."

She looked at me. "What is it?"

"I—"

"Hey, Lincoln." I turned just as General Hudson arced his hand forward.

My heart lurched. I tried to leap into the way, but I couldn't get ahead of the knife. The same knife that Jesper's thug had stabbed through my brother's heart sailed through the air and buried itself in Tamara's chest.

The panther sprang forward. Shoving the general to the floor, it clamped its jaws around his neck and ripped his throat apart. The man's arms and legs flailed against the floor before becoming still. A thin ribbon of blood trailed down a crack in the concrete.

Tamara stared at the handle sticking out of her sternum. She glanced at me, then crumpled to the floor.

"Tamara!" I dropped to my knees, scooping her up in my arms. "Tamara, oh shit. No. No. No. I'm so sorry."

From deep in the recesses of my mind, a man cried out in agony as the life drained from the woman he loved and the rest of his world crumbled.

I brushed back a strand of her hair and delivered the message the sobbing, broken man inside of me said over and over. "I love you."

She touched my cheek as a small stream of blood dribbled out of the side of her mouth. She tried to speak, her voice no more than a whisper. "I love you too. Tell Jeff I love him." Then her hand went limp and her eyes turned glassy.

Detective Mires and his uniformed men barreled into the room, their pulse guns drawn. They paused, glancing around at all the bodies covering the floor. The panther roared, and the entire squad turned and raised their weapons.

The detective held up his arms, motioning for his men to wait. "Call off your dog, Jeff."

I looked at the creature. "Fuss."

It huffed and then settled to the concrete floor. Laying its head on its folded front paws, its amethyst eyes went dark.

The men still looked wary but lowered their weapons. The detective came up and stood beside me, staring down at the fallen woman in my arms.

I gently laid her on the floor and closed her eyelids. I sat down next to her. Without looking at the detective, I said, "In the back room, you'll find scatter cameras, *your* scatter cameras actually, on the floor. They should tell you everything you need to know."

I slipped my fingers into the breast pocket of my shirt and pulled out the one I'd slipped in there, along with a folded dollar bill. I let the money flutter to the floor, then dropped the pinhead sized device in his palm. "You won't be able to see anything, but you'll hear everything that went down here."

The detective glanced at the speck in his hand and narrowed his eyes. "Don't think that just because of this you're free of all charges. Until I'm satisfied, you're still my prisoner."

I brushed back Tamara's dark hair. "If I was trying to get away, do you think I would have told you where to find us?"

He looked at me for a minute, then shook his head. "No. I suppose not."

"I'm sure there's no point now," I glanced up at him, "but you need to search for Rick. I don't think he's the ringleader, but most of what happened was because of him."

Detective Mires frowned. "You mean the guy that signed the affidavit?"

"Yes," I said, nodding. "I told you I didn't do it, and after you examine the scatter cameras, you'll know it too. He was here, but before this final round of fun, he disappeared."

The detective motioned for one of his officers to come over. He whispered something, and the man took off.

A few minutes later, the detective checked his DigiSleeve. "There's no one else on the premises. I don't know if you're just trying to throw me off or if this guy really played a part. But like I said, until I can prove otherwise, I'm not letting you out of my sight."

One of his men stepped up next to him. "Should I cuff him?"

I ignored them and continued to stroke the girl's hair as the man inside me wept. A heavy tear fell from my eye and splattered against the concrete floor.

The detective sighed. "No. Don't bother. He's not going anywhere."

CHAPTER TWENTY-SIX

LINCOLN

Reverend Darlene Boyd regarded me from behind her modest desk. "Unfortunately, I don't have a lot of time. I'm officiating a service in half an hour."

"I know, Reverend," I said. "But this is important."

She folded her hands and leaned back in her worn leather chair.

"I feel," I said, searching for the right words, "like I'm no longer 'me,' at least not the 'me' that God created."

Talk about the understatement of the century.

She nodded. "I see. Are you saying you feel reborn?"

That didn't even come close to explaining it. Unfortunately, the words did not exist. In the transfer from one body to another, some of 'me' seemed to have gotten left behind. My essence felt as hole-filled as Swiss cheese.

For a couple of hours after the three goons...woke me up, Jeff still occupied a corner of my mind. He'd told me how to reprogram the robotic panther, given me the override code to assume control of it, and fed me the German dog training commands to make it do my bidding.

At the time, I'd wondered if the two of us would eventually have to figure out dual-occupancy in a space designed for one. But shortly after Tamara died, Jeff had faded away too.

Weirdly, his absence left me feeling hollow and vacant. I'd called out, listening for his voice, but only received silence in response.

Despite being one of the lowest points in my life, things had barreled downhill from there. Trapped in a foreign body and ensnared in an alien universe, I'd spent days in custody as the primary suspect in the police's murder investigation.

It turned out that Jeff had a substantial sum of money tucked away in his bank account. My new lawyer waded through the red tape to gain access and finally posted my bail. When Detective Mires and his posse released me, I thought my situation might improve, but then the media had begun hounding me, spinning me round and round in a three-ringed circus so insane it made me lust for the solitude of the cellblock.

Worse, my widowed wife and fatherless children waited to bury my body. To them, I'd died, and in no rational universe could I explain that I still walked the Earth.

The reverend studied me as if she could read my thoughts. She adjusted her glasses. "So, what happened that led to these feelings of not being the 'you' the Lord created?"

How much time ya got? I stared straight into her eyes. "I died."

If my words surprised her, it didn't register on her face. "Yes, having a near-death experience can certainly be a life-changing event."

"No," I said, shaking my head. "I literally died."

She paused. "And with technology being what it is today, they were able to bring you back."

"Yes."

"I see," she said. "And what has brought you into my office? What answers do you seek?"

I took a deep breath. "I want to know about souls, Reverend. What can you tell me about them?"

When Ms. Boyd smiled, crow's feet formed in the skin around her eyes, making her look ancient and wise. "That particular conversation will take more than a few minutes."

"I know. The thing is, I grew up in the church. There's always been a lot of talk about saving our souls, and the tarnishing of souls, and of working hard, and being faithful so that our souls will go to Heaven."

Her smile grew. "Well, it is the church's job to see to it that you are close to God while you're here on Earth and to prepare you to meet Him in the ever-after."

I'd heard this litany tens of thousands of times before. My entire life, well-meaning people like the reverend had worried and fretted about my soul as if they alone had a monopoly on the tickets for the only holy bus in town that went to the giant enchilada in the sky.

I took a deep breath. "Yes, okay. The thing is, I remember dying, and I remember waking up. But I have no recollection of the time in between. Though in reality there was time in between, to me, the jump between the two events was instantaneous. No pearly gates. No angels singing. No bright light. But also no heat or hellfire. No pain. No nothing."

Reverend Boyd tapped the table with her finger. "You're hoping I'll tell you what happened to your soul during the 'in between?'"

"I don't mean any disrespect, but I don't think you can do that," I said.

She shrugged. "Probably not with any certainty."

I paused for a second, mulling over how exactly to phrase my question. "When you get down to it, what I'd really like to know is if we actually have souls. Are they real, or are we nothing more than just a collection of our memories and experiences?"

The reverend scratched her chin and sat back, regarding me. She pointed to a statue of a thorn-crowned figure hanging on a cross. "That man believed so. So much so that he died to cleanse our souls to assure we would ascend to Heaven when we too pass."

Unsurprisingly, the reverend had neatly sidestepped my question. I glanced at the small crucifix. *If what He believed is true and we do have souls, did I go to Heaven and come back, or did mine split like an amoeba?*

If so, then how many copies of 'me' can Rick and his goons make? Five? Ten? A million? And are they all me?

These were the real questions I wanted answered, though I didn't dare ask.

"In addition to my dying and coming back to life, my fiancée got killed." Though it had been weeks since her death, the echoes of Jeff's sorrow and agony still reverberated through my heart. As though it hadn't just been his loss, but mine as well.

I looked back up at the woman sitting behind the scarred desk. "I fought in the war. Killed my country's enemies. But this was different. I held Tamara as she died. I felt her body go limp in my arms, and there was nothing I could do about it. She was innocent. That was her crime, and that was the weapon they used to control me."

Squeezing my hands together to keep them from shaking, I said, "They also killed Lincoln and his brother, two more innocents, and they kidnapped a man who worked at my company. No one's heard from him, and the police have no leads. To make matters even worse, the men that did it got away. Now, everything I had is gone. I used to have a family. I used to have a life. I used to have…faith."

The reverend paused for a few seconds, then pulled out a scrap of paper and began scribbling on it. "I'm almost out of time. So, here's a list of scriptures. I want you to go home, read them, pray, and meditate. Once you've done this, come back and we will finish our conversation."

Disappointed though not surprised by the lack of real answers, I took the paper from her and stuck it in my pocket without looking at it. I stood and headed out of the humble office.

Before I stepped into the hallway, I turned back to the graying woman. "Thank you. You didn't answer my questions, but I appreciate you listening just the same."

"Of course." She reclined in her chair and smiled. "I can't wait to finish our conversation." A small old-fashioned clock on a nearby shelf pinged. She glanced at it and pursed her lips as she began to search her desk. "Now, where are my notes?"

I marched down the hallway but paused before pushing through the last door. Maybe I shouldn't be here. Maybe I should turn around and leave. My very presence felt sacrilegious somehow, and even if it wasn't, did I really want to see what lay beyond this entrance?

But I'd come this far, I had to finish it. Taking a deep breath, I pushed through the door and into the sanctuary of the First Congregational Church. No one but ghosts and the Holy Spirit lingered in the large room, so I stepped in front of the stage and stood before the huge cross hanging on the wall.

I considered kneeling and praying as the reverend had suggested. But the massive wooden planks wouldn't quell my curiosity any more than Ms. Boyd had. The answers I sought lay under divine lock and key and probably would remain out of my grasp forever.

I sighed and turned around, facing the pair of coffins parked at the front of the room. Looking back and forth between these two involuntary guests of honor, I stepped up next to the one bearing my brother's picture and placed a hand on its glossy surface.

"I'm so sorry I couldn't save you, Mike. I tried, but in the end, I couldn't save anyone, not even myself. I don't know when I'll be joining you again. Hell, for all I know part of me already has, but until I'm fully me again, start rockin' Heaven. Get it good and warmed up so when I do get up there, we can bring the roof down."

I turned to the second casket. The one with my picture next to it. "This has got to be the weirdest thing to ever have happened to anyone in the history of time. I'm talking to my dead self."

I took a deep breath. "Self, if a part of you...me did go somewhere else, hopefully I'll...*we'll* become whole again when this is done. Though, until then, if you could come back and fill in the missing parts, I'd really appreciate it."

I stared into the shiny surface. The handle lay just inches from my fingertips, and a weird part of me wanted to lift the lid. Wanted to see my own face staring back at me.

Talk about surreal.

As if of its own accord, my hand slid down the mahogany surface. I grasped the brass handle. As I started to open Pandora's Box, from behind me, the door at the back of the sanctuary squeaked. Startled, I dropped the lid and turned to find a woman and her three children standing in the entrance.

My heart lurched and started hammering. Tears blurred my vision, and I had to swipe at them. Every fiber in my being urged me to run to the four of them, scoop them up in my arms, and squeeze them tight.

Though it almost tore me apart, I forced myself to remain in place. If I sprinted toward them, the result would not be a tearful reunion but would end with me in ElectriCuffs.

My family came down the aisle. Melody directed our children to the front pew, where they took their seats in silence.

My wife came up to me. When she offered her hand and introduced herself, a piece of me cracked.

I forced a welcoming expression onto my face and grasped her small hand in mine. "It's good to meet you. I'm Jeff Braxton. I…knew your husband."

I'd seen the forced-smile on her face a handful of times before. Her 'brave' demonstration masked a torrent of pain lurking just beneath the surface. "Did you work with him?"

I looked into her familiar eyes, hoping beyond hope that she would see the real me. My heart called out to her. *It's me. See me, Melody. Please.* "Something like that."

I glanced at the kids—my kids—watching us before I turned back to her. Lowering my voice, I said, "You were the melody to his harmony."

She blinked. "How do you know that? No one knows that." My wife furrowed her brow as confusion crossed her face. "Who did you say you were?"

I touched her hand. "Like I said, I knew your husband."

Cocking her head, she stared at me. Suddenly her mouth dropped open, and her face grew pale as recognition flashed in the depths of her eyes.

For the shortest of moments, I thought that we could leap across the chasm. That despite having died and been brought back to life in another man's body, somehow we could pick up the slivers of our fractured world. Perhaps we could glue them back together and start over.

But I caught a glimpse of my reflection in the glossy surface of the casket. My casket. A stranger stared back at me, and the overwhelming impossibility of reality crushed my dream before the embers had even begun to grow warm.

My heart lumbered as if it had been filled with mid-winter tar. "I need to go now."

I slipped past her and had only made it a few steps when she called after me. "Aren't you going to stay for the service?"

I paused and looked back. "I'm sorry, I can't."

A thousand Lincoln Grey words waited to be said, but not one of them was appropriate coming from Jeff Braxton. I resumed trudging up the aisle and pushed through the entrance. A cold breeze ruffled my hair and billowed my jacket as I started down the sidewalk.

I didn't have a destination in mind, just away. Away from Melody. Away from my children. Away from me in the mahogany box. Away from my old life.

I didn't even bother swiping at the tears on my cheeks. "Lexi, bring the car around."

Her voice chirped from my DigiSleeve. "Okay, Jeff."

Behind me, the hinges of the church door squeaked again. Despite my logical mind telling me to run—to leave and never look back—my heart screamed at me to stop. Ignoring all intelligent rationality, I froze in my tracks and slowly turned around.

Melody stood in the entrance. The tears streaming down her cheeks mimicked my own. Uncertainty lined her face, creasing the little spot between her eyes.

An image of us huddled on our porch swing under a huge May moon bubbled up to the surface of my mind. We'd spent the evening talking, laughing, and doing a whole lot of nothing. When the sun fell and the temperature dropped, I'd gone inside for a blanket.

As I'd wrapped my wife in the soft, thick fabric, her eyes had glimmered in the lunar glow and a sly smile had tugged at her lips.

"What is it?" I'd asked.

"You take good care of me. You always have." She'd pulled my hand under the quilt, placing it on her stomach. "You're going to make a great daddy."

My heart had sighed with happiness. And when I kissed the spot, that little spot between her eyes, her warm skin had smelled of violets and the tiny hairs of her brows had tickled my lips.

All these years later—standing in the drizzle and river-chilled wind, under an ash-colored Portland sky—that memory struck a spark.

For an instant, my soul, or what remained of it, flared to life, happy and joyful for the first time in forever. Burning bright in my core, it filled my essence with spiritual heat.

Until that moment, I hadn't realized just how empty I'd been.

Melody opened her mouth to say something—what, I couldn't imagine—but before she could utter a single syllable, a digital authoritative voice cut her off. "Halt. You are under detainment."

I spun.

Ten paces away, a heavily armored drone hovered, an array of fan motors buzzed like an angry wasp while the turret of its pulse gun centered a laser light on my chest. "You are to wait here for the authorities. If you try to escape, forceful methods of restraint have been authorized."

The hornet's twin screamed down the street. It came around, flanking me and aiming its weapons at my chest and head.

My eyes lingered on the firearms brandished by the flying robots. "Under whose authority do you dare detain me?"

"The FBI and the Department of Homeland Security," the two said in unison.

A dark car slid in next to the curb, and three men in suits climbed out. Two pulled out pulse guns while the third flashed his credentials. "Jeff Braxton?"

I put my hands on my hips. What the hell else had Jeff been up to that would warrant all of this? "Yes?"

He stepped in front of me. "Hold out your hands, sir."

I glared. "Why do I need to do that?"

He pulled out a pair of ElectriCuffs from his pocket. "Because you are under arrest for a dozen counts of cyberterrorism, the release of classified information to the public, and the murder of Lincoln Grey."

My eyes flew open wide. "What? I did no such thing."

The government goon stood firm. "You tortured and killed Mr. Grey, used the information he provided to breach the Pentagon's security system, and upload a classified conversation from the server to the public domain. The rest of your charges will be explained to you shortly."

Taking a step back, I began to stammer. "I... What? No, the police investigation is still pending. There hasn't even been a trial yet."

The two gun-toting goons-in-suits moved closer.

"We are not the police," the man with cuffs said. "These are federal charges, not state. The evidence we have against you is substantial and indisputable. Now, please sir, do not make us use force. It will go much easier for you if you come along willingly."

I glared at him but held out my wrists. "I'm contacting my lawyer."

He guided me to the car and opened the door. "Requesting a lawyer is your right, sir."

I paused and glanced back at my wife.

The uncertainty on her face had been replaced with rage and hurt.

I'd hoped that the noise from the drones had drowned out the goon's words. Clearly not.

The hate and darkness in her eyes snuffed out my short-lived internal light. The shadows consumed what remained of my soul, leaving only emptiness and a sinewy trail of bland-colored smoke behind.

The agent, impatient to take me to prison or wherever, pushed me inside the car. Doors slammed as the men piled in after me.

As we pulled away from the curb, I turned and stared out the back window. Melody glared at me as we drove away. She spun on her heels, flung open the door, and marched into the church.

I continued to watch the spot where my wife had been standing until it dwindled into the distance, leaving me with nothing but my memories.

The End

ACKNOWLEDGEMENTS

First and foremost, I want to thank my fans. I love sharing story adventures with you. You make this journey so fun!

A novel is not a solitary endeavor. A lot of people spend a lot of hours in an author's universe before a book hits the digital shelves. While my latest book baby was still a zygote, I had several sets of eyes on it that provided invaluable insight and helped root out plot problems, technical issues, relationship improbabilities, and typo devils. Thank you, father, Anya, Chris, Jennica, Becky (aka Guido), and Nicole!

To my cover artist. Anita, I had no idea what the front of this book was going to look like. As always, you completely rocked it. Thank you! This book is yet another example of why Erin and I created the hashtag #AnitaIsAmazing.

I especially want to send a huge thank you to my amazing wife, Erin. The idea for this book came about during one of our conversations about everything and nothing. Erin, you and I worked through the minutia, turning the rocks of the story this way and that. You were the first and last lines of editing defense. You are my inspiration, my ideal reader, my love, and my best friend. Thank you for sharing this (and all) of life's journeys with me!

Thank you for purchasing this copy of *The Extractor: Rise of Osiris*, Book One in the Osiris Series. If you enjoyed this book by Deek, please let him know by posting a short review. If you purchased this book through Amazon, it is eligible for a free Kindle Match.

One of my favorite things about being a writer is building relationships with readers.
I occasionally send out newsletters with details on new releases, information on how to become part of my advanced reader team, as well as subscriber-only material.

If you sign up for the mailing list, you'll get a Tenacious Books Starter kit which includes a **free**, award-winning novel.

You can get your free books by scanning the above QR code with your smartphone.

Alternately, you can register at:
www.DeekRhewBooks.com/contact.html

Thank you for being a
Tenacious Books Reader!

ABOUT THE AUTHOR

Deek did not set out to be a writer. Originally, he wanted to follow his father's path as a career military man and fly for the Air Force. So, Deek spent two years in high school preparing for the ROTC. During a routine check-in, his recruiter asked about any handicaps, to which Deek jokingly replied he was colorblind. The recruiter got a funny look on his face and informed Deek that the closest he'd ever get to the pilot's seat was from the scheduling office. Ummm…no.

After that, Deek focused on his love for music—touring with a local rock band and majoring in music in college. Unfortunately, he didn't enjoy the life of a pauper, so he started secondary school over. Ten years later, he walked across the stage with a computer science degree. He now slings web code during the day to support his seven day a week writing habit.

Though he loves his job and the people he works with, Deek has been enthralled by the written word and storytelling since he picked up his first Stephen King novel, It. On his way to work one day, a scene so vivid flashed through his mind that he felt compelled to pull over and put it to paper. Having neither quill nor parchment with which to document the image, he laboriously pecked out the first chapter of his first novel on his phone.

A transplant from a rainy pocket in the Pacific Northwest, Deek now lives at the beach—where the sun shines bright, he can listen to the waves crash all day, and the air is hot and smells of the sea. He and his brilliant and stunning author bride, Erin Rhew, live a simple life with their writing assistant, a fat tabby named Trinity and a six-pound guard dog named Gus. They enjoy lingering in the mornings, and often late into the night, caught up in Erin's fantastic fantasy worlds of noble princes and knights and entwined in Deek's dark universes where nothing is as it seems.

He and Erin enjoy spending time with friends, walking on the beach, lifting weights, and adventuring.

Made in the USA
Middletown, DE
16 August 2021